John Lutz published his first short story in 1966 in *Alfred Hitchcock's Mystery Magazine* and has been publishing regularly ever since. His work includes political suspense, private eye novels, urban suspense, humour, occult, crime caper, police procedural, espionage, historical, futuristic, amateur detective – virtually every mystery sub-genre. He is the author of more than thirty-five novels and 250 short stories and articles. His *SWF Seeks Same* was made into the hit movie *Single White Female,* starring Bridget Fonda and Jennifer Jason Leigh, and his novel *The Ex* was made into the HBO original movie of the same title, for which he co-authored the screenplay.

Mister X

John Lutz

ROBINSON

Constable & Robinson Ltd
55–56 Russell Square
London WC1B 4HP
www.constablerobinson.com

First published in the USA by Pinnacle Books,
a division of Kensington Publishing Corp., 2010

First published in the UK by Robinson,
an imprint of Constable & Robinson Ltd, 2012

A copy of the British Library Cataloguing in
Publication Data is available from the British Library

ISBN: 978-1-78033-179-9 (paperback)
ISBN: 978-1-78033-180-5 (ebook)

Printed and bound in the UK

1 3 5 7 9 10 8 6 4 2

*For Don Mackey
and Vernon Shults*

PART
I

And what are you that, missing you
I should be kept awake
As many nights as there are days
With weeping for your sake?

—EDNA ST. VINCENT MILLAY, "The Philosopher"

1

Quinn had found a box of paper clips in his bottom desk drawer and was just straightening up when the dead woman entered his office.

She'd startled him, the way she'd come in without making any noise.

She wasn't what you'd call beautiful, but she was attractive, with slim hips and legs inside new-looking stiff jeans, small breasts beneath a white sleeveless blouse. Her shoulder-length hair was brown, her eyes a deeper brown and slightly bulbous. She had symmetrical features with oversized lips, a slight overbite. A yellow file folder stuffed with what looked like newspaper clippings was tucked beneath her left arm. Her right hand held a brown leather shoulder bag, the strap scrunched up to act as a handle. She'd said on the phone her name was Tiffany Keller. If she were still alive, Quinn thought, she'd be pushing thirty.

There was a kind of grim resolve to her expression, as if she'd just been affronted and was about to fire back.

The generous mouth suddenly arced into a toothy smile, and the dogged expression disappeared entirely, as if a face like hers couldn't hold such a visage for long. Quinn was left with the impression that he'd momentarily glimpsed someone else entirely.

"Captain Frank Quinn, I presume."

"Just Quinn," he said. "Like the lettering on the door, Quinn and Associates Investigations."

"I was aware you were no longer with the NYPD," she said.

"Want to sit down?" he asked, motioning with a paper clip toward one of the walnut chairs angled in front of his desk.

"I'll stand, thanks." Her smile widened. "I'm Tiffany Keller."

He continued staring at the woman while his right hand groped for the empty glass ashtray he used to contain paperclips. "You said when you phoned earlier to make this appointment that you were Tiffany Keller. Would you be the same Tiffany Keller who was a victim of a serial killer?"

"That would be me."

Unable to look away from her, he turned the tiny box upside down and dropped the paper clips into the ashtray, hearing the faint clickety sound that told him he'd hit his glass target. "Excuse me, but aren't you dead?"

"Not exactly."

Wondering where this was all going, Quinn tossed the empty paper-clip box into the wastebasket inside the desk's kneehole. It landed on recently shredded paper and didn't make a sound. "What is it you want, Tiffany?"

"I want you to find the Carver."

The Carver was a serial killer who'd taken five victims, the last one five years ago, and then suddenly ceased killing. In the way of most serial killers, he'd slain only women. His victims' nipples had been sliced off and a large X carved on their torsos just beneath their breasts. Then their throats had been cut.

At the time, Quinn had been laid up after being shot in the leg during a liquor store hold-up, and hadn't been involved in the Carver investigation. He'd followed it in the papers and on TV news with a temporary invalid's distracted interest. It had been one of his few alternatives to staring at the ceiling. If he remembered correctly, Tiffany Keller had been the Carver's last victim.

He leaned back in his desk chair and studied his visitor more closely.

She didn't wilt under his scrutiny.

"Actually I'm Tiffany's twin sister," she said.

"Then why the act?" he asked.

She smiled even wider. Lots of even white molars. Quinn would bet she'd never had a cavity. The large white smile gave her a kind of flashy cheerleader look. It would dazzle you even in the cheap seats.

"I thought one of the Carver's victims herself appealing to you to take this case might be more convincing," she said. She spoke with a hint of accent, her intonations flat and slightly drawn out. She wasn't from the Northeast. Probably someplace Midwestern. Corn country. "I'm Chrissie." *Ahm.* "Chrissie Keller. My twin sister and I were named after two of our mom's favorite eighties recording stars, Chrissie Hynde and Tiffany."

"Tiffany who?"

"She didn't use a last name. Some artists don't."

"Some artists I've met don't, either," Quinn said.

"Like pickpockets and confidence men and such?"

"Uh-huh. And impersonators."

"I didn't *have* to impersonate Tiffany," she said. "I just wanted you to think that maybe, for only a second or two, you were face-to-face with her. A victim asking that her killer be brought to justice."

"An emotional appeal."

"You got it."

"Justice is a hard thing to find in this world, Chrissie. Sometimes even hard to define. It can be a lot of work and expense, and then we might not like it when we find it."

"Or we might glory in it."

Never having been in her position, Quinn found it difficult to disagree.

"I have the means to pay you for your work," she said. "And what I want to do with my money is find out who killed Tiffany and make sure he pays for his crime. This might sound strange, but I think that's why I have the money. Why I won the Tri-State Triple Monkey Squared Super Jackpot." She shifted her weight in the stiff jeans so she was standing hip-shot. "That's three monkeys in a row three times," she said with a note of pride.

"You did that?" he said, figuring she must be talking about slot-machine winnings.

She swiveled back and forth on the foot her weight rested on, as if idly crushing a small insect. Her shoes were rubber sandals that looked as if they must hurt her feet. "I surely did. With a lucky quarter, and a good reason to win the hundred and thirty-nine thousand dollars." Her face broke into the big smile. "That's still a lot of money after taxes."

"Even here in New York," Quinn said. He leaned back again in his chair, farther this time, making it squeal a warning that it might tip and send him sprawling, make him pay for flirting with danger. He said, "Now you're on a mission."

"That I am, Mr. Quinn. Don't tell me to go to the police, because I already have. They're not interested. The Carver murders happened too long ago, and I got the impression the police don't want to be reminded of a serial killer case they never solved."

"Bureaucracies hate being reminded of their failures."

"I'm not interested in what they hate or don't hate. I'm interested in justice for Tiffany."

Justice again.

"People on a mission scare me," Quinn said, thinking he had a lot of room to talk. But what he'd said was true. He sometimes scared himself. "You're not from New York."

She looked a little surprised and licked her big red lips. "It shows that much?"

"Not a lot," Quinn said. He tapped a forefinger to his cheekbone beneath his right eye and smiled. "Trained observer."

Chrissie pulled the chair closer to the desk and sat down. She crossed her legs tightly, as if she were wearing a skirt and not jeans, or as if she thought Quinn might glimpse too much denim-clad thigh and go berserk and attack her. "I'm from Holifield, Ohio. So was Tiffany, of course. It's a small town. Most folks work for the chemical plant or for Tread-strong Truck Tire Manufacturing. Tiffany worked in the plant for a while; then she came here to New York to try to become an actress. She got killed instead." A firm expression came over Chrissie's face. Her lips compressed together over her protruding teeth and paled, but only for an instant. "I want that rectified."

"Avenged?"

"That, too. You should know, Mr. Quinn, that when one twin dies the other also dies a little. And the way Tiffany died . . . well, it's almost like it happened to both of us. Twins' deaths are special."

"Everyone's death is special to them."

Chrissie leaned forward in her chair, her hands cupped over her knees. She had long fingers, well-kept nails. No rings. "The police called the Carver investigation a cold case, Mr. Quinn. I want it heated up again. I want my mission to be your mission."

"You need to give this some thought," Quinn said. "The NYPD cops aren't fools. Most of the time, anyway. They couldn't solve the Carver murders five years ago."

"I've read about you, Mr. Quinn. When it comes to serial killers, you're smarter than the police. Smarter than anyone."

"Now you're making me blush."

"I doubt if much of anything does that," she said.

"Now you've reverted to insult."

"I didn't mean it that way. I was referring to your experience, the fact that you're a winner."

"Praise again. I'm getting whiplash."

"I'll put my faith in you, and my money on you," Chrissie said.

"Investigations go into the cold-case file; time passes. . . . They get harder to solve. I couldn't promise you much."

"I'm not interested in promises," Chrissie said. "Just results. Like you are." The smile came again, a red slash of amusement that broke into speech. "They say you're only interested in results, that you skirt the rules in ways an actual cop couldn't. That you're a hunter who never gives up." She edged even farther forward in her chair, as if she might spring across the desk and devour him with her big smile. "What do you say?"

"I give up. What do I say?"

"You say yes, of course."

"I guess I shouldn't have left it up to you."

He watched her pick up her worn leather purse from where she'd leaned it against the chair leg and reach into it for her checkbook.

He didn't try to stop her. For all he knew she was right. Right and lucky. That was why she'd won the Tri-State Triple Monkey Squared Super Jackpot.

What had he ever won?

2

It had all been so quick, and the eye could be fooled.

Pearl Kasner, acting as hostess, stood off to the side in the dim entrance alcove of Sammy's Steaks, unsure of what she'd just seen.

She'd waited patiently, making sure she was on the periphery of Linda's vision. A slender and tireless young woman with hair that dangled in natural ringlets around her ears, Linda was one of the busier food servers at Sammy's. The customers were crazy about her.

As she ran another diner's credit card, Linda casually drew what looked like a small black box from her pocket, laid it on the counter, and swiped the card a second time.

Back went the box into her apron pocket.

It was all done so quickly and smoothly that you had to be watching for it, looking directly at it, to notice it.

Pearl edged back completely out of sight and smiled.

She'd been right when she'd noticed Linda the first time. Whenever Linda was alone settling a diner's check, she would run the card twice, once legitimately, the second time to record the card's number in the device she carried concealed in her apron pocket. For several days, the customers' names and card numbers could be used safely to purchase merchandise. When finally the diners realized what was happening and notified the credit card company, they wouldn't be likely to connect the stolen number with a not-so-recent steak dinner at Sammy's.

Pearl left the foyer unattended and weaved her way between white-clothed tables and across the restaurant. She was slightly over five feet tall, with vivid dark eyes, red lips, and black, black shoulder-length hair. Pearl drew male attention, and when attention was paid, said males saw a compact, shapely body with a vibrant energy about it. Her ankles were well turned, her waist narrow. She had a bust too large to be fashionable, but only in the world of fashion.

No one who looked at Pearl was disappointed.

She approached a booth where a lanky but potbellied man in a wrinkled brown suit lounged before a stuffed mushroom appetizer and a half-empty martini glass. He was past middle age and balding, and the day Pearl started pretending to be a hostess, he had started pretending to be a slightly inebriated customer who ordered appetizers as an excuse to drink alone. That was better than drinking at the bar, where the mostly under-forty club was watching and discussing baseball. Discussing it loudly and sometimes angrily. They could really get worked up over steroid use.

The solitary drinker was Larry Fedderman, who had long ago been Quinn's partner in an NYPD radio car, and later his fellow Manhattan South homicide detective. Fedderman, retired from the department, had been living in Florida when Quinn founded Quinn and Associates. Pearl had been working as a uniformed guard at Sixth National Bank in Lower Manhattan.

They'd both stopped what they'd been doing and went to work for Quinn as minority partners in Quinn and Associates Investigations. They were the associates.

Restaurateur Sammy Caminatto had hired QAI to discover how his cousin's Visa card number was stolen, when the only place he'd used his new card and new number, before cutting the card into six pieces to keep it out of his new trophy wife's hands, was at Sammy's.

Quinn had assigned Pearl and Fedderman to the case, and they'd slipped into their roles at Sammy's. Now it looked as if they'd found the answer to the riddle of the roaming card numbers. It was in Linda's apron pocket. Which Pearl thought was a shame, because she liked Linda, who was cute as puppies, naïve, and probably being used.

"Looks like Linda's it," Pearl said to Fedderman.

He showed no reaction but said, "I'm surprised. She seems like a good kid."

"Maybe she is, but she's going down for this one. Carries a mimic card swiper in her apron pocket."

"I watched for those and missed it," Fedderman said. "She must be smooth."

"You can tell she's done it before."

"Let's not spoil her evening," Fedderman said, sipping some of his martini that he hadn't poured into his water glass. "Let's let her copy some more numbers, build up the evidence against her."

"Watch her keep breaking the law?"

"Sure."

"Doesn't that kind of make us accomplices?" Pearl asked. Since becoming an associate and not having the NYPD to cover legal expenses, she'd become cautious about exposing herself and the agency to potential litigation. Or maybe this was because she'd become fond of Linda and didn't want to compound the mess the young woman was in.

"In a way," Fedderman said, "but nobody'll know but us. And you and me, Pearl, we'd never rat each other out."

"I suspect you're half right," Pearl said.

She waited till an hour before closing time to call the NYPD, and Linda was apprehended with the card recorder in her apron pocket. It contained the names and credit card numbers of five diners who'd paid their checks with plastic that evening. Damning evidence.

As she was being led away, Linda was loudly and tearfully blaming everything on a guy named Bobby. Pearl believed her.

"Men!" Pearl said, with a disdain that dripped.

Fedderman didn't comment, standing there thinking it was Linda who'd illegally recorded the card numbers.

A beaming and impressed Sammy told them his check to QAI would be in the mail, and Pearl and Fedderman left the restaurant about eleven o'clock to go to their respective apartments. They would write up their separate reports tomorrow and present them to Quinn, who would doubtless instruct Pearl to send a bill to Sammy even though it might cross with his check in the mail. Business was business.

Fedderman waited around outside the restaurant with Pearl while she tried to hail a cab. The temperature was still in the eighties, and the air was so sultry it felt as if rain might simply break out instead of fall.

It never took Pearl long to attract the eye of a cabbie, so they'd soon part and Fedderman would walk the opposite direction to his subway stop two blocks away.

Pearl extended one foot off the curb into the street and waved, kind of with her whole body.

Sure enough, a cab's brake lights flared, and it made a U-turn, causing oncoming traffic to weave and honk, and drove half a block the wrong way in the curb lane to come to a halt near Pearl.

"It might have been Bobbie with an 'I-E,'" Fedderman said, as she was climbing into the back of the cab. "A woman."

Pearl glared at him. "Dream on."

She slammed the cab's door before he could reply.

Fedderman watched the cab make another U-turn to get straight with the traffic. He wondered if Pearl had always been the way she was, born with a burr up her ass. She was so damned smart, but always mouthing off and getting into trouble. What a waste. She'd never had a chance to make it any higher in the NYPD than he had. Fedderman was steady, a plodder, a solid detective, unskilled at departmental politics and wise enough to stay out of them. Staying out of things was another of Pearl's problems. She couldn't.

Another problem was that Pearl was a woman, and she had those looks. Her appearance drew unwanted attention, and she'd always been too hotheaded to handle it. She'd punched an NYPD captain once in a Midtown hotel after he'd touched her where he shouldn't have. That alone would have been enough to sink most careers. It hadn't quite sunk Pearl's, but there was always a hole in her boat, and she'd had to bail constantly just to stay afloat. That was why she'd finally drifted out of the NYPD and into the bank guard job. She could be nice to people ten, twenty seconds at a stretch, so it had worked out okay for her. But she'd never been happy at Sixth National. She missed the challenge, the action, the satisfaction of bringing down the bad guys, even the danger.

The way Fedderman had missed that life while chasing after elusive golf balls down in Florida, or fishing in Gulf waters and pulling from the sea creatures he didn't even recognize as fish.

Like Pearl, he'd been ripe for Quinn's call.

Fedderman smiled in the direction Pearl had gone and then walked away, his right shirt cuff unbuttoned and flapping like a white surrender flag with every stride. If he knew about the cuff, he didn't seem to mind.

He did kind of mind that there would be no more free drinks and appetizers at Sammy's.

3

The next morning they were sitting in the arrangement of desks that made up Quinn and Associates' office. Quinn was seated behind his desk, Pearl and Fedderman in chairs facing him. Low-angled sunlight invaded through the iron-grilled window and warmed the office. The Mr. Coffee over on the table in the corner was chuggling away, filling the air with the rich scent of fresh-brewed beans.

Fedderman had his suit coat off and was slouched sideways, taking notes. His right shirt cuff was already unbuttoned. That usually happened because of the way he cocked and dragged his wrist over paper as he wrote. A sunbeam alive with dust motes had found Pearl and made her more vividly beautiful than ever. Quinn wished, as he often did, that what they'd shared together hadn't ended. He liked to think that maybe it hadn't. He knew Pearl liked to think that it definitely had, for her, anyway. Could be she was right.

Quinn had made copies of the clippings Chrissie Keller had given him, and he explained the situation. Pearl and Fedderman listened carefully. This was the sort of investigation they all liked—multiple murder rather than credit card pilfering. In the world of catching the bad guys and setting things as right as possible, solving this one could make a person feel useful. If only the case weren't more than five years old. They all knew the odds of rekindling the past and nailing the Carver were long.

"I've read a lot about the mystical link between twins," Pearl said, when Quinn was finished talking. "I'd like to say it's bullshit, but I'm not so sure."

"I don't see how the mystery of twins is in any way relevant to this," Fedderman said. "Other than motivating our client."

"That's enough relevance," Quinn said, "considering we're no longer paid by the city." He looked at Pearl. "Or by a bank."

They had all stuck their necks out to create this investigative agency, and they knew it.

Three people, working without a net. No one said anything for a while.

"That was a pregnant pause if ever I didn't hear one," Pearl finally said.

Fedderman, who'd been adding tooth marks to his dented yellow pencil, glanced over at her. "Does that mean we can expect another, smaller pause?"

"Point is," Quinn said, "however a client's motivated, if it's legal and ethical, we'll gladly accept payment."

"One out of two would be okay," Pearl said.

She was ignored.

"You mentioned our client had won some sorta jackpot," Fedderman said to Quinn.

"Slot machine thing. She hit a kind of tri-state trifecta and got temporarily rich. This is how she feels compelled to spend her money."

"That mysterious twins business," Pearl said. She'd also been taking notes. She tapped her pencil's eraser on a front tooth in tiny bounces. "I remember the Carver murders, how they confounded the hell out of everyone. You looked through this stuff already, Quinn. Do you think we've really got a chance of finding the killer?"

"A chance, sure."

"It'd help if we could get the murder books outta the NYPD cold-case files," Fedderman said.

"Right now," Quinn said, "I don't think the NYPD would be very cooperative. Understandably, they don't want us stirring up something they failed to solve."

"Maybe you could talk to Renz," Pearl said.

Harley Renz was the city's popular police commissioner, and a longtime acquaintance of them all. He was an unashamed, ambitious, and corrupt bureaucratic climber. "Renz would have the most to lose if we came along after five years and solved a serial killer case," Quinn said. "In Harley's eyes, that'd be making the NYPD look like dopes."

"It wouldn't be the first time," Fedderman said. "So what would he lose?"

"Political capital. To Renz, that's like losing his own blood. In fact, it is his blood." Quinn laced his fingers behind his neck and leaned back in his chair. Maybe too far back. Pearl was watching him, waiting to see if this time he'd topple backward. Maybe hoping. "We need to have something solid before we go to Renz," Quinn said. "And some way for him to gain by us solving the case."

"Meanwhile," Pearl said, "we do our jobs, and never mind if our efforts are hopeless."

"I'll miss the free drinks and food at Sammy's," Fedderman said. "But to tell you the truth, I was getting tired of playing the alcoholic businessman. And Pearl was putting on weight."

"I'll come over there and put some weight on your goddamned head," Pearl said.

Quinn thought about settling them down so they could all get to work familiarizing themselves with the five-year-old murder investigation; then he decided against it. He knew Pearl, and she wasn't yet at the point where she would physically attack Fedderman. And experience had taught Fedderman how to tread around Pearl just out of range while sticking her with his barbs. So let them agitate each other, Quinn thought.

It was how they worked best.

4

It had been a grueling series of hot and dusty bus rides from Bennett, South Dakota, to New York City. You could measure the distance in more than miles. Mary Bakehouse didn't want to make the return trip. Ever.

She'd spent the weekend moving in to her new apartment in the East Village. Mary had enough money that she could afford the place for a while. In the meantime she'd be job hunting.

The apartment was the third-floor east unit of a six-story building. The previous tenant had been a smoker, and the scent of stale tobacco smoke made itself known at unexpected times, when closet doors were opened or summer breezes worked their way in through the window and played across the floor. The window was stuck only two inches open and wouldn't budge, so usually the living room was stale and stuffy. Mary would buy some kind of aerosol air freshener when she got a chance. Or maybe one of those things you plugged into an electrical socket and it hissed every fifteen minutes or so and deodorized the air. Something was needed. She didn't like tobacco smoke and could smell it for what seemed like blocks. She had a nose like a beagle, a boyfriend had told her once, not quite grasping what he'd said. She hadn't gone out with him again, figuring him to be mentally inferior.

A few people had warned Mary about living in this part of the Village. It could be dangerous. Mary didn't take those warnings seriously. She'd dealt with thugs before, in Bennett. They were just like New York thugs, only they wore cowboy hats.

The way she dealt with them was by showing a complete absence of fear. Mary had a sweet, heart-shaped face, a frail body, and rather sad brown eyes. A frail person who looked as if her photo belonged in an old locket. But there was something about her that strongly suggested she would hold her ground. Anything done to her would be at a cost. People with the wrong kind of thing in mind usually backed off.

Something else about Mary was that she had a gun. A .32-caliber Taurus revolver with a checked wood grip. She'd shot targets and plunked varmints with it for years on her parents' ranch. Brought it with her in her suitcase on the bus. The security people didn't check bus luggage the way they checked suitcases for airline travel. Or if they had checked her suitcase, they hadn't found the gun, rolled up in an old pair of Levi's.

The apartment was partially furnished, so moving in had been easy. She'd simply opened her suitcase and transferred her clothes to the dresser drawers in the tiny bedroom.

The bedroom smelled better than the living room, so maybe the previous tenant hadn't smoked in bed. The bed itself was a twin size, and the mattress was pretty saggy. She did always allow herself a good bed, so she would buy a better mattress and put this one in the basement storage area that went with the apartment. Her mother had advised her that a good mattress and good shoes were of prime importance. She had a new pair of Nike joggers. The mattress and a few more pieces of furniture—a table, a lamp—were all she should need. Things she'd pick out and that would make the place uniquely hers.

She slid her empty suitcase under the bed and then turned her attention to her big vinyl portfolio that held samples of her work. Mary was a graphic designer with a degree from Happer Design College in South Dakota. Her instructors had told her she was the most talented student they'd ever taught. They said as much in letters of recommendation. She realized that wouldn't make getting a job in New York easy, but surely it should make it possible. She wasn't looking for an easy time here. A chance was all she wanted.

Back in the living room, she stood with her fists propped on her slender hips and looked around.

What have you done, Mary Bakehouse?

The walls were painted a mottled off-white, and the gray carpet was stained and frayed. What furniture there was appeared to be a flea market hodgepodge, but some of it, like the sturdy old matching bookcases that stood side by side against a living room wall, looked to be of pretty good quality. The bookcases held a small TV, an odd assortment of vases, and even a few old books without dust jackets. Mary thought she'd put some flowers in those vases, and maybe even read some of the books.

This will work. It has to work!

She switched the air conditioner in the living room window on low, thinking it would partially cool that room and the bedroom while she was away running errands. There were black ornamental iron bars on some of the windows, along with a U-shaped iron horizontal bar that held the air conditioner fast in its window so it couldn't be removed except from inside the apartment. The windows that looked out over the small courtyard outside her bedroom didn't have bars on them, probably because that was the way to the fire escape. Still, there were bars on enough of the windows that from the inside at least, the apartment had the aspect of a prison.

Okay, Mary thought, the real estate people who'd warned her were probably right; it was a dangerous part of town in a dangerous city. But she wasn't the shrinking innocent they seemed to assume. Mary figured her accent made her seem more naïve than she was. She was twenty-five and had been away to college. She'd been around some.

Right now, she needed some groceries, and a few things for the bathroom, such as toothpaste, soap, and shampoo. And that air freshener. When she was finished with shopping for those items and had put them away, she'd go out and see if she could find a place to buy an easel and some art supplies. That shouldn't be hard to do in the Village. It was an artsy place.

An artsy place with bars on the windows.

Mary went into the *L*-shaped kitchen, gazed into the empty refrigerator, and decided to make a list.

As she was turning around to go get her purse in the bedroom, she noticed the large blue ceramic canisters on the sink counter near the stove. They were lettered FLOUR, COFFEE, SUGAR, and so on. Mary liked them and might have chosen them herself.

She was a tea drinker, so when she returned from the bedroom with her purse, she put her gun in the empty coffee canister.

As she was going out the door, Mary glanced back and smiled. The apartment was nothing like the ones in those old Doris Day white-telephone movies. More like the apartments in *Seinfeld*, only shabbier. But it was already beginning to feel like home.

This was going to work, Mary assured herself again, making sure the door was closed tight and locked behind her.

Everything was going to be okay.

5

"You're tearing open old wounds," Rhonda Nathan's mother said.

Pearl thought the elderly woman might begin to cry, but the unblinking gray eyes remained calm behind what looked like cheap drugstore eyeglasses.

The Nathans hadn't been difficult to trace, but the effort had been time-consuming. When their twenty-five-year-old daughter, Rhonda, had been killed by the Carver seven years ago, they'd lived in a spacious condo in the East Fifties. Rhonda's father, who'd been struck and killed by a bus three years ago, had been the family breadwinner with a partnership in a Wall Street firm. His widow, Edith Nathan, had fallen a long way to this cramped apartment on the Lower East Side.

Pearl did feel sorry for the woman. Her thinning gray hair was unkempt, her complexion sallow. The flesh beneath her chin dangled in wattles, and her figure, if she'd ever had one, had become plump in a way that reminded Pearl of infants still in the crib. Breasts seemed nonexistent beneath her stained blue robe with its mismatched white sash.

The woman's eyes were fixed straight ahead. Her soul seemed to have wandered.

"Edith?" Pearl said softly.

The unnaturally calm gray eyes trained themselves on Pearl.

"We don't mean to cause pain," Pearl said.

"But you do cause pain," Edith said. "Like a scab being ripped from a wounded heart that will never completely heal."

Pearl glanced around the humble apartment. Geraniums in plastic pots on a windowsill were obviously dead, as were roses in a cracked vase on top of the television. Live flowers in another pot in the middle of the kitchen table, barely visible to Pearl, saved the apartment's plant life from being a sad metaphor. On a shelf that ran along a wall near a cabinet full of glass curios, a color photograph of a young dark-haired woman with a bright smile was propped in a silver frame. Pearl recognized Rhonda Nathan from her photos in the newspaper clippings of seven years ago that had been delivered by Chrissie Keller.

"Like most of the families of the monster's victims," Edith said, "I long ago accepted the reality that my daughter and only child was gone from the world. Nothing will bring her back. Not fate or a prayer or a deal with God or the devil. Not you reopening the investigation. Would I trade my life for the monster's death? Yes. Would I gladly kill him slowly in the most dreadful way? Yes. But not in the heat of vengeance. More in the balancing of scales." Edith sighed and leaned back into the flowered sofa cushions. "There is a numbness in me, Detective Kasner. Has been for years. Not a depression. A numbness because something is missing."

Edith hadn't looked closely at Pearl's ID when Pearl had identified herself as a detective. It wasn't ethical for Pearl to let the woman go on assuming she was with the NYPD, but Pearl was afraid the interview might not be granted otherwise.

Seven years ago in June, Rhonda Nathan had worked late at the advertising agency where she wrote copy, alone in her office cubicle. Her body had been found there by the office cleaning service just before daylight the next morning. She was slouched dead in her desk chair, nude, her nipples removed, the grotesque and bloody *X* carved deeply into her torso beneath her breasts. Her panties had been removed and knotted into a gag, stuffed deeply in her mouth in such a way that leftover material allowed for a leg hole to be looped around her neck and knotted to hold the gag firm. It was a method that had to be the result of planning and practice. A pencil had been placed between the victim's fingers, doubtless after death, as if she'd been taking notes throughout her torture and demise. A small thing, but it carried a jolting incongruity. It was one of several examples of a gruesome sense of humor that the Carver sometimes exhibited to the police at his crime scenes. A taunter, was the Carver. Not unusual in a serial killer who assumed he was much brighter than his pursuers.

Pearl decided not to go into the details of Rhonda's murder.

"In the intervening years since . . . it happened," she said, "have any new thoughts come to you, any recollections that might be of help? Even those that you might not think important?"

"Such as?" Edith asked softly.

"Anything that became clearer to you, or that you remembered about the week or so before the tragedy."

"I'm sorry, but there's nothing. And I think about that time every night, and sometimes I dream."

"Do you recall your daughter acting strangely—or simply out of character—in the time leading up to her death? Is there someone you can think of who could have had some disagreement with her? Someone who might have had a motive?"

"Motive?" Edith seemed mystified and slightly angry. "My daughter was a girl well liked. I would say *very* well liked. Rhonda was slain by a deranged monster, Detective Kasner. It's as simple and horrible as that."

"I think you're right," Pearl said, "but the monster doesn't necessarily seem like one when he's not being . . . himself. It's possible you knew him at the time, or at least had met him."

"Rhonda had recently broken up with her boyfriend, Charles Correnwell. It would be difficult to see Charles as a killer. Anyway, he moved to live with his mother in California weeks before Rhonda was killed, and has an alibi."

Pearl knew that to be true. Charles Correnwell, on the other side of a continent, had attended a college lecture and was later drinking with friends at the approximate time of Rhonda's murder.

"Your husband . . ." Pearl began.

Edith stared at her sharply. "He's dead."

"I know, ma'am. I know the circumstances."

"We were both shattered by the loss of our daughter," Edith said, "but I'm sure Aaron's death was an accident. He wouldn't leave me, leave the world, that way."

"I wasn't thinking that," Pearl said. "I was wondering if there might have been someone with an irrational motive to get at your husband by murdering his daughter."

"I'm sure there was no one that sick among our social or business acquaintances."

Pearl said nothing, and she and Edith exchanged glances. They'd established that monsters didn't always seem like monsters.

"Someone with protective coloring, you mean?" Edith said.

"Yes, ma'am."

Edith shrugged beneath the blue robe. "I'd have no way of knowing, would I?"

"Not unless a way came to you. Sometime when you were doing something else, or just before falling asleep, or waking up. The human mind works that way, catches us by surprise."

"I've fallen asleep and awakened thinking about Rhonda

almost every night and morning since she died," Edith said. "The horror always plays out the same way, and I always wish I could have done something—anything—to prevent it. That's the worst thing about the past, that it can't be changed."

Pearl felt stymied for a moment. "Mrs. Nathan—Edith. There's so much about a person that never makes it into a police report." She leaned forward. "What was your daughter's favorite food? Did she smoke? What sort of music did she listen to? Might she have met someone online? Did she have a lot of male friends? Did she like movies?"

Edith sat more rigidly and stared hard at her, then seemed to relax. "She liked junk food—hamburgers, French fries, anything greasy and bad for her health. She didn't smoke. Drank some, but not much. Music? She liked to listen to that little girl from Brooklyn."

"Cyndi Lauper?"

Edith seemed to brighten. "That's the one."

"So happens I'm also a fan," Pearl said.

"Rhonda used her computer, the Internet, but she didn't go to chat rooms or that sort of thing. She had mostly female friends but some boys. They'd talk a lot on their cell phones. She had her cell phone pressed to her ear too much, like they all do, like it was growing there. I told her she might get brain cancer, but she didn't listen."

"None of them do," Pearl said.

Neither woman said anything. Neither wanted to hear that it hadn't mattered whether Rhonda's cell phone would have given her cancer.

"These don't sound like the kind of questions that solve murder cases," Edith said.

"Oh, but they are," Pearl told her. "Almost always it's something that didn't seem important at the time that turns out to be the key."

"Rhonda had just gotten her degree in psychology and was spending most of her time waiting tables at Sporter's, the restaurant in the next block, while she was looking for a better job. She didn't have a lot of spare time." Edith rubbed her palms on her temples, her fingers rigid. She looked exhausted. "I've sometimes wondered if that's where she met the monster, at the restaurant."

"It's possible."

"The police looked into it and found nothing."

"That doesn't mean there was nothing," Pearl said.

Seeing that Edith was almost too tired to remain awake, Pearl stood up and thanked her for her time.

"Do you really think there's a chance, after all these years?" Edith asked. Her eyes were bloodshot, swollen, and without hope.

"A chance," Pearl said. "A slight chance."

"I saw when you showed me your identification that you weren't a real detective," Edith said. "I mean, with the police."

Pearl smiled. "I'm a real detective."

"Private," Edith said. "Who hired you? Who's paying for this?"

"Twin sister of one of the Carver victims," Pearl said.

Edith flinched slightly, as if assailed by a bright and sudden light. "Twins . . . my God, how she must have suffered." She stared directly at Pearl. "She's still suffering, isn't she?"

"She is." Pearl reached into a pocket, drew out one of her cards, and handed it to Edith. "If you do think of something . . ."

Edith accepted the card and studied it. "Quinn and Associates. Is that Captain Frank Quinn?"

"It is," Pearl said. "You know him?"

"By reputation. I'm glad he's one of the people looking for Rhonda's killer."

Pearl was reminded, as she often was, of Quinn's high standing with the public because of his success in apprehending serial killers. He was halfway famous.

What next? Pearl thought. *A book contract?*

"I'll call you," Edith said.

Her voice brought Pearl back from her thoughts.

"If I think of something," Edith reminded her.

"Yes," Pearl said. "Please. Anything, however trivial. It might make all the difference."

"Reopening the investigation can't be cheap," Edith said. "The surviving twin, is she rich?"

"Not usually," Pearl said, "but she recently came into some money."

"She must feel she has to do this."

"She feels that way right now," Pearl said.

"She won't change her mind," Edith said.

6

"Her check will clear," Quinn said. "I called her bank to make sure there were sufficient funds."

They were in the office, wondering why they couldn't get in touch with Chrissie Keller at either of the phone numbers she'd given them. A message machine answered at one number, but the messages didn't seem to get through. The other number was to a cell phone and elicited nothing but a high-pitched squeal.

"What about the check for the Sammy's job?" Pearl asked.

"It's good, too. I made sure."

"We're rich," Fedderman said.

"Solvent," Quinn said.

"So why can't we get in touch with Chrissie?" Pearl asked.

"Maybe she's one of those clients who figures she'll be the one to decide when we report," Fedderman said.

"Control freak," Pearl said.

"I hate those," Quinn said.

Pot, kettle, Pearl thought, and congratulated herself for staying quiet.

"If she doesn't contact us in a day or two, we can start to wonder," Quinn said. "Until then, we stay on the case. More interviews with victims' friends and family." He glanced from Pearl to Fedderman. "You two have any luck?"

"Not so's you'd notice," Pearl said.

Even as she spoke, she realized there was something about the case that she hadn't yet noticed. It played like a bashful shadow just beyond the borders of her consciousness.

Pearl and Fedderman handed Quinn copies of their interview notes for the files, then in matter-of-fact tones told him about their reinterviewing of people close to the Carver victims. Other than the usual contradictions that could be put down to the passage of time and erosion of memory, there didn't seem to be many discernable differences between these interviews and those done years ago. Nothing that might be construed as a lead.

Quinn considered lighting a cigar but didn't. Pearl would raise hell. She hated it when he or anyone else smoked in the office.

He thought about Chrissie Keller, the way she'd come into the office. Something about her. He was getting a bad feeling about what they'd gotten into, where it might be heading. A deep sensation in his stomach that was seldom off the mark.

"Some of the friends and family didn't like being taken back to that time," Fedderman said. "You could see it in their faces, and it made your heart sad."

"That's what these assholes start," Quinn said. "It goes on for years. Sometimes for generations."

"There's still a lot of breakage there," Pearl said. "A lot of hatred." But that was what she'd expected to find. She knew Quinn was right: Untimely, violent death resonated for decades.

"Let's check these statements in detail with the earlier ones," Quinn said. "Then we can do some more reinterviewing."

"Revive some more pain," Fedderman said sadly.

"Blame the aforementioned asshole," Quinn said.

* * *

It was when Pearl was integrating the new statements into the files that she realized what had been nagging at the edges of her mind. She reached for her folder containing the copies of the newspaper clippings that had been left by Chrissie Keller.

She leafed through the clippings and stopped at those concerning Chrissie's twin, Tiffany.

Pearl was right in what had occurred to her. She felt the flush of satisfaction that was what she loved most about this work.

"There are photos of all the victims until we get to victim number five, the Carver's last victim," she said. "Tiffany Keller. Lots of clippings, but none with a photograph."

Quinn and Fedderman checked their own copies.

No photos of Tiffany.

"Coincidence?" Fedderman asked. Thinking, *Yeah, sure.* Like most cops, he wasn't much of a believer in coincidence.

"It doesn't seem likely that Tiffany's murder would generate all those news items without a photo," Pearl said.

Quinn did his backward tilt in his desk chair and went into his casual balancing act, damn near tipping. "A young, attractive victim, sexually mutilated. There'd be plenty of photographs."

He watched Pearl go at it, like a hound on the scent, though she wouldn't like the comparison. She already had her computer booted up and was online, feeding Tiffany Keller's name into her browser.

It took only a few moments to search the New York papers' archives for related items.

Unsurprisingly, Tiffany's mutilation and death at the hands of the Carver had been a major news story. And as Quinn had thought, the gory details of the crime were accompanied by plenty of vivid photographs of the young, attractive victim.

"I'll be damned," Pearl said.

"Photos?" Quinn asked.

"Lots of them."

"Chrissie must have culled out the news clippings accompanied by photos," Fedderman said.

Pearl shook her head. "That's not what I mean."

Quinn and Fedderman moved closer so they could see her computer's monitor without glare.

Quinn felt the sensation in his stomach gain in intensity.

The screen showed what looked like a high school yearbook photo of a pretty, dark-haired girl with a broad grin and slightly uptilted brown eyes that suggested potential mischief. It was a potential never realized in a life cut short by the Carver.

The caption beneath the photo was simply the subject's name: *Tiffany Keller*.

Tiffany looked nothing like her twin who had hired Quinn and Associates to find her killer.

7

"This is crazy," Pearl said, as they crossed West Forty-fourth Street toward the Sherman Hotel.

Quinn silently agreed with her. But sometimes it was a crazy world with its own kind of whatever passed for logic.

"We're interrupting looking for a killer so we can search for our client," Pearl said.

"I told you, her check cleared," Quinn said. He hastened his pace to get across the heated concrete street before a white pickup truck leading a convoy of yellow cabs reached them. "That means we're still working for her." The line of vehicles hummed and rattled past behind them, stirring a warm breeze around their ankles.

"A cashier's check," Pearl said, when they were safely up on the sidewalk. "Which means we have no way to trace her through her checking account."

"If you're suggesting we should have been suspicious of her from the get-go," Quinn said, "you're right. I don't know how it happened, Pearl, but we've both become too trusting."

Pearl knew sarcasm when she heard it, so she bit her lip and held her silence.

It wasn't smart to cross Quinn when he was being sarcastic. It could mean he was getting angry with himself, which was when he was his most difficult with other people. So

Pearl simply followed him silently through a heavily tinted glass revolving door into the welcome coolness of the Sherman Hotel's marble and oak lobby.

The Sherman was an old hotel in a difficult phase of renovation while remaining open. That brought the rates down, so there was no dearth of business despite the cordoned-off areas of the lobby where the floor was torn up, or the closed restaurant necessitating eating at the diner on the corner. The Sherman was small but had a shabby elegance about it that was being resurrected to something like its original state. Besides all the oak wainscoting and the veined marble floor and columns, there was a lot of fancy crown molding, and what looked like the original long, curved oak registration desk. Some of the black leather furniture and the potted palms placed about the lobby appeared to be new. Pearl couldn't help looking for price tags on the plants.

When Quinn and Pearl approached the desk they were greeted by a tall, elderly man in a gray sport jacket with what must be the Sherman's crest over its left breast pocket. He had thick white hair and a long, lean face with a patrician nose that was made for him to look down over. The sort of chap who would have seemed right at home in a venerable British men's club.

"Yous got a reservation?" he inquired in a Brooklyn accent.

"Wees don't," Pearl said.

Quinn gave her a warning look. Sometimes that had an effect on Pearl. Usually not.

"We're inquiring about one of your guests," he said to the clerk, and showed him identification.

The clerk gazed at the ID, then made good use of his nose. "A private detective service? Not the real cops?"

"Not yet," Quinn said. "We were hoping you'd be cooperative."

The man gazed down his long nose at Quinn for another few seconds and then shrugged. "So who's the guest?"

"Chrissie Keller," Pearl said. "I phoned about her earlier."

"Ah, yeah. You don't look nuttin' like you sounded on the phone. You sounded taller. I told you, didn't I, that she'd checked out?"

"What we were wondering," Quinn said, "is if the maid's gotten around to cleaning her room."

The desk clerk turned his back on them and punched some keys on a computer keyboard. "Keller, Chrissie. She was in room five-twelve, checked out at ten-thirty a.m. yesterday. Maid service woulda taken care of five-twelve by now."

"Do you recall if she had a lot of luggage?" Quinn asked.

"Couldn't say. But Buddy the bellhop could. He's got a photographic mind. He remembers everything."

Quinn and Pearl looked around the otherwise deserted lobby. "Do you remember where Buddy is?" Quinn asked.

The desk clerk gave him a Brooklyn-British kind of look and then went to a phone at the other end of the registration desk.

Buddy the bellhop appeared within seconds, as if he'd been waiting for his cue. He was a short, middle-aged man with a stomach paunch that ruined the effect of a blue and red uniform that made him look like an officer in Napoleon's army. It even had epaulets. He glanced from Quinn to Pearl and smiled broadly. When he reached them, he looked about in mild confusion for suitcases to be carried.

The desk clerk explained to Buddy that only information was wanted. Quinn described Chrissie Keller.

"I remember her," Buddy said. "Nice lady, tipped okay."

"Luggage?" Quinn asked.

"Big red Samsonite hard shell with wheels. Also a black nylon carry-on, looked like the kinda thing that might hold a notebook computer. She was wearin' jeans and a yellow silk blouse."

"What color eyes?" Pearl asked.

"One brown, one blue." Buddy grinned hugely. "Naw,

I'm funnin' you there. I don't remember her eyes. The rest of it, though, you can count on it bein' right. I got a—"

"Yeah, we know."

"The suitcase was heavy. She was plannin' on bein' around for a while."

"You help her with the suitcase when she checked out?" Quinn asked.

"Naw, she just wheeled the thing out to the curb an' piled into a cab. The carry-on was slung over her arm with her purse. The purse was brown leather. Kinda scuffed. That was the last I seen of her."

Quinn thanked Buddy and turned back to the desk clerk. "Anybody been in five-twelve since Chrissie Keller?"

"Only the maid."

"Mind if we have a look?"

"At the maid?"

Pearl dead-eyed the desk clerk, which seemed to scare him.

"Don't mind at all," he said. "Yous see our rooms, you'll maybe wanna stay here sometime. But yous won't find nuttin'—not the way our maids clean up after a guest."

"Still," Quinn said with a smile, "you never know."

"I guess not," the desk clerk said. "Yous might find lint or a hair or somethin'."

"You'd be surprised," Quinn said.

"No, I wouldn't. I watch all those forensic crime-scene shows on TV, read mysteries about how crimes are solved." He appeared thoughtful. "There a crime been committed here?"

"We're trying to find out," Quinn said.

Buddy accompanied them in the elevator and led them to 512, where he opened the door and then hung around as if expecting a tip. Habit, Quinn supposed.

"The bathroom's in there," Buddy said, motioning toward a closed door. "There's your television. There's a refrigerator right there stocked with—"

Quinn gave him a look that shut him up. Buddy grinned, shrugged, and left the room.

Quinn and Pearl looked around. The room was neatly arranged; it had to be, since most of the furniture was fastened to the walls. The maid had indeed been thorough. The scent of Lemon Pledge still hung in the air, and there wasn't the slightest trace of dust.

Pearl checked the tiny bathroom and found it smelling of bleach and gleaming and spotless. Even the grout between the blue tiles looked clean. She wished she had a bathroom like it. Hers was about the same size but was comparatively cruddy.

Quinn was impressed. "The maid emptied the wastebaskets, and it looks like she polished their insides," he said.

"Waste of time," Pearl said.

Quinn wasn't sure if she meant the wastebasket polishing or the room search.

They went over the room thoroughly, but not with much enthusiasm, deftly staying out of each other's way because they'd done this dozens of times in dozens of rooms.

The desk clerk was right: the maid's thoroughness had neutered the room when it came to anything like a clue. There was nothing that might be of help. Not lint, not a hair. Nothing.

"Chrissie's away clean," Pearl said. "She did a number on us."

Quinn knew she was right. But what kind of number? And why?

Two blocks away from where Quinn and Fedderman stood, a man was standing staring in the window of a luggage shop.

A trip to someplace interesting, where I've never been before. That's what I should do, take a trip. Pack a bag and get

*out of this city, at least for a while. Someplace in Europe. Or
the Caribbean, if I can find an island that—*

Air brakes hissed, drawing his attention.

He watched the young woman step down from the bus
that had stopped near the corner. She was in her thirties,
with dark eyes and luxurious shoulder-length dark hair that
bounced with her generous breasts as she took the long,
lurching step down to the pavement. Her dress was pale
green, made of some kind of thin material that clung to her
body in the light summer breeze.

How gracefully she moved. So like a cat. Her high heels
flashed as she extended her long legs with each stride, her
calf muscles working like silk.

Dancer's legs, he thought. Maybe she was a dancer.
Maybe she was—

He realized he'd begun following the woman without
even thinking about it. As if some part of him had already
made the decision that their lives and her death should converge.

No, goddamn it!

He stopped walking, using all his willpower to avert his
eyes from the woman.

I don't do that anymore.

I don't even have a hard-on.

He turned around and started walking in the opposite direction the woman was going. He didn't even glance back at
her for one last look. One additional memory of her he could
recall in detail at least for a while. He walked faster, length-
ening his stride, pounding his heels down hard as if testing
the resiliency of the sidewalk.

I don't do that anymore.

I don't have to do that anymore.

But he found himself recalling the way her hair and her
breasts had bounced as she'd stepped down out of the bus.

He smiled. Even though that part of his life was over and
he was somebody else now, it did no harm to remember. To

think about how things were, or even how they might have been. Even how they might be. After all, he wasn't the one who'd stirred up the past and started the thoughts playing like movie scenes in his mind. Scenes that he was in or was simply observing, looking at them usually from above, as if he'd been a spirit in the room.

Thoughts . . .

Thoughts never hurt anyone. How could they? They weren't real. You couldn't even touch them.

And sometimes you couldn't stop them.

But he did stop thinking about leaving the city.

8

Even though she'd brushed her teeth, the aftertaste of last night's scotch that she'd used to relax and make herself tired remained. Pearl didn't mind. She knew she was having trouble sleeping because she was on the hunt with the pack she knew and in strange ways loved. Or was it the hunt that she loved? Either way, she liked it that her internal engine was running like a separate heart.

The engine had awakened her early from her disturbed slumber, which was why she was the first one in the office this morning.

Pearl sat down at her gray steel desk and booted up her computer. She'd done some research at home on her laptop, so she copied files from her flash drive to her desk computer. That completed, she replaced the flash drive in her purse and set to work running Internet searches for information pertaining to Chrissie Keller.

When that failed she got up and went over and poured coffee from the brewer's glass pot into her personalized ceramic mug, then added powdered cream and stirred until not much of it floated on top. Her second coffee of the morning. Cop pop.

She glanced at her watch. Almost nine o'clock, and she was still alone in the office. *What the hell?*

Then she remembered that, instead of meeting at the office this morning, Quinn and Fedderman were going to the East Side to interview some witnesses. Pearl might be alone a while longer.

She sat down again at her computer and sipped her coffee while she idly typed "the carver, serial killer" into her browser and began another Internet search.

Most of what came up she'd already seen, but there were a few unfamiliar sites. She sighed, sipped coffee, and visited the first one. It had to do with a butcher's theft of Christmas turkeys from a halfway house for ex-convicts in 1997 in Miami.

Off to a good start.

The next link took her to a site that sold exotic wood carvings of birds. As she continued to link from one site to another, they became more and more remote from her subject. Still, she kept on. Sometimes doggedness turned the trick. Give Pearl the right haystack and she'd find the needle.

The word "carver" alone eventually linked her to "Initials Carved in Trees," which linked her to "Initials of the Famous," which linked her to "Initial Reports," categorized by city, which linked her to "Crimes against persons reports, Detroit PD," which linked her to an amateur crime site called "Initial Attempts" that featured cases where inept beginner criminals had been interrupted during their attempted crimes. It featured photographs of an astounded would-be teenage burglar blinded by floodlights, one leg draped over a window ledge, a sack of loot in his hand; and a security camera shot of a would-be robber fleeing a convenience store empty-handed while a large dog snapped at his heels.

And there was something else.

Pearl sat forward. There was a blurry photo of what appeared to be a slender young woman. Her face wasn't clearly visible. There was a brief accompanying news item that made no reference to the photograph but reported that a woman named Geraldine Knott, twenty-two years old, had been attacked by a masked assailant in the parking structure of her apartment. He'd struck her, straddled her, then drawn a knife and begun telling her exactly what he was going to do with it, including severing her nipples.

Something had caused the assailant to break off his attack and flee. Possibly it had been the coincidence of sirens, as police arrived at the building across the street after being called on another matter. Ms. Knott was discovered when a woman who also lived in the building entered the parking structure and noticed her slumped and dazed on the concrete floor. The news report said the victim had a broken collarbone, was suffering from extreme stress, and was hospitalized in stable condition. An artist's sketch of the attacker, based on Geraldine Knott's description, would be in the paper soon. The date of the news item was April 7, eight years ago. Shortly before the Carver began his horrific string of murders in New York.

Pearl ran a search of the Detroit paper archives and easily found another item about the Geraldine Knott assault, accompanied by the sketch artist's rendering of her attacker. He was wearing a balaclava that covered his head and all of his face but his eyes. There didn't seem to be anything special about the eyes. Geraldine Knott couldn't recall their color.

All in all, Pearl thought, the sketch was useless. Nevertheless, she printed out what she had, three copies, for Quinn, Fedderman, and herself.

Ten minutes later, Quinn and Fedderman came into the office. The sultry summer air came with them, thick as syrup. Both men were damp. Quinn's hair stuck out every which way and was glistening with rainwater, and his blue tie was spotted. Fedderman's customary wrinkled brown suit looked even more rumpled than usual. When he walked past

Pearl's desk she noticed he smelled like a wet dog. Maybe the suit, maybe Fedderman.

"Raining again out there?" Pearl asked, knowing the answer was obvious but wanting to rub it in.

Quinn and Fedderman ignored her. Quinn nodded toward the computer.

"What are you doing?" he asked, walking over to remove his rain-spotted suit coat and drape it over a brass hook on the wall near his desk.

"Running a computer check on one Geraldine Knott," Pearl said. Not telling them everything up front, letting the geniuses work for it.

"Why?" Fedderman asked, shambling over like a curious hound and staring at Pearl's computer monitor.

Pearl didn't answer but pointed to the paper-clipped printouts on her desk corner.

"Read those," she said.

Fedderman and Quinn both read silently, then looked at each other.

"Holy Jesus!" Fedderman said.

"Not Him," Pearl said. "Me. This came up on an Internet search for the Carver while you two were frolicking in the rain."

"Holed up eating doughnuts," Fedderman said. "And we brought one for you."

"I don't see it."

"Fedderman ate it," Quinn said. "Just as we turned the corner and pulled in to park out front."

Fedderman shrugged.

Quinn laid his copy of the printout back on Pearl's desk. "Great work, Pearl. Stay on it. Find out everything you can about Geraldine Knott."

Fedderman grinned and pulled a greasy white paper sack from where it was jammed in his suit coat pocket. He placed it on Pearl's desk.

"For you," he said. "Chocolate icing. A cake doughnut, so in case you want to dunk, it won't come apart in your coffee. Don't believe everything you hear. We're always thinking of you."

"Yeah," Pearl said.

But thinking what?

She thanked Fedderman, opened the grease-stained sack, and removed the sticky doughnut that had been in Fedderman's pocket.

It smelled like a wet dog.

9

Mary Bakehouse maneuvered toward the doors of the crowded subway car, wielding her large, flat imitation-leather artist's portfolio vertically like the prow of an icebreaker to forge ahead. A man with breath smelling of onions pressed tightly behind her, pushing her even faster than she wanted to go. A bead of sweat trickled down her ribs. Someone stepped on her toe.

Nothing like South Dakota.

She'd barely gotten out onto the platform when the doors hissed closed behind her. Walking away, she heard the train squeal and roar as it pulled forward and picked up speed. The public address system was repeating something no one from any country on earth would understand.

Mary was exhausted from her two job interviews, and not very optimistic. An ad agency had told her that things were slow, but maybe. An architectural firm had candidly told her they simply weren't hiring, and in fact the man who had posted the want ad in the paper's classified section had himself been laid off and was leaving at the end of the week.

As she trudged up the granite steps to the entrance to her apartment building, she was beginning to think she'd chosen precisely the wrong time to attempt a move to New York.

The lobby, which was really more of a vestibule, was at

least quiet. She pressed the up button for the elevator and settled her weight equally on both tired legs. In the building above her cables thrummed, but the brass arrow floor indicator on the wall over the elevator door didn't budge.

As she waited patiently, she heard footsteps descending the nearby stairs. Somebody in a hurry.

But at the landing just above the lobby, the sound of hurried soles on rubber stair treads suddenly ceased, as if whoever had come down from upstairs was standing absolutely still, waiting for something.

For me to leave?

The landing was out of sight, but Mary thought she could hear someone breathing heavily, almost asthmatically.

A man. She was sure it was a man. Not only because of the loud breathing but because of the sound his soles had made on the stairs, a rapid, repetitive clomping that was almost like a machine gun firing. As if he was simply letting his weight tilt him forward and catching himself with each step. Most women didn't take stairs that way.

The elevator arrived, unoccupied. Mary hurried inside and pressed the button for her floor. When the steel door had glided almost shut, she thought she heard the footfalls continue on the stairs. It was obvious now that whoever was on the landing had been waiting for her to clear the lobby so he or she wouldn't be seen leaving the building.

Mary told herself there could be a dozen reasons for that, none of them concerning her.

As the elevator rose, she glanced down and saw that the dusting of fine hairs on the backs of her arms was standing up. Suddenly she had to swallow.

I guess this means I'm scared.

She told herself that rationally she had no reason to be afraid. If someone wanted to use the stairs instead of the elevator and not be seen, that was fine with her.

Unless her apartment had been burgled.

Well, she'd soon see if that had occurred. She almost smiled. If a burglar had chosen her apartment to break into, he'd be one disappointed thief. She had little worth stealing.

No, that wasn't quite true. She remembered her Dell notebook computer sitting right out in plain view on the desk in the living room. But even that was over five years old, hopelessly obsolete to anyone familiar with electronics.

Still, if it was gone, she'd have to replace it.

This is absurd. Nothing's been stolen and I am not *afraid!*

When she left the elevator and reached her apartment door, she studied it and saw no sign that it had been forced. She tried the doorknob, and it wouldn't turn. The door was still locked, as it should be.

Even if she hadn't been afraid, she felt a huge relief.

Imagination. Too much imagination because I'm creative.

Curiosity overcame what was now merely a vague unease, and she unlocked the door and opened it. Drawing a deep breath, she stepped into her apartment.

An encompassing glance told her that everything was okay. Nothing seemed to have been disturbed since she'd left to go job hunting this morning.

Telling herself she'd been a big baby, she closed the door to the hall and locked the dead bolt, then fastened the chain. She crossed the room and yanked the drapes open wider so more of the early evening light spilled in through the window.

She looked around more carefully. There were the throw pillows stacked as they'd been on the sofa, so she could prop her feet up while watching television. There was her empty orange juice glass she'd forgotten to carry back to the kitchen this morning, precisely where she'd left it on the coffee table, resting on a magazine so it wouldn't leave a ring.

She went to the window air conditioner and switched it on maximum, enjoying the cool breeze gradually generated by the humming blower. When she turned around her gaze went to the nearby desk, checking to make sure her computer was still there. She knew that it was, yet she still had to look.

And there was her computer.

But its lid was raised and it was on.

Doubt crawled like an insect up the nape of her neck. She was sure she'd shut down the computer this morning. But she must not have. There it was, not online but with the desktop icons displayed against a field of blue.

Mary went to the computer and laid her hand over it. She felt no warmth. Might that mean it hadn't been on very long? Shouldn't it be warm if she'd gone away and left it on for hours? She wasn't sure. She hadn't actually experimented to find out. How could she know?

She switched on the desk lamp, then sat before the computer and went online. She moved the cursor and clicked on the computer's history.

The sites recently visited were familiar. Her e-mail from when she'd checked for messages this morning, the *Times* and *Post* online editions. eBay, to do some looking but not buying. *USA Today*, to find out what was happening outside New York.

All the sites were ones she was sure she'd visited the last time she'd sat at the computer this morning. It didn't appear that anyone had gone fishing for her personal information.

On the other hand, she knew the entire contents of her hard drive might have been copied to an external disk drive, or even a flash drive, and she'd have no way of knowing.

And she was sure, *sure,* that she'd left the computer this morning with its screen dark.

But how sure was anyone of anything?

Mary got up from the desk and made herself look through the rest of the apartment, extending a tentative hand and switching on lights as she went, even though it wasn't yet dusk. She looked in closets, even peered under her bed, before she was satisfied that she was alone.

She settled into the sofa and worked off her shoes, trying to relax. But she was still afraid—and angry.

It wasn't so much that someone—the man on the stairs?—might have entered her apartment; it was more as if he'd entered her life.

There were plenty of dangerous nut cases in the human turmoil of the city. She'd been warned about them often enough. In the closeness and press of Manhattan, any woman was bound to pass at least some of them on the crowded sidewalks every day.

She knew that some men became fixated on certain women with merely a glance. For them it was like obsessive love.

She knew that some men killed the thing they loved.

10

Quinn was finishing his tuna melt and fries supper at the Lotus Diner when Thel, the waitress, approached him without her glass coffeepot.

"Your friend Pearl's on the phone," Thel said.

"Can you bring it to the table?"

"I can yank it outta the wall and bring it to you—then what you do with it is your business."

Thel took kidding okay, but she always shot back. She was a middle-aged, dumpy woman in a dead-end job. Her forehead was folded into a permanent frown, and the deep etching around her mouth wasn't laugh lines. Her teeth were yellowed and needed braces she'd never be able to afford. Being a smart-ass was what got her by in the world. It was what she had, and she worked it hard, sometimes making customers angry. The diner owner liked Thel, so she got by with her attitude act, especially after he'd learned that in some perverse way it actually attracted customers. And it didn't hurt that the owner was at least slightly afraid of Thel.

Quinn wasn't afraid of her. He pretended not to have heard her, dabbed at his lips with his white paper napkin, and then slid out of the booth. His cell was turned off so he could eat in peace. Pearl and Fedderman had known where to find him, but they wouldn't have bothered him unless the call was at least somewhat important.

He knew where the phone was mounted on the wall near the doorway to the kitchen, at the end of the counter. As he approached it he saw that the receiver was unhooked and lying on the floor. He gripped the cord and hand-over-hand pulled up the receiver like a fish he'd caught and held it to his ear.

"That you, Quinn?" Pearl's voice.

"Me," Quinn said. "Straight from my tuna melt and coffee. Tell me this is important?"

"As your sandwich, you mean?"

"I'm getting enough crap from Thel, so don't push it. What's going on?"

"Thel? You mean that woman hasn't been fired by now? With her attitude and that mouth?"

"*You* hang on—why not her? Why'd you call, Pearl?"

"Harley Renz phoned here. He wants you to get back at him at his office like yesterday or sooner."

"Get back at him?"

"*To* him. You know what I meant, Quinn."

Thel has infected us all. "Renz say what it is he wanted?"

"You, to call him." Pearl sighed her loud telephone sigh, as if dealing with a teenage obscene caller. "He *is* the police commissioner, Quinn. Maybe you should deign to return his call."

"You got a point," Quinn said, and hung up.

He depressed the old wall phone's cradle button, then let it bounce up before he punched out Harley Renz's direct line at 1 Police Plaza. This was no time to goof around with Pearl. Harley *was* police commissioner, so maybe he did have something important to say.

Or ask.

Or demand.

As he listened to the phone chirp on the other end of the

connection, Quinn glanced over and saw that Thel had gone from where she'd been wiping down the counter and eavesdropping on his conversation. Now she was standing by his table, which she'd completely cleared, and was ignoring him while scribbling on her order pad, figuring his total.

And her tip.

The chirping in Quinn's right ear was replaced by Harley Renz's impatient growl.

"'Bout time you returned my call."

"What's this about, Harley?"

"Your investigation," Renz said. "I want you to stop it. Refund your fee. Tell your client it's over."

"Can't."

"Why is that?"

"Can't find my client."

"You mean she's lost? Like missing keys?"

"Like a missing client."

After a long silence, Renz said in a soft but strained voice. "Just stop your investigation, Quinn. As of now, this phone call. I don't care if you never find your client. Never, never, never. Do I make myself clear?"

"Never," Quinn said, and hung up.

Mary Bakehouse had gotten over most of the uneasiness about the time she'd come home and found her computer on. She simply must have left it on that morning and not realized it. There was no point in looking for things to make herself afraid.

On the surface, her situation was getting better. A couple of job interviews had left her with the impression the human resource directors might actually call her. And the tobacco smoke smell was finally out of her apartment. Or was she simply getting used to it?

She couldn't be sure sometimes that after being away for a while and entering the apartment, she didn't for just a second catch a whiff of the awful scent. Mary hated smoking. Her favorite teacher in primary school, a heavy smoker, had died of lung cancer when Mary was ten. It had left quite an impression on her, as well as a loathing for the tobacco industry and smoking in general. Maybe that was all she was smelling, her hate.

The city itself seemed harder for her now, more dangerous. She hadn't felt that way until she'd been accosted last week by a homeless man who'd politely asked for any loose change she might have. Mary hadn't had any change, but the man wouldn't take no for an answer. His attitude quickly changed, and he'd grabbed the sleeve of her raincoat and yanked her back toward him when she tried to walk away.

She couldn't forget the look in his faded blue eyes. There was raw hatred there, and when he began raving incomprehensibly about her "selfishness," spraying her face with spittle, she felt herself returning that hatred. How could she not?

That day the city became in her mind a more menacing place. Dark doorways suggested danger. As did heavy traffic, street vendors of questionable goods, panhandlers, men who stared vaguely but knowingly at her in the subway train as it raced rocking and squealing toward its destination.

In the subway, it was one man in particular. She saw him almost every time she rode, as if they were on the same timetable, though Mary had no particular schedule. She supposed he might be one of the homeless who virtually lived belowground in the subway system. He was unshaven, and his clothes were threadbare. He wore a gray baseball hat with its bill pulled low, so that he observed her from shadow and with half-eyes that never blinked. Once—quite deliberately, she was sure—he slowly licked his lips and then smiled at her. It was a message she loathed and feared. He seemed to feed on her fear, as if he were drawing it across the swaying subway car to his inner evil self. He was hungry for her fear.

She'd tried not to work herself into a dither. After all,

wearing beard stubble was the current style among male movie and TV stars, and some *new* clothes were doctored to look faded and threadbare. Even unwashed. This was an era when celebrities looked like bums.

But this man smelled like one of the dispossessed. A rank odor of stale perspiration and urine emanated from him. The stench of the desperate and dangerous.

Mary almost collapsed with relief when the man remained seated and unmoving and didn't get off at her stop.

Thank God! Let him pick on some other woman now. Let some other woman feel her carefully nurtured armor drop to her feet with her heart.

After the unsteadiness of the subway car, the concrete platform felt firm and safe beneath her feet.

She glanced back and saw that the man was watching her through the train's smeared and scratched window as she joined the crowd moving along the platform toward the steps to the street. She'd tried to show no reaction, but she knew she had, and he'd seen it.

That was what infuriated her, that they could do this to her and enjoy her fear.

Mary was a strong woman—she knew she was. Yet lately she'd been afraid almost all the time, even unconsciously. Sitting in warm sunlight she'd become aware that she had her shoulders hunched and feel chilled, and she'd realize it was because of her fear.

In the beginning she was certain she'd never return to South Dakota except to visit, but now she wasn't so sure. There was nothing to be afraid of in South Dakota. No buildings crowded together and blocking the light; no teeming sea of uninterested faces; no daily news accounts of unspeakable horrors; no brick corners she was afraid to turn.

That was what, if anything, might drive her from the city. Her fear.

She would never have believed it of herself.

11

After entering her apartment, Mary Bakehouse engaged the dead-bolt lock and fastened the chain. She draped the gray blazer she'd been wearing (an essential part of her interview outfit) over a hanger in the closet, then stepped out of her high-heeled pumps.

Mary was returning from three fruitless job interviews. She'd been told after each that they might call her, but she knew better. She had received no callbacks. Nothing had panned out. The economy. That was her problem, she was assured by well-fed men and annoyingly lean, suited women. The bad economy was making jobs scarce and competition for those jobs fierce. "You almost have to sleep with someone," a greyhound of a woman who'd been waiting with Mary to be interviewed had confided to her in a whisper.

Not that, Mary thought. She'd return to small-town life and small ambitions before engaging in thinly disguised prostitution.

She changed into jeans and a loose-fitting blue T-shirt lettered DEATH CAB FOR CUTIE, advertising one of the group's concerts from two years ago in Tulsa. She'd bought it cheap and on impulse from a street vendor, figuring it matched her mood.

Mary poured herself a glass of iced tea from the plastic

pitcher she kept in the refrigerator. She carried the glass into the living room and slumped on the sofa, automatically reaching for the remote.

She watched cable news for a while and didn't in the slightest feel buoyed by it. Switched it off.

Misery doesn't really love company.

After staring at the opposite wall for a few minutes, she got up and went back into the kitchen and placed her half-empty glass on the sink counter. Her thirst was slaked, but now she was hungry. Lunch had been a street vendor's pretzel and diet soda, so an early supper was in order.

There's nothing in the fridge.

The deli again.

A glance out the window told her that dusk had moved in, and the drizzle that had started just as she'd arrived at her apartment building had stopped. Playing it safe, she got an umbrella with a telescoping handle from the closet and carried it as she left the apartment. It had rained once today; it could rain again.

The deli was only two blocks away and around the corner. As she walked she decided to have the orange chicken again. It was the best thing they had for takeout, so why not eat it two evenings in a row?

She picked up her pace. She could almost smell the narrow takeout buffet that ran down the center of the diner.

Nose like a beagle.

When she was in the brightly lit deli she felt better. She spooned some of the orange chicken from its heated metal pot into a white foam takeout container, then some white rice. She thought about buying a *Daily News* when she checked out at the register, then decided she shouldn't spend the money and left the newspaper lying in its rack. Next to it was the last *City Beat,* one of several smaller New York papers that competed in a city hooked on information. It was a giveaway that made money from advertising space, including personal ads. Mary scanned the personals sometimes and let her imagination roam, but she was a long way from calling any of the numbers.

She picked up the tabloid-style paper and slid it into the bag with the takeout container and unopened bottle of soda.

Something didn't feel right to Mary as she was walking home from the deli. She wasn't sure why she was uneasy, but she picked up her pace.

It didn't take her long to reach her building. Or to ride the elevator up to her floor and lock herself inside her apartment.

She leaned with her back against the door and felt better. She was home. Safe from whatever was out *there*.

She drew a deep breath and picked up a peculiar odor. Not of tobacco smoke. Something else. Faint but persistent, and definitely *not* the orange chicken

More like stale perspiration.

Urine.

The man from the subway!

She reined in her fear and made herself think. What was she going to do? Go back outside where there was more danger? Then what? Go to the police? Tell them she thought someone was in her apartment because she'd smelled an unfamiliar odor?

Sure, they'd believe her and send all units.

She sniffed the air again and detected no odor other than the food from the foam takeout container.

My imagination?

Surely. Must have been. Must!

She shut her mind to the faint odor that she *might* have smelled and moved away from the door and deeper into the living room.

She drew a deep breath and felt better.

Fear had to be faced. And, damn it, she could face it!

Mary placed the foam container on the coffee table and

willed her fear-numbed legs to take her where she wanted to go. Where she knew she *must* go.

She made herself look everywhere in the small apartment. Under the bed, in the closets, behind the closed shower curtain. As she flung the plastic curtain aside, the murder score from the movie *Psycho* screeched through her mind, almost making her smile. She let the curtain fall back into place. Not so afraid now.

There's no one here. Just me and my overactive imagination. Picture this viewed from above, like in a Hitchcock movie—a foreshortened, fearful woman scurrying about in a maze of cubicles, peeking here, peering there. It's almost laughable.

There were a few more places to look. Extremely unlikely hiding places. Mary decided not to explore them. She told herself she was no longer so afraid that she had to look everywhere in the apartment.

I've made enough of a fool of myself.

He was in the living room.

12

Quinn figured he'd better call Renz back. If this investigation was going to stop, and it turned out it shouldn't have, he wanted to make it clear that it was going to be the albatross around Renz's neck.

"Which investigation do you want me to stop?" Quinn asked Renz, on the phone in the Lotus Diner. He turned his body in toward the wall, in case Thel, still over by his booth, might be eavesdropping as she figured up his check. "The one with the dog that ran away with the clues?"

"That one sounds interesting," Renz said, "but I think we both know I'm talking about the Carver murders."

"Carver murders . . . is that the one with the guy who raped and sliced up his victims?"

"See, you *do* know."

"Was a long time ago."

"It'd seem like yesterday if you were one of the victims. If they'd had any tomorrows."

"Why would you want us to back away from that one, Harley? It must be in the NYPD cold-case files."

But Quinn knew why. The politically attuned Renz, who at the time of the Carver murders had been a police captain overseeing the investigation, didn't want one of his notable unsolved cases dredged up from the past to bedevil him in the present and future.

"There's been enough human suffering over those murders," Renz said. "The families should be left alone."

"My impression is that the families would still like to see the killer found and brought to trial."

"Yeah, yeah. Closure and all that." Sensitive Harley. "We both know what the families really want is for us to kill the bastard."

"That, too," Quinn said. "What *you* really *don't* want is for somebody to break this case, after you and the rest of the NYPD and your political hacks worked the publicity pump and made it bigger than Son of Sam and then failed to get anywhere with it."

"How cruel and direct," Renz said. "And accurate. Right now I'm especially vulnerable, with the wolves after my job. My political enemies within the department are breathing hot air down my neck. That prick Nobbler would love to have a big unsolved case that happened during my tenure as police captain to use against me. He'd use it to nail me to the cross." Nobbler was Captain Wes Nobbler, an NYPD bureaucratic climber with apparatchiks throughout the department. Nobbler was almost as cynical and ambitious as Renz.

"Always political reasons," Quinn said. Political infighting was one of the main reasons he was no longer with the NYPD.

"Everything's political."

Like having a maniac sit on your chest and slice off your nipples.

"Not everything, Harley."

"Don't stand on principle here, Quinn. There are plenty of people in and out of the NYPD who don't want the Carver case reactivated and will do whatever's necessary to keep it where it belongs—in the past. I'm talking powerful people, Quinn."

"Like you?"

"Like me. Be glad I'm your friend. Listen to me on this one."

"How did you know I was on this case, Harley?"

"Get serious. I'm the goddamned police commissioner, and I didn't inherit the position. I came up out of the streets just like you did, only I rose higher because I was more realistic. I understood the realities of the job. I've got eyes and ears everywhere in this city."

"I owe something to my client," Quinn said.

"You owe your client jack shit. You owe something to yourself. The idea is to stop this train before it builds up steam and the media notice the smoke. If you don't help do that you might wind up under the wheels."

"Along with you."

"Naw, I know the engineer. I might even *become* the engineer."

"These railroad metaphors are getting on my nerves. Can we try the airlines?"

"No. Let's keep the airlines grounded and speak plainly: Drop the Carver investigation or you'll regret it. Whether I regret it too shouldn't make any difference to you. Think about yourself instead of your dreamland ethics. Give your client her money back, if that's what's bothering you."

"How do you know it's a she?"

"You and your other two monkeys have talked to people, and we've talked to the same people. Didn't it occur to you some of those victims' families might contact us after you stomped all over their peace and well-being and reminded them of their grief?"

It had occurred to Quinn, only he doubted that Pearl or Fedderman had mentioned the identity of their client. And he was sure he hadn't. It was possible that Renz was keeping a loose tail on Quinn and his detectives, even possible that a search without a warrant had been done at the office. Quinn made a mental note to be more careful locking up, and to make sure the office computers hadn't been violated.

"It's the twin sister," Renz said. "Full of all that psychic bullshit about twins being so close they can read each other's thoughts even if one of them's dead." Renz made a mock shivering sound. "Spooky, spooky. Take my advice and return the bitch's retainer, tell her it's no use. Once this shit gets into the news it'll be too late. The River Styx'll be crossed."

"I think you mean the Rubicon," Quinn said. "That's the river you cross when you can't turn back. The Styx is the river you cross when you're dead."

"Never mind that. Can I be sure you got my message?"

"Sure, Harley. I'll sleep on it."

"That'll have to be good enough for now," Renz said. "But let me know early tomorrow morning so I can be sure. Not that you got a choice, but you're a stubborn bastard."

"I'll call you."

"I'll be waiting. And Quinn, I know my rivers."

13

Mary attempted to scream, but the sight of the man from the subway right there, in her apartment, turned her throat to stone. She couldn't breathe, much less scream.

And he *was* the subway man. The same wrinkled, soiled clothing. The same baseball cap with its bill worn low so he seemed to be staring at her with half eyes. The same bristly beard stubble. The same horrible, frightening stench of stale sweat and urine. Of the street. Of everything about New York that was raw and dangerous.

He seemed as shocked as Mary for a moment; as if he could hardly comprehend finding her in her own apartment. It was as if *she'd* surprised and frightened *him*. As if *she* didn't belong.

He actually smiled. His teeth were crooked and yellow, one of the upper incisors broken half off. As he stared at her, he ran his tongue over his lower lip.

He bent low at the waist and removed something from just inside his pants cuff. When he straightened up, Mary saw that he was holding a knife with a long, thin blade. A boning knife, she knew. She had one something like it in her own kitchen drawer.

Was it her knife?

No. Hers had a wooden handle. The handle on this

knife—what she could see of it inside the man's hand—was steel, like the blade.

Mary inhaled again to scream, and the man moved quickly toward her. It was all so fast, as if film frames had been skipped. Suddenly his forearm was pressed vertically against her upper body, between her breasts. It was the arm that held the knife, and she could feel the cold steel of the blade against her throat. The knife point probed eagerly beneath her jaw, not quite breaking through flesh. If he pushed upward the knife would go into her mouth, through her tongue and the roof of her mouth, into her brain. She could imagine it. Could almost *feel* it.

Mary was still too paralyzed with fear to scream. She felt her bladder release and the warmth of her urine trickling down her legs.

The man with the knife became aware of her mixture of terror and humiliation, and his smile broadened. She was his entertainment, and she was performing well, his smile said. He wasn't tall and didn't seem particularly muscular, but Mary could feel his strength like a current as he moved her a step backward with a shifting of his slender but powerful arm.

Any second he might use the knife.

She managed to make a few gasping, hoarse noises, almost like a bagpipe bellowing, but muted. She had never known such fear was possible.

Leaning his body weight into her, he walked her backward, through the living room, down the short hall to her bedroom. Her entire body was trembling as if electric shocks were running through it.

The bed! Once I'm on the bed I'm lost!

Without warning he shoved her hard, and she staggered backward, catching her heel on the carpet, losing her balance.

She was on her back on the hard wood floor before she

knew what had happened, and the back of her head ached as if her skull had fractured in a thousand fragments.

He straddled her, seated on her stomach, waving the knife before her eyes so she'd be sure to see it.

He clutched the front of her T-shirt and yanked it up, exposing her breasts. She wasn't wearing a bra. With his free hand he clamped her nipple between thumb and forefinger and squeezed hard.

Then his weight was lifted from her, and she could breathe easier.

Through her pain and dizziness Mary realized she was looking up at the man's back, at the dark crescents of perspiration stains on his shirt beneath his armpits. She watched him move quickly toward her bedroom window, knowing as she did so that the air was different in the room. Warmer and more humid.

The window's open. I left it unlocked, and now it's open.

She shifted her gaze and saw that she was right. He'd left the window open where he'd gained entrance from the fire escape.

He looked back at her, and their gazes locked. His unblinking eyes were hypnotic. Snake to mongoose.

With a surprising grace and confidence he let himself out through the window, moving backward and not taking his sullen, greedy eyes from her. Beneath the half-moon eyes was the broken-toothed grin, as if he had her completely in his power and knew every evil thing about her, all the secrets of her body.

She was his for the taking, that grin said. And when he was ready, he would take.

Mary understood that and knew she was helpless to do anything about it.

Still lying on her back, she managed to prop herself up on her elbows and watch the man outside the window. He turned away from her, and began his descent on the black iron fire escape. She could barely hear the leather-on-metal scraping of his shoes as he scrambled down and away from her. She was safer with each of his hurried steps.

She dropped so she was flat on her back again and lay silently for a while, then rolled onto her side. When she tried to stand up her headache exploded behind her eyes, and she sat down on the floor near the bed.

Using the mattress to lean against, she finally managed to pull herself up to where she was sitting hunched over on the bed. She stretched out her hand and without looking found the phone on the nightstand, dragged the receiver from its cradle, and held it in her lap. She pressed it between her thighs so it wouldn't drop to the floor. Her head flared with pain again as she turned slightly and focused her bleary vision on the base unit. She pecked out nine-one-one on the keypad.

Her voice was strangled, but she was sure she'd included her address in her rambling, choking conversation with the 911 operator.

Mary heard herself begin to sob. Her body shuddered, and she leaned back into deeper and deeper darkness.

There was a clock by the phone. Though it had seemed like seconds, she knew that fifteen minutes had passed and the police were pounding on her door.

14

He'd dropped silently from the iron fire escape into the courtyard and made his way through the narrow passageway on the side of the building to the street. No one had seen him, he was sure. And even if someone had noticed him, they'd never be able to recognize him. He was away clean. Things hadn't worked out as he'd planned, but he was safe.

He hadn't wanted to hurt her. Not at this point. He'd only wanted to learn more about her.

Her name was Mary. Mary Bakehouse. He knew that much from riffling through the contents of her desk. He knew where she banked, how much she owed, where she left her laundry, that she had family in godforsaken South Dakota. He'd seen photographs of her and her country relatives, the Bakehouse clan, and a close-up of lovely Mary wearing a white blouse buttoned to her throat and grinning with every tooth. Desk drawers could be so revealing.

He'd been about to switch on her computer and learn even more about her when he heard her out in the hall, fumbling for her door key.

He'd barely had time to sweep everything back into the drawers and push them shut, then conceal himself before she'd entered.

She'd diligently searched the rest of the apartment before

returning to the living room, where he'd decided to reveal himself.

He'd known she'd be frightened but not so exquisitely. She was his, and she knew it immediately. The knowledge had stopped her throat and silenced her with its terrible truth.

That was why he'd taken his time. He wasn't going to harm her, but she didn't know that. He was in control. He could manage an orderly exit. She wouldn't have much of a description to give to the police. Probably not enough to pick him out of a lineup and certainly not enough to make a positive identification. He'd be well away and in the clear.

Dressed in clothes from his respectable wardrobe and clean shaven, his artificial dentures removed, he was reasonably confident he could pass her in the street or sit opposite her on the subway, and she might suspect he was the same man but she couldn't be sure.

From now on, uncertainty would be her constant companion. Even in her dreams she would doubt.

Thoughts. She would be the victim of her thoughts, just as he was of his. Thoughts couldn't hurt anyone, but she wouldn't know that. Not in her heart. Not for sure.

Walking swiftly toward the corner where he could hail a cab, he smiled. Mary Bakehouse might never be sure of anything else in her life.

That he could do such a thing to her, and so easily, the special power that he had, gave him a partial erection. He bent slightly forward as he walked so no one would notice. And if they did, so what?

The power and control . . .

His erection persisted. Mary would find the mess in her desk drawers and know he'd examined their contents, but that was okay. He wanted her to know. Ultimately, that would work for him.

She'd probably report their encounter to the authorities, but she'd soon find out they really couldn't do anything about it, and they certainly couldn't guarantee it wouldn't happen again.

That would make her feel even more powerless.

Within a few minutes he was seated comfortably in the back of a cab, the incident with Mary Bakehouse fading behind him.

Thoughts were all they'd dealt with tonight, not blood. Later might come the blood. He knew that. He could deny it. He could fight it. But he couldn't be sure of the outcome.

Maybe he'd pay Mary Bakehouse another visit, and maybe he wouldn't. She knew that he might, and that made the night a triumph.

He hadn't set out to hurt her, and he hadn't. Still, in a way, their encounter had been a success for him. Ask Mary Bakehouse, and if she could bring herself to be honest, she'd admit that.

Whether she lived or died depended entirely upon his whim. He remembered her complete loss of control, the warm urine escaping her body. They both recognized at that moment her fetid, trickling surrender.

She belonged to him. She understood that in the very depths of her soul, in the dark recesses of her brain where the demons played.

That was enough for now.

It wouldn't look like much in the morning *Times* or *Post,* if it even made the papers. And it wouldn't be mentioned on TV news. After all, there was no tape. There'd been no chance for some techie geek with a phone camera to be standing nearby creating a video stream.

Mary had been treated well by the police and the hospital staff. At the hospital she'd been given a thorough examination, and what they referred to as a rape kit had been used on her to confirm that she hadn't been penetrated.

After the ordeal at the hospital she had given a carefully detailed and recorded statement. Through it all she could sense a genuine concern, but also a workaday disinterest. Hers wasn't the first story like this they'd heard. No one had actually told her that, but it showed.

The incident would be merely another apartment break-in in New York. The intruder had been surprised by the occupant and frightened away. Nothing had been taken. No one had been seriously hurt. Mary's encounter with a man who might have killed her would be barely worth a mention in the media. In the grand and sweeping maelstrom of the city, it wasn't at all important.

Except to Mary.

Quinn sat up late at the desk in his den and let his thoughts roam. A cigar in a glass ashtray was playing up a thread of smoke that dissipated before it reached the ceiling. A half-drunk cup of coffee sat on a round cork coaster. The cup was Spode and a survivor of his time with his former wife, May, who was married now to a real estate attorney in California. Their daughter Lauri was in California, too, but in a different part of the state. Quinn figured May and Lauri seldom, if ever, saw each other, but he couldn't be sure. Lauri had ditched her musician boyfriend Wormy, and as far as Quinn knew was concentrating on her studies at Muir College in the northern part of the state. When last he heard Lauri was studying journalism.

He drew on the cigar, exhaled, and concentrated less on his personal life and more on the case. On the desk was a yellow legal pad, as yet unmarked. Quinn picked up a ballpoint pen and began to make notes as he went over the case in his mind. Sometimes seeing things in some kind of order, in print, made them clearer.

Tiffany Keller had years ago been the last victim of the Carver.

Her twin, Chrissie, won the Triple Monkey whatever slot-machine jackpot and found herself suddenly moderately wealthy. She decided to use the money to find her sister's killer. Or, more accurately, to avenge her sister's death.

The NYPD had demonstrated no interest in reopening the case.

Chrissie, after pretending to be Tiffany's ghost to get Quinn's attention, had finally admitted who she was and hired Quinn and Associates to find the Carver.

After paying a handsome retainer, Chrissie had then disappeared.

Chrissie had deleted any and all photographs of Tiffany from news items in the folder she'd left with Quinn.

Photographs on the Internet revealed that Chrissie and Tiffany looked nothing alike.

Renz had phoned and tried to warn Quinn off the case.

Quinn jotted on the legal pad that Chrissie was not to be trusted. There was no need to write a reminder about Renz.

Quinn placed his cigar back in the ashtray and leaned back in his desk chair to look over what he'd written on the legal pad.

None of it aided him in any kind of understanding.

Too early, he assured himself. But that didn't alleviate the uneasy feeling deep in his stomach.

He placed the legal pad in the shallow center drawer of the desk, then slid the drawer closed. His cigar was smoked down to a nub, so he took a final pull on it, then snuffed it out in the ashtray. A sample sip of his coffee revealed it to be too cool to drink.

He was weary, but not tired in a way conducive to sleep. Maybe he should walk over to the Lotus Diner, drink a hot chocolate, and trade insults with Thel, if she was working late.

Better, he decided, to lock up the apartment and call it a night. That way he could sleep on what he'd written on his legal pad. Maybe something would occur to him in his dreams, and he'd remember it tomorrow morning and everything would make sense.

Then he remembered that nothing ever entirely made sense and went to bed.

15

The first thing Quinn saw when he entered the Lotus Diner the next morning was Thel. She was in her usual acerbic mood, which was somehow reassuring.

After a breakfast of biscuits, a three-egg cheese omelet, bacon, and two cups of coffee, Quinn walked from the Lotus Diner to the office on West Seventy-ninth Street. Dr. Gregory, whom Quinn infrequently saw at the doctor's medical service over on Columbus, would hardly have approved of the meal, but he'd endorse the walk.

The morning hadn't yet heated up and was beautiful. Sun glinted off the buildings and made vivid the canvas canopies over entrances and outdoor restaurants. Produce and fresh-cut flowers in outside stands sweetened the air. The bustle and rumble of the city was background music for millions of dramas. The city in its entirety was a bold and brassy Broadway musical and didn't know it.

Even the exhaust fumes smelled good to Quinn. It was the kind of morning that promised hope, at least for a while, though he realized it could be a con, like the rest of the city. New York liked to trick people. Even astound them.

Pearl and Fedderman were already in the office. Pearl was hunched over her computer, dark eyes fixed on the monitor, her outstretched right hand deftly moving her mouse on its pad as if playing on a Ouija board. The low-tech Fedderman was slouched at his desk reading a newspaper. The trespass and assault at Mary Bakehouse's apartment was mentioned in the *Post* police blotter section, but it hadn't made the *Times*. Not that it would have meant anything to Fedderman, who was reading the *Times* anyway. He'd probably be too busy today to read any other newspaper.

Nor would it have meant much of anything to Quinn, who had other things on his mind.

"No phone messages," Pearl said, glancing over at him.

Quinn grunted and went over to the table where the occasionally gurgling brewer sat. He poured himself his third coffee of the morning.

"We thought maybe our missing client Chrissie might have called," Fedderman said.

Quinn wandered back to stand between their desks, sipping coffee that would never be as good as the stuff at the Lotus Diner.

"Feds and I have a bet," Pearl said. "He thinks we'll never see Chrissie Keller again. I think we will, and there'll be an explanation for her disappearance."

"What kind of explanation?" Quinn asked.

Pearl smiled. "Not necessarily one we'll believe."

"What if she can't contact us because the Carver's made sure it's impossible?"

Pearl had considered that and saw it as unlikely. But there was no ruling it out. "It's something to keep in mind," she said, "but I do lean the other way. From the beginning, Chrissie struck me as the disappearing type. Not playing straight with us from word one."

"Meanwhile," Quinn said, "she's still our client. We're spending her money, so we'll continue to work the case, no matter what Renz says."

They both looked at him.

Fedderman folded his paper closed and said, "Renz?" As if a rare and unpleasant ailment had been mentioned.

Quinn told them about yesterday evening's phone call.

When he was finished, Fedderman said, "Is that guy ever, for even one second, not a self-serving prick?"

Quinn shrugged. "He's a politician."

"Didn't I just say that?"

Pearl sat staring and smiling slightly at Quinn. She didn't have to ask whether they were going to continue on the case. Instead she said, "How are we going to work it?"

"I'm about to make a phone call," Quinn said. "And not to Harley Renz."

It hadn't taken him long to dig up Cindy Sellers's direct line at *City Beat* from when she'd badgered them on a previous case.

She answered on the second ring. Quinn guessed a muckraking reporter had to stick close to the phone. Or possibly his call had been patched through to a mobile phone.

When Quinn had identified himself, Sellers's voice became wary. "Always a pleasure to hear from you, Captain."

"Not 'Captain' anymore," Quinn said. "I've opened up my own investigative agency."

"That's right, I heard." She waited a few beats. "Well, anything I can do to scratch somebody's back who's willing to scratch back . . . ?"

"What I always liked about you was that it wasn't necessary to do a verbal dance getting to the point. You're honest in your own special way."

She laughed. "But I like dancing with you, Quinn. You tromp on my toes now and then, but what the hell."

"You like dancing with Harley Renz?"

"Oh, he's an amazingly deft dancer. But you know that."

There was a smile in her voice. She knew he wanted something, or he wouldn't have called.

"To the point," Quinn said, "I have some information that might interest you."

"So interest me."

"There you go—very direct."

"You be too, why don't you?"

Quinn almost smiled. Sometimes Sellers could be as much of a smart-ass as Pearl. "Remember the Carver murders?"

"Sure. Serial killer, five or six years ago. One of the few in this city that you didn't catch. In fact, didn't that killer—"

"He was never caught," Quinn interrupted. "But it turns out that was only round one. The case has been reopened, and we think he can be caught now."

"New evidence?"

"We can't say."

"What made the NYPD reopen the investigation?"

"It didn't. We did."

"We?"

"Quinn and Associates Investigations."

Sellers was quiet for a moment. "And the NYPD doesn't like you meddling."

"That's it."

"Renz told you to fold your tent."

"Uh-huh. He doesn't want the department and its illustrious police commissioner to be embarrassed by dredging up an old case the police were unable to solve. He's afraid of the negative publicity, so he's pressuring us to halt our investigation."

Cindy Sellers laughed. "No point in that if the information's already out in the media, based on information from anonymous sources, of course."

"That's the game," Quinn said.

Sellers said, "I'll play. But there has to be a quid pro quo."

"You'll be first in the media to know everything," Quinn said. "Starting now."

"And I'll be in on the finale? If there is one."

"There'll be one," Quinn said, "and you'll be there."

Again one of Cindy's silences. There weren't many; she tended to think on the run, asking questions along the way.

"Somebody must have hired you," she said at last.

"The killer's last victim had a sister. A twin."

"*A twin!* And the surviving twin is your client?"

"Uh-huh."

"Wonderful! The surviving twin wants vengeance. It's almost poetic. It's as if the murderer killed only half of his victim, and now the other half—"

"However you want to play it," Quinn said.

"We have an arrangement, Quinn. Tell me more."

And he did. Not everything, of course, but just enough.

After hanging up, he absently wiped his hand on his pants leg, as if Sellers had salivated over the phone.

Fedderman was grinning at him. "Renz is gonna be so mad he might catch fire."

"Give me a can of gas," Pearl said, rather absently.

She was gazing at Quinn in a way he recognized, thoughtfully and slightly disturbed, as if she'd again discovered a new facet of his deviousness.

"This will work out," he assured her.

Now there was something cautionary in her look, warning him that he'd done something possibly unwise as well as distasteful. Her "If you lie down with dogs . . ." look.

"I can put up with fleas," he said.

She nodded and turned back to her computer. She'd known exactly what he'd been thinking. Incredible.

Maybe her mouse pad *was* a Ouija board.

"My, my, my," Pearl said, reading over additional information about Geraldine Knott, the young woman who'd survived an attack eight years ago in Detroit by an assailant very much like the Carver.

She remained seated at her computer. Quinn and Fedderman were standing behind her, looking over her shoulder at the monitor. They were all reading the old news item from the archives of a Detroit newspaper. It was accompanied by another blurred black-and-white photo. In this one Geraldine Knott was standing and leaning sideways, as if hoping the camera's aim would miss her, holding both hands covering her face.

This account of the attack was more detailed. It described how her masked assailant had gotten her on the ground and straddled her, kneeling on her upper arms to pin her to the parking garage's concrete floor. He'd then shown her a knife and explained to her what he intended to do with it. As the news item quoted the tearful intended victim: ". . . slice off my nipples, do some creative carving on me, then carve me a big smile under my chin." Fortunately for Geraldine Knott, her attacker had been frightened away.

"He mentioned carving twice," Quinn noted.

"Could be early Carver," Pearl said. "Or maybe some sicko imitating him."

"Except this woman was attacked before anybody'd ever heard of the Carver," Fedderman pointed out.

"Maybe this guy *had* heard of him and was imitating him even before he became famous," Quinn suggested.

Pearl said, "The odds on that are about the same as Fedderman wearing both socks right side out."

"Did I do that again?" Fedderman asked automatically, glancing down at his ankles and tugging up his pants legs.

"Sure seems like this could be our guy," Pearl said. "The way he showed the knife and told her what he was about to do, getting his jollies by scaring the hell out of her. Or maybe our sicko saw this news account when it was fresh in a Detroit paper and it stuck in his mind."

"I'd bet on Feds's socks," Quinn said.

"Then you think this was early Carver?" Pearl asked.

"I don't know."

Fedderman unconsciously glanced down at his feet again. "So what are we gonna do with this information?"

"Put it in the hopper," Quinn said, "along with everything else we know or think we know."

"And then?" Fedderman asked.

"Wait and see if someday it makes sense."

16

Holifield, Ohio, 1992

Jerry Grantland, thirteen years old last week, lowered himself from his bedroom window onto the soft carpet of lawn. He glanced at the luminous green hands of his Timex watch. One o'clock a.m.

That was the time it usually happened.

If it was going to happen.

There were clouds, and the moon was only a sliver, like a glowing shaving from a larger carving. Jerry knew that once he made it across the dark stretch of lawn that was the shadow of the house, cast by the softly illuminated streetlight out near the curb, he'd be in almost total darkness. The rest would be easy. There was a wooden picket fence running the property line between his house and the Kellers' side yard, but it was only four feet high. The nimble Jerry could be over it in seconds and on his way into the shadows of the overgrown honeysuckle bush.

The bush would conceal him until he made it past the rosebushes and into the yews, where he could squat unseen in the darkness outside the Keller twins' bedroom window.

He knew where the twins, a year younger than he was, slept in their matching twin beds with their brass headboards. Tiffany's bed was against the far wall, Chrissie's nearer the window.

Jerry found his familiar, comfortable place to squat on his heels and peer beneath the partly drawn shade into the room.

Both girls appeared to be sleeping beneath thin white sheets that were pulled all the way up to their chins.

Jerry thought it unlikely that they were sleeping. Like him, they were probably waiting.

He watched as both girls stirred and stiffened. Tiffany sat straight up in bed and then lay down again. Both twins curled onto their sides, pretending to be asleep. The window was raised slightly to let in the night breeze, and Jerry thought he could hear the faint rustle of the sheets as the girls' young bodies moved beneath them.

Jerry let his thoughts about the Keller twins roam free, as he often did. If the twins knew what they did—and what was done *to* them—in his imagination, they'd be appalled. But they wouldn't be surprised. In some ways they were interchangeable. In others—

As he always did when it happened, Jerry drew in his breath.

The bedroom door had opened and closed silently.

The twins' father, Mr. Keller—Ed Keller—was like a shadow in the room, but a shadow with substance.

Jerry swallowed and stayed as still as possible at the window. He'd been sure Mr. Keller would enter the twins' room. Mr. Keller was some kind of salesman and was out of town a lot. Whatever he sold had something to do with cars, with Detroit; that's what either twin would say when Jerry asked about their father.

Mr. Keller had been away on business most of the week, and this was his first night back. That was how Jerry knew he'd visit the twins' room. After being out of town for a while on one his sales trips, he almost always paid the twins a visit.

The tall shadow that was Mr. Keller moved to Tiffany's bed. Chrissie, in her own bed, turned away, drew her knees up almost to her chin, and held the wadded sheet tightly against her ears. She was facing the window, but Jerry was sure she couldn't see him, the way her face was screwed into an ugly mask, her eyes clenched tightly shut.

Behind her, shadows began to move on the far wall. Holding his breath, Jerry leaned slightly forward.

Within minutes the rhythmic, writhing dance of light and darkness on the wall became more urgent, wilder. It was impossible to know what was shadow and what was Tiffany or her father.

He could hear a soft moaning through the window and couldn't be sure if it was Tiffany or Chrissie.

The writhing and moaning continued in a madder and madder rhythm. Jerry was hard now, and he lowered his right hand and stroked himself. Within minutes he'd reached orgasm.

The movement of the distorted figures on the wall finally slowed, then stopped altogether.

The tall shadow that was Mr. Keller straightened up from Tiffany's bed. It moved toward the window, but Jerry, secure in the knowledge that he was invisible in the darkness and shelter of the yews, stayed motionless and continued to watch.

Mr. Keller rested a hand briefly on Chrissie's shoulder. He knew she'd been awake, been listening. Jerry thought that almost surely she hadn't been the only one in the house who'd heard. The twin's mother must have heard *something* of what happened over and over in the twins' room.

She must know.

The world of adults. Jerry wasn't sure if he'd ever understand it.

He watched as Mr. Keller crept to the bedroom door, opened it, and merged with the darkness beyond it, closing the door behind him.

Neither twin moved for a long time, and then Chrissie re-moved the wadded sheet from her ears and sat up in bed. She looked over at Tiffany, who lay facing away from her, pre-tending to be asleep.

Chrissie lay back and pretended to sleep herself.

Jerry backed away from the window and made for the dark patch in the lawn where he could cross unseen into his own yard. He would return to his bed, where he'd pretend he'd never left the house, that he was asleep like the twins.

Everyone pretending, as the night moved toward morning and another day.

17

New York, the present

"We need to get together off the record," Harley Renz had said to Quinn over the phone. That was why Quinn was in Bryant Park, on Forty-second Street and Sixth Avenue, next to the library.

Bryant was a pleasant green oasis surrounded by concrete in a busy part of town. Quinn sat on a bench not far from where a group of people were playing some kind of game where players tossed heavy balls underhanded and palm down, so reverse English would cut down the distance they rolled when they came to earth. Every once in a while about half the players would jump up and down and hug each other, but Quinn couldn't see that much had been accomplished.

Harley had entered the park from Sixth Avenue and was trudging steadily in Quinn's direction. His general sagginess made him appear a lot heavier than he was. Maybe because of his face, which was jowly and sad-eyed, with a fleshy mouth usually arced down at the corners. Gravity was not his friend. The expensive blue suit he had on might have helped if he'd bothered to button its coat. Now and then the

breeze off the avenue whipped the coat sideways and revealed the thin leather strap of a shoulder holster.

He spotted Quinn and veered slightly to set his course
more directly toward the bench, swinging his arms in his peculiar restricted way, as if he were carrying a heavy bucket
in each hand.

When he was about ten feet from Quinn, he showed his
bloodhound smile. Sunlight sparked off one of his canine
teeth. "I thought you'd be smoking one of your Cuban cigars, Quinn."

"Isn't it illegal to smoke in a public park?"

"Damned if I know," Renz said. He pulled a cellophane-
wrapped cigar from his shirt pocket, unwrapped it, and
stuffed the torn cellophane back into his pocket.

"Not to mention that Cuban cigars are illegal."

"Not to mention." Renz bit the end off the cigar and spat
it off to the side, then fired up the cigar with a silver lighter.
The tobacco burned unevenly and made a soft sizzling
sound, the way cheap cigars often did.

"Somebody have a baby?" Quinn asked.

Renz exhaled and held the cigar off to the side, as if even
he was put off by its odor. "If you'd tell me your source for
the Cubans, I wouldn't have to smoke these dog turds." He
sucked on the cigar again, rolled the smoke around in his
mouth and then slowly released it. "'Course, I don't know
now if I can still trust you."

"You never could," Quinn said.

"But I thought so for some things, which is why I'm disappointed in you." Renz clamped the cigar in his teeth and
from a side pocket of his suit coat drew out a folded, crinkly
City Beat and handed it to Quinn.

Quinn had seen the paper's morning edition but pretended
he hadn't. TWIN SEEKS KILLER OF OTHER SELF, proclaimed the
headline. Quinn scanned the story of the resurrection of the

Carver investigation and vengeance delayed. It was spirited prose.

He handed the paper back to Renz. "Cindy Sellers. Where does she get that stuff?"

Renz stared at him as if they were playing poker and Quinn might buckle under pressure and display a tell. "Somebody's talking, is where she's getting it."

"Maybe," Quinn said, unperturbed. "Or maybe she's making it up."

"Whatever her source, Sellers has decided to be a pain in the ass."

"First Amendment," Quinn said.

"Yeah, yeah." Renz wadded the *City Beat* into a tight ball and arced it gracefully into a nearby trash receptacle. He sat down heavily on the opposite end of the bench, causing it to rock slightly on uneven ground. "Whatever her source, she's gonna continue writing this crap," he said.

"That's like her. She can't be trusted."

Renz looked over at the people tossing the balls and giving them backward spin. "What the hell are they doing over there? Bocce ball? Is it goddamned bocce ball?"

"I don't know," Quinn said. "It's something else in life that puzzles me."

"But you're the sort who figures things out. For instance, you must know that with Sellers writing and blabbing about the Carver investigation all over town, the rest of the media wolves are gonna be hunting in packs. My assistant tells me our phones are already lit up with calls from the papers and television news. I had to make sure I wasn't followed here by media schmucks."

Quinn nodded. "Yeah, Sellers has changed things. Heated them up."

Renz puffed on his cigar, then glanced at the glowing tip with satisfaction. "That's why I'm reactivating you and your team. Or, to be more specific, the NYPD is hiring Quinn and

Associates Investigations to help work on the reactivated Carver case."

Quinn was surprised, but he shouldn't have been. Renz could always be counted on to come up with some kind of bold countermove. Usually one that furthered his career. "So the popular and daring police commissioner goes outside the NYPD again for the public good and safety."

"You forgot *imaginative,*" Renz said.

"Imagine that."

"Our arrangement has proved successful in the past. And when you weren't on the Carver case, we weren't able to close it. This time around, I'm hitching my wagon to a winner." Again, Renz's doglike smile. "I'll get some NYPD shields to you so you and your team can come and go at crime scenes unmolested, maybe wrangle some free doughnuts."

"Is there a possibility of discussing whether I agree to this?" Quinn asked.

"Not really, considering Cindy Sellers has shot our previous agreement all to hell. It isn't worth much now that the media seem to be getting shovelfuls of information on this case. Matter of days before our more vocal members of the public—some of them political office holders—will be demanding that the case actually gets solved."

"You've gone from trying to scare me off this case to hiring me to continue my investigation," Quinn pointed out.

"That's called being outmaneuvered."

Quinn had nothing to say to that. After all, the investigation was not only going to continue, but at an accelerated rate. So who'd been outmaneuvered?

"You'll be initiating the NYPD investigation and consolidating it with what you have so far," Renz said. "I'm assigning a detective team to work with you. You'll be lead detective, of course. And you'll report to me."

"Do I have a choice?" Quinn asked again.

"Stop asking me that. It's annoying. You don't want a choice. You got what you wanted." Renz watched the people playing with the wooden balls for a while. "There was a lot of spin on that ball you tossed me the other day," he said.

"Conversational ball, you mean?"

"Whatever."

They both sat quietly observing the people playing the mysterious game with the balls.

"I think they're trying to knock their opponents' balls out of a circle," Quinn said.

"The thing to remember," Renz said around the smoldering cigar wedged in his jaw, "is that, like in most games, they take turns."

Quinn had been warned. It didn't much concern him.

Renz nodded knowingly and smiled his jowly smile, then stood up from the bench and sauntered toward Sixth Avenue.

Quinn sat watching him walk away. He knew that when it was Renz's turn, the ambitious police commissioner would make the most of it. And he wasn't above playing out of turn.

It must be liberating to be so blithely corrupt.

As soon as Renz had disappeared, Quinn lit a Cuban cigar.

18

"It's better than having him shut down the investigation," Quinn said, after returning to the Seventy-ninth Street office and telling Pearl and Fedderman about his conversation with Renz.

The air conditioner wasn't very efficient, and the air was still and muggy and smelled, as it often did, of subversive cigar smoke.

Fedderman had his suit coat off and his tie knot loosened. The top button of his shirt was undone. Pearl had a shimmer of perspiration above her upper lip that somehow looked good on her.

Neither of Quinn's two detectives was crazy about the idea that the NYPD had landed with both flat feet in the middle of their investigation.

"Did we plan for this development?" Pearl asked.

"Not exactly," Quinn said. "We'll have to improvise."

"They do that in comedy clubs," Fedderman said.

"We'll try not to make it funny."

"At least we'll be working with Vitali and Mishkin again," Fedderman said.

The NYPD homicide team of detectives Sal Vitali and Harold Mishkin had shared the load with Quinn, Pearl, and Fedderman in a previous serial killer case. The gravel-voiced, intense Vitali and the deceptively meek Mishkin were a crack team and meshed well with Quinn and his crew.

Pearl, who'd been working her computer, sat back and stretched her arms, clenching and unclenching her fists as if she were working little exercise balls. "It'd be nice, though, if we had a client."

"We do," Fedderman said. "We just can't find her. Pearl keeps checking her computer, but Chrissie's not on Face-book or YouTube or any of the other mass Internet connectors. There are some people there looking for dates, though, so Pearl's not giving up."

"I got a YouTube for you," Pearl said.

"Wouldn't doubt it."

Pearl fumed. Fedderman liked that. Quinn didn't, but he hesitated in acting as referee when Pearl and Fedderman went at each other. Their frequent bickering seemed to stimulate their little gray cells.

"Ease up," was all he said, and not with much conviction.

Pearl swiveled slightly in her chair to look directly at him. "Did you mention to Cindy Sellers that we can't seem to locate our client?"

"Slipped my mind."

"Sure it did." Pearl knew better than to believe that. Hardly anything slipped Quinn's mind.

Having forgotten for now about Fedderman and his jibes, Pearl smiled. Quinn thought she was beautiful when she smiled while still flush with anger. It was amazing the way she could switch gears like that. Like speed-shifting a race car.

"She called here while you were talking to Renz," Fedderman said.

"Sellers?"

"The same. Pearl took the call."

"I can't stand that woman," Pearl said.

"That's just because she has no taste, compassion, or ethics," Fedderman said.

"I can stand you," Pearl said. "Barely, sometimes, and in short doses, but I can stand you."

Quinn was getting fed up with the verbal rock fight. What were they, in high school? But he knew it was because they were stymied in their investigation. Couldn't even find their client. "What did Sellers want, Pearl?"

"The usual. Answers. I didn't give her any."

"What did you give her?"

"That high school yearbook photo. The one we found on the Internet when we realized Chrissie hadn't included any in the clippings she gave us. Sellers wanted a photo of Tiffany to run with her *City Beat* story."

"Did Sellers bitch because you gave her such an old photograph?" Fedderman asked.

"No. She'll do what we did: scour the Internet and build her own file of photos."

"She's probably good at that," Fedderman said. "It's what reporters do nowadays. Not much legwork left in the job. Not like being a cop."

"Hmph," Pearl said, which irritated Fedderman. It was hard to know if she was agreeing or disagreeing.

She sat forward. "I went through the clippings Chrissie gave us again, to make doubly sure, and there were photos of all the victims except for the last. Then I went on the Internet again." She wrestled her chair up closer to her desk and worked her computer. "There are some great shots." She moved the mouse across its pad and clicked it. "Like this one. It's from an old *Daily News*. Looks like a studio portrait when she was still a teenager. Tiffany sure was a terrific-looking kid."

Quinn angled to his left so the glare from the window didn't obscure the image on Pearl's computer screen. He stepped closer.

The image was of a news item with the victim's photo inset on the right. Tiffany's name was printed beneath the black-and-white head shot of a pretty brunette with dark eyes and a glowing and somewhat naive smile. *Young woman with a bright future,* the caption should have read, rather than *Latest Carver victim.*

"Exactly the Carver victim type," Pearl said. "Attractive, with dark hair and eyes, good cheekbones, generous mouth."

You, Quinn thought, but didn't say it.

"Tiffany fits right in. Our client does, too, but not exactly."

"She can't be Chrissie," Fedderman said.

"So who is she?" Quinn asked. "And why's she done a runner?"

"I might be able to answer your first question," Pearl said. "As I recall, she never said she and Tiffany were *identical* twins. She *is* Chrissie Keller, Tiffany's fraternal twin."

"She sure let us assume they were identical twins," Fedderman said. "I mean, with her story about wanting Quinn to think at first he was looking at one of the Carver's victims. Shock persuasion."

"Feds is right," Quinn said. "She led us in that direction."

"So she lied," Pearl said. "My God, what a surprise!"

Quinn and Fedderman looked at each other.

In a corner of his mind, Fedderman had mulled over Pearl's suggestion. "Pearl's got a point," he said. "They might be fraternal twins. But me, I'm not so sure."

"Either way, she's been dicking around with us," Pearl said.

"Still is," Fedderman said. "Playing a game."

"We'll give her game," Pearl said.

The two detectives' animosity was forgotten, lost in the fervor of the hunt. Quinn almost smiled. *Cooking now . . .*

"We need to find out why she lied," Fedderman said.

Pearl nodded. "We need to find *her.*"

19

The Carver sat in his room in Midtown Manhattan and watched the long, angular shadow cast by the afternoon sun move as inexorably as fate across the wall of the building across the street.

He'd taken to sitting in the same comfortable imitation Herman Miller chair and studying the same view.

It wasn't really much of a view—simply rows and rows of windows. In the way of countless rows of windows in New York, they overwhelmed the eye so that all of them seemed impersonal, at least from a distance.

The Carver used high-powered Bausch & Lomb binoculars to close that distance and get to know on a more personal basis the people in the offices across the street. The interesting people, that is. Not the simple working drones. They didn't provide much entertainment.

But the interesting people were something else. Of course, it took time and a lot of watching to locate the interesting ones; and the intriguing thing was, a few of the drones, after you watched them for a while, turned out to be interesting once you got to know and understand them.

There was the insurance guy who spent most of his time masturbating or tossing darts at a poster of Angelina Jolie. The woman office manager who, locked in her own office, drank to excess and was having a hot affair that involved bondage with one of her female underlings. More conventional romance was a regular feature on the other side of a windowpane where the building stair-stepped to rise another ten floors. There a middle-aged bald man—the Carver had never figured out what sort of position he held—had at least three sexual trysts per week with a long-legged blond woman who was quite spectacular and didn't seem to frequent that floor of the building except for services rendered to the man.

A high-priced prostitute?

No. She didn't have that look about her, and she didn't carry a purse or large bag. She seemed to work elsewhere in the building, though the Carver had never figured out where. She was definitely one of the interesting people.

Considering the size of the building, all of this didn't really seem an excessive amount of interesting activity. In fact, it was barely enough to keep the Carver occupied. Most of those whom he considered his unknowing "family" held some fascination, but less each day. They all seemed to be on treadmills of risk and relentlessness that would result in wearing out their luck. And like everything else, luck *did* eventually wear out.

The Carver knew when not to push his luck. When not to use it up unnecessarily. And that resulted in a knack for sensing exactly when to leave the party.

He had left the best party of his life at precisely the right time. He'd gotten away with murder. Five times. While the police were aimlessly dashing around and bouncing off bad ideas like blind mice. He was proud of that.

The experts were wrong, of course. Serial killers didn't necessarily finally fall victim to their compulsion. Sometimes it worked just as it was supposed to, exactly as they wanted it to work. They fed their compulsion, and they became sated.

He hadn't been much alarmed when television and newspapers suddenly became more interesting. When he learned that the Carver murders were being reinvestigated, and by Frank Quinn.

The Carver had always regretted that the famous serial killer hunter was injured and laid up in a hospital, or pensioned off and involved in litigation, during the time of most of his greatest achievements. Quinn hadn't had a chance to hunt for the Carver. The famous detective had been gunned down and seriously injured at the scene of a completely unrelated crime. A mundane liquor store holdup.

But Quinn was on the case now, years later, when the trail was so cold that solving the crimes would be almost impossible.

None of what had happened more than five years ago mattered much now, or provided any sort of handle for a reopened investigation. Time had built a wall and then an impenetrable fortress around the Carver.

Maybe it was because he was invulnerable that he avidly followed news of the present investigation. Possibly he was waiting for news of Mary Bakehouse. So far, none had appeared. He had spared her, but always she'd carry a part of him with her because now he *was* a part of her. He lived in her brain and being. That might be a burden too heavy for her, too painful. She would probably try to hide from that burden, run from it, maybe all the way to the other side of the country. But it wouldn't work. He would always be with her. He wouldn't be surprised if he picked up the paper one day and read of Mary's suicide. Perhaps he'd claim her as a victim after all.

Would it all begin again then?

No! He was finished with those times, those deeds. Thoughts. That was all he had now, and all he wanted. He didn't need Mary Bakehouse's death to fuel old embers. He could think about her any time he wanted, any way he wanted.

Mary was why he followed the news. Mere curiosity.

But he knew better. He tracked the news because old memories had stirred, and what lay dormant in him all those years, since what he'd considered to be his last murder, had slowly awakened and was pacing in his breast, sharing his heartbeats. A demon roused from its dreams.

He found that frightening.

He found it exhilarating.

Pearl surfaced from her subway stop that evening and trudged through the humid dusk toward her apartment. The softened light gave the city a dreamlike quality, as if she were viewing it through a fine screen. What did they call it in theater? A scrim. This momentary surreal view of New York was beautiful, in its way. It painted a place where any dream might come true, as well as any nightmare.

The meeting with Vitali and Mishkin had left Pearl feeling vaguely dissatisfied, though she didn't know why. The two NYPD detectives had listened carefully while Quinn filled them in on the investigation and then gave them copies of whatever paperwork there was, including the clipping files given to them by Chrissie Keller—if the woman had been Chrissie Keller. Vitali and Mishkin had turned copies of the murder books over to Quinn and Associates. Everyone had been polite and professional, and nothing had really changed except that there were two more warm bodies on the case, representing Harley Renz's political ass-covering. Nobody knew any more after the meeting than before.

"At least," Harold Mishkin had said from under his brushy, graying mustache, "we're all getting paid. I mean, with the economy and all."

"That's something," Quinn had said, exchanging glances with Sal Vitali, who was grinning.

"Harold always takes the practical view," Vitali said.

Pearl couldn't keep her mouth shut. "It isn't practical to have a client we can't find, while we're investigating murders that happened over five years ago, committed by a killer who, for all we know, is dead or living in another city."

"What?" Vitali growled in his gravel-pan voice. "You wanna quit?"

Pearl sighed. "Can't."

"The economy," Mishkin said.

"Not the economy," Pearl said.

Vitali winked at her and shrugged. "We soldier on."

"Only practical thing to do," Quinn said, standing up.

And the meeting was over.

He watched his detectives trail from the office. They looked eager but tired. They knew that most of the case, the hardest part, still lay ahead of them. Phase two of the investigation had begun. It was one of those forks in the road nobody would consider significant until they looked back at it while driving over a cliff.

PART
II

From their folded mates they wander far,
Their ways seem harsh and wild:
They follow the beck of a baleful star,
Their paths are dream beguiled.

—RICHARD FRANCIS BURTON, "Black Sheep"

20

Pearl stopped and stood on the curb, waiting for a traffic light to flash the walk signal. Her gaze fell on a glowing sign in a window across the street: HITS AND MRS. She'd been walking past the place forever and noticed now for the first time that it was a lounge. Its wide front window was dark because of narrow-slatted blinds behind it. The only thing displayed in the window was the glowing red sign.

She was more thirsty than hungry, and she'd had enough lack of progress for one day. Hits and Mrs. looked respectable enough, maybe because it was next to Love Blooms, a florist specializing in weddings. Pearl wondered if she was the only one who saw a connection between the two businesses. Might they be in cahoots?

After the meeting with Vitali and Mishkin, featuring Quinn's stoicism and Fedderman's usual bullshit, she decided she owed herself a drink. She changed direction and crossed the intersection at a ninety-degree angle to her previous course, not quite beating the light.

A car horn blared at her, and voices shouted something indecipherable. Pearl didn't bother to look, but raised her middle finger in the general direction of the racket.

Inside, Hits and Mrs. was softly lighted, with the long bar

on the right and booths on the left and in back. Indirect lighting glowed from sconces that vaguely resembled seashells. There were fox-hunting scenes on the paneled walls, and the stools and booths were upholstered in dark green leather or vinyl. About half the booths were occupied, as were three of the bar stools. It seemed all in all a sheltering boozy place where people went after dinner or the theater, or simply to unwind. Everyone looked reasonably like an upright citizen.

Pearl sat on a stool about halfway down the bar, and a too-handsome red-vested bartender with the air of an out-of-work actor sauntered down and took her order for a draft Heineken, every move a pose. Pearl thought, *Guys like you are all over this city, their numbers exceeded only by cockroaches.*

When her draft beer arrived, she took a long drink from the frosty mug and immediately felt better.

Resting the mug on a cork coaster, she looked the place over in the back bar mirror and decided she liked it. There was nothing pretentious about it except maybe the fox-hunting scenes, and there was a weighty, restful silence and no canned music. No TVs mounted everywhere showing endless tapes of sporting events.

The other three drinkers at the bar were on Pearl's right, two men and a woman, each separated by at least one bar stool. All three noticed her glance taking them in and seemed not to care. The woman actually smiled slightly and nodded to her.

When Pearl averted her gaze and was lifting her mug for another sip of beer, she saw that there was another drinker at the bar. She hadn't noticed him before because he was on her left, near the bar's end, and was seated where there was a dim spot in the lighting.

He was a slender man with thick white hair neatly parted and combed to the side. Pearl was intrigued by the way he was dressed—neatly pressed gray slacks, tailored blue blazer

with gold buttons, a white shirt with cuffs that flashed gold
cufflinks. Among his accessories were a gold ring and wrist-
watch, and what appeared to be a red ascot. The guy looked
more like money and leisure than anyone she'd ever seen.
Everything but a yachting cap.

He got down off his stool and walked toward her, moving
in the graceful, deliberate manner of someone who'd had social dancing lessons at some snooty prep school.

*Great! Just what I need. Some Casanova asshole trying
to hit on me when all I want is a peaceful place to drink.*

When he got closer she saw with some relief that he was-
n't wearing an ascot; it was simply a generously cut, mostly
red paisley tie fastened in what might be a big Windsor knot.
He was older than she'd at first thought, maybe sixty, with
regular features and a tanned face just beginning to weather
in a way that would only make him appear more distin-
guished. Pearl mentally projected and decided that in a few
years he'd look incredibly worldly and handsome. He had
angular pale blue eyes that seemed amused. She stared straight
ahead, watching him in the back bar mirror, and waited for
the pickup line.

"This is it," he said.

"It?"

She continued looking at him in the mirror, watching him
studying her. The two-dimensional reflected scene in the
smoky mirror reminded her of how the city had looked in
the lowering dusk.

"The pickup line," he said.

"It didn't work."

He smiled, very handsomely. "You haven't given it a
chance to sink in."

Time to discourage this guy, right now.

"I'm a cop," she said.

"Great."

"Vice," she said.

He slid onto the stool next to her. "Fine. I could use some advice."

At first she didn't understand; then she had to discipline herself not to smile. "That's 'vice.'"

"Ah! As in human foible."

"As in if you don't stop bothering me I'm going to arrest you for haranguing a police officer."

"You mean I've committed a haranguing offense."

"I mean you're about to get your ass hauled off to the punitentiary."

"That's very good," he said, brightening. "And fast. Brains and beauty."

"But not necessarily in that ardor."

"Wonderful!"

My God, I'm playing this idiot's game.

But there was something about him. Something suggesting that the smooth banter was on a surface of deeper water and he was . . . trustworthy? Perhaps he was being amiable only for the sake of amiability, without a hidden agenda.

Pearl was no fool. She had to wonder. Had she encountered an admirable genuineness or a real talent for deceit? She couldn't help herself. Couldn't contain a smile that broke through her somber demeanor and gave her away.

Even she had to admit it was a "yes, I am interested" smile.

It's because he came at me playing a game.

Pearl, always analyzing. A game player herself.

Had he somehow known that?

"I'm Yancy Taggart," he said, offering his hand.

She gave up, looked into the blue eyes directly, and shook the strong, dry hand. "Pearl."

He didn't ask for her last name, but within ten minutes she gave it to him.

Chatting with this guy turned out to be so easy. It was as if they both had scripts and magically knew all their lines. The prep school where he'd had his dance lessons had sanded off all his rough edges. There was no awkwardness about Yancy Taggart, and no one could for long feel awkward in his presence.

They sat for a while at the bar and then carried their drinks over to one of the booths where they wouldn't be overheard. Taggart was clearly a practiced charmer, but Pearl figured she'd had enough experience with his type that she could handle him. Still, she was amazed by his poise and smooth patter, and how he so casually pried personal information from her. If he wasn't the world's greatest salesman, he was a con man.

"You know I'm a cop," Pearl said, over yet another frosty mug, "but you haven't told me what you do."

"So take a guess."

"You're a salesman."

"In a way."

"I know what way," Pearl said with a grin.

"I'm a lobbyist," he said. "For the National Wind Power Coalition. I've been assigned to convince people of wealth and influence to commit funds to an effort to convert New York City to wind power."

"You mean windmills on skyscraper roofs?"

He smiled. "Not exactly. They'd be cowled units computerized always to face the wind. And they could be incorporated into existing architecture to protrude from the walls of buildings and take advantage of the winds that often blow along the avenues. The generated power could be made to supplement the grid and—" He broke off his explanation. "Whoa. You don't really want to hear the technical details of the concept."

"Will it really work?"

"I haven't the slightest idea."

"But you're lobbying for them."

"I'm a professional lobbyist. It's my job to convince people."

She grinned. "Sort of like a defense attorney who knows his client is guilty."

"Exactly. Only I don't know for sure that wind power *isn't* the answer. Nobody really knows the answer. I just pretend to."

"That's terrible!"

"Only if the wind power project won't work. And I don't know that it won't."

"The point is, you don't know that it will."

"That's a difficult one to get around," Yancy admitted. "That's why the coalition hired a professional lobbyist."

"That isn't ethical, Yancy."

"I'll grant you that. But being a lobbyist, I lobby. I have a sliding code of ethics."

She laughed. "Jesus! Those aren't ethics at all. They're just—"

Pearl was interrupted by the first four notes of the old *Dragnet* series.

"My phone," she explained, digging her cell from her purse, thinking there must be a pun in there someplace, a cop with a cell phone.

She saw that the caller was Quinn.

When she answered, he said, "Pearl, we've got a dead woman in the five-hundred block of West Eighteenth Street. You better get down here."

"Chrissie?" she asked.

"No. But it looks like the Carver might be active again."

Oh, God! "On my way."

"Coming from your apartment?"

"Sure am," she replied, keeping her personal life personal.

"Vitali can have a radio car sent for you."

"It'll be faster if I take a cab," Pearl said, with a glance at Yancy Taggart.

She broke the connection before Quinn could reply.

"Crime beckons?" Yancy asked.

Pearl was already sliding out of the booth. "Yeah. Sorry, I've gotta go."

"You look upset. Not bad news, I hope."

"Not for me," Pearl said. And she realized she meant it. Though she had compassion for this latest Carver victim—if it turned out Quinn was right—a part of her was also glad this had happened. It meant the investigation had gotten off the dime. The game was on.

"So you really are a police detective."

"I really am."

"Shall we meet here tomorrow evening about this time?"

"We shall," Pearl said.

Maybe he did have a yacht to go with his sliding ethics. Sometimes that was where sliding ethics led, right to a yacht.

"Bring your handcuffs," she heard Yancy call behind her, as she was moving toward the door.

That was how it began.

21

While the cab she'd flagged down bounced and jounced over Eighth Avenue potholes, Pearl thought not about the murder scene she was speeding toward, but about Yancy Taggart. She found that odd.

Would he meet her?

Did she care?

Never one to lie to herself, she figured the answers were yes and yes.

Why did this guy appeal to her? He was probably at least fifteen years older than she was, and not her usual type.

Then she realized what might be the basis of the attraction. Taggart was sort of an anti-Quinn. Where Quinn was duty-bound and relentless, Taggart didn't mind whiling away a morning over coffee and a racing form in a bar. Taggart would gamble his money; Quinn chanced every other kind of gamble but didn't like the odds of house games. Taggart was slim and graceful—even languid—in posture and attitude; Quinn was lanky but powerfully built, stolid, calm, and intense. Taggart dressed stylishly and was neatly groomed; Quinn always looked like what he was—a cop in a suit—and his hair looked uncombed even when it was combed. While Taggart was elegant and classically handsome, Quinn was somehow homely enough to be attractive.

Maybe, she thought, Yancy Taggart was what she needed to chase Quinn completely out of her thoughts.

In time she might chase them both from her thoughts.

Pearl saw the yellow crime-scene tape, and her thoughts were jolted to where she was, and why. She asked the cabbie to pull to the curb half a block from the tape. She wanted to take the scene in as she walked toward it from a distance. Sometimes it was smart to begin with the long view.

Several radio cars were parked at crazy angles to the curb, as if they were the toys of some giant child who'd tired of them and walked away, leaving their colorful roof bar lights flashing. Beyond the police cars, Pearl could see Quinn's black Lincoln with two wheels up on the curb to allow the remaining lane of traffic to pass. She noticed for the first time that the old Lincoln had whitewall tires. She hadn't thought they made those anymore. But Quinn would know where to get them. Like his Cuban cigars.

The Lincoln's engine was still ticking in the heat as she walked past it. Inside the trapezoid of yellow tape a group of large men huddled over what looked like a bundle of clothes on the sidewalk.

When Pearl got closer, she saw that the bundle was a woman.

One of the men standing over the dead woman was Quinn. He spotted Pearl and motioned her over. A uniform held up the tape so she could duck under it like a boxer entering a ring. He gave her a look, as if he might wink at her. Didn't the idiot think she'd ever seen a corpse before?

This part of Eighteenth Street was being improved or marred—depending on your point of view—with neo-modern architecture, most of it angular glittering glass and metal, some of it appearing precariously balanced. The building the body was next to was an almost completed condominium project. According to the plywood sign leaning against the wall near the silvered glass door to what would become the lobby, it was The Sabre Arms. The optimistic advertising didn't mention price.

Quinn nodded to Pearl and moved over to make room for her in the huddle. Pearl nodded back. Quinn's sport coat collar was twisted in back, and he needed a shave. It struck Pearl again how different he was from Yancy. Yancy the lobbyist with the gift of gab and the sliding ethics. Quinn the taciturn engine of justice with a moral code like Moses that sometimes transcended the laws of man.

Pearl shook off her flash of dubious insight and refocused her mind on her work.

Julius Nift, the obnoxious little medical examiner who looked and acted like Napoleon, was bent over the dead woman. Pearl didn't bother nodding hello to him.

Her gaze slid past him to the victim, and her stomach lurched. The corpse was wearing ragged clothing. Her face was dirty, her fingernails black, her brown hair a tangle. A homeless woman. Pearl felt pity well up in her as well as horror. What must be the woman's panties had been knotted and used as a gag, and a slender shaft of silver protruded from the dead woman's mouth, apparently a handle.

"It's a spoon," Nift said. "She died with a silver spoon in her mouth."

"Might she have choked on it before her throat was cut?"

"We'll have to wait till later to find out for sure, but I doubt it. There are no other signs of asphyxiation. No cyanosis, petechiae, or distended tongue." Nift spoke in a tone suggesting Pearl should have noticed this lack of symptoms herself.

The woman's threadbare dress was torn open in front to reveal her breasts and stomach. Her nipples had been sliced off, and there was the bloody *X* carved on her midsection, beginning just below a point between her breasts. There was a gaping wound in her throat, like a scarlet necklace. She appeared to have been in her late forties, had a crooked nose, prognathous jaw, and wouldn't have been attractive even cleaned up and twenty years younger. *Odd*, Pearl thought; all the other Carver victims had been attractive women.

Nift had been peeking up at Pearl, amused by her discomfort.

"She had a face like a mule," he said, "but you can see she had a pretty good rack, even with the nipples gone."

"You're such an asshole," Pearl said. "Are the nipples gone from the scene?"

"Unless you're standing on them," Nift said.

Pearl doubled up a fist.

"Pearl," Quinn said, cautioning her. He'd told her before she should let Nift's remarks roll off her. She shouldn't give the nasty little M.E. the pleasure of getting under her skin.

She knew Quinn was right. That was Nift's game, using his gruesome trade to rattle people with his sick sense of humor. All cops used dark humor to help them cope with some of the things they saw in the Job, but Nift pushed it from diversion to something that filled a twisted need.

Pearl's fist unclenched, and she flexed her fingers. But she still wouldn't have minded choking Nift until she saw some cyanosis.

Nift smiled.

"How long's she been dead?" Quinn asked.

"I told you—"

"For Officer Kasner."

"More than ten hours. I'll be able to know more when I get her in the morgue where I can play with her." For Pearl.

"Any identification on her?" Pearl asked Quinn.

But it was Nift who answered. "Are you kidding? No purse or wallet. Every pocket is empty. This little number probably hasn't slept indoors in weeks, maybe months. She's been screwed over every which way, and if she did have anything on her person, her killer probably took it."

"A shitty life," one of the plainclothes detectives said.

"And a shitty death," another added.

"You guys homicide?" Quinn asked.

"Vice. We heard the call and were only a few blocks away, so we came over to see what there was to see."

"And I've seen enough," the other vice guy said, but he made no move to leave. "What's with the spoon?"

"A bad joke," Quinn said.

"In bad taste," the first vice guy said.

Quinn gave him a look that induced both vice detectives to fall silent.

"There isn't much blood considering her throat's been slashed," Pearl said.

"Very good," Nift said. "That's because she was killed with a single stab wound to the heart." As he spoke he absently probed one of the damaged breasts with a pointed steel instrument. The expression on the corpse's face was one of mild insult.

"Why don't you close her eyes?" Pearl said.

"Why don't you ask her some questions? I'll do my job, you do yours. She can't see, just like she can't talk."

"Her body was stuffed behind the big plywood sign leaning on the building," Quinn said, before Pearl could reply to Nift. "We figure she was killed late last night or early this morning. Nobody spotted her until half an hour ago."

Pearl noticed a woman wearing a gray jogging outfit with a hooded sweatshirt standing across the street, staring at them. Her arms hung at her sides, and she didn't move. Her face was in shadow, but something about her seemed familiar.

"Who found her?" Pearl asked.

"Woman who lives across the street. Her hat blew off, and she chased it and happened to glance behind the sign. She's in her apartment over there with a uniform keeping her company. She's still in shock."

Pearl could understand that. Right in the middle of all this art-gone-mad architecture and expensive renewal, an ugly reminder of poverty and death might be especially jolting.

When Pearl glanced back across the street, she saw that the woman in the jogging outfit was gone. She'd been simply an onlooker who'd stopped to stare. Yet there was that familiarity. Pearl was certain she'd seen the woman before in the course of this investigation, somewhere standing in the shadows. *Shadow woman*, she thought.

Fedderman suddenly appeared. His suit coat was wrinkled, and where he might have worn a tie was what looked to be a spaghetti-sauce stain. Behind him were Mishkin and Vitali, looking like a bemused accountant tailed by one of the brothers in *The Godfather.*

It was going to be crowded inside the crime-scene tape, so the two vice guys nodded their good-byes and left.

The three detectives who'd just arrived took in the scene. Fedderman's face was a blank. Vitali looked keenly interested. Mishkin, who had a notoriously weak stomach, went chalk white and turned away.

"Bring them up to date, Pearl," Quinn said.

"Can I have the body?" Nift asked.

"If you want it," Quinn said. To Pearl: "Make sure there's nothing interesting under it."

"Like a nipple or two," Nift said.

He straightened up to his full Napoleonic stature and motioned for the waiting paramedics to remove the body.

Quinn walked off to the side and punched out a number on his cell phone. He stood at the edge of the crime-scene tape with the phone pressed to his ear.

"Who's he calling?" Vitali asked. "Everybody's here except Eliot Ness."

Pearl shrugged. She didn't know for sure who was on the other end of Quinn's phone conversation, but she figured that if she guessed Cindy Sellers, she wouldn't be far wrong.

The devil getting her due.

22

Quinn's phone call from Nift the next day at the office shed more light on the dead woman found on Eighteenth Street. She'd had a high alcohol level in her body, along with traces of methamphetamine. Cause of death was the stab wound in her chest. The slicing off of her nipples and the X carved into her abdomen had occurred after death, as had the slit in her throat. Probably the same knife had been used to inflict all the injuries.

"Was she stoned when she died?" Quinn asked.

"It's doubtful. She wasn't legally drunk, and the meth wasn't enough to have made her stoned. I'm not saying she used these two substances simultaneously. The meth stays in the blood one to three days, in the urine even longer."

"Time of death?" Quinn asked.

"I make it between midnight and three a.m. Something else, Quinn, she displayed all the signs of heavy drug use over a long period of time. And not just meth. She was a real veteran, and on the way out. Needle marks on both arms and between her toes. Hadn't bathed in at least a week. This cunt probably smelled better dead than alive."

"She was somebody's daughter or sister," Quinn reminded him, "so why be such a contemptible asshole?"

"Hey, I'm somebody's son. Don't have a brother, though.

Don't get your undies all twisted, Quinn. I'm just trying to get across to you the deplorable shape this vic was in even before she was spoon-fed and offed. If the killer hadn't gotten her, she wouldn't have lasted much longer on her own."

"Any identification yet?"

"No. Who'd want to claim her?"

"Would your mother claim you?"

"You would have to ask her nice."

"Anything else?"

"Yeah. Next time try to get me a higher class of victim."

Nift hung up before Quinn could reproach him.

That was okay. Quinn had other things on his mind.

Quinn sat staring at the phone on his desk, letting his mind continue to work on the conversation with Nift.

The death of the Chelsea woman certainly bore the Carver's signature, except for the fatal stab to the heart. And the Carver had inflicted the breast and torso injuries *before* slitting his victims' throats.

Was the Carver getting soft?

Not likely. That wasn't the way with sadistic killers.

All but one of his other victims had been killed indoors, in their apartments, except for Rhonda Nathan, who'd been killed at work in her office. Possibly he'd learned his lesson. Maybe for some reason he'd had to kill the Eighteenth Street woman outdoors, and wanted to minimize the flow of blood. There would be nowhere to wash up after maiming her breasts and abdomen and then slashing her throat, and blood tended to spurt from the large arteries in the neck. The stab to the heart had been relatively neat. It would cause immediate death and minimize blood flow from subsequent wounds.

A warm flow of air stirred the papers on Quinn's desk as Pearl entered the office and nodded a good morning to him.

"Doughnut?" she asked, holding up a Krispy Kreme bag.

He told her no thanks and said he'd just hung up on Nift.

"Glad I didn't have to talk to the little asshole this early in the morning," she said. She went over to the coffee brewer and poured some of the strong black liquid into her mug. The trickle of coffee caught the lamplight for a moment and glowed a beautiful translucent amber. Pearl added powdered cream, which did not look so inspirational going in.

While she sat at her desk dunking a doughnut, Quinn told her about his and Nift's conversation.

She licked glaze from her fingers. "We could have a copycat killer, what with the news about the investigation being reopened." She deftly flicked her tongue over the back of her thumb. "Could be some psycho thinks he can have a free one by blaming it on the Carver."

"Or the Carver has simply changed his M.O. after all this time. His compulsion would demand that the essentials remain the same, but he might change the details. He might be more practical."

"Huh?" Pearl sipped at her coffee.

Quinn told her his theory about the killer minimizing the bloodshed so he'd be less likely to have noticeable and incriminating stains on his clothes or person.

"Maybe," she said, but she sounded dubious. She glanced around. "Where's Fedderman?"

"He drove the unmarked down to Eighteenth Street. Gonna talk to the people who live and work around where the body was found. Maybe somebody noticed something. Mishkin's down there, too."

"How about Vitali?"

"He's at a precinct house utilizing the vast resources of the NYPD."

"Or reporting to Renz."

"Better Vitali than me," Quinn said.

He noticed that Pearl had left a glazed doughnut untouched on a paper napkin on her desk. As he gave in to temptation and parted his lips to ask her for it, his phone rang again.

This time it was Vitali.

"Waddya got, Sal?" Quinn asked.

Vitali started telling Quinn about the postmortem results on the Eighteenth Street victim, but Quinn interrupted him and said he'd already talked with Nift.

"Something new, though," Vitali said. "We just got a positive ID on the dead woman. Turns out her prints were on file. Maureen Sanders, forty-four years old, no listed address, unmarried, probably unloved. She's got a sheet. Two arrests for cocaine possession a year ago. Three arrests for prostitution the year before that. One conviction on the drug charges. She was on parole, but her P.O. hadn't seen her in months."

"A street person."

"Street junkie," Vitali said. "I'm still trying to find family. And by the way, that spoon that was jammed in her mouth— it was real silver."

"Part of a set?"

"At one time, sure. But it looks old and like it might have been knocking around secondhand shops and flea markets for years. Good for *Antiques Roadshow,* but not much of a clue."

"Died with a silver spoon in her mouth," Quinn said. "Ironic humor. It fits the Carver. Let's get a morgue photo to the media. Maybe somebody'll claim Maureen Sanders." Quinn thought of Cindy Sellers. "And Sal, soon as you can, will you fax that photo to me?"

"Sure."

"I've got Mishkin down in Chelsea with Fedderman, canvassing the neighborhood where we found Sanders's body. You gonna need him?"

"I thought it'd be a good idea to run a check of violent crimes in South Manhattan for the last six months," Vitali said, "see if anything similar to the Sanders killing went down. I could use Harold for that."

"I'll send him to you," Quinn said.

He hung up the phone and stood up to slip on his suit coat. He and Pearl could drive down to Eighteenth Street in the Lincoln. On the way, he could fill her in on what Vitali had found.

He remembered the doughnut on Pearl's desk and turned to ask her about it, but he saw that it was gone. She was licking the back of her thumb again.

"Let's go," he said. "We're joining Feds and Mishkin."

She stood up, took a final sip of coffee, and wadded the white paper napkin the doughnut had rested on. She dropped the napkin into the Krispy Kreme bag, which she wadded and dropped into the wastebasket beneath her desk. It made the lightest of sounds in the metal wastebasket.

"You eat all those doughnuts?" Quinn asked.

"Yup. All three."

"You're gonna die of a sugar high."

"About the time you die of doughnut remorse."

Had she somehow known he was about to ask for the remaining doughnut? It was eerie sometimes, the way Pearl could almost read minds.

He didn't mention doughnuts again as they went out to where the Lincoln was parked in front of the office.

As they were pulling away from the curb, Quinn said, "You putting on weight?"

Pearl smiled.

23

Quinn and Fedderman were in the field. Pearl spent much of a rainy afternoon alone at the office, working at her computer. The new alliance with the NYPD gave her access to select databases, but so far she hadn't learned much more that was useful about Maureen Sanders.

Not that she hadn't learned some things. Sanders's fingerprints and arrest record led to her connections with various welfare agencies in New York. Slowly her background had come to light on Pearl's computer monitor. She'd been born in 1966 in Kansas City, Kansas, to parents who'd died within a few months of each other five years ago. Maureen had attended Kansas State University and at age nineteen had been expelled after falsely accusing her history professor of sexually assaulting her. Days later she was arrested for possession of cocaine, but claimed the drug had been planted in her car. Maybe it had been, because the charge was later dropped.

Still, it was easy to read between the lines that Sanders had developed a serious drug problem. After her expulsion from KSU she'd attended the University of Missouri for two months before dropping out. Then she seemed to have given up on higher education. Sanders had worked for three years as a waitress in a Columbia, Missouri, restaurant and then was arrested for stealing from her employer. She moved to

San Francisco and worked off and on as an exotic dancer.
Eight years ago, after her first arrest for prostitution, she'd
left San Francisco for Las Vegas, supposedly for a job as a
dealer in a casino.

There the thread of scant information played out. Pearl
could find no record of Maureen Sanders in Las Vegas. She
seemed to have been in suspended animation somewhere
until she was arrested twice for prostitution in Trenton, New
Jersey, three years ago. Again a gap after she failed to report
to her probation officer. She appeared on New York welfare
rolls two years ago, and was arrested twice on drug charges.
For whatever reason the charges in New Jersey never followed her to New York, just as the California charge hadn't
followed her to New Jersey, perhaps because she lived on
the streets and had no known address. Pearl guessed that
until the move to New York Sanders had been able to sustain
herself through prostitution. Then her drug habit and
lifestyle had taken their physical toll and made that kind of
work impossible.

Pearl sat back and watched the summer drizzle running
blurrily down the window facing West Seventy-ninth Street.
She thought about what a familiar and dreary life Maureen
Sanders had lived. Hers was a tragedy too often played out
in New York, and doubtless in every big city. She happened
to have fallen victim to a killer rather than to a bottle or a
needle or a bitterly cold winter.

Pearl got up and started to pour herself a cup of coffee,
then decided against it and made a cup of instant hot chocolate instead. It looked so dreary outside that chocolate
seemed the better choice to improve her mood.

She returned to her computer and decided to take a break
from researching Maureen Sanders. She'd probably learned
all she was going to anyway. Besides, simply reading about
the woman's wasted life was depressing as hell and had
probably more than the weather resulted in the choice of
chocolate over coffee.

Pearl let her fingertips drift idly over the computer's keyboard, barely touching the hard plastic. The rain continued to fall and began making a steady dripping sound on something metallic outside the window.

Casually—or so she told herself—she keyed in the name Yancy Taggart.

She soon became so engrossed in her search that she'd taken only an initial sip of her chocolate.

Yancy's full name—apparently his real name—was Yancy Rockefeller Taggart. He'd been born in 1954 in Pasadena, California. (Twelve years older then Maureen Sanders, yet he seemed so much younger.) Pearl was relieved when she was unable to find a police record. He had a business administration degree from Brandon University, served four years in the Coast Guard as something called an information officer, and finished his tour of duty in Norfolk, Virginia. Back in civilian life he'd gone to work in public relations for Philip Morris, then lobbied for the company when it became Altria. He was actually registered in Washington, D.C., as a lobbyist, though he'd lived at the time in North Carolina. Two years ago he'd moved to New York City and shortly thereafter resigned his position at Altria.

Lobbyist. What sort of man would admit to being a lobbyist? And for a tobacco company?

Of course, now he lobbied for some kind of wind power consortium. Curiously apropos.

Pearl worked her keyboard, then the mouse.

Though it didn't list all its employees, there really was a National Wind Power Coalition.

Pearl let out a long breath and sat back in her chair.

So it's true. Everything he told me is true. He actually is a lobbyist for something called the National Wind Power Coalition, headquartered in New York City. Windmills on skyscrapers. Maybe it's possible. At least some people think so. Maybe not Yancy, their lobbyist, but some people.

Pearl closed the windows she'd visited, then clicked on

the computer's history and deleted everything pertaining to
Yancy Taggart. He was her own personal business, certainly
not Quinn's or Fedderman's.

She *had* wronged Yancy. As much as called the poor man
a liar. Why did she always treat men's small talk or compli-
ments as lies or insults? Had she become too cynical?

She decided to call Yancy and suggest they go to dinner
tonight. He'd accept her invitation. They'd dine and sip wine
in a nice, quiet restaurant, and he'd almost surely find some
excuse to try to smooth talk her into going with him to his
apartment.

Pearl decided that she'd go. Not without a bit of a hassle,
but she'd go.

She was reaching across her desk to call Yancy's number
when Quinn's desk phone rang.

Pearl punched the glowing button that directed the call to
her line. She told the caller he'd reached Quinn and Associates Investigations.

"It's Sal," Vitali said in his gravelly voice. "Quinn
around?"

"Just me at the moment. You got Quinn's cell number?"

"Yeah, but you'll do. I was just being polite. I'd much
rather talk to you."

"You're so full of bullshit I'm surprised grass doesn't
grow on you."

Damn it! There I go again!

"Be that as it may," Vitali said, "you guys need to know
something. Harold was working his computer, doing some
cross-checking with violent crimes against women in and
around New York. He found an interesting one. Woman
named Mary Bakehouse, attacked in her Village apartment
three nights ago by a guy who was about to work her over
with a knife, when he was scared away by something.
Could've been our guy."

"Three nights ago, you said?"

"Yeah. The uniforms who took the call said she was scared shitless, had a hard time even telling them what had happened."

"You'd think she'd have wanted police protection."

"The guy warned her not to tell anyone, and she took it seriously. Besides, she was embarrassed as well as terrified. Not all women are like you, Pearl, with a set of balls."

"Aw, that's one of the nicest things you ever said to me, Sal. Should I adjust my protective cup and go talk to this shrinking violet?"

"Pearl, I meant it as a compliment."

"I know, Sal."

"Harold and I were gonna go talk to the victim while there's still time today. I just wanted to keep you guys informed."

"Thanks," Pearl said. "I'll let Quinn know."

"Okay. We'll check with you tomorrow. And Pearl . . ."

"What?"

"You okay, Pearl?"

"Fine. Very good, in fact. Balls and all."

"I didn't mean about that."

"Then why would you ask?"

"I dunno. You seem distracted."

Pearl almost blushed. *Jesus!*

"I'm fine, Sal. Just tired from sitting at my computer. Learning some sad facts about Maureen Sanders."

One part of her mind still thinking about calling Yancy, she told Vitali what she'd discovered about Sanders.

"Hell of a life," he said, when she was finished.

"Not unlike a lot of others."

"So true, Pearl. Talk to you tomorrow."

After she'd replaced the receiver, Pearl sat at her desk quietly thinking.

She *had* been distracted, by thoughts of Yancy Taggart,

and shrewd Vitali had sensed it with his cop's finely tuned ear.

Enough of this, she told herself. She'd focus in, do her job. She'd call Quinn and fill him in on what she'd learned about Maureen Sanders, and about the possible earlier intended victim Vitali and Mishkin had uncovered.

She stretched out her arm and reached for the phone. There would still be time enough tonight for the improbable but apparently genuine Yancy Taggart.

Is his middle name actually Rockefeller?

Quinn had left Fedderman and gone home to think. He sat at the desk in his den, a cup of coffee before him. No cigar, though.

Maybe that's what was wrong. Why he couldn't get his mind going. He needed a cigar.

He got one of the Cubans from the mini-humidor in his desk drawer, used his guillotine cutter on it, and fired it up. He sat back and watched the smoke writhe toward the ceiling.

After tapping his fingers on the desk for a while, he sat forward and got his legal pad from the flat drawer. He looked over what he'd written so far, then drew a line beneath it. Beneath the line he wrote:

> *Maureen Sanders dies, wounds unlike those*
>   *made by the Carver, too shallow, silver spoon*
>   *in her mouth like Carver's sick humor. Carver*
>   *older so more hesitant?*
> *Mary Bakehouse attacked before Maureen*
>   *Sanders. Carver frightened away?*

Quinn still didn't know a lot about the Bakehouse woman. Sal and Harold would fill him in later. But it wasn't the Carver's style to leave a survivor behind. One slash of the knife was all it would have taken, and then run, run, run.

Chrissie still missing. Carver victim?

Quinn stared at the yellow legal pad. *Too many question marks.* He tossed the pad onto the desk and leaned back in his chair. Clamped the cigar between his teeth.

Watching the smoke's writhing dance toward the ceiling, he thought about where he was, what he was doing. He remembered how May hated for him to smoke inside. May was still here, part of her, even though they'd been divorced for years. May and Lauri, when Lauri was small . . . good years.

Then the loneliness, and then Pearl.

Then the loneliness again.

Quinn could still remember Pearl here. Her presence still haunted the apartment. He would wake up sometimes thinking about her. She was so vibrant, and could be so loving when she wasn't . . . pissed off about something. Pissed off about everything, in fact. Pearl was not a contented person. She was a driven and obsessive one.

Quinn had to admit that he was obsessive, too, but in a larger, more comprehensive way. Not minute by minute, like Pearl. Not with a short fuse like Pearl's.

And not with insight like Pearl's. It was almost as if she had little antennae all over her, picking up other people's silent signals. Whatever else she was, she was a hell of a detective.

Quinn leaned back farther in his chair and smiled around his cigar, thinking about their life together here in this apartment. Dinner with friends, taking long walks, going to the theater and then coming back here and making love as pleasurably and slowly as if there were no numbers on the clock and they'd never have to leave the bed. The look in Pearl's eyes after making love, so dark and unimaginably deep. If you could somehow see clearly in those dark depths you might glimpse the far end of the universe.

The truth was, he'd like to return to those days.

The truth was, he didn't see much hope for that to happen.

Pearl saw to that.

He continued watching the smoke curl toward the ceiling and thought about Pearl.

Jesus, she can be a bitch!

24

The air conditioner was off, and the apartment was miserably hot. Mary Bakehouse sat bent forward on the remaining chair and looked up at Vitali and Mishkin. The sofa remained, along with whatever else had been there when Mary had rented the place furnished. It wasn't much. The rest of what she'd bought to decorate or furnish the living room was gone. Two sweaty guys in identical wrinkled gray pants and white T-shirts huffed and puffed their way out the door carrying a mattress. A cardboard box with a lamp shade and some knickknacks in it sat near the door, almost close enough for the movers to trip over.

Sweat was rolling down Mary's heart-shaped face as she struggled for words. *A sweet woman*, Harold Mishkin thought. Sweet and under a terrible strain, knowing her ordeal might not be over. The kind of visitor she'd had, sometimes they came back.

"Did he tell you directly he wasn't finished with you?" Mishkin asked.

Mary Bakehouse appeared momentarily thrown by the question. "Not exactly, but he gave the impression he could come back anytime he wanted. That he could do whatever he wanted to me."

"They often give that impression," Mishkin said, "but usually they don't return." *Not that we can be sure about that.* "They get their kicks knowing you'll worry about them for a long time."

"Sadistic animal!" she said.

"That sums him up. But knowing what he's about, you don't have to worry so much. Scaring their victims is often the object of their sick game. He'll probably move on to some other unsuspecting woman."

"Do you really think so?"

"Absolutely. There's no shortage of potential victims out there. He's probably done with you. Besides, you're moving. He's not gonna go to the trouble of tracing you in a city so full of potential victims."

Vitali waited patiently for Mishkin to finish his comfort patter. His partner seemed compelled to console crime's victims, especially the more vulnerable, and women in particular. In her heart of hearts this woman knew her attacker might very well return and finish what he'd started. Maybe he'd follow her to the gates of hell to torture and kill her. It all depended on what kind of whack job he was, and who knew the answer to that?

When Mishkin had finally run down, Vitali glanced around at the now minimally furnished apartment. "Is that the only reason you're moving, so he can't find you?"

"Yes," Mary said. "At least it will make it more difficult."

"Could you identify him if you saw him again?" Vitali asked.

"I think so, but I can't be sure. I saw him clearly, but it all happened fast, and . . . my God! I was confused."

"Of course you were," Mishkin said.

"Describe him as best you can," Vitali said.

And she did, obviously growing more afraid as her words caused her to relive what had happened. Watching her, Vitali understood Mishkin's point of view. He felt himself growing angry at the attacker.

What has he done to your sleep, Mary Bakehouse? To your dreams?

"Did you get the impression you surprised him?" Vitali asked. "Or do you think he was waiting for you?"

"Waiting. But I can't be sure."

"Any sign that you interrupted a burglar?"

"No."

"Nothing missing?"

"No, I don't think he was a burglar. He seemed more interested in me than in stealing anything."

Vitali looked at her previous statement. "You said he had a knife."

"Yes. I think he had it strapped to his ankle." She described the knife, how her attacker had drawn it and used it to threaten her. Held it before her eyes so she had to look at the sharp blade. A boning knife, made to cleanly separate flesh from bone and gristle.

"Did he describe to you what he was going to do with the knife?" Vitali asked.

Mary Bakehouse turned pale. She shook her head no. "He didn't say anything to me. Not all the time we were together. It was like there was a spell, as if some terrible thing would happen if either of us spoke. He smiled. He seemed . . . amused."

"Excuse me for asking this," Mishkin said, "but . . ."

"Go ahead," she said. "Ask what you must."

"It's just that I need to confirm something. You said he pinched your right nipple?"

The embarrassed shrinking of Mary Bakehouse made Mishkin feel miserable for having asked. This should have been Sal's question.

She nodded silently.

Vitali gave Mishkin one of his "I'll take it, Harold" looks. Mishkin was getting as uncomfortable as the victim.

"He waved the knife around while he held it in front of you?" Vitali asked.

Another nod.

"Did he try to make it seem as if he was about to . . . cut off the nipple?"

"Of course he did! That was the whole idea!" She bowed her head and began to sob silently.

Mishkin got down on one knee in front of her as if he might be about to propose marriage. He pressed one of her hands in both of his. "It's all right, really. We've got to ask you this stuff. We don't like it any more than you do."

"The hell you don't!" Mary Bakehouse shouted at him.

Mishkin recoiled, stunned. He scrambled to his feet and backed away. "We don't! Honest . . ."

"Harold." Vitali's voice, cautioning. Then, to the victim: "Ms. Bakehouse, it could be very important that we know these things. Or at least have some sense of them."

She sniffed and then wiped her perspiring forearm across her nose. Her hair was a tangle in the heat, wild bangs plastered to her glistening forehead.

"He wasn't going to cut me," she said in a meek and beaten voice. "If he'd wanted to, he would have. Instead he just got up off me and made his way out the window and down the fire escape."

The two guys were back from taking out the mattress. They paused inside the door and gave Mary Bakehouse and the two detectives a look, as if to ask if Mary needed help. *Chivalry*, Vitali thought. This woman seemed to bring that out in men, a keen desire to protect her. Even Harold, least likely of dragon slayers, had his chest puffed out.

"Here," Vitali said, ignoring the movers and handing one of his cards to Mary Bakehouse. "If you think of something—"

"Or if you feel you need help," Mishkin interrupted, handing her one of his cards, too. "You make sure you call us. We can have somebody at your side in a hurry."

The two burly movers swaggered off into the bedroom. A

single damsel in distress could be divvied up only so many ways.

Mishkin rested a hand briefly on Mary Bakehouse's trembling shoulder, and the two detectives thanked her for her time and cooperation and left her sitting hunched over in her chair.

"That tears your heart out," Mishkin said, when they were outside on the sidewalk.

Vitali shook his head. "Don't have a coronary, Harold. We were only questioning a witness."

"You think whoever assaulted her was our guy?"

"I dunno. He made it look like he was going to help himself to a nipple. Our man likes souvenirs. But he didn't cut her."

"Why do you think he bolted?"

"Probably because he didn't like the setup. I think she might have come home unexpectedly and surprised him, which means he wasn't in complete control. Hadn't made the encounter happen on his terms."

"Or he might've been waiting for her, just like she said, and only wanted to scare her that time," Mishkin said. "But that doesn't mean he wouldn't have gotten carried away and eventually killed her."

"True," Vitali said. "But it still doesn't seem like the Carver. Doesn't *feel* like him."

"I've gotta agree with you," Mishkin said, opening the driver-side door of their unmarked. "But at the same time, we can't absolutely rule the subway guy out."

"If it actually *was* the man from the subway who attacked Bakehouse."

"If," Mishkin agreed, and waited while Vitali walked around the car and got in next to him.

"What's your gut feeling?" Mishkin asked.

"Same guy," Vitali said.

"Yeah," Mishkin said.

When Vitali had fastened his seat belt, Mishkin started the engine.

"What a science our job is, Sal."

Vitali grunted agreement. "Drive, Dr. Mishkin."

Mary followed the mover down with the last cardboard box packed with the detritus of her life, from the apartment that had once seemed a haven. In a strange way, moving away from here was more of a wrench than when she'd left home to come to New York. That had been a matter of choice. This move was a necessity. If she didn't make it, she would never feel safe in her home again.

Of course, she wasn't positive she'd feel safer in her new apartment, on a higher floor, with a full-time doorman, where she was off her usual subway route and would have to be traced to be found. She didn't think the subway man would go to that trouble. Probably he chose his targets at random.

Or so she told herself. She knew that if she were the object of some kind of sick fixation he might go to whatever trouble he had to in order to find her, his unholy grail.

She carried the seed of fear he'd planted in her with his eyes and the glint of the knife blade. What would he do to her if he did somehow manage to find her?

Mary knew that wherever she went she would ask herself that question, terrified of the answer. The subway man hadn't harmed her, but he'd certainly considered it. She was nothing human to him, merely something to satisfy a sick whim, a plaything of his dark desires. He could see her as that and only that, an object. And he wasn't the only one. There were others out there just like him, looking at her the same way, thinking the same dark thoughts. Every day, everywhere she went, they could simply look at her and know how vulnerable she was. People like them could see her as what she had become, could sense her injured soul the way carnivores could sense their prey.

In head and heart she knew that.

And knowing it had changed everything for her.

She shut the street door and tried not to look back.

25

Pearl deliberately drank too much wine.

Three glasses of an expensive pinot noir.

She'd made up her mind and eaten lightly during dinner at Russeria's, only a few short blocks from Yancy's apartment on Fifth Avenue.

He'd suggested the restaurant, somehow knowing this would be the night. Had she in some way signaled him? Pearl wondered if it was particularly easy for men to read her mind. Quinn—

Well, never mind Quinn.

She took another sip of wine. Dessert was on the way, a chocolate flan rimmed with whipped cream and raspberries.

Yancy had told her his apartment overlooked Central Park, Of course it would. And someday it would be windmill powered. It was difficult for her to believe completely, or to *dis*believe completely, anything this man said.

Well, maybe nothing he said was the whole truth and nothing but the truth. That was usually the way it turned out in criminal court.

Not that Yancy was a criminal. Ethics weren't exactly law.

As they were eating their desserts, she studied him across the table. He was impeccably dressed in a dark tan sport coat with neatly creased taupe slacks, a white shirt, and a maroon knit tie. A matching maroon handkerchief peeked from his jacket pocket. He reminded her of the seasoned, sophisticated Cary Grant. Around the time that airplane chased him.

"New York also has steam," he was saying, "running underground through much of the city. Remember when that underground steam pipe blew a few years ago near Grand Central?"

Pearl did. It had been a terrific explosion, followed by a gusher of superheated steam and water that reached as high as the nearby Chrysler building. People had gawked in disbelief. People had panicked. There had been at least one death.

"It was quite a demonstration of power unleashed in the wrong way," Yancy said. "But that kind of power can have positive uses. It's already used to provide heat and electricity, but not to its full potential. The coalition is considering ways to tap into that steam system even more, expand it out of the city so that someday it will hook up to similar steam systems, get it turning turbines to produce unheard-of amounts of energy. I have a few people close to the governor interested." He grinned. "I guess we'll call ourselves the National Wind and Steam Coalition."

Wind, steam, and bullshit, Pearl thought. But he did seem enthusiastic about his work.

She told herself that with Yancy, *seem* was the operative word.

"Do you really think that's possible?" she asked. "Turning the city's underground steam system into a kind of subterranean Hoover Dam project?"

He toyed with his fork. "Oh, I don't know. I can make it sound possible, so maybe it is."

She helped herself to a small sampling of her flan, watching him watch her lips work on the smooth silver spoon.

He gave her his handsome smile, the blue eyes. "But why am I talking about work? You're so much more important than that."

"More important than wind and steam power? You sure of that?"

"Of course, Pearl. What you have makes the whole world go round, not just a few windmills or turbines."

She sipped her wine and leaned over the table to look closely at him. "Are you lobbying me?"

He nodded. "I admit it. Are you susceptible to a bribe?"

She nodded back. "Like a two-term congresswoman."

"Going to finish your dessert, Congresswoman Pearl?"

"No, just my wine."

He gave some sort of silent signal to the waiter, who appeared with their check. Yancy paid cash and left an outrageous tip, probably to impress Pearl.

Within a few minutes they were outside on the sidewalk, in the hot night. She was slightly lightheaded from the wine. Things were moving swiftly. It was apparent that Yancy didn't want her to have second thoughts.

She knew that wasn't going to happen. The red wine and chocolate flan were having their combined effects on her, and she felt marvelously . . . compliant.

She didn't feel that way often, so why not lean back and enjoy it? A person couldn't keep her guard up all the time.

He flagged a cab that appeared as mysteriously as had the waiter.

"I thought your apartment was only a few blocks away," Pearl said.

"It is, but we shouldn't walk when we can ride."

"Smaller carbon footprint," said the congresswoman.

"We'll walk next time," Yancy assured her.

In the back of the cab he kissed her, then nibbled at her earlobe and gave it a little nip.

"What was that all about?" she asked.

"Earmark."

"You do stay with a theme."

"You're the theme," he said. "The theme, the overture, and the entire symphony."

Being played like an instrument, Pearl thought. *It's not just a figure of speech.*

His apartment was on Fifth Avenue and did indeed have a view of the park. The apartment was spacious, with plush rugs over a gleaming hardwood floor. There were brown leather upholstered chairs, glass-topped tables, modern prints on the walls. A Mondrian that looked real over a fireplace that didn't. Over in a corner there was even a gleaming grand piano.

The overall impression was one of comfort, order, and wealth.

But just an impression of the apartment's living room was all Pearl got, or wanted.

The bedroom was vast, with a king-sized bed with a brown leather bench at its foot. White walls, beige drapes, a thick cream-colored duvet.

No mirrored ceiling, thank God.

Had she expected one?

In truth, she was still trying to understand this guy.

In bed he was dominant but gentle, bringing her close to orgasm and then letting her fall back, turning her in on herself so that every thought other than of what he was doing fled from her mind. He toyed with her, and she amused him in a way that excited her.

He brought her closer, closer to where she wanted to be, and didn't let up.

Didn't let up.

A woman in the room called his name in her voice.

When they were finished he rolled lightly off her and kissed the ear he'd nibbled in the back of the cab. They looked at each other across the topography of white linen that was the landscape of lovers.

He didn't ask her how it had been for her, but she could see the question in his eyes.

"Profound and fun," she said.

He smiled. "In equal measures?"

She thought about it. "Yeah, I'd say. Only one complaint."

He appeared startled and hurt. "Oh? What's that?"

"Your hair didn't get mussed. Not one single hair on your head."

She turned to him, laced her fingers through his thick white hair, and made it a wild tangle.

She was amazed to see that he had dark roots.

26

It had taken forever for night to fall. Jerry and his mother were the only ones in the house.

Jerry Grantland's father seldom bothered to show up on his scheduled visitation days. This day had been no exception. It had passed without explanation, without even a phone call, without Jerry or his mother even mentioning his father.

Jerry lay silently in bed, waiting for his mother to turn off the *Jeopardy!* rerun on television in the living room. He could barely hear the low murmur of voices and rustle of applause from the TV, but he could see the crack of light beneath his bedroom door and knew she was still up. Probably she was drinking another of the mixture she made from club soda and the bottle of gin she kept in the cabinet above the sink.

An hour passed. Two. He could hear his mother snoring now and thought she'd probably sleep all night where she lay on the sofa. That was how it usually worked when she watched *Jeopardy!* and drank the gin drink.

Jerry rolled over onto his side and checked the clock with its flipping lighted numbers by his bed. It was twenty minutes past midnight. Jerry knew he should wait until about one a.m. That was usually the time it happened, when Mrs. Keller was asleep. Of course, if you watched the clock it would never flip to the next minute. Instead of watching, he closed his eyes and thought about Mrs. Keller. Jerry realized he had an erection, and he wondered, with a wife like Mrs. Keller, why did Mr. Keller do the things he did?

But then, why did Jerry's mother do some of the same things? Adults were a mystery to Jerry. Someday, he was sure, the mystery would be solved. When he was an adult.

At ten minutes to one he could no longer stay in bed without jumping clear out of his skin. He got up, slipped into his jeans, and put on his tennis shoes without socks. Though it was a hot night, he got a dark shirt from his closet and wore it untucked over the white T-shirt he slept in.

Silently, he went to his bedroom window and raised it. The window moved smoothly in its wooden frame and made no sound. Two days ago, while alone in the house, Jerry had lubricated it with some of his mother's Crisco from the kitchen.

The window screen unlatched from the bottom and swung upward, allowing him room to slip beneath it and drop the few feet to the yard.

It was a moonless night and dark, just as he liked it. The mosquitoes were out, but they didn't bother him much. Off in the distance he could see a shimmering cloud of moths circling a street light. They looked oddly like snowflakes caught in a whirl of wind.

He crept a few feet away from the window, then ran and disappeared into the dark void that was the unbroken lawn between his house and the Kellers'.

Then he was in the blackness and shrubbery at the side of the Kellers' house, near the twins' bedroom window. Sharp-edged holly bush leaves scratched his bare arms as he moved sideways into the comparative softness of the yews.

The yews were his cover and his shelter. He'd come to feel as at home in them as if he were some wild and nesting animal. Though he knew he was risking everything by being there, he still somehow felt more secure where he was than anywhere else in his world. He belonged there, in the concealing blackness and cover of the shrubbery. What he was doing couldn't be so wrong if he belonged there.

As if on signal, katydids in the surrounding trees began to sound their ratcheting shrill mating call. Jerry was glad. The racket made it less likely that he'd make some slight noise and be discovered.

He was at the window now. The shade was lowered almost all the way, as it usually was. A gap was left so it wouldn't knock over Tiffany's collection of ceramic animals on the inside sill. The bottom of the shade was an inch above the giraffe, leaving plenty of room for a view.

Squatting on the soft earth, Jerry settled into a comfortable position so he could peer into the bedroom without moving or making a sound. He wasn't worried about being noticed; there was always a night-light glowing softly in the twins' room, making it brighter inside than out. If somebody inside did happen to glance his way, he was sure that if he didn't move he'd be invisible behind dark reflecting glass. Experimenting with his own bedroom window had taught him that much. Night turned bedroom windows into the kind of mirrors you saw in the movies and on TV, where the police questioned suspects and then left them alone to comb their hair or examine their teeth, but they couldn't see the cops standing behind the mirror looking right at them.

Jerry was where the cops usually stood. Safe unless for some reason the light changed.

Mr. Keller had begun early tonight. He was already in bed with Tiffany. The bedroom was shadowed and dimly lit, so that Jerry couldn't make out exactly what was going on. But the shadows writhing on the wall beside Tiffany's bed made it obvious what was happening. As Jerry watched, breathless, he moved his hand down to caress himself.

The shadow show became more frantic and violent, and

Jerry was sure he could actually hear the squeaking of bed-springs.

Mrs. Keller has to know what's going on. She has to. . . .

All the time Mr. Keller was doing things to Tiffany, Chrissie lay curled on her side, facing away from her sister's bed but not seeing Jerry. Her eyes were open and blank, and she was sucking her thumb. As old as she was, she was sucking her thumb.

When Mr. Keller was finished with Tiffany he got up from his bed and adjusted his white boxer shorts. He moved toward the window, and Jerry's heart leaped and he drew back, ready to bolt into the shadows between the houses. He held his breath and made himself be still.

But Mr. Keller wasn't looking at the window; he was looking at Chrissie. Jerry saw something looped in his hand. His belt. He hadn't worn his pants to the twins' bedroom, but he'd brought his belt.

He yanked Chrissie roughly so she lay flat on her stomach, then raised her nightgown and pulled her panties down. She didn't resist or change expression.

Mr. Keller bent low and said something to her, probably warning her to be quiet. Then he began beating her bare buttocks and the backs of her thighs with the belt. With each blow her body tensed and relaxed, tensed and relaxed, and then it stayed tense as the beating continued. Jerry understood how she must feel. He realized he was weeping silently, and his fingernails were digging into his palms so deeply that it hurt.

When Mr. Keller was finished, he worked Chrissie's nightgown back down so that it covered her buttocks. Then he sat on the edge of the bed, leaned down so his face was near hers, and kissed her cheek. He stood up, caressed her hair, and then turned and walked from the room. He closed the door slowly and carefully behind him.

Jerry wondered where Mr. Keller was going now? To Mrs. Keller? They slept together, Jerry was sure, but their bedroom was upstairs, impossible to see into from outside. He could only guess what they might be doing.

Chrissie lay motionless for a while, and then she turned onto her side, facing away from Jerry. Across the room, Tiffany was lying on her side, facing Chrissie and the window where Jerry watched. The twins lay that way and stared at each other, their expressions blank. Jerry didn't think either of them spoke.

He'd reached a climax. He could feel the wetness at the crotch of his jeans.

Controlling his shakiness and shortness of breath, he backed away from the window, into the scratchy holly bushes. Sweat beaded on his face. Perspiration or tears stung like acid at the corners of his eyes.

Everywhere in the night the katydids screamed their relentless mating call.

Jerry turned and ran into the darkness, toward his own window, his own home.

The screams of insects followed him. As did the darkness.

27

"I suppose you're mad at me," Chrissie said, standing before Quinn's desk.

Her attitude seemed that of a teenage girl caught breaking curfew, rather than that of an avenging huntress talking to hired help.

They were in the office alone. Quinn had looked up, surprised, when she'd entered. She was slightly bedraggled from the heat, and at first he hadn't recognized her. Her sleeveless white blouse clung to her narrow upper body, and a strand of her dishwater-blond hair dangled over one eye. She was wearing jeans that looked genuinely well worn, and brown leather sandals that looked brand new.

In the vacuum of his surprise, she managed a half smile and said, "I could never do that."

He didn't know what she'd meant at first, and then realized she was referring to what he'd been doing at his desk—trying to balance a checkbook. "Seems I never could, either."

She went from smiling to looking guilty. "I know you've been trying to get in touch with me."

"You have blue eyes now," Quinn said. "And short blond hair."

"Before, I was wearing brown contact lenses and a brown wig. There was a certain facial resemblance to begin with, don't you think?"

"Not really," Quinn said.

He sat calmly, trying to figure out her game. He couldn't.

"Usually it's the other way around," he said. "The client is *too* available and badgers the detective agency for reports on any kind of progress."

She nervously shifted her weight from one foot to the other, like a tennis player anticipating a serve. Seeking a point of balance.

"I'm sorry for making myself scarce," she said. "Really."

"Maybe you had a good reason for disappearing."

"I'm not sure it was good enough. I knew after a while that you'd probably looked up photos of all the Carver victims and figured out that I'd sort of misled you into thinking Tiffany and I are—were—identical twins. What scared me was that it might not have occurred to you that we were fraternal twins. That you might simply think I was an imposter. That I'd lied to you."

"That's what you did," Quinn said. "You lied."

"More like misled you." She gnawed on her lower lip for a moment with her overbite. *"Misled?"* She tried the word again.

"We won't quibble over it," Quinn said.

"But then I ran. I'm not very brave lately."

"But you came back."

"When I saw in the news that the Carver had killed that woman down in Chelsea, Maureen Sanders, and then attacked that other woman, I couldn't stay away. I had to find out what you'd learned."

"It's pretty much all in the news."

She stared at him. "You're playing it closed-mouthed.

Now you don't trust me." Her contriteness had disappeared to be replaced by anger.

He had to grin. "Should I trust you?"

"Maybe not. But I *am* your client. Don't you have some kind of legal obligation to tell me everything you know?"

"Legal and ethical. Unless there are special circumstances."

"Such as?"

"The client disappearing."

She tucked her fingertips into her jeans pockets and looked glum as well as bedraggled. The blond hairdo he couldn't get used to looked damp and stuck to her head.

"You know the police are actively involved now," he said.

"Yeah. I didn't want that to happen. They'll screw things up, don't you think?"

"Possibly they will." He toyed with the ballpoint pen he'd been holding during his assault on the checkbook and bank statement. "But we didn't have a choice. When Maureen Sanders was killed and sliced up using the Carver's M.O., the police naturally made the connection and reopened the investigation. And that includes all the Carver murders, including your sister's."

"They couldn't catch the Carver the first time around, so I don't have much hope they'll do any better this time. They should have stayed out of it."

"Politics are involved," Quinn said. "As well as that pesky thing called the law."

"Well, I don't see much point to it. Maybe you can explain to me all that's happened, tell me what my money's bought."

Quinn studied her, not wanting to be taken in again. Her sudden mood changes and apparent ignorance of the law didn't fool him. He knew she wasn't nearly as naïve as she appeared.

He put down the pen and pointed to the nearest desk chair, Pearl's. "Roll that chair over here and sit down."

She did, and he brought her up to date on the investigation.

"So who's this mystery woman who's been shadowing the investigation?" Chrissie asked, when he was finished. "Any ideas?"

Quinn had deliberately mentioned Pearl's shadow woman. "One theory is that she's you."

Chrissie seemed surprised, but she might be good at that. She appeared to think about what he'd said, absently rubbing her chin. It might have been a feigned gesture, but he'd seen her do it before, unconsciously. Quinn noticed that she wore no rings on either hand—no jewelry at all, at least that he could see.

"Well, I can understand why you might have thought it was me," she said, "since you couldn't get in touch with me for a while. But I can tell you honestly it wasn't me."

"It also occurred to us that something bad might have happened to you and you couldn't contact us."

Now she seemed embarrassed, and not a little bit pleased. "I hadn't thought of that, truly. It didn't occur to me that my disappearance might alarm you. But I am touched by your concern."

She wasn't being sarcastic. She'd meant it, he was sure.

Don't be sure. Don't take for granted that anything this woman says is true.

"So where were you?" Quinn asked.

"Oh, nowhere or not doing anything that has anything to do with any of this," Chrissie said.

While Quinn was mentally diagramming her sentence, Chrissie stood up from Pearl's chair and tapped the side of the small brown leather purse she was carrying.

"I've got my cell phone turned on again," she said. "You have my number."

"Where are you staying?"

"I'm looking for a new place now. I'll let you know." She exhaled loudly and smiled. "I'm glad we're on the same page again. Do you need any more money?"

He shook his head no. "We're fine for now." He tapped a knuckle on the checkbook and statement spread out before him on the desk. "I think we are, anyway."

She took a step closer to the desk. "I do want, more than anything, for my sister's killer to be brought to hard justice."

"We all do."

She nodded, shifted her weight awkwardly, and made for the door.

"By the way," Quinn said, "you needn't have worried. We had it figured that you were a fraternal twin."

"I should have known," she said. "You do have a reputation."

"Pearl suggested it."

"*Cherchez la femme.*"

She was smiling as she went out.

28

A woman who lived in the building where Mary Bakehouse had been attacked contacted the police. She claimed to have remembered something that might be important. Her name was Ida Frost. Mishkin had interviewed her before and was skeptical.

Still, any lead might be worth following.

Vitali knocked on the apartment door. Mishkin moved closer so if she was looking through the peephole Ida Frost might recognize him.

She opened the door almost immediately. She was a small, stooped woman close to eighty, with gnarled teeth that didn't spoil a bright smile. As she peered up at Vitali and Mishkin, her eyes were bright and alert.

She stood back so they could enter. It was warm in the apartment but not uncomfortable.

"I made brownies," she said.

She left them abruptly and scurried toward what they assumed was the kitchen.

Vitali and Mishkin exchanged glances.

Then Ida Frost was back, using two hot pads to hold a large rectangular pan of brownies generously dusted with powdered sugar. They smelled delicious.

"Hot from the oven," she said. "My mother's recipe and her mother's before her." She offered the pan.

"Can't say no to all that history," Mishkin said. He delicately lifted one of the end brownies.

Vitali, thinking that for all they knew the brownies could be poisoned, smiled and shook his head no. Ida Frost moved in on him with the brownies. He raised a hand, still smiling. The edge of the hot pan was almost touching his tie. She was smiling up at him insistently, still advancing. If he didn't back up he'd have a brownie pan scar on his stomach.

"These are great, Sal," Mishkin said. There were brownie crumbs and powdered sugar in his bushy mustache, on his tie. "You oughta try one."

Vitali gave in and helped himself to a brownie. Ida Frost withdrew from his personal space.

"You said on the phone that you recalled something," Mishkin said, and took another bite of brownie.

"Did I? Oh, yes." Ida Frost looked at Vitali and at the half a brownie in his hand. "Do they meet with your approval, Detective?"

Vitali growled around a mouthful of brownie that they did.

"What was it you recalled?" Mishkin asked.

Ida Frost appeared puzzled.

"You called the precinct house and asked for Detective Mishkin," Vitali reminded her. "You left a message saying you remembered something about the Mary Bakehouse case and were calling as we'd requested."

"I liked Mary," Ida Frost said. "I wish she hadn't moved away."

"Probably it's better for her that she went somewhere else," Vitali said.

Ida Frost seemed to consider that; then she smiled. "Yes, she's probably safer if she moved out of the city. People in these big apartment buildings don't seem to know each other, don't have the time. Everyone's always rushing around wrapped up in their own thoughts, busy, busy. I'm afraid we lead very insulated and uncaring lives."

"We should all take better care of each other," Mishkin said.

"Yes. We all share the guilt, in a way."

"We all agree that's true," Vitali said dismissively, trying to keep the Frost woman and Mishkin on point and hurry things along. What was it with Harold sometimes? "About your phone call, ma'am . . ."

Ida Frost's smile widened. "Am I a suspect?"

"Gosh, no!" Mishkin said, helping himself to another brownie.

She saw that Vitali had finished his brownie and advanced on him again with the pan. Though she had a slight limp, she was fast off the mark. "Do take another, Detective. They're sinfully delicious."

"They should be against the law," Mishkin said, and he and Ida Frost laughed.

Vitali took another brownie in self-defense. Or so he told himself, the brownies being hell on his diet. "You did call the precinct house," he reminded Ida Frost. "What was it you remembered, ma'am?"

"A hat. I understand the thug who attacked Mary wore a hat." She paused for what might have been dramatic effect.

"A hat," Mishkin said.

"I saw a man with a hat that very evening, standing outside and looking suspicious. I passed him when I went out for my daily walk."

"What time was that, ma'am?"

"Why, I couldn't say."

"Was it still light outside?"

"Outside, yes."

"What did he look like?" Mishkin asked.

"He was . . . just a man in a hat. A cap, rather. A baseball cap."

Mishkin glanced over at Vitali and almost imperceptibly

shrugged. He couldn't recall if he'd mentioned to Ida Frost that the attacker had worn a baseball cap. "Do you remember the color, ma'am?"

"Blue, or perhaps gray. Or both. Now that I think of it, It was a Brooklyn Dodgers cap, I'm sure," Ida Frost said. "I spend enough time in Ebbets Field, I should be able to recognize a Dodgers cap."

"The Los Angeles Dodgers, you mean, ma'am?" Vitali asked. There was powdered sugar on his brown suit coat. "The Dodgers haven't been in Brooklyn for a long time."

"I attended the games often with my father when I was a young girl."

"We all miss the Dodgers," Mishkin said.

"The man in the cap. He might have been Pee Wee Reese."

Mishkin grinned broadly. "Say, you're a real Dodgers fan."

"I've always been partial to Pee Wee. Would you like a glass of milk with those brownies? I have nice cold milk for all my visitors."

Vitali and Mishkin regarded each other. Vitali had powdered sugar on his suit and the back of his right hand. Mishkin had more of the white dusting on his mustache and tie. Probably some on his white shirt that wasn't visible unless you looked closely. Some of the powdered sugar on Mishkin had drifted down and was on his right shoe.

"Milk would be great!" Mishkin said, and Vitali seconded him.

Ida Frost set the pan of brownies on a magazine on the coffee table and hurried off again to the kitchen. The two detectives shook their heads silently. They were going to get nothing of value from this witness other than brownies. Ida Frost was one of the older, lonely women who inhabited many of Manhattan's small, rent-controlled apartments. What she wanted was company, somebody to appreciate her brownies. She had found two such people. Alleviating her loneliness might have been the sole purpose of her phone call.

Mishkin helped himself to another brownie while Vitali stood brushing at the powdered sugar on his suit coat with the backs of his knuckles, making more of a mess.

"Pee Wee," Ida Frost said to them, when she came back from the kitchen with two tall glasses of milk on a tray, "would never have harmed Mary Bakehouse."

Not Pee Wee, they agreed.

After leaving Ida Frost's apartment, Vitali and Mishkin slapped at their clothes to rid them of powdered sugar, trailing a white haze as they strode toward the elevator.

They both saw her at the same time, a woman standing watching them from beyond the elevator, near the end of the hall. She was wearing a dark raincoat and a dark hat with the wide brim bent low so her face was in shadow.

As if she'd just noticed them, she turned and walked quickly away, rounding the corner at the end of the hall and passing out of sight.

"I'll go after her," Vitali said. "You take the elevator and beat her to the lobby, Harold. We'll have her between us, and we can flush her out."

Off he went.

The elevator was already at lobby level and took its time rising to where Mishkin waited.

When it arrived at his floor he quickly stepped in and punched the lobby button, then the button that closed the elevator door.

The elevator stopped at the floor below, and a woman with two identical corgis on red leather leashes got in. One of the corgis began licking Mishkin's right shoe.

Another floor down, an elderly but alert-looking woman with an aluminum cane boarded the elevator. She and the woman with the Corgis ignored each other. No one paid the slightest attention to Mishkin except for the corgi licking his shoe.

When they reached lobby level, Mishkin, out of habit and because they crowded past him, let the women and the two dogs exit the elevator ahead of him. He stepped out just in time to see the door to the stairwell burst open and a panting and heaving Vitali come skidding out.

Both men looked at the street door shutting slowly on its pneumatic closer as the women and dogs disappeared into the night.

"I don't want to hurt your feelings, Sal," Mishkin said, "but I think our shadow woman beat you down the stairs and got out of the building."

"How did you get your shoe wet, Harold?"

"Huh? Oh. Dog."

"She's probably gone, Harold, but maybe she didn't leave at all. Let's get some uniforms down here to check the building."

Two hours later, all the occupants and apartments were accounted for. The shadow woman had escaped again.

"I don't understand it, Harold," Vitali said, as everyone was leaving the building. "I was really flying down those stairs."

"Don't feel bad," Mishkin said. "She had a good head start."

They pushed through the pneumatic door out into the night.

Three radio cars were still parked at the curb. Two uniformed cops were lounging against one of the cars, and three more cops were standing around nearby on the sidewalk, chatting.

Ida Frost emerged from the building, wielding her pan of brownies.

29

In the Nickel Diner on Broadway in TriBeCa, Joyce House laid out a breakfast of eggs, pancakes, and coffee for the good-looking guy.

That was how she'd come to think of him, because that was what he was—good-looking. He was slightly built, with a mop of curly black hair and magnetic blue eyes, and always dressed a bit showily and expensively. This morning he had on designer jeans, pointy-toed boots that looked like they were ostrich skin, and a tailored short-sleeved black shirt with white buttons. His silver belt buckle was in the form of a soaring eagle. A silver stud earring glinted in each earlobe. *Just this side of ghetto fabulous*, thought Joyce. But somehow the good-looking guy could bring it off.

Joyce was no slouch in the looks department herself. She was medium height, trim, and buxom, eye candy even in her yellow and white server's uniform. She had straight brown hair with bangs, a perfect pale complexion, and widely set eyes that were like calm dark lakes.

Mick, the diner's owner and overseer of the kitchen, leaned down to look at Joyce through the serving window. His beefy red face was perspiring after a busy breakfast hour. Mick had one of those florid complexions, as if his tie were always too tight and choking him. It was almost ten o'clock, and the diner was empty except for an elderly couple at a table near the rear, and the good-looking guy in a front booth by the window.

"We stay slow," Mick said to Joyce, "why don't you come back and help with the dishwashing?"

Joyce nodded. It was their usual routine. She didn't know why Mick even bothered to ask.

Alice the cashier would remain at her place behind the counter to greet any customers who happened to wander in during the void between breakfast and lunchtime. Alice was a gum-chomping, henna-haired former stock trader who'd opted out of the world of finance five years ago to live a simpler life with Mick. For years they'd been going to get married someday.

"I see you and Mr. Hotshot over there," Alice said, "and I can't help thinking I'm looking at two of God's beautiful creatures. He's been coming in regular for a few weeks now. He ever put any moves on you?"

"None that I noticed," Joyce said.

"You think he might be gay?"

"Hmmm. No."

"Married?"

"Irrelevant."

"So maybe you oughta go over and talk to him. Strike up a conversation about his pancakes. If you don't, I will."

Joyce laughed. "Yeah, you will. With Mick in the kitchen with all those knives."

"He might be in show business or something," Alice said, watching the good-looking guy fork in a bite of pancake. "Now that I look at him, I think I might've seen him in something."

"He might need more coffee," Joyce said.

She lifted the glass pot of decaffeinated from its burner and approached the good-looking guy, who was chewing and staring out the window.

He caught a glimpse of her reflection in the window but didn't turn around, letting her come to him.

"Top you off?" she asked.

He counted to three and swiveled around on the booth's hard wooden seat. Gave her a smile. "Pardon?"

"Your coffee, I mean."

"Sure." He nodded toward the pot. "That decaf?"

"Sure is. Always the pot with the orange top." She poured steaming coffee into his half-full cup. "My friend over there thinks you might be somebody. I mean, in show business."

He laughed. He had very white, very even teeth, made to appear still whiter because he apparently spent time in a tanning salon. And there was something about his hair, like maybe it wasn't so dark and had been dyed. So it could be he was a celebrity who had to be careful about his appearance. He didn't look like the type to be in any kind of outdoor work. Theater in the park, maybe.

"You're an actor," she said.

Big smile. "Yes, I'm Brad Pitt."

Joyce gave him his smile right back. "Well, I guess that makes me Angelina Jolie."

He added cream to his coffee from the little silver pitcher on the table. "Would you really be Angelina if I were Brad?"

The coffeepot was getting heavy, so she set it down. "Why not? That would be kind of a perfect world."

He kept his smile as he leaned back and studied her more closely. It made her uneasy, but not in a bad way. "A perfect world . . ."

"But it sure isn't that," she said. She picked up the coffeepot, keeping her elbow in tight and back so her right breast strained her uniform blouse.

"Don't go away," he said.

She felt herself heat up like the decaf, and her heart started to hammer.

"Work to do," she said. "Sorry."

She turned away, hoping to hear his voice calling her back. Waiting . . .

I'm hard to get, hard to get but worth it. . . . Come on. . . .

"If you go away," he said, "I'll have to order something else to make you come back."

Ah! She grinned. She did feel like one of God's beautiful creatures. The good-looking guy made her feel that way.

She turned back around to face him, being careful to keep a neutral expression.

"I wanted to talk, is all," he said.

"About what?"

"Why is it called the Nickel Diner? There's nothing on the menu that's a nickel."

"They always said about Mick, the owner, that he never saw a nickel he didn't pick up."

"Interesting. See, we talked and I learned something."

She smiled. "I didn't."

"Well, we haven't talked long enough. Don't you ever get lonely? Don't you sometimes just want somebody to talk to?"

She put the coffeepot back down on the table. "Yes and yes."

"What size shoe do you wear?"

Huh? "Seven," she said. "Why?"

"I can get you shoes. I'm in New York to help design a new shoe store."

"You're not an actor?" She feigned disappointment.

"Close," he said. "Shoe business."

"God!" she said, and rolled her eyes.

But she did like a man with a sense of humor.

"I can get you shoes," he said again. "You like pumps?"

"Joyce!"

Alice's voice from behind the counter. When Joyce looked over at her, Alice made a sideways motion with her head toward the kitchen. A signal that Mick might be taking an interest in where Joyce was, what she was doing. Mick could make a big commotion, like a major storm with thunder but no lightning. Except maybe if he thought she was flirting with a customer. Then there would be lightning to go with the thunder. He had a thing about that, said it was one of the *shalt nots* in the diner Bible.

"I really better get back to work," she said to the good-looking guy. "The boss doesn't like even the thought of the help getting to know any of the customers too well."

"We don't know each other *too* well. But I'd like to get to know you better. It's not just the pancakes talking, Joyce. I mean it."

She almost asked how he knew her name, and then she remembered Alice had just called her. Also, it was on all his breakfast checks along with a little smiley face.

"I'm Loren Ensam," he said, holding out his right hand. It was narrow but long-fingered; he had a pianist's hands.

She shook the hand, feeling its surprising strength though he didn't seem to have squeezed very hard.

"Joyce House," she said.

"Got a phone number, Joyce?"

"*Joyce!*" Alice called again. With more desperation this time.

"When I go over and total your check," she said, "I'll write it on the copy you keep."

He smiled up at her. "Okay. I'll be honest. I'm in the middle of an ugly divorce, and it wouldn't be to my advantage if my soon-to-be ex learned I was seeing another woman. And if your boss found out about us, you might lose your job and I'd have to find another breakfast stop. So we'll have a secret relationship."

"Sounds like fun." Joyce was already moving away from the booth.

"Oh, it can be," she heard him say behind her.

Of course, he'd never seen Mick blow up.

When she was back behind the counter, Alice grinned at her and said, "So how'd you do?"

"He's married with three kids," Joyce said without hesitation.

She didn't like doing it, but how could she not lie to Alice, who slept with Mick?

Joyce realized that her life had suddenly become more complicated. Secrets, lies, sex. Well, not sex yet. But it was inevitable.

Joyce was looking forward to all of it. She felt an inner turmoil that she didn't at all mind. What was happening was like out of a book, too good to be anything but fiction.

What if he doesn't call?

After she totaled up his check, she wrote her name and drew her customary little smiley face above it. The smiley face didn't seem as happy as usual. She saw that her hand was trembling.

He'll call. Why wouldn't he?

Below her name, on the check's customer receipt, she meticulously printed her phone number, even the area code so there would be no doubt. If Mick was watching, he'd probably think she was diligently itemizing prices.

Careful not even to glance at the good-looking guy, she walked over and laid the check on his table.

He'll call. He's got my number.

30

The entire team, including Vitali and Mishkin, were in the office. They were sipping coffee, passing around Krispy Kreme glazed doughnuts, and talking over the appearance—then disappearance—of the shadow woman in Mary Bakehouse's old apartment building yesterday.

"I can't quarrel with your tactics," Quinn said, "one of you giving chase on foot on the stairs, and the other taking the elevator down to the lobby, so you have her trapped in a squeeze."

"Couple of things might explain why the tactic didn't work," Fedderman said. He was half sitting on his desk, trying not to dribble more coffee on his tie as he dipped a doughnut. The journey from cup to mouth was perilous, and he wasn't having much luck. "The elevator was too slow, and it's possible our shadow woman is young and spry, or Sal has lost a step in his advancing age."

"Screw you," Vitali said in his gravel-pan voice.

Quinn raised a hand for silence and motioned for Fedderman to continue.

Fedderman dribbled more coffee, just before hastily fitting the last bite of a soggy doughnut into his mouth. He chewed, gulped, and continued. "Another possibility is she ducked into one of the apartments on the way down and managed to stay hidden while the building was searched."

"Or became somebody else," Pearl said, bringing everyone up short. Doughnuts froze in midair.

"Whaddya mean?" Vitali asked. "She got into an apartment where nobody was home and posed as a tenant?"

"Might even *be* a tenant, for all we know," Pearl said.

Pearl thinking outside the universe. Quinn almost smiled.

"I see what she means," Mishkin said. He was seated in Fedderman's chair. "Since we don't have the slightest idea who this woman is, she might be anybody. Very illuminating angle, Pearl."

"It's like she reads minds sometimes," Fedderman said.

"The shadow woman, or Pearl?" Mishkin asked, looking slightly confused.

"Don't pay any attention to him," Pearl said. "You haven't been around Fedderman long enough to realize he's full of shit."

"You have been around Sal a long time, though," Quinn said to Mishkin. "You think he mighta been slow enough coming down those stairs that the shadow woman made it out of the building before either Sal or you reached the lobby?"

Mishkin looked at Sal, obviously torn. Sal had some gray in his hair now, and he'd developed a slight stomach paunch. The truth demanded that Mishkin dis his partner.

"Yeah, that could be," he said. Then: "Sorry, Sal."

"Maybe it was the brownies," Vitali said.

"Brownies?" Pearl asked.

Vitali shrugged. "Never mind."

"Brownies and doughnuts, Sal. You're not gonna be any faster on stairs next year."

"Give him a break," Fedderman told Pearl. "You don't fit so well anymore into your—"

"Enough, Feds," Quinn said.

Pearl was glowering at Fedderman. "I'll show you a whole new way to eat that doughnut."

"Let's wrap this up," Quinn said. He knew the uneasy truce between Pearl and Fedderman, while conducive to progress, could sometimes become genuinely hostile. The trick was to prevent spark from becoming fire—or explosion. "Anybody got any theories on the shadow woman's identity?"

"You mean if we had to guess?" Mishkin asked.

"Sure," Quinn said. "Who knows? Maybe we'll all guess the same person."

"My guess is Chrissie," Fedderman said. "She hasn't played straight with us yet."

"The woman in Bakehouse's building coulda been Chrissie," Vitali said.

"My guess is Cindy Sellers," Pearl said.

"Or somebody we haven't met yet," Mishkin said. "Like a relative of one of the other victims. Or maybe she's Tiffany's ghost."

Pearl looked curiously at Quinn. "So what's your guess?"

"I'm not in the guessing business," Quinn said. "This isn't some kind of party game."

"You're in the double-crossing pain-in-the-ass business," Pearl said.

Vitali said, "What if we'd all guessed the same woman?"

"Then we'd try to figure out why," Quinn said. "And maybe we'd have something."

"Like Tiffany's ghost," Pearl said.

She jumped at the first four notes of the immortal *Dragnet* theme. They were coming from her purse where it rested on the corner of her desk. She scooped up the purse and fished the phone out, peered at it to see who was calling.

Somebody at Golden Sunset Assisted Living.

Her mother. Just what she needed while she was in a murder investigation brainstorming session.

"Jesus!" Pearl said.

"Better pick up then," Fedderman said.

* * *

Pearl made the connection, put the phone to her ear, and said hello, all the time moving toward the door.

"Pearl?"

Her mother, all right.

"Reception's better outside," she said to the dead-eyed stares she was getting.

"Did you say something, Pearl?" her mother asked.

Fedderman grinned. The others simply looked at her. Pearl went out the door.

Outside in the morning heat, she said, "I'm pretty busy, Mom."

"It's never busy here in nursing home hell, Pearl."

Her mother insisted on referring to Golden Sunset Assisted Living as a nursing home. Pearl had become tired of contradicting her. Absently wandering along the sidewalk toward Amsterdam, it occurred to her that cell phone reception outside the office really was noticeably better.

"Pearl?"

"I'm here, Mom, but I can't talk long. I'm interrogating a suspect. You're breaking up some anyway."

"Can't talk long? Is one of the criminal element more important to you than your own mother, dear?"

"You know better than that."

"But do *you*, dear?"

"Did you call for a—"

"Yes, for a reason. His name is Yancy Taggart."

Huh? How could her mother know anything about Yancy? Know Yancy even existed?

"I speak, as you know," her mother said, "of the fancy shmancy Yancy. The man, so called, you've been wasting your time with instead of spending it with a fine man like *Doctor* Milton Kahn, or even your mensch policeman Captain Quinn, who is—"

"He's not a captain any longer, Mom. He's not with the NYPD."

"Not exactly and precisely, but still—"

"How did you find out I was seeing Yancy?"

"Not from a little bird, dear. Mrs. Kahn, Milton's aunt here at the nursing home, as you know, has a sister who has a half sister who has a daughter who frequents a lounge where the Yancy lizard does his womanizing. She saw your photograph during one of her visits here at the nursing home and recognized you from when she saw you at another lounge with the Yancy lizard."

Pearl was furious. "It's nobody's business where I was or who I was with, especially not the business of this niece twice removed or whatever the hell she is."

"No, dear. Mrs. Kahn's sister's half sister's—"

"I don't give a damn, Mom!"

"Don't use abusive language, dear. Did it make you feel better? Did it?"

No, it didn't. "Yancy's not a lizard. He's a lobbyist!"

"Well, dear, if you would look in the dictionary—"

"If Mrs. Kahn would look in the dictionary, she'd find the definition of busybody!"

"But facts are facts, dear, whatever their source, and it seems to me that it's my motherly duty to at least make you aware that the Yancy lizard you're going out with sees other women."

"I see other men, Mom."

"But sequentially, dear. Sequentially. There are rumors about the Yancy lizard, some of them bordering on the perverse, if you understand my meaning, which, while only speculation at this juncture, might in all honesty turn out to be true, so you might take a step back and reconsider your relationship."

"By 'speculation' you mean guessing," Pearl said. "I'm not in the guessing business." *Quinn's words. Quinn, damn you!* She hated it when men got inside her mind, especially Quinn.

"I'm in no way accusing anyone of anything in any way

improper, Pearl, but a mother knows things because a mother knows, and there is a motherly duty to make a daughter aware, and to—and I'll come right out and say it—warn a daughter when a ship, figuratively speaking, is about to smash apart on the rocks of romance in a sea so rough—"

Pearl broke the connection and turned off her cell phone. Couldn't help it.

Pearl had walked faster and faster while talking and wandered far. When she returned to the office, Vitali and Mishkin were gone. Quinn and Fedderman were at their desks.

"Your mom doing okay?" Quinn asked.

Like you care!

"You look angry, Pearl," Fedderman said.

Pearl didn't bother to answer. She *was* angry, at her mother, at Mrs. Kahn, at Mrs. Kahn's . . . whatever she was. At Fedderman, at Quinn, at all men.

At all men!

What did she really know about Yancy?

She stalked over to the Mr. Coffee and poured herself a mug of the steaming brew, muttering to herself.

"Say what?" Fedderman asked, overhearing but not understanding.

"I said there's nothing wrong with lobbyists," Pearl said, adding powdered cream and stirring violently enough to slosh coffee over the cup's rim.

Quinn and Fedderman looked at each other, puzzled.

"We're all God's creatures," Fedderman said.

Pearl fixed him with a look, and he smiled slightly.

Saving his life.

31

They'd had sex. Pearl stood at the window in Yancy's apartment that overlooked the park across the wide avenue. The bedroom was cool, but she could feel the sun's heat radiating from the windowpane. The sun was about to set, and the park was gilded. She watched foreshortened people walking on the sidewalks almost directly below, some of them couples. In the park, two kids on skateboards were terrorizing pedestrians on the winding path.

Pearl had the white linen sheet from the bed draped around her toga style. Behind her, Yancy still lay in bed. Something in the *Times* had caught his interest, and he was staring at it raptly, not paying much attention to Pearl at the moment. Nothing like the attention he'd paid her until ten minutes ago.

She turned away from the window and looked at Yancy and his nude, tanned body. He appeared younger than his supposed age, still lean and muscular. And God knew he had the endurance of a young man. Still, he displayed the experience of an older man. She smiled. Yancy was a man full of contradictions, but they made for quite a lover.

How could she trust a man like this?

You took the leap, now live with it. Stop being a cop all the time.

He folded down a flap of newspaper and glanced over at her. No reading glasses. Young eyes. Or maybe Lasik.

Pearl being observant, a cop.

What's he so avidly reading?

"You look inquisitive," he said. "Anybody ever tell you that you resemble a little terrier when you look inquisitive?"

As a matter of fact they had, but Pearl didn't see it as something Yancy had to know.

"I was just wondering what interested you so in the paper."

He laid the *Times* open over his lower body as if he were modest, which he wasn't. "This Carver character," he said. "A guy stops killing years ago then suddenly starts up again. Is that normal for serial killers?"

"Not much is normal with people who sequentially kill other people." *Sequentially, dear. Sequentially.* "Or with obsessive people who have more than one sex partner at a time."

He looked at her oddly. "We both agree on that, Pearl. But you're a cop, difficult as I find that to believe, and I thought you might have some insight into the criminal mind. Killers' minds."

"I'm not a cop anymore, Yancy. Private investigator."

"You don't look like a private dick, sweetheart. C'mon over here." He beckoned with his right hand, sunlight glinting off his gold ring.

"Think about wind power, Yancy."

"I'll take that for a yes."

She had to laugh, but she moved no closer to the bed.

"I couldn't help noticing something about you," she said.

"That would be my third testicle?"

"No, your hair."

"You mean the way it never seems to get messed up? It's trained that way. Took years. I've been combing it the same way since I was twelve and wanted to get in Amy Dingle's pants."

"I bet you were a terror at twelve."

"Amy Dingle would say so."

"But that's not what I meant about your hair. I noticed it's naturally black and you dye it white."

"Oh, sure. That's so I look older. Lobbyists who are gray eminences get taken a lot more seriously. Gotta play the role, Pearl."

"Live a lie, you mean?"

"No. Live a version, is all. But you could call it a lie. Play your lie well; that's where the honored roll."

"I don't think that's the exact quotation."

"It is if you're golfing, Pearl."

"Which I am not."

"It's an inexact world."

"Yancy, you are the most nimble liar I have ever met."

"You make me blush."

"Not so anyone would notice."

"Make me bulge, I mean."

"That I notice."

Still she moved no closer to the bed.

"Do you happen to know anybody named Kahn?" she asked.

"Sure, Dr. Milton Kahn."

That rocked her back a step. "Where do you know him from?"

"Met him yesterday. He sat down next to me at a bar and struck up a conversation. Introduced himself. Warned me about you."

Huh?

Peal felt anger rising in her like hot lava. "Warned you?"

"Said you had serious personality problems and you were trouble. Didn't go into detail. Winked at me. We had a tacit understanding, being men of the world."

"Didn't you ask him what he meant?"

"Didn't care what he meant. Still don't."

"Did you tell him that?"

"No."

"What *did* you do?"

"I considered punching him in the nose."

Pearl felt mildly excited by the prospect of men fighting over her, then was angry at herself. She wasn't some cuddly teddy bear carnival prize.

Still . . .

"*Did* you punch him?" she asked.

"No. I talked him into buying me a drink and tactfully sent him on his way. Teach him a lesson."

Pearl figured that wasn't exactly a duel fought for her honor. But it was something.

Yancy smiled at her. "You look lovely as a Roman concubine."

Pearl moved closer to the bed.

There went the toga.

32

Mick would have a cow if he knew what she was doing.

Joyce House had started work at six that morning, and she was tired. She knew Loren was waiting for her across the street and around the corner. That way he wouldn't be visible from the diner.

Mick and his rules, she thought. The guy had his good points, but he was a diner dictator.

She yelled a good-bye to Sheila, who would take her shift for the dinner customers. They were always less numerous than the breakfast and lunch crowd. That would be true even this evening—corned beef and cabbage night.

Tired as she was, when Joyce crossed with the light and Loren stepped from the doorway of a men's clothing store, the sight of him charged her with energy.

They came together with a fierce hug. He kissed her forehead and then her lips.

She ran her fingers through his dark hair, then smiled and pushed away from him, turning her head. "Let's get farther away from the diner before any of that, Loren."

He laughed. "Why? You think someone followed you?"

"It's possible. Maybe your ex-wife hired detectives."

Still grinning, he kissed her again on her forehead. "She and I are beyond that point," he said.

"The point of no return?" She'd heard the phrase earlier that day on CNN and it had stuck in her mind. There was something haunting and scary about it. Perhaps because she knew she had passed it.

"Exactly," he said.

"If I were her, I'd fight to hold on to you."

He looked more serious, his blue eyes downcast. "There was a time she might have tried, but not now. And since I met you, there's been no doubt in my mind that my marriage is over."

Without either of them making a conscious decision, they began walking together along the crowded sidewalk.

"I've got a surprise for you," he said, and held something out in his right hand.

"Theater tickets!" she exclaimed.

"You mentioned you like the theater, so I thought I'd surprise you. We're on tomorrow night for *Manhattan Nocturne.*"

She squeezed his arm. "That's supposed to be great!"

He patted her hand. "Orchestra seats, sixth row."

"You shouldn't have, Loren. They must have cost a fortune."

"You're the fortune," he told her.

She walked beside him in the hum and bustle of the city, thinking it was amazing how he always knew what to say to her. As if he could read her thoughts. He must feel as she did, that the more time they spent together, the more they belonged together, belonged to each other. Sixth-row orchestra Broadway tickets. They certainly hadn't been cheap. It pleased her immensely that he'd invested so much in her.

Loren was smiling inwardly, sensing the happiness and possessiveness emanating from Joyce. He knew things she didn't know, and he was enjoying that.

It was power.

It amused him that Joyce was contemplating tomorrow

night, and her future beyond then. He knew she'd have no future beyond tomorrow night.

Manhattan Nocturne would be her last Broadway musical.

Vitali was at the wheel of the unmarked Ford he and Mishkin were returning to the vice squad. The two detectives would be sorry to see the car go. It was five years old, had a mismatched quarter panel painted with primer, and was one of the few unmarked city cars that didn't scream its police presence.

"We got one more thing to do today, Harold," Vitali reminded his partner, as he maneuvered the car around one of the city's long, jointed buses. *Those things are too damned big for this city.*

"You've got one more thing," Mishkin said. "Renz never wants to talk with me."

"What I tell him comes from both of us, Harold."

"Meaning if things go wrong, I'll drown in the same soup you do."

Vitali grinned. "That's pretty much it, crouton." He straightened out the car and left the bus behind. "Renz is supposed to have met with Quinn earlier this evening."

"So Renz might know more than we do."

"Not the kinds of things he wants to know."

"You ever feel like a spy or something, Sal? I mean, Quinn's a straight guy. I don't like ratting on anybody, but I especially don't like ratting on him."

"He knows we've got no choice," Vitali said. "It's like a game. He knows everything we tell Renz, anyway. So no, I don't feel like a spy. And you shouldn't, either. We're not actually ratting on Quinn. It's not like he's Valerie Plame or anything."

"Who's that, Sal?"

"No one, Harold. Ancient history."

"Oh, I know who you mean. Plum, isn't it? Wasn't her name Valerie Plum?"

Vitali drove for a while silently.

"Might have been, Harold," he said at last.

"When you get done talking to Renz," Mishkin said, "he's gonna talk to that little media scum, Cindy Sellers. Set her off writing some bullshit about the shadow woman."

"That's the deal, Harold. Round and round we go. Like rats in a cage."

"Hamsters, I think you mean," Mishkin said.

"Hamsters," Vitali agreed.

"I feel like a rat sometimes," Mishkin said.

"She seems to have disappeared," Fedderman said. He was standing up and putting on his suit coat, preparing to leave the office.

"Our shadow woman?" Quinn asked. He'd just come from meeting with Harley Renz in the Campbell Apartment bar in Grand Central Station, where they'd had some of the best martinis in the city and Quinn had brought the police commissioner up to date on the investigation.

"Our client," Fedderman said. "I wanted to pump her for some other names. Common acquaintances she and her twin might have had. Been trying to call her all day on her cell."

Quinn realized Chrissie had never let him know where she was staying. Her cell phone was the only way to contact her, and now it appeared she'd rabbited again.

But why?

"Her cell's turned off," Fedderman said.

Quinn nodded and went over and sat behind his desk. "We've got a client not to be trusted, Feds."

"Yeah. Whaddya think her game is?"

"A different one from the one we're playing."

"Like chess and checkers."

"We need to make sure we're chess," Quinn said.

"Anything else going for today?" Fedderman asked.

"No. Go on home and get some rest. Or go see a movie or Broadway play."

Fedderman looked off to the left, as if calling on his memory. "I haven't seen a Broadway show since *Cats.*"

"What'd you think?"

"One good song, but I can't remember it." Fedderman waved a good-bye, his shirt cuff flapping like a flag, and went out onto West Seventy-ninth Street.

Quinn watched him—tall, disjointed, with a head-bowed, lurching kind of walk—pass the window along with the steady stream of pedestrians trudging home from work. Fedderman always seemed to be pondering. Probably he always was.

Quinn settled back in his desk chair and got a Cuban cigar from the humidor in the bottom left drawer.

He fired up the cigar and sat for a while smoking, knowing that tomorrow morning Pearl would probably bitch about the lingering tobacco scent.

He pondered for quite a while himself, searching his memory, but he never was able to recall the one good song.

33

When Quinn got to his apartment he found that he wasn't tired. Too much adrenaline in his blood. Too much coffee. And probably the cigars didn't help.

He stayed away from both as he went to his den, sat behind his desk. He couldn't help noticing that the apartment was stuffy and smelled like cigar smoke. May would raise hell if she still lived here. So would Pearl. Women didn't seem to like cigars. Was there some Freudian reason?

Freud would probably say so.

Quinn got his legal pad from the shallow middle drawer. He read over and thought about what he had so far:

Tiffany Keller years ago, last victim of the Carver.
Her twin, Chrissie, wins the Triple Monkey what-
   ever slot-machine jackpot and finds herself
   suddenly moderately wealthy. Decides to use
   the money to find sister's killer. Or, more accu-
   rately, to avenge sister's death.
NYPD demonstrates no interest in reopening the
   case.
Chrissie, after pretending to be Tiffany's ghost to

*get attention, finally admits who she is and
hires Q. & Assoc. to find the Carver.
After paying a handsome retainer, Chrissie
disappears.
Pearl notices Chrissie deleted any and all
photographs of Tiffany from news items in the
folder she left with Quinn.
Photos on the Internet reveal that Chrissie and
Tiffany looked nothing alike.
Renz phones and tries to warn Q&A off the case.*

Then there was the notation that Chrissie was not to be trusted. Well, nothing had changed there.

The next entry on the legal pad read:

*Maureen Sanders found dead, wounds unlike
those made by the Carver, too shallow, silver
spoon in mouth, like Carver's sick humor.
Carver, but older so more hesitant?
Mary Bakehouse attacked before Maureen
Sanders. Carver frightened away? Chooses more
helpless victim Sanders?
Chrissie still missing. Carver victim?*

Quinn noticed as he had the last time he'd used the pad that there were too many question marks.

He picked up a pen from the desk and added on the legal pad:

*Renz tries to shut down case.
Q. calls Cindy Sellers to help pressure Renz to
continue investigation and so info flows both
directions.*

Chrissie returns. (Brown eyes now blue—used
  contacts to look more like Tiffany.)
Shadow woman almost caught in Mary B. apt.
  bldg.
(Trust no one.)

That was about it, Quinn thought, putting the pad back in
the desk drawer. He wasn't sure whether to call it progress or
additional frustration.

He went into the kitchen and poured himself two fingers
of Famous Grouse scotch in a water glass, added some ice
cubes.

Then he went in to watch television. A French movie was
on PBS. Quinn was partial to French movies. You never
knew what direction they were going to take. So like life.

"You should move in with me," Yancy said to Pearl.

"We hardly know each other."

"We know each other superficially, and that's the best
way."

They were having breakfast in his kitchen. Pearl had
made cheese omelets. She had a lacy but functional apron
tied around her waist. Yancy had wanted her to wear it and
only it, but she'd demurred and gotten dressed in slacks and
a knit pullover before donning the apron. She hadn't felt so
domestic in years.

"I mean," Yancy continued, "you're spending your nights
and parts of your days here anyway, so why shouldn't you
throw some clothes in a suitcase and stay here with me?" He
was showered and fully dressed in shirt and tie, looking at her
as if all he saw on her was the apron. Theater of the mind.

She took a bite of omelet and chewed for a while, letting
him think she was mulling over his proposition. "It isn't so
simple, Yancy."

"So bring some furniture."

"I don't mean that. It's the . . ."

"What? Appearances?"

"No, I don't give a rat's ass about appearances. I'm talking about how it'd be between you and me."

"It'd be the way it is now, only more of it."

"No, it wouldn't be exactly the way it is now. We'd soon become . . . a couple."

He smiled handsomely at her with his refreshing blankness. "Yeah, I can count."

"What you're proposing is something like a marriage. In fact, if we lived that way long enough it'd become a common-law marriage."

He forked in more omelet, then swallowed and took a sip of coffee. "A legal technicality."

"I'm not cut out for marriage of any kind."

"I wouldn't say that. You're a hell of a good cook. And you look terrific in that apron."

"Ugh! See, you're trying to domesticate me already."

"Like a wild mare in a corral," he said.

Horse analogies while I'm wearing an apron like June Cleaver? What the hell does he mean by that?

This was the kind of thing that could be a problem. While Yancy was ostensibly transparent, there were times when he thought in ways that baffled her. Or was that simply a complicated way of saying he was devious and a skilled liar?

Pearl warned herself: *Don't make a two-sided problem six-sided. For that matter, don't create a problem where there's no problem at all.*

An amused comprehension glowed in his blue eyes. "Do you think I'm too old for you?"

"No. You don't seem too old for anybody."

"Maybe you don't like the white hair," he said.

"It's more the dark roots."

"I explained why I—"

"Yeah, but it seems dishonest."

He seemed mildly surprised. "It's not dishonest. Not even illegal, immoral or fattening. It's simply me, slightly altered for convenience."

"But you seem to alter almost everything for your convenience."

"Why not, if it's convenient?"

She smiled to temper any insult. "To tell you the truth, darling, everything you say is subject to doubt."

"That kind of consistency is hard to find in a man. Anyway, truth is an amorphous concept."

"You do tell the kind of lies I like. Practical lies."

"So move in with me. We'll tell the neighbors we're siblings. Let them think we're doing unspeakable things to each other."

Yuk! Yet Pearl had to admit there was something about such a charade that tickled her perverse side. Not the notion of sibling sex—that was absolutely repugnant. But its very repugnance made it kind of appealing as a pretend way to put one over on the neighbors. Yes, horrifying the neighbors could be fun.

No, no, no!

But for a moment the devil in her mind had considered it. That was the sort of thing that made her uneasy about being so close to Yancy. He seemed to understand her entire spectrum of emotions, and he could play it as if it were a harp. That made her feel vulnerable. Floating a sister-brother illicit relationship rumor as a diversion while simply living together. Quinn would never suggest such a sick thing, even jokingly.

Serious, obsessive Quinn.

It struck her again: Maybe Yancy's appeal was that he was so unlike Quinn.

So what's wrong with that?

"If it would make you feel better," Yancy said, "we could tell people we've been married twenty years. Even have families out there from previous marriages. And in-laws. Though I don't have any of either."

More lies.

"Do you have any family in the area?" he asked.

Pearl hesitated. But why lie like Yancy?

"Just my mother," she said. "In New Jersey."

"No kidding? I'd like to meet her. You know what they say, if you're going to pretend to be married to a woman, you should meet her mother."

"No," Pearl said, "you shouldn't."

"So think about my offer," Yancy said.

"This is me thinking," Pearl said. She stood up from her chair and began clearing the table, even though there were a few remaining bites of omelet on Yancy's plate. "I've gotta get outta here and go to work."

Yancy sat back and crossed his arms, watching her and grinning lewdly.

"That apron!" he said. "There's something about a really sexy woman wearing an apron."

"Try thinking of something else."

"Washing the dishes bare-breasted?"

"Don't ever do that in front of me," Pearl said.

34

Renz had finally relented and agreed to talk to the woman. Now he wasn't sorry.

Her name was Adelaide Price, and she was from Detroit. In several letters to Renz she'd explained how she'd been attacked six years ago by a masked assailant. She'd fought her way free and crawled from her apartment into the hall. Her attacker had followed and dragged her back. Then, for some unexplained reason—possibly fearing she'd been seen in the hall—he broke off the assault and ran.

She'd turned the attack into an opportunity. After a locally bestselling book, degrees in psychology and criminal justice, and a series of media appearances, she'd become a frequent guest on Detroit TV as an expert on crime and criminals. Her fame had lasted more than fifteen minutes. She was good for ratings and someone to be taken seriously.

Now she was badgering Renz for an assignment as profiler in the reopened Carver investigation. Not only was she personally politicking for the job, she'd enlisted the help of several prominent people in Detroit who might know several prominent people in New York. That got Renz's attention.

Finally he'd agreed to see her for a number of reasons, not the least of which were her references. Her freelance work as a crime psychologist and profiler had led to several arrests and convictions in Detroit, and a Captain Mark Drucker had given Adelaide Price the highest of recommendations. So high that Renz suspected that Drucker, an old friend of Renz's who was a notorious womanizer, had an intensely personal reason for helping Adelaide Price. That was okay with Renz. He owed Drucker a favor, and in the world of Renz and Drucker, favors owed and paid were the currency of the realm.

And here she was.

Adelaide Price was surprisingly attractive, in her thirties, tall, with honey blond hair, brown eyes somehow made to appear blue with violet eye shadow, and full red lips. Her build was slender but athletic, and she had long, shapely legs that showed well in the short brown skirt she wore.

Renz smiled at her, and she smiled back. If Drucker had gotten into her pants, Renz could understand his motivation.

"We need to be honest with each other," he said.

She nodded and gave him a glance with her brown-blue eyes. She knew how to use those eyes so she seemed to be gazing up at Renz even though they were seated on the same level.

"Honesty above all," she said.

Renz thought that was just what someone dishonest would say. He decided to give her a taste of honesty to see how she'd react.

"Okay," Renz said. "My understanding from people I've talked to in Detroit is that you are an ambitious, hard-driving bitch."

"That's pretty much true," Adelaide Price said. "And my friends call me Addie."

Her sexy, throaty voice reminded him of someone he couldn't quite place.

"We're not friends yet," he said, "but I'll make it Addie. You can call me Commissioner Renz."

Adelaide—Addie—appeared unmoved by his snub. "My reason for wanting this assignment is due to my ambition," she said. "It does run strong in me. I never saw wanting to get ahead as a crime. Or a liability."

"It's an asset," Renz said, recognizing her as one of his own. "So in terms less general than mere ambition, tell me why you want this assignment."

"I don't consider ambition mere, but I get your point. Vengeance figures into it, too."

"You think it was the Carver who attacked you in Detroit?"

"It might have been, the way he displayed a knife, waved it around. There had been another woman attacked that way in Detroit, maybe by the same man. He was scared away that time, too. But in all honesty, it's mostly ambition that prompted me to politick for this assignment. I think there could be a book in this. I've already talked to an agent who'd be interested in handling it."

A book . . . Renz had never considered that. A book about his exploits, his rapid climb from patrolman to the top of the NYPD. Maybe he should consider trying to get an agent, a book contract. He could always find some schmuck to write the thing.

"This sicko who attacked you and this other woman," he said, "if it was the same guy. He was never apprehended?"

" 'Fraid not."

She uncrossed, then recrossed her long legs. The swishing sound of nylon on nylon was almost enough to give Renz an erection.

"I think you could use me," she said.

My God, yes!

Renz's reaction didn't show on his saggy features, but he was sure Addie Price was aware of her effect on men.

"Now that you understand me," she said, "why don't you give me a better idea of what to expect if I am assigned to the case?"

Now they were down to it. Trading this for that. The quid pro quo. Renz's favorite part. Renz's world.

"You could expect to report to me and only me," he said. "And secretly."

"I would be your unofficial undercover operative."

"*Unofficial* is what you need to remember. But let's not forget *confidential.* This part of our conversation never took place."

The way she smiled and nodded, he could tell she was used to this kind of conniving and in fact enjoyed it. The way he did. He wondered if they might have even more in common than he'd first thought. Who could predict where their relationship might lead? Perhaps it was possible to have a soul mate even without a soul.

"I already have two NYPD detectives working with Quinn and his team," he said to her legs. "They're supposed to report to me the way I'd want you to report."

"And do they?"

"I can't be sure."

"You don't trust them?"

"Can't."

"Why not?"

Renz raised his gaze to meet her eyes. "Frank Quinn can be a very persuasive guy. People tend to fall in behind him. Also, he's not the kind of man you cross. Even hardened cops like my detectives might be afraid to get sideways of him. He locks on to his target like a radar-guided missile fueled by obsession, and he doesn't always operate strictly within the law."

"Is that why you hired Quinn?"

"Yeah. He and I understand each other, go way back."

"Boys' club."

"Sure."

Renz suddenly realized who her voice reminded him of—the young Lauren Bacall, vamping it up with Bogie. She was making Renz feel as if he were in a movie. Nice feeling.

They looked at each other for a long moment. Renz's heartbeat quickened.

"There's something else, isn't there?" Addie Price said.

Soul mates. "Yeah, there is. There's another reason I can trust my two guys on the case—Vitali and Mishkin—only so far. It's because I've moved up in the NYPD and become police commissioner. I'm seen mostly as a politician now, and not so much as a cop. My blood doesn't run completely blue, so I'm no longer a member of the club. Not to guys like Vitali and Mishkin, anyway."

"They good cops?"

"The best. Same way with Quinn and his team. They can be a pain in the ass, even to each other, but they get the job done."

"Any of them bendable?"

"No. They're all dead honest."

"Good. That makes them predictable."

"I wouldn't say that," Renz said. "Honest isn't always legal."

"I'm looking forward to meeting Quinn, if I'm hired."

"You're hired," Renz said. "Same terms as Quinn and his team. They're working out of Quinn's agency over on West Seventy-ninth Street."

"I know where it is."

Renz gave her his hound-dog smile. "I'll bet you do. I'll call Quinn today and tell him you're part of the team. Don't be surprised if they don't welcome you like a long-lost family member."

"I'll win them over," Addie said.

"I don't doubt that for a moment. You'll be the crime psychologist and profiler on the case."

"And your reliable spy," Addie said. "Not being a member of the club."

"You and I have our own club," Renz said, standing up while he didn't have an erection.

Addie unwound herself and stood up from her chair, smoothed down her skirt over those long thighs.

"Okay," she said in her Lauren Bacall voice. "Our own private club. Maybe with a secret handshake. Or something."

Renz sat back down fast and watched her see her own way out.

35

Joyce House lay in bed and stared up at the cracks in her bedroom ceiling. They were barely visible in the dim light, and through eyes still teared up slightly by the intensity of the sex she'd just experienced with Loren.

The pattern above was familiar to her. The fine network of cracks in the white plaster was like a road map to her future. She imagined the cracks as highways seen from a great distance, with varied destinations and important intersections. She knew precisely where she was now. If she turned left, she'd be traveling toward a dark wood. A right turn would take her to a city on a beach, where everything was bleached clean by the sun. Continuing straight would take her to a city exactly like New York.

Beside her Loren lay breathing evenly, sleeping from the efforts of their sometimes frenetic lovemaking. She'd known during the happy-ending play they'd seen, *Manhattan Nocturne*, and during dinner afterward, that he expected to leave the restaurant and walk with her to her apartment. She'd done nothing to discourage the idea.

Good thing. She hadn't suspected he was such an expert in bed.

She'd been inebriated from too much wine at dinner. She smiled. No, she'd been drunk, actually. That was the reason why her memory was foggy. Part of the reason, anyway. In her mind, the night had been layer after layer of fantasy, yet she knew it had happened. Loren had used only his tongue on her, sending her into frenzies of passion. *A down payment*, she thought he'd said. Well, if this was his idea of foreplay, bring it on.

Back to the ceiling road map.

Right now, the New York highway seemed a good one to stay on.

She imagined herself speeding along it toward a wonderful tomorrow. The fine crack in the ceiling was the road to a better world.

The road curved and rose and dipped into darkness, and she was asleep.

She awakened from a dream of bulk and weight pressing her upper body into the soft mattress.

No dream! Real!

She tried to sit up but couldn't.

For an instant she panicked. Then she realized the weight she felt was Loren's body, nude but for his white undershirt. He was seated on her with his knees on her upper arms, his bare buttocks just beneath her breasts. The room had gotten warm, and he was perspiring. The bedroom was no longer dim. He'd switched on the small shaded lamp on her dresser.

He had an erection and was smiling down at her.

One of his games.

Okay, she'd play. Though she wasn't so sure of this game.

But if it's going to be anything like last night . . .

She let her body go limp and returned his smile. His eyes, his smile, were so wonderful. She uttered his name in near reverence, and he held a forefinger to his lips in a signal for her to be silent. With his other hand he gripped her cheeks between thumb and forefinger and gently forced her mouth open.

He's going to use his tongue again. . . .

Now he was stuffing something into her mouth. Material. Silky.

With a start, she realized it was her panties. He'd knotted them and forced the bulky knot between her parted lips. The instant she tried to turn her head to the side, he stretched the panties and somehow tied them behind her neck. The knotted nylon went deeper into her mouth, behind her teeth. The maneuver was done so deftly that she knew he'd practiced it or done it many times before.

Joyce didn't like this game. Not so far, anyway. She fought off a wave of nausea and tried to keep calm so she wouldn't gag on the bunched material.

This is disgusting!

If he persisted in playing rough she'd have to tell him about it, let him know in no uncertain terms that it wasn't for her. And there was something else about the wadded panties being stuffed into her mouth. She'd heard or read something. . . .

In the news?

Oh, God! No, No, NO!

He leaned closer to her, and she could feel his warm breath on her face. Smelled the sex on it, their sex.

She shook her head wildly and moaned through the wadded cloth, trying to tell him she didn't understand what they were doing, what he wanted. Trying desperately to plead.

He shifted his weight forward, and his knees bore down harder, firmly and painfully pinning her arms to the bed. He was gazing down at her fondly as he held out something for her to see.

He spoke through a smile. "Let me tell you what I'm going to do with this knife."

Softly and in minute detail, he described to her everything as he was doing it, until she was no longer listening.

36

More heat this morning, and Quinn thought that if it got any more humid things might start to float.

"So there are slight differences in the M.O.s of the Sanders killing and the earlier murders," Fedderman said. His bald pate was perspiring beneath his comb-over. "The Carver's been on vacation, and he's rusty."

Pearl was perched with her haunches on the edge of her desk. She was the only one of the three who looked reasonably cool. In fact, Quinn thought she looked great today, wearing tight beige slacks, a yellow blouse made of some sort of silky material, and white shoes with some heel to them—not like her usual clunky black cop shoes. Her lustrous black hair was combed back and held by some sort of round silver barrette, and her makeup had been applied with obvious care. It all made her look more like Pearl than ever. She hadn't just piled out of bed, showered, and dressed damp this morning. What was she up to? Quinn was afraid to consider.

"Feds is right," she said. "People change over time. Even serial killers."

"He hasn't changed enough," Quinn said.

Pearl shrugged in the silky blouse in a way Quinn liked. "It's not as if we might mistake him for some other guy who de-nipples women, carves the letter X on them, and slits their throats."

"Maybe, but unfortunately there are more than a few guys who wouldn't mind meeting those requirements."

"Anyone else happen to see her at the crime scene?" Fedderman asked.

Pearl looked at him. "See who? What the hell are you talking about?"

"Our shadow woman. Dressed in gray. She was standing across the street when we were talking with Nift. I saw her, looked away when Nift said something, and when I looked back she was gone."

"Running outfit with a hood?" Quinn asked.

Fedderman nodded.

"I had more or less the same experience."

"I noticed her," Pearl said. "But what makes you think she wasn't simply some woman from the neighborhood who was out running and stopped to see what all the commotion was about?"

"No," Fedderman said. "There was definitely something creepy about her."

"Because you wanted to see something creepy. The shadow woman was on both your minds."

"My mind doesn't fool itself that easily," Fedderman said.

"How would it know?" Pearl asked.

She walked over and got a cup of coffee. Fedderman watched her. Quinn watched them both, like a man watching inclement weather developing.

The door opened, and a woman stepped inside.

Everyone looked at her.

She looked as put together as Pearl, but that was about all they had in common. This woman was tall and slender—a fashion model's build. She was wearing a dark gray blazer and lighter gray slacks. Shoes with silver buckles and flat heels. On top of the model's body was a model's face, strong-featured with prominent cheekbones, full lips, and intriguing eyes that appeared blue at a glance but were actually brown.

She smiled, but before she could introduce herself, Quinn said, "This is Adelaide Price." He nodded toward Pearl and Fedderman as he introduced them, and then himself. "Ms. Price is going to join us," he said.

Pearl didn't like surprises from Quinn. They usually meant impending trouble. "What do you mean, 'join us'? Are we all going out for a doughnut fest?"

"It's Addie," the woman said. "I'm glad to meet you all, and doughnuts sound all right to me."

Pearl didn't like the husky, sexy voice, like a cat seducing mice. She also didn't like the way the two mice were staring at the woman.

"I'm assuming Commissioner Renz contacted you about me," Addie said.

Quinn seemed to drift up out of his trance. "He did, Addie, but I haven't had a chance to fill in Pearl and Feds—Fedderman."

"Just Feds is okay," Fedderman said to Addie. Got him a smile.

Addie Price sat in the client's chair while Quinn explained to Pearl and Fedderman that she was now part of the investigation as a crime psychologist and profiler. She'd had plenty of experience with the Detroit police and as a freelancer and media personality. She'd written a book. Without being too obvious, he made it clear to them that this was Renz's idea and they had no choice.

"I've already met Vitali and Mishkin," Addie Price said, when Quinn was finished.

"Great," Quinn said. "I've got a desk coming for you, Addie, but it won't get here till this afternoon. Pearl and I will be in the field this morning, and Feds can bring you up to date on the case."

"I'm already somewhat up to date on it," Addie said. "I have a special interest."

"Renz explained that," Quinn said.

Pearl waited for him to say more, but he didn't. Neither did Addie Price.

"We're becoming quite a task force," Pearl said in a neutral tone.

A profiler assigned by Renz. One who'd be taking an active part in the investigation. Pearl didn't like this a bit.

"Whatever it takes," Fedderman said. He was not going to be on Pearl's side when it came to Addie Price. "We can use my desk," he said to Addie, "and we need to get you a coffee mug with your initials on it."

"Gold ones," Pearl said.

Addie gave her a look. It was easy to read: *We're sisters in a man's world. For God's sake, give me a chance.*

"What's with this book?" Fedderman asked.

Addie made a pass at looking modest. "Oh, it's one of those dry academic things. *Crime Profiling in the Context of Modern Society.* It's a padded version of my doctoral dissertation."

Pearl thought, *Jesus H. Christ!*

"Pearl and I will be down in Chelsea," Quinn said, "seeing if we can find somebody who knew Maureen Sanders or saw or heard anything unusual. Maybe some of the other street people around there knew her."

He got his suit coat from where it hung on a wire hanger and draped it over his arm. A few long steps and he was at the door.

"Good to meet you, Addie," he said. He held the door open for Pearl.

"Welcome aboard, Addie," Pearl said, with a wide, warm smile. "We can use all the help we can get."

Thinking, *Spy.*

* * *

They took Quinn's Lincoln for the drive downtown. He got behind the steering wheel as Pearl opened the door on her side and slid in to sit next to him. She fastened her seat belt and stared straight ahead.

Quinn didn't drive away immediately. They sat with the engine running almost silently, the car's air-conditioning fighting the good fight against the heat. Pearl didn't feel like a caution from Quinn, but she could sense one coming.

"She seems nice," she said, not looking over at Quinn. Perhaps she could divert this conversation with a modicum of bullshit.

"This is Renz's idea," he said. "He's the unseen hand running the investigation."

"I didn't notice his name on our stationery. Or Addie Price's."

"Or Vitali's or Mishkin's," Quinn said. "We find ourselves working for the city, Pearl. Not just for our periodically disappearing client."

"Think there might be a conflict of interest there?"

"Not unless our client's involved in a crime."

"Hmph," Pearl said. She finally looked over at Quinn. "You *do* realize Addie Price is probably Renz's way of keeping tabs on us. His own personal Mata Hari."

"Yes, I realize that. I also realize she can be a valuable conduit for feeding whatever information we want to Renz."

Pearl couldn't help laughing, partly in disgust. "You are such a devious bastard, Quinn."

"You probably forget from time to time." He slipped the shift lever into drive and pulled the big Lincoln away from the curb. "Something else about Addie Price, Pearl, is she might be damned good at her job."

"She's good at something," Pearl said, and settled back in her seat.

Halfway down Broadway to Chelsea, dark clouds blew in, and vast shadows moved against the buildings and across the wide street. Thunder rumbled like distant lions. People on the sidewalks began walking slightly faster and sneaking looks at the sky as if they might be caught at it and punished with a bolt of lightning. Shop owners with sidewalk displays busied themselves lowering awnings or steel shutters to keep merchandise dry. Judging by the spotless windshield, not a drop of rain had fallen, but already several street vendors were hawking umbrellas. The kind that flipped inside-out with the first brisk wind and were useless ever after.

"Storm coming," Quinn said.

"You think?" Pearl said, each word like a splash of acid.

"Jesus, Pearl, lighten up."

Pearl said, "You're looking at the light me."

37

Holifield, Ohio, 1994

Hardware Hill had started out the cold winter morning with a frozen crust on the surface of five inches of snow. By the time Jerry Grantland got there with the American Flyer sled he'd almost outgrown, the kids who'd gotten a snow day off school and used it for winter hijinks had made an icy mess of things.

The hill was city property, a wide thirty-degree plane leading to a shallow lake. But for the prospect of an icy dunking at the bottom, it might have been designed for sledding.

During the winter the city stacked bales of straw along the lake's edge to keep overenthusiastic sled riders from zooming onto the frozen surface or into the frigid water. Often there were bonfires at the edges of the hill to warm those who stayed long or managed to find their way beyond the straw-bale barrier. At the top of the hill was the back of Munger's Hardware Emporium, where many of the wooden sleds, plastic saucers, even skis were sold. During winters with lots of ice and snow, Munger's did very well and paid the city a lot in taxes. Everybody enjoyed themselves sledding, battling in snowball fights, or making money.

Jerry was dragging the sled behind him by steering ropes he'd fashioned from clothesline. He was wearing his old green parka with the fur-edged hood, a black watch cap, thick corduroy pants, and rubber boots with metal clasps.

He waited for a clear path all the way down the hill, then held his sled with both hands off to his right side and ran. With each stride he bent his knees a little more until he was running in a crouch. He flung himself forward and at the same time brought the sled around so it was beneath him. He landed on it and lay on his belly, gripping the steering rope that was fastened to the sled's wooden yokes. All very smooth.

The sled moved slowly at first and then began picking up speed. It was going to be a good run.

He glided past two girls seated on a slower sled. Hit a slick spot and flashed past some little kids rolling in the snow. He was really traveling now. The cold breeze was getting inside his hood, causing his ears to sting.

At the bottom of the hill, he chose not to crash the sled into the hay bales, as did many of the sledders. Instead he yanked the rope back with his left hand and shifted his weight to the right, raising the leading edge of the sled's left steel runner. The sled veered sharply to the left, dug into the snow, and tipped abruptly to the right, spilling Jerry off and into the soft bale.

Perfect!

He stood up and brushed snow off his coat and pants, then wiped away some that had sneaked under his collar.

That was when he saw another sled bearing down on him. A slight figure in a blue parka was lying flat on it. Chrissie Keller, staring up at him, grinning widely and screaming for him to get out of the way. He knew it was Chrissie even at a distance. She was the twin who wore her thick stocking cap rolled up at the bottom. He had cataloged in his mind details like that about the girls.

"Jerrrry! Move!"

He could have, but why? Her sled wasn't traveling that fast, and if he lifted his feet and pretended he was trying to dodge the sled, he might land against the bale in a bundle with the sled and Chrissie. The prospect created a familiar tightening in his groin.

He yanked his right foot back just in time so the sled's runner wouldn't glide over it, then acted as if he'd lost his balance and landed on top of Chrissie and the sled. They rolled and lay in each other's arms at the base of a bale. The sled was upside down on top of them.

Everything but the sled was soft. Nobody hurt.

They were both grinning.

"You okay?" Jerry asked.

"Nothing broken," Chrissie said.

"You sure?"

They struggled to their feet, helping each other up, and brushed away the snow.

"I'm sure," Chrissie said. He could see her breath fogging in the cold air.

"Sometimes you can't tell till you feel," Jerry told her. He pulled her close and slid his hand beneath her parka. Her sweater had come untucked, and he felt the warm soft flesh of her firm belly.

To Chrissie, the hand might as well have been carved from ice. "Jerry, damn it! Stop!"

But he didn't want to stop. And right now didn't even care if someone noticed.

She gripped his wrist and pushed his arm and hand away. The effort caused her to lose her balance and fall, dragging him down with her. They sat in the snow with their backs against the bales.

"You afraid somebody might see?" Jerry asked.

Chrissie made no attempt to get up. "It isn't right. I don't want you to do that again."

"We all have our secrets," Jerry said, watching his own breath fog in front of his face.

"You and me aren't gonna have that one."

"I know your secret," Jerry said. He swallowed. "I've got the same one."

She looked horrified for a few seconds; she knew what he meant, and briefly thought about confiding in him. He could see the indecision in her eyes.

Tell me, Chrissie. We'll tell each other. That'll make it all right. Or at least better.

Her lips parted slightly, and then her expression hardened.

"I don't know what you're talking about, Jerry."

"Yes, you do." He took a deep breath, gathering courage, and tried to kiss her.

She shoved him away violently and attempted to stand, but her feet shot out from under her and she fell back down.

"Damn you, Jerry! Don't try that again! Ever!"

"I didn't know you cussed. Knew you did other things, though."

"You're too old for me, Jerry."

"What? A year?"

"You'd be too old for me if I was thirty and you were thirty-one."

He gave her a look that scared her. "If we were those ages . . ."

"What?"

"Nothing."

She stood up on her own and stayed on her feet, brushing the snow off her parka. "Keep that in mind, Jerry. Nothing. Not if you were the last boy on this earth."

"We're the same," he said.

She acted as if she didn't know what he was talking about, but she did know. He was sure she knew that he watched sometimes at night. Both twins knew.

"We're the same," he said again. "You, me, and Tiffany."

And suddenly Tiffany was there, on a sled that looked

brand new. Its curved steel runners were still painted bright red. The red was so vivid against the white snow.

Almost in the instant she appeared, Tiffany deftly turned the sled sideways and dragged her boots in the snow. She came to a smooth stop and stood up, holding the sled on end and leaning on it.

"You, me, and Jerry what?" she asked her twin.

But Chrissie was gazing beyond her, toward the top of the hill.

All three of them looked.

The twins' father stood staring down at them, his feet spread wide and his fists propped on his hips.

"Nothing," Jerry said.

Dragging his sled by its steering rope, he began trudging back up the hill, but at an angle, away from Mr. Keller.

"Nothing!" Chrissie echoed behind him.

The desperation in her voice stayed with him always.

"You were talkin' to Chrissie Keller," Jerry's mother said, when he'd returned home. He'd struggled out of his snow-crusted coat, hat, and boots and left them piled on the floor in the mud room off the kitchen.

Still in her white terry cloth robe, his mother was seated at the kitchen table, her hands invisible in her lap.

"Sure," Jerry said. "She lives next door and we go to the same school."

An empty bottle flew through the air and crashed into the wall beside him. It was his first realization that his mother was drunk. Usually she started in heavily with the gin in the early evening, when she was off work from her waitress job at Vellie's, where they served only breakfast and lunch. But today was her day off.

The throwing motion had caused her robe to open, and

one of her breasts was entirely visible. She automatically pulled the robe closed with a quick motion of her right hand.

"I ask you a question," she said, "don't give me a shit answer."

"I wasn't—"

She raised her right hand palm out and shook her head back and forth violently. "You hear me? I mean, you *hear* what I said?"

"Yes, ma'am."

Jerry knew that if he agreed with her about everything without making it too obvious, kept everything smooth if delicately balanced, she'd become sleepy and get tired of picking on him.

Either that or . . .

"Chrissie's father saw you talkin' to her, called on the phone, and said you musta told her somethin' that made her upset. Said Chrissie was cryin'."

"I didn't—well, maybe I did. But if I did, I didn't mean it."

"You tryin' to get in that young bitch's britches?"

Jerry felt himself go red. "Mom!"

"Britches bitch's." She threw back her head and laughed at her unintentional rhyme.

Then she stopped laughing. "I don't want trouble with the neighbors, you unershtan'?"

It was the first word she'd slurred. This could become worse.

"Yes, ma'am," Jerry said.

She stood up unsteadily. The gin bottle she'd thrown at the wall had been empty. The one in her left hand was half empty. Not a good sign.

"'Cause you don't have a father around don't mean you can go misbehavin'," his mother said.

"No, ma'am."

She peered at him as if through the wrong end of a telescope.

"I mean, yes, ma'am."

"It don't mean you ain't got nobody to whip your worthless ass when you need it."

Jerry didn't know what to say. He could only nod, hoping it was the right thing to do.

It wasn't.

His mother weaved her way out of the kitchen and returned with a slender wooden switch about a yard long. It was actually a hickory switch, which seemed to dignify and make acceptable what she was about to do to him. *Taught to the tune of a hickory stick* . . . Jerry knew all the words to the venerable schoolyard tune. Spanking was simply part of disciplining a boy, in his mother's mind. Or in the mind of anyone who might inquire or in any way come to Jerry's aid.

Spare the rod . . .

That wasn't going to happen in the Grantland household.

"Bedroom, young man," his mother said.

Jerry went.

"Need to learn how to hold your tongue," his mother said behind him.

Jerry knew what to do. It took him only a few minutes before he was standing shivering, wearing only his socks. The top of one was still wet where snow had worked its way inside his boot.

His mother stared at him until he bent over the foot of the bed, his elbows on the mattress.

"I wouldn't do this if I didn't have to," his mother said. "If you didn't make me."

Jerry clenched his eyes shut and waited.

The wooden switch hissed like a snake as it cut through the air.

Over and over again. After each hiss came the sharp *snap* of the switch whipping into the bare flesh of his buttocks and the backs of his thighs. The pain became a constant fire.

She shouldn't be doing this to me. I'm too grown up. It isn't fair. It isn't right.

Jerry knew enough not to make a sound. He'd adapted to the pain enough so that he could remain silent except for an occasional whimper that escaped on its own and didn't seem to his mother to count. Clenching his teeth hard enough to break them, he could smell the sweet reek of gin on his mother's breath as she began to labor at her task.

She spread her slippered feet farther apart to gain leverage. Jerry had to be disciplined, didn't he? Best thing for him in the long run.

The lashes with the switch began coming further apart. His mother's breath was now ragged, rasping harshly with each inhalation. She was making more noise than Jerry.

With his eyes closed, Jerry stared into the darkness inside him, waiting for it to be over.

But for the pain, it might have been happening to someone else.

Sometimes it did happen to Chrissie Keller, whose father loved her.

Jerry stayed in his room after the whipping, lying curled on his bed and listening to the rain that had begun falling and would soon melt the snow. If the temperature dropped below freezing again, there would be an icy mess outside.

For some reason he was drained of strength in his mother's presence. She could do what she wanted with him. It was . . . infantile, and he was ashamed.

He didn't move for several hours. The rain hadn't exactly stopped; it now sounded more like sleet.

He heard the rattle and jingle of a car with chains on it, loud enough to be in the driveway.

The car stopped. Jerry didn't bother looking out his window to see who might be driving. It would be a man he wouldn't recognize. Or worse, one that he did. A car door slammed, and he heard someone on the porch. The doorbell didn't chime, but he heard the door open.

A few minutes later his bedroom door opened and his mother stuck her head in. She had on a dress now, and her hair was combed with bangs carefully arranged on her forehead. She was wearing makeup.

"I'm going out for a while, sweetheart," she said. "There are leftovers in the refrigerator if you get hungry."

Jerry didn't move. Said nothing.

After about twenty seconds he heard the front door open and close and the sound of footfalls on the porch. The car in the driveway started up, and he heard the faint jangling of its tire chains again as it backed out to the street and then drove away.

To be on the safe side, he counted slowly to a hundred before getting up and going to his mother's bedroom. The pain was still there, and he moved slowly.

The bedroom was warm, as if she might still be there with her body heat, and it smelled of rose-scented powder and spiced sachets.

When he was in front of his mother's dresser with its tall mirror, he turned his body slightly and saw that there were bloodstains on the seat of his white Jockey shorts. Red lash marks patterned the backs of his pale thighs.

He smiled at his image in the mirror and then bent low and opened the dresser's bottom drawer.

38

New York, the present

Pearl had been first to arrive and was alone in the office. A soft summer rain had begun to fall. It changed the colorful street scene outside the first-floor window from realism to impressionism. The light in the office was made soft by the wavering rain running down the glass panes. It was a light you could almost reach out and feel.

"It's insane," Pearl's mother said over the phone.

Pearl squeezed her cell phone almost hard enough to break it. "I thought you'd want to know. You're always so interested in my personal life, and now I'm changing my address."

"To move in with the Yancy lizard. Not wise, Pearl."

"It's a decision of the heart, Mom. Like when you married Dad."

"Heart, shmart," her mother said. "Your father—and I still miss him dearly—and I were engaged for two years before we were married. Besides, it had all been arranged."

"Well, I'm not married to Yancy, and anyway, marriages aren't arranged anymore. At least not in this country. We've made progress in that regard."

"You have noticed the divorce rate, Pearl?"

"But the murder rate among spouses has fallen," Pearl lied.

"What does Captain Quinn think of this new living arrangement you propose?"

"I've told you, Mom, Quinn is no longer a police captain. And he doesn't know about it yet."

"I know in my mother's heart—as do you in the heart of a dear daughter—that Captain Quinn would not approve."

"So what?"

"So you are not heeding the opinion—which you know he has—of a man of the world who has sailed harsh seas and endured storms and developed a weather eye, and would tell you that over the horizon—"

"He doesn't even know Yancy."

"He knows many Yancys, dear. And their victims."

"You haven't met Yancy, either, Mom. How could you possibly know any of these terrible things about him?"

"I know those who know of him, Pearl. Word passes from mouth to ear, and the word is not good. Mrs. Kahn's cousin's son, himself not a young man with the highest prospects, has been in the Yancy lizard's presence many times in the places where such people congregate, and Mrs. Kahn's cousin's son, once a psychology student at New York University until a so-called misunderstanding about purloined university property brought about the end of his scholarly pursuits, has seen and heard and has some insight into the Yancy lizard's lies and deceptions and total lack of responsibility. He has seen the Yancy Lizard with women other than yourself, imbibing and laughing, and it would logically seem—"

"Mom, I'm not the only woman who goes into bars and imbibes and laughs."

"And you would not be the only woman to fall prey to a reptile of the night and—"

"Gotta go, Mom. Police business."

Pearl flipped the lid closed on the cell phone.

* * *

She could talk with her mother about personal matters only so long before snapping and saying things she'd regret. Pearl had learned not to let it reach that point. Not as often as before, anyway. And she hadn't exactly lied about police business. She *was* in the office where, as of late, police business was conducted.

She was sliding her cell phone into her pocket when it vibrated in her hand.

She smiled when she saw that the caller was Yancy.

"Still love me?" she asked with the phone to her ear.

"If you'll do certain things," Yancy said.

"You know I will."

"Then it's a match. Did you mention to your mother you were moving?"

"I did. She isn't happy about it. Isn't happy about you and me."

"She hasn't even met me," Yancy said in a puzzled voice.

"She thinks she knows you by reputation."

"Nobody *knows* anyone by reputation. Introduce us, honey. I'll win her over."

"You can't win over everyone you meet, Yancy."

"Sure I can. She probably just heard something negative about me from someone jealous 'cause I've got you. Believe me, I can clear up any misunderstanding and change her mind about me."

"She called you a reptile of the night," Pearl said.

"Well, that's nothing. Just a figure of speech. I can turn her around."

Pearl saw one of the passing impressionist figures out in the street veer in toward the doorway, lowering and folding an umbrella. A figure tall, rangy, yet hulking. Quinn arriving.

"I need to go now, Yancy. Crime needs attention."

"So do I, darling."

"Yancy . . ."

"Always willing to step aside for crime. Tonight?"

"Tonight."

Pearl slid the phone into her pocket just as Quinn was coming through the door. He nodded a good morning and shook water from his black umbrella before depositing it in an old metal milk container that had been pressed into service as an umbrella stand.

Pearl watched as he walked over and poured a mug of the coffee she'd brewed. He added powdered cream, stirred, sipped, made a face. It was all an act because she'd made the coffee. They both knew cops drank any kind of black sludge for coffee and it was all the same to them.

"Got those notes on our witness interviews from yesterday organized?" he asked, drifting over and settling in behind his desk.

Pearl went to her desk, got the folder of witness statements, and laid it on his desktop.

"I thought I might find Cindy Sellers and talk to her," Pearl said. "I still think she's a good bet to be our shadow woman."

Quinn laced his fingers behind his neck and leaned his head back into them, moving his elbows back and forth and stretching. "Sellers is good at denying things," he said.

"I'm good at seeing through fake denials."

"You are at that." Quinn looked closely at Pearl for the first time this morning. She was well put together today, dark slacks, light tan blazer, black hair brushed back to a knot at the base of her neck. He remembered how surprisingly long her hair would be when she loosed it from that knot. The way it would tumble to below her shoulders and close in an oval frame around her face, making her eyes look larger, softening her features.

"Quinn?"

She was still waiting for his response.

"Can't hurt," he said. "You might learn something while Sellers is lying to you. Go ahead and talk to her woman-to-woman."

"Woman to piranha," Pearl said.

Quinn figured she was waiting for him to ask which woman was the piranha, but he was too smart for that.

As she was going out the door, she glanced back and for just a second pursed her lips and arranged her features in what was unmistakably a kind of fish face. Knowing as she often did exactly what was in his mind.

Quinn pretended not to have noticed and started leafing through the material she'd placed on his desk.

He didn't look up until he heard the door close. Mumbled something that might have been, "Piranha . . ."

39

Quinn thought Pearl had returned, but when he looked up he saw that Addie Price had entered the office. Her hair was damp from the rain, but its mussed condition somehow improved her looks. Her jeans and green tunic looked good on her, too. She grinned and wiped rainwater from her brow and said hello to him.

"Morning," Quinn said. Then, "Sorry about your desk. It's still on order."

"That's okay. I can continue doubling up with Fedderman for a while." She crossed the room and then sat on the edge of Pearl's desk, not at all the way Pearl habitually perched there. Addie's lanky body looked more comfortable, maybe because her legs were longer than Pearl's and one of her feet was flat on the floor. "Anything new?"

"Nothing," Quinn said.

She straightened up. Her roomy tunic was damp and clung to her in front, and he wondered if she was wearing a bra. All that material, he guessed probably not. And with that coltish figure, she probably wasn't much in the boobs department.

What am I, fifteen?

"I'll continue to familiarize myself with what we have," Addie said. Then caught herself. "If that's okay with you."

"It's what I was gonna suggest," Quinn said. "A fresh eye, maybe something will jump out at you."

She walked around the desk and booted up Fedderman's computer, then got some of the murder books from the file cabinet. Fedderman's password was the same as everyone's in the office and posed no problem. She sat down and busied herself, appearing to compare information in the files with what was on the computer. Looking for inconsistencies. That was so much of their work, Quinn mused, searching for inconsistencies. God knew there were a hell of a lot of those in the world.

After about half an hour, Addie glanced over at Quinn and caught him looking at her. She had to know she was attractive; she smiled as if she were accustomed to being studied by men.

Quinn smiled back. "Sorry. I didn't mean to stare. I'm used to seeing Feds sitting there. You're an improvement."

"That could be a sexist remark." Still smiling.

"If you're offended—"

"I know. I can go—"

"No, no!" Quinn laughed. "I was gonna apologize, is all."

"Well, you might do that over lunch."

He shot a glance at his watch. "It's only ten-thirty."

"I know. I thought we'd get our reservation in early." Another nice smile. Something enigmatic about it. About her.

Quinn wasn't sure what was going on. Was she coming on to him, or was his ego trying to convince him of that? It would be just like his ego, setting him up to play the fool.

"We could discuss the investigation," she said. "A business lunch."

"Okay. If you like Italian, I know a place we can walk to."

"That would be nice," she said.

"I'll call and make the reservation," Quinn said. "Noon okay?"

"Uh-huh." Addie concentrated again on whatever she was doing on the computer.

Quinn knew Addie was a trained psychologist. Was she up to something? Probably she'd picked up that he was still halfway hooked on Pearl, even though it was no secret that Pearl was going out with this Yancy character. Was she trying to move in on Pearl?

Quinn rejected the thought. Male ego again. Most likely Addie was trying to get a line on him so she could manipulate him.

He looked over at Addie. She was glancing back and forth between the computer monitor and her open notebook, copying something with a stubby yellow pencil.

Quinn told himself not to be so damned suspicious of a woman who simply wanted to lunch with a colleague. After all, they did have plenty to talk over, and she was ambitious and eager to learn.

He called Pasta Paradiso over on Columbus and made a reservation for noon; then he got up and went into the washroom near the table where the coffee brewer sat. After rinsing off his face, he looked at his bony, homely features in the mirror above the washbasin. He'd roughened as he got older, and didn't see himself as a prize. It was unlikely that Addie was interested in him in a potentially romantic way. He combed his hair with his wet fingers and dried his hands on a paper towel.

After wadding the towel in a tight wet mass, he tossed it toward the wastebasket, telling himself that if it went in he'd be lucky the rest of the day.

It bounced off the metal rim and landed on the floor.

When Quinn returned to the office, Addie was still at Fedderman's desk. A woman was seated in the client's chair in front of Quinn's desk.

He stopped in mid-stride and stared.

The woman was attractive, with dark hair and eyes, and looked like Tiffany Keller, who was dead.

Not again!

When he regained his composure and moved closer he saw that this woman was older, in her forties. There were fine crow's feet at the corners of her brown eyes, and the beginning of that tendon tightness beneath the chin that happens to some women in their forties. Time touching lightly for now, exploring for vulnerabilities. Quinn's quick assessment suggested to him that she'd probably be attractive all her life.

Her figure inside her two-piece blue outfit was trim. Her legs were shapely, and she wore medium heeled pumps. Dressed as if going for a job interview.

When Quinn approached, she stood up and managed a nervous smile. They shook hands. Her grip was cool and firm. Behind her, Addie was watching, interested. If she'd had antennae they would have been fully extended.

"I'm Erin Keller," the woman said. "Chrissie's mother."

Quinn motioned for her to sit back down, then went behind his desk and settled into his swivel chair.

He held his silence, leaving it up to her to start the conversation.

"I'm aware that Chrissie hired you," she said. Another tentative smile. "I've been following the case in the news, back in Ohio."

"Then you know," Quinn said. "We're looking for Chrissie."

"She left without any notice? Any indication of where she was going?"

"She simply dropped out of the investigation and our lives," Quinn said. "Didn't answer her cell phone or call, and checked out of her hotel."

"There must have been a reason. There's a reason for everything."

"Is there?"

Erin Keller gnawed on her lower lip for a few seconds. "When Chrissie left Holifield, I wasn't surprised. She'd won all that money. She was restless. And I'm afraid her desire to see her sister's killer brought to justice became an obsession. I mean, with so much money she suddenly realized she could actually *do* something about finding the monster."

"Easy enough to understand," Quinn said.

"She said that since it was gambling winnings, and usually she didn't gamble, it meant she was *supposed* to avenge Tiffany's murder. Otherwise, she wouldn't have won. It was her mission."

"I can understand that, too."

"I'm not sure I can. Whatever she accomplishes, it won't bring Tiffany back. Or any of those other young women."

Behind Erin Keller, Quinn saw Addie still sitting motionless, listening, her expression giving away nothing. Quinn saw that she was wearing tortoiseshell-rimmed glasses. He'd never seen her with glasses before. It was as if she wanted to see everything possible that was going on between Erin and Quinn.

"After Chrissie left home," Erin said, "I found some New York travel brochures in her room, along with copies of old news clippings about Tiffany's . . . passing. You must know how I felt . . . feel about this." Tears brimmed in her dark eyes. "Both my daughters. In a way, the monster claimed them both. Tiffany was tortured and killed, and now Chrissie's disappeared. . . . Maybe it was meant to be. You know, twins, destiny . . ."

"That I don't understand," Quinn said.

And neither does anyone else.

Addie stood up, and Quinn thought she was going to comfort Erin. Instead she nodded to Quinn and quietly walked from the office. As if it had occurred to her that she might be eavesdropping on something personal.

More likely, Quinn thought, Addie had decided Erin

might open up and reveal intensely personal information if she was alone with Quinn. Suspects could spill information like that when they got emotional.

"Even before I saw on the news what was happening here in New York," Erin said, dabbing at her swollen eyes with a wadded tissue she'd produced from a small purse, "it wasn't difficult to figure out where Chrissie had gone."

Quinn stood up and walked around the desk. He patted the back of Erin's cool hand. The blue network of veins was very near the surface. "It will be all right, dear," he assured her. "We intend to find Chrissie, and to find Tiffany's killer."

"Before he finds Chrissie?"

It was a possibility Quinn so far hadn't given much weight, but maybe he should. The killer—Maureen Sanders's killer—might be searching for Chrissie as they were.

And vice versa.

Either way it was an explosive situation.

"Chrissie did strike me as a young woman who could look after herself," he said.

Erin, still teared up, nodded.

Quinn went to the file cabinets. He withdrew the file of newspaper clippings Chrissie had given them and laid it on the desk where Erin could reach it.

"She brought us these," he said.

He remained standing, and opened the file so the two of them could examine the contents.

"You've probably seen some of these before," he said.

"Most of them," Erin said.

She examined the file's contents, idly turned the last clipping in the folder, and there was a sketch of Chrissie.

"That's one of dozens of copies," Quinn said. "We had that done by a police sketch artist. We're using it to help search for her."

"Her?" Erin Keller said, looking confused.

"Chrissie. For some reason she—"

"This woman?" Erin asked, placing a finger with a painted pink nail on the sketch.

Confused, Quinn nodded. "We think it's a reasonably good likeness."

"Maybe it is, but it isn't Chrissie. This woman looks nothing like Chrissie. Or Tiffany."

"She told us she and Tiffany were fraternal twins. They wouldn't necessarily look anything alike."

"My daughters are—were—identical twins."

"They were . . . alike?"

"Identical means identical. Especially when it came to Tiffany and Chrissie."

Quinn moved around the desk and sat back down heavily. He leaned backward in his chair and for some reason wished he could light up a cigar. But it wasn't the kind of thing to do now, in front of Erin Keller.

Who the hell is our client?

"Whoever this woman is," Erin Keller said firmly, "she isn't Chrissie."

PART III

And all my mother came into mine eyes
And gave me up to tears.

—SHAKESPEARE, *Henry V*

40

Pearl took a few steps inside the door and stopped to look around.

The offices of *City Beat* looked like the set of one of those 1930s movies wherein all the characters talked like machine guns. The small newspaper occupied the third floor of what appeared to be a mostly deserted redbrick office building in Lower Manhattan. There was an arrangement of battered green steel desks littered with papers. Journalists were seated at most of them, working away or swinging this way and that in their wooden swivel chairs to talk to—or yell at— colleagues. Above the turmoil, ceiling fans slowly rotated.

The entire hectic scene was palely lighted by fluorescent fixtures dangling on chains. Nobody was chewing on a cigar. No one had a pencil stuck behind his or her ear. And there were computers on the desks instead of bulky black type-writers. Other than that, Pearl felt as if she'd wandered into a production of *The Front Page*.

Cindy Sellers, medium height with short brown hair, wearing a beige skirt and a white blouse with a man's red tie, made her way between the desks and emerged from the sea of activity and chatter and shook hands with Pearl.

"We're getting close to press time," she said, by way of explaining all the frenzy.

"I appreciate you taking the time to see me," Pearl said, as Sellers led her toward a small cubicle partitioned off with metal-framed frosted glass.

Sellers glanced back over her shoulder and smiled. "The pleasure's mine. You might be the story."

Pearl also smiled. *Stop the presses! Pearl says . . .*

But she knew she wasn't at the *New York Times.*

"My office," Sellers said when they were in the comparative privacy of the cramped cubicle. She plopped down behind her green steel desk and motioned for Pearl to take the only other place to sit, a hard wooden chair that looked as if it might have been manufactured by some religious sect that considered sitting a sin.

Pearl sat.

Sellers gave her a grin. "This is where I look at you and say 'shoot.' But I guess that's a dangerous thing to say to a cop."

"Some cops," Pearl said.

"Fire away, Detective."

"I'm wondering if *you're* the story," Pearl said.

"How so?"

"The shadow woman."

Sellers acted surprised, then emitted what might be described as a guffaw.

Yes, Pearl thought, *a guffaw.*

"You're way off track," Sellers said, "but I can see how you got there. And I'm not going to tell you where I get my information."

"I can imagine," Pearl said. "We have loose lips all over the place."

"I'm having such a good time, not to mention a good payday, writing about the mysterious shadow woman that you think I manufactured her. I don't do that kind of thing, Pearl, I'm a journalist. A professional." Sellers waved a hand as if trying to flick something sticky off her fingertips. "All that mishmash in the outer office might look like confusion and something lightweight, but we all take it seriously. Call us naïve and altruistic, but we have ethics."

"Such bullshit," Pearl said.

Sellers grinned. "Okay, I was lying. Half lying, anyway. What we're most interested in is a story, and if I'd thought of inventing or becoming a mysterious shadow woman, I might have. But I didn't." She made a big show of crossing her nonexistent heart with the tip of her forefinger. "Honest."

"You didn't stick a needle in your eye," Pearl said.

"If I had a needle . . ." Sellers rolled her chair back a little so she had room to cross her legs and swivel slightly this way and that. "What made you think if you came here and asked me I might tell you the truth?"

"I believe in the direct approach."

"Me, too. How you getting along with your new profiler?"

"Addie seems okay."

"Just okay?"

"Now you're trying to manufacture a story."

"What I told you about my profession, it wasn't all bullshit, Pearl. I think you know that. You and I are in kind of the same business—we dig, and we know how to dig. We find out things."

Pearl decided to take the bait. "What have you found out about Addie Price?"

"Probably nothing you don't know. She was attacked in Detroit and would have been killed, but her assailant broke off the attempt and fled."

Pearl sat silently.

"Our girl made the most of things, turned her brush with death into opportunity. She earned degrees in criminology and psychology and made contacts in the local media. Became a minor celebrity, blabbing about her theories on radio and TV whenever a serious crime was committed. Beyond that, I don't know much else about her."

"You've got it pretty much covered," Pearl said.

"Anything you want to contribute?"

"Nothing that I could. What is it about Addie that interests you?"

"I'm not sure. Just a feeling that something about her isn't right. Do you have the same feeling?"

"No," Pearl lied.

"I deal in favors made and repaid," Sellers said. "That's why I took time out of my busy day to talk with you. Why I just told you what I know about Adelaide Price. And I think I put your mind at rest about your theory of me being the shadow woman. All I want in return is for you to tell me whatever else you find out about Addie Price."

"Whatever's connected to the investigation and newsworthy, you mean?"

Sellers shrugged. "Oh, sure. I'm not interested in her personal life."

Both women laughed.

Then Sellers said, surprising Pearl, "You and Quinn aren't completely over."

"Maybe not as far as he's concerned," Pearl said. "But yes, we're over."

Sellers winked. "Because of Yancy Taggart?"

Pearl felt the rush of blood to her face and knew Sellers would enjoy having made her blush. "How do you know about Yancy?"

"I told you, it's my business to find out things. Yancy's getting it on with one of the investigating officers, so he might become part of the story."

"I don't agree."

"Well, Yancy's got a way of becoming a big part of whatever he gets involved in. You'd be surprised at his connections, with his lobbying for those crackpots who want windmills on skyscrapers."

"They aren't crackpots, and it's not windmills. They're wind turbines, and it makes more sense than it seems to when you first hear it."

Sellers grinned silently at her.

"Well, maybe not," Pearl said.

"What I know about Yancy is he's damned convincing. He can make those wind turbines seem like good sense, at least long enough to pry money from wealthy donors. If he was still a tobacco industry lobbyist, everybody'd still be smoking."

Pearl deadpanned it and said nothing. For all she knew, Sellers was trying to confirm things she didn't know for sure. Or maybe she had some other motive.

"Guys like Yancy can be exciting," Sellers went on. "Full of charm and schmaltz. Oh, sometimes they have other sides you wouldn't expect, redeeming facets to their personalities. But then so does everyone else. Hell, you wouldn't believe it, but sometimes I have a kind heart."

Pearl gave her a level look. "Are you trying to get me deeper in your debt by warning me about Yancy?"

"Warning? No, that'd be too strong a word. I would say, though, a man like that, who's been around and plays around, you need to be careful." Sellers stood up, indicating that they'd talked long enough and she had to get back to newspaper biz. "But you're a cop. You've been around, yourself, and you understand people. You sure don't have to be warned. But it wouldn't hurt if somebody who sometimes knows more than you do was kind of looking out for you."

Pearl knew the game. Sellers was offering to feed her information about Yancy in return for whatever information Pearl might give her about the investigation. Or about Addie Price. After all, both women dealt in information.

For the first time since entering the modest, stifling cubicle, Pearl wondered if this conversation was being recorded. Sellers was the type who probably recorded everything. And used it whatever the consequences. *Well, the hell with it*, Pearl thought. She was sure she hadn't said anything incriminating or even out of line, and she didn't intend to.

Pearl stood up. "Thanks, but I can pretty much look after myself."

"I would agree with that," Sellers said. "And I hope we've cleared up that shadow woman thing."

"Sure," Pearl said.

Sellers walked her out through the maze of green desks, swivel chairs, and maelstrom of activity, staying slightly ahead of her in the manner of a guide escorting someone through a dangerous jungle.

Lies, lies, lies, Pearl thought, all the way back down to the street and the jungle outside.

After leaving the offices of *City Beat* Pearl used the unmarked she was driving to swing by her apartment. Her conversation with Cindy Sellers had upset her more than she wanted to admit.

Once inside the apartment, she decided simply to eat an early lunch there and then do some work on her laptop at the kitchen table. There was no need for Quinn to know her exact whereabouts. If he wanted her, he could contact her on her cell phone.

When her shoes were removed and the air conditioner had cooled and dehumidified the kitchen, she settled down at the table with a container of sharp cheddar cheese, some crackers, a cold can of Diet Coke, and her notebook computer.

Since Cindy Sellers revealed that she'd probed into Yancy's affairs, and Cindy was the fourth estate's dubious representative, Yancy was part of the investigation. Therefore Pearl was working on the investigation. Right there at her kitchen table, cheese and crackers and all.

She smiled, knowing Quinn wouldn't buy that line of reasoning.

That was okay; she didn't plan on having to sell it to him.

She snacked with one hand and worked the computer

with the other, following links from relevance to remoteness and learning everything possible online about Yancy Taggart, registered lobbyist. She was driven by a desire to dig deeper, to know everything Cindy Sellers knew and more.

So at one time Yancy had lobbied for the tobacco industry. Well, so what? He'd probably believed in the merits of smoking the same way he believed in wind-powered skyscrapers.

Pearl followed obscure links and visited sites she hadn't seen before.

Yancy seemed to have been honest and forthcoming. He'd told her about the tobacco industry job, and a lot of other things that she confirmed. He did hold a degree in communications and had put it and his ebullient personality and deviousness to good use. Pearl could find nothing to suggest that he was or had been married, or that he'd fathered any children.

There was a photograph of him posing with half a dozen successful business types in suits, and with correspondingly beautiful women, at some sort of convention two years ago in Miami. His arm was about the waist of a gorgeous blond woman with a dress that looked already ripped half off. The men were identified in the photo but not the women.

Humph, Pearl thought.

She fed the other five men's names into Google and worked for another two hours. Three of the men were fellow lobbyists, one was in insurance, and the other was mayor of a small town in Texas. All innocuous enough.

Yancy seemed never to have crossed swords with the law in any serious manner.

Pearl drained the last of the warm Coke and shut down her computer. Then she closed the laptop's lid, sat back, and smiled as she thought about Yancy.

Passed!

Realizing she was still hungry, she ate another cracker.

What was that? Music?

She listened more closely, fitting the faint notes together. The theme from *Dragnet*. Coming from her cell phone in her purse, where she'd left it on the arm of the sofa in the living room.

Pearl got up from the table and dashed out of the kitchen. She made a beeline for the phone and snatched it up, flipped it open, and pressed TALK all in the same motion.

"Where are you Pearl?" Quinn asked.

"Climbing into the unmarked, on the way to the office," Pearl said. *Lies, lies, lies.*

"You have another destination. We've got another Carver victim."

One last cracker and Pearl was on her way.

41

Traffic on Broadway slowed Pearl, but she cut over to Second Avenue, imperiled the lives of a few pedestrians, and reached Lower Manhattan in good time.

The address Quinn had given her was an old brick building with a red granite facade. There was the usual assortment of unmarked and radio cars pulled in at odd angles to the curb in front of the building, along with an ambulance. Two paramedics sat inside the ambulance with the engine running to keep the air-conditioning going. The vehicles' emergency lights were still flashing, along with the roof bar lights of one of the radio cars.

Three uniforms were standing at the wide concrete steps leading to the entrance, two with their feet propped on the first step. Pearl flashed her shield and one of them, a young guy with a nose like de Bergerac's, told her the floor and apartment numbers.

The victim's apartment was close enough to the elevator that as soon as Pearl stepped out of it she was there. Fedderman and Harold Mishkin were standing in the hall outside the open apartment door. Fedderman acknowledged Pearl with a nod. Mishkin smiled wanly at her. He had the mentholated goo he used at murder scenes rubbed into his mustache beneath his nose. It was almost enough to make her eyes water.

"Quinn and Sal are inside," Mishkin said.

So were the techs from the CSU, dusting and plucking, picking and bagging. The ballet of the white gloves. Careful where she stepped and what she touched, Pearl made her way through the apartment living room and down the hall, glancing in the bathroom to make sure that wasn't where the body was.

Quinn and Sal Vitali were in the bedroom, standing at the foot of the bed and watching Nift, the repugnant little M.E., examining the victim. The smells of blood, feces, and the beginnings of decay were strong. Pearl understood why Mishkin had used his mentholated cream.

The victim was lying on her back nude, blood on her chest and caked black beneath her on the sheets. Her throat had been sliced almost ear to ear. Even through the blood, it was obvious that her nipples had been removed and a large X was carved on her body so that the intersection of its straight lines was between her breasts. The breasts themselves were undamaged by the X.

Pearl wondered what the bloody X could mean. X marks the spot? The victim has been canceled? Or was it an initial? *Xavier*?

It might be none or all those things.

Probably they would never know until they had the killer.

"Meet Joyce House," Sal said in his deep, gravel voice. "She was a waitress at a place called the Nickel Diner. Thirty-two years old, unmarried, lived alone."

The victim was the Carver's type. Between twenty and forty, brown hair, attractive. Her brown eyes were fixed as a doll's eyes. They were widened in horror though she was grinning. Her throat was grinning, anyway, where it had been slashed. Her mouth—

"What's that in her mouth?" Pearl asked.

"A gag," Nift said, without looking up at Pearl. Then he

did look up and grin, nothing like the victim's ghastly grin but in its way almost as ugly. "Her wadded-up panties."

Pearl looked over at Quinn and Sal. The Carver had used his victims' wadded panties to silence them.

"Look over on the dresser," Nift said.

They did, and saw a simple house of cards. Quinn went over and looked closely at it. The card house was made of face cards, all of them turned out so the fragile structure was colorful. The rest of the deck was stacked neatly next to it, a popular brand of playing card that would be impossible to trace. Quinn knew it was a given that there would be no fingerprints on the cards.

"Get it?" Nift asked. "House of cards . . . Joyce House . . . another gag, like the one in her mouth."

"I'd like to stuff something in your mouth," Pearl said.

"I'm always available," Nift said, laughing.

"He's returned to form," Quinn said.

"He was always a jerk-off," Pearl said.

"I meant the Carver, with the panties gag," Quinn said. "Stay on point, Pearl."

Sal said, "He was rusty with the Sanders woman."

"He's getting back in the groove," Nift said, tapping the slashed throat with a pointed silver instrument.

Pearl instinctively winced. *Don't hurt her!*

"His taste is improving, too," Nift said. "This one was a honey when she was alive. Look at that set on her. She was built like you, Pearl."

"How would you like to be dead like her?" Pearl said.

Nift smiled.

"What about those bruises on her arms?" Quinn asked.

"Something pressed down hard there, pinning her to the mattress," Nift said. "Probably the killer's knees. My guess is he straddled her and placed her arms like that so she couldn't interfere with what he was doing to her."

"You mean that happened while she was alive?" Sal asked.

Nift looked at Pearl when he answered. "Oh, yeah, she felt everything. He probably took his time with her. She must've been scared shitless." He nodded toward the victim's lower body and the stain where her bowels had released after death. "In fact—"

"Shut your goddamned mouth!" Pearl said.

Quinn looked over at Pearl and then stared hard at Nift.

"I would do that," Quinn said.

Nift shrugged and continued his work on the body. He was obviously amused at having made Pearl lose her cool.

"Got an approximate time of death?" Vitali asked, keeping his voice calm and trying to put a damper on everyone's emotions. Keep the focus of the conversation on business. He knew about Pearl. Unstable dynamite.

"She's been dead at least twelve hours," Nift said. "So she's slightly ripe. That's why your partner Mishkin isn't in here."

"Only one of us needs to be here," Sal said.

"I can get closer on the time of death after I get her to the morgue," Nift said. He'd seemed to have caught something in Sal's voice that suggested he'd better back off. "It won't be long. There's a rush on this one, and I'm squeezing her into my busy schedule."

"Who found her?" Pearl asked.

"Neighbors complained about the smell coming from the apartment, through the vents," Sal said. "The super let himself in, then saw her and let himself out in a hurry. Harold went downstairs and got his statement."

"Any signs of rape?" Quinn asked.

"No signs of penetration, but this might have started out as rough sex and got out of control." Nift straightened up, gave his nasty little grin, and touched his crotch. "One thing's for sure: this one got it rougher than she wanted."

Pearl took a step toward the bed where Nift was again bending over the victim. Quinn extended an arm, and she stopped, knowing he wouldn't let her get any closer to Nift.

He'd grab and restrain her. She didn't want Quinn's hands on her. Right now, not any man's hands. She wanted her hands on Nift.

"Haven't seen her nipples anywhere," Nift said. "Our guy took his usual souvenirs. He's building quite a collection."

Nift straightened back up and stepped away from the bed. He dropped the steel instrument he'd been probing with into a container with the others that he'd used and then peeled off his latex gloves. "I'm finished playing with the young lady until the postmortem. You can have her removed anytime you want. Do what you will with her." He stuffed the inside-out gloves into the container with the instruments and closed it. "Just remember her last date's with me."

"Necrophiliac prick," Pearl said.

Nift seemed unperturbed. "Well, I enjoy my work." He smiled at Pearl. "You might enjoy my work, too."

Pearl made a move toward Nift, but there was Quinn's big arm, like a barrier at a railroad crossing.

Pearl stopped and took a deep breath. She pushed at the arm, but it didn't give. That was okay. By now she didn't want to move it.

"Try your line of bullshit on a live woman and see what happens," Pearl said from where she was safe behind Quinn's arm. Safe not from Nift, but from doing something to him she'd regret.

Nift finished gathering up what he needed and picked up his black medical bag. "My perverse charm works on the live ones, too," he said to Pearl. "It's all in knowing how to get under their skin. Once their emotions are aroused, who knows what else they might want to feel?"

He winked at her as he went out the door.

Quinn and Sal looked at each other. Might Nift be right in his cynical approach to women? Arousing their ire to kick-start their other emotions. Getting their engines started, so to speak.

"Asshole!" Pearl said under her breath.

Apparently the technique didn't work with Pearl.

"It's his game," Quinn said. "He wants to get a rise out of you, Pearl. You shouldn't play along."

"If you just did your job and ignored his bullshit, it'd be easier for you," Sal said.

"You saying I don't do my job?"

Sal raised both hands. "No, no . . ."

"Nift is a born shit disturber," Pearl said.

"Okay," Quinn said. "We all agree on that, along with everybody who ever met Nift. Let's calm down and remember where we are."

Where they were was in a room with the dead.

The three detectives took a long last look around. Nobody's gaze lingered on Joyce House.

The techs had finished with the body and almost with this room, leaving only slight evidence that they'd been there. They still had to disassemble and dust the house of cards, but no one doubted they'd find only glove smudges.

"Time to talk in-depth with the neighbors," Sal said. "Nift wants to do a rush job. Should I give word the body can be removed?"

"Not yet," Quinn said. "Conference in the hall first about who talks to which tenants."

"The lady can keep Nift waiting," Pearl said.

The two men smiled.

Not Pearl.

42

Joyce House's neighbors didn't provide much help. The crime had taken place behind a locked door and in the privacy of the victim's bedroom. The victim had been gagged. No shot had been fired. No blow had been struck with a blunt instrument. No body had crashed to the floor. Perhaps there had been the snick of blade on bone, but aside from that the sharp knife had done its work in silence.

A woman who lived down the hall from Joyce said she'd noticed Joyce walking on the street near her apartment building with a man a few days ago. But other than saying he was medium height and weight, she couldn't help. It had been raining, and both Joyce and the man had been walking into the downfall, holding their open umbrellas low so their faces were visible only in glimpses.

Other than that brief sighting, none of Joyce's neighbors could recall seeing her with a man.

EMS paramedics had removed the body. The crime scene unit had left, and Joyce's apartment was sealed. Most of the yellow crime-scene tape had been removed, and only one uniformed officer stood watch near the building's entrance. Onlookers had drifted away.

There was nothing more to hold their interest.

Yet when Quinn, Pearl, Fedderman, and Vitali left the

building they saw a woman standing very still across the street and staring at them. She was wearing a gray windbreaker and a dark blue baseball cap. Her arms were crossed, and her weight was on one leg. Her attitude was that of someone waiting.

A black car suddenly turned the corner and veered in toward the curb in front of the building.

Mishkin in the unmarked. He'd driven over to the diner where Joyce House had worked and interviewed people there who knew her.

The arrival of the car, and Mishkin getting out, temporarily distracted everyone's attention. When they looked back across the street, the woman was gone.

Vitali said, "Shit!" and jogged across the street. Pearl followed.

Fedderman began to tag after them, but slowed after a few steps and looked around with his hands on his hips. Sal ran all the way to the end of the block and rounded the corner.

Quinn had looked up and down the street and didn't see much hope for catching up with the woman. There were too many ways she could have gone to lose them.

It didn't take long for Pearl and Fedderman to return.

Sal came back within a few minutes, breathing hard. "Gone like a ghost," he said.

"Our shadow woman?" Mishkin asked.

"Could have been," Quinn said. "If it was just somebody stopping for a moment to gawk, she wouldn't have made herself disappear so soon. It had to be that she didn't want us to catch her."

"More grist for Cindy Sellers's print mill," Pearl said.

"How will she find out—" Mishkin began, then stopped. The others were looking at him. They were hardly going to omit mention of the woman's presence in their report to Renz; they all knew Sellers would get the information from him. Being secretive simply meant to delay the information in making its predictable circuit.

"Maybe we're getting spooked," Pearl said. "People move when you're not looking at them all the time, so that when you glance back they're gone. It's just that we're looking for this woman. We're almost expecting to see her, and maybe that's why we do."

"That didn't look like a mirage Sal was chasing," Quinn said.

"She always wears something so you can't see her face," Fedderman said.

"What was it this time?" Pearl said. "A baseball cap. Some disguise. What? Were we supposed to think she was Derek Jeter?"

"She had the bill pulled down," Fedderman said. "Wore it facing full front and down so her face was in shadow."

"I wear my Mets cap that way when the sun's in my eyes," Pearl said.

"But you were right here with us, so we know it wasn't you," Fedderman said.

Pearl gave him a dead-eyed look. "I hate it when you play dumb, Feds. And it really isn't necessary."

Mishkin smiled slightly, and Vitali gave a gravelly laugh.

Pearl had both hands clenched into fists. Never a good sign.

"What'd you find out at the diner?" Quinn asked Mishkin, getting the conversation on another track that wouldn't lead to a train wreck.

"Everybody loved Joyce," Mishkin said.

"They mention anyone she seemed to love back?"

"No, but it's not the kind of place where the servers mix with the customers except to see they get their food and checks." Mishkin shoved his hands in his pockets and rocked back and forth on his heels. "The owner-operator of the place, a guy named Mick, seems to have a thing about his employees getting too friendly with the customers, like they're going to conspire to steal tidbits from the kitchen."

"So if Joyce and anybody she met at the diner developed a relationship, they might keep it secret so she wouldn't lose her job."

"Which means our killer might be a frequent customer at the diner," Fedderman said. "We should check out the regulars."

"Actually," Quinn said, "I was thinking of anyone who might have *stopped* eating there."

"The dog that didn't bark in the night," Pearl said.

Fedderman said, "Dog? Night?"

"Think we should go back there?" Pearl asked, ignoring him.

"For breakfast," Quinn said. "As I recall, Joyce worked the early shift. You and Feds go there tomorrow and have the special on the city. Then talk to the boss and whoever else might have worked some of the same hours as the victim."

Pearl made a face. "Breakfast with Fedderman. Just how I wanna start the day."

"It'll be like a date, Pearl," Fedderman said with mock cheer.

"It'll be like most of your dates," Pearl said. "All you'll get is indigestion."

Quinn glanced around. "Since you're all here, it's a good time to inform you about another development."

And he told them about Erin Keller.

43

Back at the office, Quinn gave his detectives, including Vitali and Mishkin, the name of Erin's hotel, the Melbourne, and more fully described his meeting with her.

They all listened closely, temporarily forgetting about the heat and the humming and occasionally hammering air conditioner.

They were particularly interested in Erin's reaction to their client's photograph.

"So now we've got two missing women," Sal said. "Chrissie and whoever impersonated Chrissie."

"And they look nothing alike," Fedderman added.

The phone on Quinn's desk rang. He nodded at Pearl, and she picked up the receiver. "Quinn and Associates."

The phone greeting still didn't sound familiar to Quinn; he'd been too long in the NYPD.

Pearl held the receiver out to him and silently mouthed, *Renz.*

"You got anything fresh on House?" Renz asked when Quinn had gotten on the line.

"Nothing that would excite you," Quinn said.

"I had a rush preliminary done on the postmortem. The victim was alive up until the time her throat was slashed. There was plenty of blood on the panties stuffed in her mouth, but it was all hers. CSU found some hairs that might be anybody's. The place had been wiped of prints here and there, where the killer must have touched things. Also there were some glove smudges. There was a wine bottle in the trash. Merlot. No prints on that, and no DNA. Couple of wineglasses in the dishwasher, also clean of prints. Some red wine in the victim's stomach, too. Same as what was left in the bottle. Musta been a party."

"Up to a point," Quinn said.

"Or an edge. We got the hairs, anyway, some of them with follicle attached, so we got DNA samples. We get a suspect and make a match and we might have our killer."

"Getting the suspect is the problem," Quinn said, thinking if the suspect had ever been in Joyce House's apartment at any time before the night of the murder, the hair and DNA match could have come from an earlier visit and not be much in the way of hard evidence.

"Looks like they came home to her place with a bottle of wine—or she already had the bottle there. Then they had drinks, maybe cunnilingus sex, and murder. They musta known each other, had some kind of ongoing relationship."

"If they didn't meet that night. And if she wasn't raped."

"Nift is pretty sure she wasn't raped. Didn't anybody know who she was screwing?"

"Nobody we've found so far," Quinn said. "She might have had some kind of secret relationship."

"A married man?"

"Or somebody where she worked. The guy who runs the place and his employees don't seem likely. But she'd pretend not to know a customer who was a lover. Her boss had a strict policy of not mixing pleasure with business, and that kind of affair might have caused her to lose her job."

"Love will find a way," Renz said. "You checking on the diner's regular customers?"

"We're on it," Quinn said, deciding not to go into detail with Renz.

"It's worth pursuing," Renz said. "Way to go about that is to check and see if any of the regulars suddenly stopped eating there, so if he was banging Joyce House they could keep it a secret."

"Good idea."

"How's our girl Addie Price working out?" Renz asked.

"Fine. She knows her job."

"She came highly recommended. And she's media savvy, too. Listen close to her if she has ideas on how to handle the wolves."

"Wolves like Cindy Sellers?"

"I've got that wolf domesticated," Renz said.

Quinn almost laughed into the phone. He turned his head so Renz wouldn't hear.

"Partly, anyway." Renz might have heard something. "Keep me up on things, Quinn."

Quinn said that he would, and they ended the conversation.

Quinn filled everyone in on what Renz had told him about the postmortem and CSU findings.

"We got diddly shit," Vitali said.

"Except for the dog-in-the-night angle," Fedderman said. "That one's worth pursuing."

"That's what Renz said," Quinn told him.

"Now I am worried," Fedderman said.

Two hours later, Fedderman dropped a sheet of copy paper on Quinn's desk. "That dog in the night didn't hunt. The owner and employees said there were three regular customers that recently stopped coming into the diner where Joyce House worked. Two were women. We did an Identi-Kit on the third."

Quinn studied the image the police artist had created from voice description. An average-looking man, short haircut, firm chin, neither too fat nor too thin.

"Make a good spy, wouldn't he?" Fedderman said.

"Yeah. He look familiar to you?"

"Uh-huh. But he's got one of those faces."

"I guess that's it," Quinn said.

"No way to trace him from the diner," Fedderman said. "Mr. Nobody."

"Maybe he planned it that way."

"But probably he's just a guy," Fedderman said. "Mighta found a hair in his food and started eating someplace else. Could happen to anyone."

"So could what happened to Joyce House."

Quinn seated himself at his desk in his den that evening. He already had a cigar burning, and was carrying a glass containing Famous Grouse over ice with a splash of water. He was in his socks, and his shirt was unbuttoned halfway down and untucked. Comfortable.

When he was settled, he slid open the desk's middle drawer and withdrew his yellow legal pad. He didn't see a pen, so he picked up a reasonably sharp pencil that had toothmarks and a worn-down eraser. He noticed it was the exact yellow as the legal pad.

Beneath *(Trust no one.)* he began to write in his sloppy but legible hand:

Enter Addie Price. Renz spy?

Enter Erin Keller. Sees Chrissie photo—not Chrissie. Our Chrissie not even related to Tiffany.

Two Chrissies missing now. Fake Chrissie and real one.

Joyce House body found.

Shadow woman appears again at crime scene.

Quinn dropped the pencil and leaned back, studying the legal pad. It told him nothing, but it raised an uneasy feeling. There was a lot about this case that wasn't right. Nothing fully formed in his mind yet, but not right. He couldn't quite grasp the solution to the puzzle, but it was there ahead of him. He could sense its amorphous presence even if he couldn't see it.

He concentrated on his cigar and scotch and felt oddly satisfied. He was getting somewhere, even if he wasn't sure where.

It had to be soon. A person could wait only so long, could only fight off such a compulsion so long. Not to give in to it was to be devoured by it. He'd never dreamed it could be like this, that the *need* could come on so suddenly and be so powerful.

The bothersome thing was that the times, the women, were coming closer together and without predictable intervals. Predictable intervals made it easier to plan. To be in control.

Control was what it was all about. Control bestowed by destiny. Once begun, if it was meant to happen, it would.

Not to give in to it was to be devoured by it.

Joyce House had been the best. She'd struggled with her fate enough to make it interesting, to satisfy the need, but not so much as to make things truly difficult and perhaps more dangerous.

The change in her eyes hadn't occurred too soon, and when it came it was complete. She was already dead and knew it. All that was necessary then was the acting out, and she readily gave herself up to that. She was ready to end it, to end herself, to end the future, past, and present, and to begin the forever.

Perhaps because Joyce had been so satisfying, the need

was back sooner than anticipated. Not a demon fully formed, but forming.

Joyce's image played on the screen of the mind, her eyes when she saw the knife and understood the inevitability of the blade, when she felt the caressing point of the blade, the course of the blade.

The blade.

Her eyes.

Her eyes.

It had to be soon.

44

They'd had dinner and red wine at Orzo's, near Pearl's apartment. She'd had the four-cheese ravioli special, and Yancy the lamb and new potatoes. Before leaving the restaurant, Yancy had gone to the bar and bought a second bottle of merlot. He carried it in a plain brown paper bag as they walked toward Pearl's apartment.

Pearl let Yancy set the pace, which was moderate. It was a calm, cool evening, with a light fog that had settled in while they were inside the restaurant. The glow of streetlights was starred, and there was a halo around the service lights of cabs. Pearl thought it would make a nice illustration for a don't-you-wish-you-were-in-New York card.

When they came to an intersection and stopped walking to wait for a traffic signal, Yancy shifted the paper bag to his other hand, as if it was heavy.

"There gonna be a celebration?" Pearl asked, nodding toward the bag.

Yancy grinned down at her. "Could be. I've got a surprise for you."

The signal changed, and they crossed the street.

"I'm glad you didn't ask what," Yancy said.

"I don't believe in pointless questions," Pearl said.

"I'll ask most any kind. Is your mother getting any more used to the idea of me?"

"She doesn't get used to ideas. She's still dismayed that I'd take up with a scoundrel like you, and frankly so am I. But we don't always have a choice in these matters."

"Good thing for scoundrels like me." They were silent for a few paces. "Did she really call me that—a scoundrel?"

"I don't think so," Pearl said. "It might have been wastrel."

"Ah. Better."

"You *are* a lobbyist," Pearl said.

"For green power."

"Does it really matter to you what kind of power you represent?"

"Actually, not in the slightest. I'm a hired advocate. I believe everyone should have the chance to have his or her case made. Every organization or special interest group. I do that professionally. Like a lawyer."

"There are a lot of lawyer jokes."

"Lots of cop jokes, too."

"Ouch."

Half a block of silence followed. It was a silence heavy with expectation. Pearl realized the palms of her hands were sweating. Something about that damned Yancy. Maybe her mother had a point.

They were almost to Pearl's apartment.

Yancy said, "A good dinner, some wine . . . I thought it would lighten the mood."

"The mood is light," Pearl said.

"Doesn't feel like it."

Pearl stopped walking and moved around in front of Yancy. She kissed him on the lips, used her tongue, felt his hand close tightly on the nape of her neck.

She drew back, smiling up at him.

"There's the mood," she said.

He bent and kissed her on the forehead. "Perfect."

They held hands the rest of the way.

* * *

As soon as they entered the apartment, Pearl kicked off her shoes.

Yancy stooped and placed the bag with the bottle of wine on the floor and then pulled her to him, and they kissed as they had out on the sidewalk. He worked the zipper in the back of her dress as smoothly as if he'd practiced it hundreds of times.

With a faint rustling sound, the dress slid down, and she lowered her arms so it would fall all the way and puddle at her feet. He hugged her to him again, and his right hand slid beneath her panties and over the smooth contours of her hips and buttocks. His left hand was at her back. Her bra strap came undone, and the bra slid down and almost off her breasts.

Jesus! Does he have three hands?

The bra slipped all the way off seemingly of its own volition, so its straps were at the crooks of her elbows, and he bent his body and kissed both her nipples. He stepped back, smiling at her, and she lowered her arms so the bra dropped to the floor with the dress.

Yancy left her panties on—for now. Before she knew it, he'd picked her up and carried her into the bedroom. She heard the soft crinkling sound of paper and realized that somehow he'd managed to pick up the bag containing the wine bottle.

After laying her gently on the bed, he removed the bottle from its bag. She saw that it had already been uncorked to the point where the stopper would slide from the neck with minimal effort. Two plastic wineglasses from the restaurant were also in the bag.

"For later," he said, arranging the bottle and glasses on the nightstand.

"Let's think about later . . . later," Pearl said.

For a brief moment she wondered again if her mother might be right.

Then she forgot all about her mother.

* * *

Afterward Pearl lay on her back, gazing sideways across her pillow at Yancy. He was still breathing hard from the exertion of their lovemaking, staring up at the ceiling as if in deep thought.

"We've reached later," Pearl said.

He looked over at her and smiled. Then he sat up and swiveled on the mattress so he could reach the wine bottle and glasses. He poured one glass, for her. She sat up and scooted so her back was against her wadded pillow and the headboard. She accepted the plastic wineglass and sipped. The wine tasted, even *felt* good, on her tongue and throat, after the way they'd made love. It was a good combination, she thought, sex and wine. Probably people had been enjoying it for centuries.

Yancy stood up from the bed and stared down at her with a combination of admiration and careful consideration, as if pondering whether to ask her to pose for a photograph.

Then he turned and walked from the room.

"Aren't you going to have a glass?" Pearl asked.

"First the surprise," he said, glancing back at her over his shoulder.

Pearl sighed, sipped, and waited.

It was such good wine, and strong. And relaxing. She tilted back her head and breathed deeply of the scent and warmth of both their bodies, and felt contentment. Yancy, she had to admit, knew how to treat a lady.

When he returned to the bedroom, still nude, he held one hand behind his back. Carrying something as he approached the bed.

Pearl smiled at him, but he didn't smile back. He had an odd, serious look on his handsome face. Seriousness didn't look right on him, like a hat that was way too big.

"Yancy?"

He raised his forefinger to his lips to signal silence and then sat down near her on the bed.

He brought his hand out from behind his back.

With a crash of knowledge that took her breath away, she saw what he was holding and knew exactly what it meant.

He opened the small, square box with rounded corners, removed a diamond engagement ring, and slipped it on her finger.

45

Holifield, Ohio, 1996

Summer and Saturday night at Holi-Burger. It was the place to cruise. The restaurant itself was a glass and brick box of a building, mostly glass, brightly lighted inside. It was as if it had been set up as a display case to show the workers in their yellow T-shirts buzzing about like bees behind the counter, and the two lines of customers waiting patiently to pick up or place their orders.

The restaurant was set in the center of a large blacktop lot. Parking spaces were marked with yellow lines along the lot's perimeter, leaving room to drive in a circle about the building without going out onto the county roads or the street of small commercial buildings that bordered the north side of the lot. Always there was a trickle of show-off vehicle traffic at Holi-Burger, but especially on Friday and Saturday nights.

Holi-Burger was neither a drive-in nor a drive-through. Though there were a few tables inside, most of the food served there was carryout, and people usually ate it sitting in their parked cars. Those who wanted to watch the cruisers would back their cars into parking spots.

The vehicles that were actually owned by teenagers were

usually customized. Cars were chopped to create lower roof-lines or raked forward on jacked-up suspensions. Pickup trucks sported oversized knobby tires that looked as if they belonged on a tractor. The family cars borrowed for the night were generally less interesting, the newer ones looking as if they'd just been driven home from the dealers.

Jerry Grantland sat parked in his mother's eight-year-old green Chevy Impala, definitely not cruiser material. It was scraped and dented along one side from when it had been sideswiped two years ago. Jerry's mother, Miriam, had chosen to keep the insurance payment and leave the car unrepaired. It ran just as well with its exterior damage, and she needed the money.

Idly chewing on a cheeseburger and sipping a large fountain Coke from a soggy waxed cup, Jerry watched the slow and proud parade of vehicles. As a vintage red Mustang went past, its driver, a fat kid with a military buzz cut, glanced over and gave Jerry the finger. The gesture of disdain was for no reason Jerry could figure out. Most of the other drivers stared straight ahead, imperious in their art projects on wheels.

A jacked-up Ford pickup cruised past, deep maroon and gleaming in the sodium lights rimming Holi-Burger's lot. Adam Clement was behind the steering wheel. He was a year older than Jerry, tall and painfully skinny, with scruffy blond hair and thick glasses with oversized frames.

Jerry paused in his chewing and sat forward. Someone was in the truck's high cab with Adam. As it rolled past, Jerry caught a glimpse of the passenger. A girl. He could tell that much by her size and hair. And she looked like Chrissie Keller.

Chrissie had been hanging out with Adam and his group lately, so maybe the two of them were going together.

Jerry didn't see what Chrissie saw in an awkward bean-pole like Adam. And it wasn't as if he was a genius. Adam was always getting special help, and he spent more than his share of time in detention. So what was the appeal? Jerry didn't think it was Adam's truck that Chrissie liked. But then with girls, women, who could tell?

Jerry waited patiently for the maroon truck to come around again. The Chevy's windows were down, and he could hear revving engines, voices, a cacophony of music from radios. Someone had the Indians' ballgame on the radio, the announcer's voice somehow finding its way through the muted riot of sound. A huge summer moth lit on Jerry's left elbow. He flicked it away and drew in the arm he'd had propped out the window.

He got a better look at the maroon truck this time around and was pretty sure Chrissie was in there with Adam.

In fact, absolutely sure.

But he was wrong, and he found out immediately.

A gray Voyager minivan bounced over the concrete lip of the driveway and rolled to an open parking space about fifty feet from Jerry's. Chrissie got out, waited for a break in cruise traffic, and strode quickly and purposefully toward the restaurant. She was wearing a white tank top, cut-off jeans, and what looked like floppy rubber thongs, the kind with the little strip of rubber that went between the toes. Her brown hair bounced as she walked. The way the jeans were cut so short, it made her tanned legs look incredibly long.

Jerry was one of the few people who could tell the twins apart within seconds rather than minutes. He'd spent plenty of time observing—studying—them. Chrissie walked gracefully but with a slight forward lean and her elbows tucked in farther than Tiffany's.

Jerry had been so sure, even though he hadn't gotten a clear look. But he had no doubt now that it was Tiffany in the truck with Adam.

He watched Chrissie enter the restaurant and join the line at the counter where orders were placed.

Jerry took a deep breath, climbed out of the Chevy, and jogged across the lot toward the restaurant.

He was able to be next in line, right behind Chrissie, standing so close he could smell her perfume or shampoo. Better than that was the faint heat and scent of her perspiration.

She pretended she hadn't seen him, but when it was impossible to ignore him any longer she glanced at him, nodded, and turned away again.

He didn't know what to say, so said simply, "Chrissie."

She turned back to look at him. "Hi, Jerry."

His throat was tight, and he had nothing to say. "Got the minivan, I see," was all that squeaked out.

She didn't bother answering his inane question.

"There's a, uh, dance next Saturday," Jerry managed to say.

Golden legs moved at the bottom of his vision as she shifted her body to look at him. "No, Jerry."

"Why not?" he asked. "Really, why not?"

"Why not what?"

"Why won't you go out with me?"

"I don't want to."

"But—"

"Drop it, Jerry."

"I mean, really?"

Jerry's face was warm. *God! What a conversation!* His throat always constricted and made it difficult to talk to Chrissie.

"You two wanna order?" the middle-aged guy behind the counter asked. He had a puffy face and obviously dyed black hair combed forward in bangs to conceal a receding hairline.

"We're not together," Chrissie said.

She ordered a double hamburger, fries, and a diet Coke, then laid out the bills and exact change on the stainless-steel counter.

"You're number one-ten," the counterman said. He scooped the money from the counter and placed it where it belonged in the cash register.

Chrissie got her receipt and moved well to the side. Jerry followed. They were near a window and far enough away from the order line and tables that they wouldn't be overheard if they kept their voices low.

"I mean, really," Jerry said again.

"We both know you're a sicko, Jerry. A voyeur. That's somebody who watches people while they do it."

A hot coal of embarrassment began to burn in his stomach.

He felt like turning and walking away, but he didn't.

He glared at Chrissie. "You watch what happens to Tiffany and don't do anything to stop it. Then you get your bare ass whipped and like it, and you call *me* a sicko?"

Oh, he could talk to her now. His anger made it possible.

And it felt good.

Chrissie looked astounded. "Like it? You actually think I *like* it? And you obviously like to watch it. That just shows what a sicko you are."

"But you know I'm watching."

"What's that supposed to mean? We always leave the window raised a little so there's air circulation. It'd look funny if we closed it all the way."

"Chrissie—"

"One ten!" proclaimed a voice behind the counter.

Chrissie moved away from Jerry, picked up a white paper sack and plastic-lidded cup from the counter, and stalked from the restaurant.

Jerry stood fuming. The guy behind the counter grinned at him and shrugged, as if to say, "Women."

Jerry burst from the restaurant.

Women!

Women! Women!

By the time he reached his mother's car, Chrissie was already driving the gray minivan from the lot. Its tires squealed as she made a right turn on the county road.

Jerry stood and watched the boxy vehicle speed away.

Fine! Does she think I might follow her?

He lowered himself into the Chevy and started the engine. As he looked up he saw the maroon pickup truck cruise past again. The girl in the cab with Adam was plainly visible this time, and didn't look anything like either Tiffany or Chrissie.

Jerry wondered if he'd been expecting to see one of the twins in the truck with Adam, expecting it to be Chrissie. Was his mind playing tricks? Was he nuts? A sicko, like Chrissie said?

The glowing coal in his gut burst into flame. He almost bent the ignition key starting the car's engine. *Women!* He slammed the shift lever into drive and floored the accelerator, burning rubber as the big car squealed from its parking space. Jerry barely missed hitting a blue and cream Chrysler, gleaming like an Easter egg. Horns blared at him as he turned left on the street bordering the parking lot.

He ran a stop sign, his foot still mashing down on the accelerator. Wind swirled in the car, ruffling his hair and cooling his perspiring face, promising freedom. Speed was an intoxicant. If he could drive fast enough, far enough, he might outrun his troubles.

A lineup of low buildings, then Munger's Hardware and the gas station, flashed past, and he was out of the business area.

The road leveled out before his headlight beams, inviting speed. Jerry accepted the invitation, feeling the car sway as he steered it through a series of gentle curves.

There was a jolt as the right front wheel jumped the pavement and sank into the soft shoulder, causing the steering wheel to spin and almost break Jerry's thumb. He tried to stamp on the brake pedal, but he was bouncing around so much in his seat that he missed it and the car picked up speed.

The right fender scraped a tree with a harsh metallic sound, slowing the car not at all. Jerry's foot found the brake pedal, and he mashed down on it so hard that he pushed himself back into the upholstery. There was a series of hard jolts, and a tire must have gone flat. Jerry could hear rubber beating and flapping around like crazy in the wheel well. The car fishtailed and nosed down sharply as it lost speed. The steering wheel was like a trapped thing trying to slip from his grasp, fighting him as he tried to control it.

Then it stopped fighting.

Everything stopped.

Remained still.

The car's right front was lodged in the ditch running parallel to the street. The engine was dead. Jerry could hear crickets ratcheting nearby.

He got the door open even though it stuck for a few seconds and made a loud metallic *ponk!* Pushing hard on the door, he climbed out into the suddenly motionless world. His thoughts were still speeding, still a jumble. He stood dizzily and was afraid he might fall, so he extended his left arm and his hand found the car's smooth metal roof. He leaned on it, not hard, just enough to steady himself.

Jerry looked back and saw that the tree he'd thought he scraped was actually a metal mailbox on a wooden post. Post and mailbox lay on the grass.

Someone's lawn . . .

It was beginning to sink in to Jerry that he was in real trouble.

The porch light came on at the nearest house. A dog, off in the distance, began a high, insistent barking.

A man with a flashlight came out of the house with the porch light and walked toward Jerry.

In the opposite direction, down the street, a car rounded the corner and came toward the accident scene. Red and blue lights on its roof began to flash.

Jerry felt his heart rise to his throat and expand.

The man with the flashlight was close now. He walked gingerly, as if his feet hurt, and was wearing wrinkled pants,

a baby blue pajama top buttoned crookedly, and blue corduroy slippers. He was old and had a gray buzz cut.

He looked at Jerry and didn't seem mad. In fact, he
seemed to sympathize with Jerry.

"You got somebody you can call?" he asked.

"I guess my mother."

"A boy's best friend," the man said.

"Goddamn you, Jerry!"

The leather belt cut through the air and bit into his bare
buttocks. His mother grunted like an animal with the effort
of swinging her arm. She was so furious she was almost sobbing.

"Goddamn you! You know I need that car for work! Goddamn you!"

The belt whirred through the air again and raised a welt
on the back of his right thigh. He looked back and saw tears
tracking down his mother's face. "What did you think you
were doing? Goddamn you!" Another half grunt, half sob.
He could smell the gin sweet on her breath.

He heard the swish of the belt again.

Jerry gritted his teeth and endured the pain. He tried to
move away from it inside his mind, letting it happen to
someone else. He wished he could be a different Jerry standing way off to the side and observing. It wasn't that his
mother didn't love him. She was angry and had every right
to be, and she'd been drinking.

This was his fault. Whatever punishment he got, he de-
served.

He'd read someplace how somebody who'd been in a
POW camp had learned to survive the beatings administered
by his captors by being able to accept the pain. Almost to
welcome it. Then to like it.

"Goddamn you, Jerry!"

46

New York, the present

The office door opened and closed, admitting a surge of warm air that mixed with the only slightly cooler air provided by the valiantly struggling air conditioner.

"You're late," Quinn said.

Pearl glanced at her watch: 9:22. She didn't bother answering Quinn, but instead walked to her desk and sat down. There was an erectness of posture and a quickness in her step that meant something.

Anger?

Fedderman and Addie Price were at Fedderman's desk, Addie standing and peering over Fedderman's shoulder at his computer screen.

Quinn, seated at his own desk, had already dispatched Vitali and Mishkin to step up their search for both Chrissie Kellers, and they had left in their unmarked car.

Pearl began shuffling through papers on her desk and rearranging items on its surface. She was in one of her moods and obviously wasn't going to say anything. It appeared that something profound had happened.

The office was warm and smelled faintly of cigar smoke (Quinn falling victim to his secret vice). The air conditioner had cycled and was down to a barely audible hum. There was even a lull in the background sound of traffic outside. The silence was becoming so thick it threatened to solidify like concrete.

Fedderman cleared his throat. "Rough night, Pearl?"

Pearl stopped what she was doing and looked over at him as if he'd spoken a foreign language.

"Those look like tea bags under your eyes," Fedderman said, by way of explanation.

Pearl shrugged and ignored Fedderman, returning to her work.

Quinn grew more curious. He stood and walked over to the coffee brewer set up on the corner table. Casually, he poured two mugs of coffee, one for himself and one for Pearl in her initialed mug. He added powdered cream to hers, the way he knew she liked it, and carried both mugs over to her desk. He set hers on a cork *Kiss Me Kate* coaster near her computer keyboard.

He took a sip of his own coffee. It was too damned hot and burned his tongue.

"Something wrong?" he asked Pearl.

She looked up at him and smiled, surprising him.

"Something right." She held out her left hand.

He saw the diamond on her ring finger, but at first didn't comprehend its meaning.

He did know he'd misinterpreted Pearl's silence, and her mood.

Addie Price had walked over from Fedderman's desk and was examining the ring from about five feet away. She was smiling, too.

"You're engaged!" she said.

Pearl beamed and bobbed her head in a yes.

Quinn thought, *Uh-oh!*

Fedderman had stood up and wandered over. "Congratulations, Pearl," he said sincerely.

Pearl thanked him.

Quinn and Addie joined in with their congratulations.

"So that's why you were late this morning," Fedderman said.

Here was a remark that could be taken in different ways, but Pearl let it slide.

"And the lucky man is?" Addie asked, as if she were hosting a quiz show. Everyone there could guess even though they had a hard time believing.

"Yancy Taggart," Pearl said.

There! It was true. Out in the open and everyone would just have to get used to it

Nobody spoke for a moment. Then Quinn said, "Congratulations to Yancy, too."

"When's the wedding?" Addie asked.

Pearl noticed that Addie had changed positions with Fedderman and was now standing near Quinn. "We haven't decided on a date yet. It'll probably be in Las Vegas."

"A gamble," Quinn muttered.

"What?" Pearl asked sharply.

"Nothing," Quinn said. "Talking to myself."

He looked again at her left ring finger and figured the diamond for at least a full carat—if it was real. Who could tell, with a fiancé like Yancy Taggart?

"Very nice ring," he said.

"I think so," Pearl said.

Fedderman offered his hand for Pearl to shake.

Addie moved closer and kissed her on the cheek. "Well, I think it's wonderful!"

"I do, too!" Pearl said.

Quinn sent forth a smile and nodded, but Pearl caught the hurt expression in his eyes and felt a stab of . . . something. Guilt? Sympathy?

Regret?

No, damn it! Not regret!

"While our happy world spins on," Quinn said, "so does Chrissie Keller's and the Carver's."

"Anything I need to know?" asked the latecomer Pearl.

Quinn thought there was plenty, but said, "Sal and Harold are working the Chrissie disappearance. We were going to coordinate witness statements on the Joyce House murder and follow up on anything that doesn't coincide."

"Think Renz would want it done that way?" Pearl asked. She knew the wily commissioner would prefer to have his NYPD minions, Vitali and Mishkin, working the actual murder cases rather than searching for the Chrissie Kellers.

"He's not running the investigation in the field," Quinn said. "I am."

Pearl understood Quinn's thinking. For more than the obvious reasons, he was determined to stay in charge of the investigation. The closer he was to the Carver murders, the more control he'd have over what knowledge flowed to Renz. Knowledge was leverage, and who knew when that might be needed?

"It's all the same case," Quinn said. "Or Renz wouldn't have assigned us Sal and Harold. And Addie."

Pearl decided that Addie, now seated on the corner of Fedderman's desk, was definitely looking at Quinn in a contemplative manner. Putting on quite a leg show, too.

With Pearl engaged, Quinn had become fair game, and he might welcome solace. Addie knew Quinn was hopelessly stuck on Pearl, and he'd feel injured and rejected. She, seemed ready to play the rebound.

Well, it was nothing to Pearl.

So she told herself. Quinn was so obsessive and tunnel-visioned when he was on the hunt, he would never be able to see or defend against the obvious ploys of a woman like Addie operating on the periphery of his attention. Busy stalking his own quarry, he would be easy prey for her.

So go to it, Addie, and good luck. It's all the same to me.

But Pearl couldn't deny the stirring in her heart and mind. The subtle anger and . . . possessiveness?

My God, jealousy?

She told herself she had nothing to be possessive or jealous about. Quinn didn't belong to her in any way. And, more importantly, she didn't belong to him.

Damn it, she didn't!

47

Lilly Branston stood in her Park Avenue apartment that she'd soon be unable to afford and assessed her possibilities.

The apartment was luxurious, near MoMA, in a much-desired area. Lilly had done well selling high-end real estate for the Willman Group until the markets soured. Both the stock market and the real estate market.

New York City real estate prices and demand had held up longer than anyone had a right to expect in a declining market. Then had come the big slide down in the stock market, followed by the financial turmoil and the bailouts.

It got worse as Wall Street came apart and the layoffs started at the brokerage and financial houses. As far as the real estate market went, Wall Street had caught up with Main Street, and Lilly was out of a job.

She soon learned that it wasn't going to be easy getting reconnected. Real estate prices had come back slightly, but most of the agents still active, and the agencies still surviving, were suffering declines in business. People simply weren't moving, or buying, in a drastically down market.

Lilly was still in her thirties and attractive, slimly built with dark brown hair and eyes. Her oval face with its perfect bowed lips and narrow nose looked as if it belonged in a medieval painting. She had, in fact, worked as an artist's model to make extra money during college. While doing so she'd met her husband, the one she'd helped put through law school, and who had then used his skills to gain maximum advantage during their divorce. He was now practicing corporate law in California, married to the woman who'd tutored him in tort law so he could pass the bar. From the divorce on, Lilly had thought of it as "tart" law.

No children from that mess, fortunately.

Lilly had learned her lesson, and out of necessity found that she had a gift for selling real estate. She'd started with residential property in New Jersey, and soon went on to the more lucrative area of luxury condos and co-ops in New York City. She'd helped to make the Willman Group one of the most successful agencies in the city. But her sales and listings had shrunk. Now they'd repaid her by putting her on reduced commission—which in the Willman Group was tantamount to being fired.

Lilly wasn't surprised. She'd learned long ago how the world worked. Sometimes you ate the little fish. Sometimes you *were* the little fish.

After a month of unemployment, Lilly realized she was lonely. Misery really did yearn for company

What she wanted was a man. Someone she could talk to, lean on, rely on. Someone who'd screw her senseless in this senseless world.

Lilly didn't like thinking that way, but circumstances were harsh and she couldn't help it. She weighed her chances. Even though she had time on her hands, she didn't want to spend it in singles bars or popular pickup spots like bookstores or produce departments in grocery stores. She was almost forty and tired of that kind of mindless dance.

Then chance played a hand. When she was reading a glossy *Executive World* magazine in her dentist's waiting room, she noticed something that immediately made sense to her. It was a small ad for a company called CC.com. Reading on, Lilly learned that "CC" stood for *Coffee and*

Conversation, an online matchmaking service. It advertised in select places so that narrowly targeted people could use a special password and meet similar people. Thus philatelists could meet philatelists, ballroom dancers meet ballroom dancers, real estate professionals meet real estate professionals. Lilly saw C and C as an opportunity not simply to meet a man with whom she had something in common, but perhaps the chance to network her way back to a new sales job with actual potential.

The best thing about C and C, according to the ad, was that it guaranteed complete privacy. Its clients contacted each other directly rather than through C and C. That way there was no record, nothing that might embarrass you or jump up and bite you during some future job interview.

The next afternoon, after a job interview she knew was hopeless, Lilly visited the C and C website, registered, and paid a reasonable fee. She screened the profiles of various male hopefuls. She settled on Gerald Lone, a handsome man (or so he'd referred to himself without going into detail) who'd sold commercial real estate for a large agency in the Midwest. For the last three years he'd had his own small agency in the city. According to him, the real estate market in New York still had pockets of profitability, if one knew how to find them. And knew how to sell.

Lilly smiled when she read that. Contacting Gerald Lone might in itself be a moneymaking proposition.

Thinking of it that way made his personal profile seem like one of those thinly veiled advertisements for escort service employees. That was okay with Lilly. The prospect of employment, along with the prospect of sex, made meeting this guy seem all the more desirable. Possible ulterior motives didn't scare her away. If he was trolling for a good salesperson as well as a good time, that might work with Lilly.

Lilly walked over to the full-length mirror in her apartment's tile foyer and tried to observe herself as someone might on their first meeting. She was wearing black three-inch heels that gave her ankles a graceful turn and made her five-foot-six frame seem tall. Her dress was simple and black but obviously expensive. She'd bought it at Saks last year after closing on an uptown condo unit. Her jewelry was silver and modest, a small diamond and opal ring and hoop earrings. No necklace. The skillfully tailored cut of the dress did its own wonders with her neck, making it look even longer and more elegant than it was.

Beautiful swan.

That's what someone would think on first meeting her.

She hoped.

Gerald Lone sat in a booth in the coffee shop of the Worthingham Hotel near Times Square. The Worthingham was old but still fashionable, and its room rates were competitive with those of the older bargain hotels that were still hanging on in the area. Its restaurant, which looked out on throngs of tourists and Times Square characters streaming past, was small and intimate, with wooden booths that had tall backs that ensured privacy.

In front of Gerald was a cup of hot chicory coffee, which from time to time he sipped from as he kept an eye on the restaurant's street door as well as the entrance from the hotel lobby. He had only Lilly's description from her CC.com profile. Like many of the women, and more than a few men, who were C and C clients, Lilly had declined to post a photo of herself online.

Gerald understood. Dating services still carried a slight stigma with some people. And with most clients, as with Gerald, the whole idea was anonymity. With the direct e-mail contact, there would be no C and C record of who'd met whom, nothing to connect one client with another unless someone connected one individual computer with another.

Not likely, since the computer Gerald had used to contact Lilly was in an Internet café and ensured privacy.

It was a good system, he'd decided. One without exposure to personal risk. Like could find, contact, and meet Like.

Or someone pretending to be Like.

Gerald Lone settled back in his chair, sipped, and waited.

And just when he was about to give up and conclude that she wouldn't show, there she was.

It had to be her. The description, including the black dress, was precise.

She was older than he'd expected. Surely closing in on forty. But not at all a disappointment. Confident. Smart. Put together. Long, graceful neck like a swan's. The kind of neck he'd like to—

She spotted him immediately and came toward him, smiling as she drew near. He liked her smile. It was that of a woman up for adventure.

Smiling back, he slid out of the booth and stood up. He was the taller of the two, even though she was wearing high heels.

When they shook hands and looked into each other's eyes, he was sure she would be his next. Everything would work out fine.

She was the one.

48

"We saw her again," Fedderman said, when everyone had reported back to the office. This was the time for the evening summing-up and for setting the strategy for the next day.

Dusk was beginning to envelop the city, and no one had bothered to switch on the overhead fluorescent fixtures as one by one the desk lamps were turned on. The light in the office was less official and revealing in the muted illumination. It had a shadowed yellow cast that created soft side lighting. Maybe it was because of the concealing and flattering lighting that the mood was more relaxed.

"*Her* being our shadow woman?" Quinn asked.

"Right. Pearl and I both saw her just after you left to drive back here. She was standing across the street again, near where she was last time. Had her arms crossed, the way she does. Just then one of those two-piece buses like short trains went past, and when we could see across the street again, she was gone. But she'd been there, watching."

Watching what? Quinn wondered. The three of them, Quinn, Pearl, and Fedderman, had simply stayed in Joyce House's apartment building most of the time, when they weren't visiting witnesses in surrounding buildings to clear up inconsistent statements regarding the time leading up to and including House's murder. Nothing useful had been learned, other than additional confirmation that any two people could see or hear the same things quite differently.

"So did you go after her?" Mishkin asked Fedderman.

"Pearl did, but it wasn't much use. She'd had plenty of time to lose herself in all the traffic and people headed home from work."

"It looked like she was wearing the same gray outfit," Pearl said. "Gray sweats, and a blue baseball cap worn low over her eyes."

"Yankees cap?" Vitali asked.

"Could have been Mets," Pearl said. "They're both blue." She felt like adding that if they knew which team the woman rooted for, they could search the ballpark next time there was a home game. But she knew Vitali wasn't an easy target for sarcasm like Fedderman. The gravelly voiced little bastard would catch on to what Pearl was doing and maybe take offense. Vitali was laid-back, but he could also bite back.

Addie, who'd worked a computer and answered the phones in the office all day, said, "There are lots of blue ball caps floating around that aren't connected to sports teams. Maybe it was even one of those generic caps you buy at sidewalk sales. The kind that come straight from where they're made and haven't been stenciled or embroidered with anything yet. A lot of them are from China."

Pearl thought, *We're really zeroing in on this cap. Stick to profiling, toots.*

Quinn was looking at Pearl, maybe in a cautioning way. Or maybe he was still pissed because of her engagement to Yancy. Pearl hadn't meant to hurt his fragile male ego, and when was the last time *he'd* proposed marriage to her?

"What about the missing Chrissies?" Quinn asked Sal and Harold.

"I'm afraid they're still missing," Harold said. "The phony Chrissie's hotel room was long ago cleaned and has had two guests stay there since her disappearance. Any DNA evidence we gathered wouldn't tell us much, even if there happened to be any after the maids did their spit-and-polish work."

"Our assumed actual Chrissie was never even in New York, for all we know," Sal said. "We checked with her hometown police and sheriff's department. There's nothing on her, no sheet, no friends or neighbors who say anything negative or revealing about her—or about her mother, for that matter."

"What about the father?" Pearl asked.

"Long gone after the divorce. You know how it works. Tiffany's death tore up the family. There was no way it could survive intact. The father was a sales rep for an auto parts company and moved to Detroit."

Detroit, Pearl thought. Where Geraldine Knott was attacked years ago by a man who was probably the Carver. Where Addie Price was also attacked, possibly by the same man, then fought for her accreditation, worked as a profiler, and went on to a career as a local media talking head. A bit of a coincidence.

Pearl filed the information away in the back of her mind.

Quinn stood up behind his desk and stretched, clenching and unclenching his powerful hands as if to make sure they still worked. "We'll do legwork again tomorrow," he said, "and see what, if anything, comes of it. Pearl and Feds can go back to House's neighborhood and haunt it, see if our shadow woman turns up again. Maybe even find out who she is and what she wants."

"It'll probably be in tomorrow's *City Beat* that she was spotted across the street from where Joyce House was murdered, and then disappeared again," Pearl said. She shot a look Addie's way, letting Addie know she was under suspicion, at least as far as Pearl was concerned. Addie had learned Pearl's game and ignored her.

"Maybe I'll call Cindy Sellers and tell her about the latest shadow woman sighting," Quinn said. "It might shake something loose out there. Could be that somebody else in the neighborhood saw our mystery woman and knows who she is."

"Could be," Pearl agreed.

And the killer is going to shoot himself outside 1 Police Plaza and leave a confession.

"So we sleep on it," Quinn said.

Everyone was ready for that. Chairs groaned. Notebooks snapped shut. Desk lamps began winking out, and someone switched on the fluorescents for the last one out the door to switch off.

Quinn stayed behind so he'd be the last to leave. Pearl was next to last. He watched her go out the door without looking back, not bothering to say good night.

She was no doubt irked by his reference to Cindy Sellers. Quinn couldn't understand why. They all knew what kind of journalist Sellers was, and that she had informants in the NYPD. Informants everywhere, in fact.

Quinn watched Pearl walk past outside the window that looked out on West Seventy-ninth Street. In the illumination from headlights and the nearby streetlight, her expression was serious and her dark eyes were trained straight ahead. The breeze blew a lock of raven-black hair across her forehead, and she instantly brushed it aside. Then she was out of sight.

He sat feeling the loss of her presence like a dull ache.

They were in business together, so Pearl would be in his life as long as that lasted. In his life during their working hours, anyway.

For now, he'd settle for that because he had no choice.

But when Pearl became Mrs. Yancy Taggart, would she continue with the agency? Would she feel the same drive she and Quinn felt now?

Or would she no longer need the hunt? Would she no longer share the feeling that at least some of what was wrong with this screwed-up, dangerous, and unfair world had to be set right, and that for some reason accomplishing that was their responsibility?

Would Mrs. Yancy Taggart think that way?

Quinn knew it was possible, even likely, that someday soon Pearl would walk out of his life for good.

On a practical level he should be able to live with that, but he had no idea how.

49

They'd each had two glasses of wine, white and red, with a gourmet dinner at Le French Affaire. Or had Lilly had three? Two glasses of red? She wasn't sure, and it wasn't like her to lose count.

She'd dressed up for this meeting, this date. No simple black outfit for this one. She was wearing her pale blue Aghali silk dress, with a low neckline and a skirt cut on the bias so it showed a lot of leg without seeming too immodest. When she'd tried the dress on, the sales clerk had described her as an asymmetrical dream. Her ivory cultivated pearl necklace set off the dress and her pale and flawless complexion. A touch of Givenchy dabbed between her breasts and here she was. Ready for the jousting of the heart. Ready, as ever, to close the deal. *Watch out, Gerald Lone.*

Gerald, sitting across from her, turned out to be charming, and obviously a skilled jouster himself. He was witty and involved in conversation, with a direct manner of looking at her—*into* her—that caused something inside her to stir in a way she hadn't felt in a long time. He seemed, on this first meeting beyond mere chat and coffee, to be . . . well, a man who was her equal. Lilly had, in her mind, encountered few of those.

They were both players with the same objective, who didn't

waste time or talk. Neither wanted to reveal too much information during the usual blather about finding things in common. Gerald had described his occupation as "helping to put pieces back together in the financial community," but avoided going into detail. Lilly had told him she was in "high-end" Manhattan real estate, but didn't mention that she was at the moment virtually unemployed. She figured a few secrets at the beginning of a relationship didn't matter. Neither of them was searching for a lifetime soul mate.

On the other hand, if things developed as swimmingly as they were going now . . .

Or maybe it was the wine.

Whatever, they were still taking each other's measure, like two characters in a sophisticated play, having a grand time and ad-libbing the scene as they went along. No script for tonight, but the Cole Porter mood should be maintained.

"There's a German Expressionism display at MoMA," Gerald said, over raspberry sorbet.

"Maudlin stuff," Lilly said. "I love it." *Keep him off balance.*

"Didn't you mention that your apartment was near the museum?"

"I did," Lilly said. "Maybe we should take it in. German expressionism can be very erotic." Stealing the play from Gerald. Staying in charge. She was getting a kick out of this verbal exchange with pretentious sharp swords. Two deft fencers.

Gerald smiled and glanced at his watch. It looked like a gold Rolex, but who could tell these days, with all the brand-name knockoffs floating around New York?

"I believe that at this hour the museum is closed," he said.

"It is. I was thinking about in the morning."

"After breakfast at Benentino's?"

"After we screw each other's brains out."

That took him slightly aback. But he recovered nicely, as she knew he would.

"You are a Lilly and not a shrinking violet," he said with a smile.

She nibbled at her sorbet and took a sip of wine, enjoying herself immensely. "My sense is that we're both people of intelligence and experience. People who don't waste time but go in short order to the quick of matters."

His smile became a grin. "That would be my impression of you," he said. "And I admire that. In all honesty, I admire you."

"And I you."

"And not only your mind."

She leaned across the table, letting some cleavage show, and gripped his right hand gently with both of hers. "Do we really want to finish dessert?"

"The wine," he said. "It's too good to waste." He held up the bottle and studied it. "Almost empty. I know what. I'll order a bottle to go, and we can enjoy it at your place."

"Afterward," Lilly said.

He laughed. "Let's drink to that and then leave."

Lilly laughed with him as he poured what was left of the wine into their glasses. She studied him without seeming to do so.

He always has something to say. He should be selling something other than himself, with his gift of gab. Or be a politician. Or lobbyist. He should be in something that requires copious amounts of blarney.

And for all she knew, maybe he was.

"Is that you, Pearl?"

Pearl winced when she heard her mother's voice. That would teach her to rush to the ringing phone and snatch it up as soon as she entered her apartment.

"Me, Mom." She slumped down on the sofa and used each foot to work the shoe off the other.

"What I called for was an awful thing I learned," her mother said in ominous preamble.

Pearl went cold with sudden alarm. "Something happen? You okay, Mom? I mean, your health?"

"My health, never a finely tuned mechanism, is not so good insofar, as the doctors say, the mind affects the body, which it does."

There was something not only in her mother's words but in the tone of her voice. Pearl sensed something wrong that didn't at all concern her mother's physical well-being.

"So what's affected your mind, Mom?"

"My *peace* of mind, you mean, dear. As a mother grows older she forgets more and more, to be sure, yet we grow in motherly wisdom."

"You think you're missing a piece of your mind, Mom?"

"Are you being facetious, dear?"

Pearl wasn't.

"It was the news I heard," her mother said. "News that skewered your mother's troubled heart like a sword."

"We're at war?"

"Worse. Much worse. My only and lovely daughter is, as it came to me, even to me, here where I sit alone—and should I not have been the *first* rather than last to hear?— that she is engaged to the reptile Yancy Taggart."

"Quinn told you," Pearl said, her anger rising.

"Only when I called him to check on your health and well-being, as I do frequently from here in my isolation. He assumed that I'd already been told, being, as I am, your only mother."

"I was going to call you tonight and tell you the news, Mom. I just got home."

"Tell me the tragedy, you mean. You may take it, Pearl— and I offer this with love and even some small hope that the consummation of such a proposed legal and unblessed union will not occur—that I do not approve of the match."

"If you spent some time with Yancy, Mom, took the time

to really get to know him, you would approve. I guarantee it."

"The mongoose approves of the cobra, and in point of fact is fascinated by the cobra, just before the strike."

"I'm not a mongoose, Mom. I've never even seen a mongoose. And Yancy is not a cobra"

"A reptile is a reptile, dear."

"I'd like for you to meet and talk with him before you lock yourself into that conclusion," Pearl said.

"People met and talked with Hitler. Hitler loved to talk. Loved to ensnare people in the webs of his lies. He could fascinate people and make them do anything he wanted for every evil purpose. Sound familiar, dear?"

"Maybe if you talked to Yancy you would fall for him like Mussolini did for Hitler," Pearl said.

"I discern insubordination, dear."

"I'm sorry, Mom. I just want you to give Yancy a chance. He and I would both like your approval. It's important to us both."

"Both? You and your mother? Or you and the reptile?"

"The rep—to me, and to Yancy, it's important."

"Yet you would marry without such approval?"

"Well, yes."

"You were always headstrong and in some ways heart weak, Pearl."

"The wedding will be in Las Vegas, Mom."

"Too far away for your mother to attend, even if, God willing, I am alive at that time and not dead of broken wishes for my only daughter. Wishes that she would come to her senses, and see before her a man like Captain Quinn."

A bitter column of bile rose in Pearl's throat. "He isn't a captain, Mom."

"Nor is he a reptile, dear. And neither is Dr. Milton Kahn."

"Now there we disagree," Pearl said.

"Perhaps if you would stand back from your unfortunate

betrothal and truly analyze the situation, our disagreement would blow away like smoke. An engagement can be a wonderful thing, dear, or it can be a steel trap about to spring shut."

"Mom, Yancy and I—"

"Love *can be* such a trap, Pearl."

"Mom, please reconsider how you feel about this."

"I have considered and reconsidered, Pearl. How I feel, what I see, is a reptile in the marriage bed alongside my daughter. The thing has a reptile's greedy eyes, a reptile's sharp teeth, a reptile's tongue."

Pearl felt herself getting excited. "Sometimes two people, even if one of them is a reptile—"

"My heart is heavy, Pearl."

"So is the phone, Mom. I'm hanging up."

And Pearl did.

A gift, Gerald thought, as they walked from the restaurant, Lilly weaving ever so slightly and leaning on him from time to time, he with a brown paper bag tucked discreetly beneath an arm. She was smiling slightly.

He kept his anticipation—and his thoughts—nicely hidden. *Why not tonight?*

There were times when things were made unexpectedly convenient, and one had merely to make slight adjustments. Maybe luck. Maybe destiny. He believed in both.

He did not believe in spurning a gift from fate.

Seize opportunity when you find it.

He could act on short notice. He could improvise.

He hailed a cab, and they kissed long and passionately in the backseat. His arm snaked around her, and his hand found its way beneath the low and graceful neckline of her dress, found the softness of her breast and the sensitive tender nipple.

By the time they got to her apartment he could convince her of anything.

While she was undressing in the bedroom, he told her he'd get the wine ready for them, put it on ice so it would be cooling while they were doing everything but that. She giggled and agreed and directed him to her high-tech European kitchen.

He glanced around the kitchen. Very nice. White pine cabinets that matched the paneling, brushed aluminum twin ovens, lots of pale green floor tile laid on the diagonal. There were three dark green oval rugs with brown strands woven through them. Throw rugs. Usually the most dangerous thing in the home. Not tonight, though.

Gerald knew he had to remember everything he touched. Everything. He was careful to stay in the center of the room and let his eyes explore.

There was the refrigerator, looking like part of the paneling. He didn't bother opening it, but instead placed the wine bottle, still in its paper sack, on the granite sink counter. Using a decorative dishrag for a makeshift glove, he rummaged around for a few minutes more in Lilly's kitchen before finding what he'd really come for.

The drawer where she kept her knives.

50

Pearl didn't really believe in God, not all the way. But she felt blessed. Lying in her bed with the light out, she contemplated why.

Not everything was going perfectly. The investigation seemed to present more of a riddle every day. Her mother figured to be a bigger pain in the ass even than Pearl had anticipated. And Quinn was taking her engagement to Yancy harder than he might have.

What right had Quinn to feel any remorse or regret? He and Pearl had been good together, but only sometimes. Other times . . . best not to think about those.

It was the sometimes that still bothered her. She turned over violently in bed, fluffed her pillow as if it were a piñata, and clenched her eyes shut. Her feeling of benevolence from above was fast dissipating. A person shouldn't think too much about life.

Pearl had always regarded life as a predicament. Lately, because of Yancy, it had seemed less so. Pearl had decided she could cope. The one sharp stone, the one thing in her new reality that prodded and bothered her, was Quinn. Why wouldn't he grow up? They'd been lovers, and now she was going to be married to someone else. That was the profound and simple fact. She could live with it, and Quinn would have to learn.

Her problem, though she seldom confronted it directly, was that despite her engagement to Yancy, the crashing finality of her relationship with Quinn, wasn't . . . well, final. Somewhere in her heart was an indestructible fondness for Quinn, and, try as she may, she couldn't ignore it.

She was alone in her bed, the one she'd once shared with Quinn. Yancy was in Albany at some kind of meeting or convention about alternative energy sources. Right now he was probably charming people and yammering about wind power, she thought. She smiled into her pillow. Thinking of Yancy—that was the antidote for Quinn. If her mother liked Quinn so well, let *her* marry him.

The thought appalled Pearl, and she rolled over again on her back.

She stared at the ceiling and tried again to feel blessed. Couldn't quite make it.

She didn't like sleeping alone. Never had.

It was something genetic, maybe. Like being human.

The Carver was impressed with this one. Lilly Branston was uncommonly strong. Kneeling on her arms had failed to prevent her from struggling. He'd had to knock her about, then rip some strips off a sheet and use them to bind her. Then, when he'd stuffed her panties into her mouth, she'd attempted to bite him. No quit in Lilly.

Breathing hard from his efforts, he assumed his kneeling position, his knees pressing down on her bound arms. He was safely back within the ritual.

In control.

He held up the thin-bladed boning knife he'd found in her kitchen drawer so she had to look at it. Grinning down at it, he pretended to pluck a hair from his head and slice it with one quick stroke of the blade.

He aimed his grin at her.

She glared up at him without fear. Without curiosity. She knew what was going to happen. She'd been tricked. She'd been had. There was going to be a penalty. As they locked eyes, a subtle glow came into hers. He recognized it easily as hate. Deep down from the depths of hell hate. It amused and excited him.

He moved the knife closer to her face so it was almost blocking her vision, but not quite. He wanted to see her eyes.

He smiled before her hate, and he knew that if she could break free she'd attempt to kill him.

He waved the knife from side to side. "I'm going to explain a few things to you while I'm doing them," he said.

When he deftly removed the first nipple she began to scream. Firmly gagged as she was, the sound could barely be heard in the bedroom, much less outside the condo walls. He adjusted the gag. He didn't want her to inhale any of the rich silk material and choke on it.

He placed the nipple in a small plastic bag, letting her see he was leaving the bag unsealed, and talked to her some more, taking his time, stringing out the enjoyment. There was no hate in her eyes now, only horror.

When he was finished, he was pleased to see that while Lilly had bled profusely, there was little blood on him. He'd been nimble and escaped most of the arterial blood when he'd slit her throat.

He was surprised to notice that he was sweating. Lilly's still body also was coated with perspiration where it wasn't bloody.

Hard work. She'd managed to make it hard work for both of them.

Well, she'd paid the price.

He climbed out of bed and went to the window, parting the drapes he'd closed before beginning Lilly's final ordeal. Then he opened the window as wide as it would go. This was part of his plan. The only facing windows were blocks away. It was highly unlikely that anyone would happen to glance out of one of them and into this particular window. He returned to the bed and stood by Lilly's body, noting as before with satisfaction that the angle of the drapes made it impossible to see the bed from outside.

There was a slight breeze in the room now, which he enjoyed as it played over his damp body. The open window would serve another purpose; he didn't want this one to be discovered too soon, and the stench of putrefaction and feces from the relaxed sphincter wouldn't be noticed right away in the building if some of the odor escaped through the window.

He began the methodical process of wiping away his fingerprints. He'd been careful as always, his mind neatly filing away in his memory everything he'd touched. When that was finished he'd go into the bathroom and use the shower, nude but for a pair of white latex gloves. When that was done he'd place the fresh lily he'd brought with him in his victim's hair. The finishing touch and a riddle for the police.

Then he'd get dressed and be on his way. Into the city. Into the night. Part of the dark.

He had to admire Lilly. She'd never really given up until her last, paper-thin breath. She'd been a fighter.

He bet Pearl would be, too.

51

Addie came bustling in out of the night, surprising Quinn.

She was surprised herself. She hadn't expected to see him sitting behind his desk, bending over paperwork in the narrow island of light from his lamp.

"Go ahead and smoke your cigar," she said, surprising him again.

They were alone in the office. She'd come in to work late, as she often did, and he'd come in to reread and reorganize some of the case files. He'd been contemplating how nice it would be to light up a Cuban cigar and lean back in his desk chair. It would help him think. He hadn't realized that, to Addie, his thoughts were so transparent.

She was smiling as she walked over to her desk. Hers and Fedderman's.

She leaned back with her haunches against the desk and crossed her arms beneath her breasts. The way she stood made her skirt hike up so a lot of leg showed. Quinn had noticed before how small-breasted women sometimes tried to compensate by taking pride in and showing off their legs.

Sexist thought. He mentally slapped his wrist.

"You've been absently feeling your shirt's left breast

pocket," she said, "as if there should be something in there. You've been licking your lips, and your eyes keep going to the drawer where you keep your cigars."

"You notice a lot of detail," he said.

She gave a small shrug, still smiling. "My job."

"So what else have you noticed?"

"That this place is set up more like precinct squad room than an office."

He glanced around and laughed. "I guess that's natural. NYPD blue runs in my blood."

"The past keeps its hold on us," she said. "You're the major partner and run the place, so maybe you should have your own private office."

"I wouldn't like that. I might lose touch."

"You could at least smoke a cigar whenever you wanted one."

"There is that."

"And maybe if you broke more from the past it might help you to accept change."

"You mean quarters, nickels?"

"You know what I mean. Treating a serious problem lightly is one way not to face up to it."

He reached into his desk drawer and drew out a cigar. It was in a brushed aluminum tube that looked like some kind of ammunition. He closed the drawer but didn't yet part the sections of the tube to get to the cigar. He regarded Addie, knowing where the conversation was going.

She didn't seem to mind being regarded. She sat all the way up on the desk now, with the heels of her hands on its flat surface so her arms were propped straight and made her shoulders high and narrow. The skirt had worked even higher. One of her legs was rhythmically pumping so the back of her high-heeled shoe barely struck the desk and made a repetitive soft bumping sound in the quiet office.

"We're talking about Pearl's engagement," he said.

She nodded, giving him that faint little smile that came mostly from her eyes. "That engagement is quite a change for Pearl, and for you."

"Me?"

"Because of the way you obviously feel about Pearl."

"I'll cope," Quinn said.

"It'd be easier with a cigar, I bet."

She sat watching him, waiting, the leg still pumping.

He opened the aluminum tube and removed the cigar. Opened the desk drawer again and got out a cutter to snip off the tip. He didn't have to rummage for matches. There was always a book of them next to where he kept his cigars.

The cutter that he used looked like a miniature guillotine. He worked it and was pleased to see that it was still sharp and efficient.

"Ouch!" Addie said. "What brand are you smoking? Marie Antoinettes?"

"It was a gift," he said, holding the cutter up so she could see it clearly and then returning it to the drawer.

"From Pearl?"

"From another cop who liked cigars but had to quit them."

Quinn held the cigar, but he didn't light it.

"Pearl wouldn't mind," Addie said. She didn't seem surprised by his hesitation.

Quinn smiled. "She might."

"She couldn't. She wouldn't know."

"She might."

"It doesn't make any difference now," Addie said. Her tone was patient, as if she were speaking to a contrary child.

"It—"

"No," Addie said calmly, "that's over. It'd be better all around if you recognized that and accepted it."

The psychologist in her coming out.

Quinn sat looking into her eyes, into her smile. A man might become used to that smile warming his world, might become addicted to it. His gaze slid down to her leg, still tapping out its rhythm, its message, softly, softly on the front panel of the desk.

He clamped the cigar between his teeth and struck the match. Touched flame to the tip of the cigar and got it burning smoothly with a couple of deep draws. He leaned back in his chair and relaxed.

"Satisfied?" she asked.

"Almost. I've learned to settle for that. It has to do with recognizing and accepting change."

"There is no *almost* when it comes to satisfaction." The smile again. So knowing and hinting of secrets. So invitingly erotic.

She stood up suddenly from the desk, tugged her skirt down, and smoothed it over her thighs. There was an air of embarrassment about her now, but it wasn't real. "Sorry. I shouldn't have broached the subject of you and Pearl. I know how it is—old loves, like old habits, die hard."

"Sometimes they take us with them," Quinn said.

She seemed alarmed. "This conversation is becoming morose."

"I was talking about cigars," he said.

"Thank God for that."

"Addie, I would never—"

"I know. I didn't really think you would."

She gathered up some papers and stuffed them into a file folder, straightened and aligned whatever was on the desk top, then bent down and picked up her purse. She stayed bent over a few seconds longer than necessary. Quinn knew he was being worked, and she didn't seem to mind if he knew.

She told him good night and walked to the door. She was obviously aware that he was watching her, but she wasn't putting on any kind of show now. All business.

At the door she turned and said, "Maybe we'll make some progress tomorrow."

"On the case," Quinn said.

"Sure. What else would I mean?"

When she was gone, some of the air seemed to go out of the office with her.

Quinn drew on the cigar and tried to blow a smoke ring. He failed. He tried again, without success.

He watched the formless smoke drift toward the ceiling and thought about Addie thinking he might be contemplating suicide because of Pearl.

He thought about God.

He wished God would pay more attention to New York.

52

"The killer is moving up in the world," Fedderman said.

Vitali had called and woken Quinn a few minutes past midnight with the address of the latest Carver victim, Lilly Branston. It was in a towering condo development on Park Avenue. The building was a pre-war honey, with a four-story granite façade topped by a tan brick and ornate pale stone structure thrust into the night sky. There was the usual cluster of radio cars, unmarkeds, and emergency vehicles outside, parked at crazy angles so it looked as if they'd all arrived at once and a massive collision had been barely averted.

Quinn nodded hello to a uniformed officer he knew, but used his ID to enter the lobby with Fedderman.

Impressive, the lobby. Cooler than the night. Pink-veined beige marble, brown plush carpeting, and polished copper elevator doors.

"A place like this," Fedderman said, "there's gotta be a doorman."

"There is. Sal said he gets off at ten. The doorman claims he saw the victim leave by herself about six. Didn't see her return."

"Maybe she met her killer and brought him back to her place after ten."

"Maybe the killer knew it was safe after ten," Quinn said, "and came calling on his own." He glanced up and around. "Any security cameras covering the entrance?"

"Yeah, but they're live, and nobody was watching the monitors."

Quinn flexed his jaw muscles and nodded.

Mishkin was standing by one of the elevators. His rumpled brown suit appeared too large for him. His eyes were pools of sadness. Even his bushy mustache seemed to droop a little, or maybe it was the mentholated cream caught in it.

"You look tired, Harold," Fedderman said.

"Trying to find some meaning in slaughter wears a person down," Mishkin said. "She's on eighteen." He pressed the elevator's up button. "This one had a lot to live for. Tragic . . ."

It was well past midnight, and they were the only ones in the elevator. No one said anything as it ascended to the murder floor. Rising to hell—it didn't feel right.

As they stepped from the elevator on eighteen, Quinn noticed an open door down the hall. A uniformed cop stood nearby, and bright light from inside the apartment cast faint moving shadows over the carpeted hall outside the door. Just beyond the open door was a small upholstered bench, and alongside it a tall stone urn with brown artificial pampas grass protruding from it.

A man about twenty who would always look about twenty at a glance sat slumped on the bench. He was wearing seriously faded and patched jeans, a fresh-looking untucked white shirt with vertical green stripes, and moccasins without socks. His straight brown hair was a tangle that might or might not have been an effort at style. He was staring at the floor with the intensity of a man watching an ant farm.

"That's Stephen Elsinger," Mishkin said. "He's the kid who called nine-one-one. Saw some of what happened through the victim's window. Trust fund baby, lives over on Lexington."

"That's in the next block," Quinn said.

"Stephen's got a powerful telescope," Mishkin said. "He was in the habit of observing the victim."

"Spying on her."

"Stephen wouldn't put it exactly that way, but yeah. She was masturbation material, is my impression."

Quinn liked the sound of this. "He saw her murdered?"

"Not exactly."

Quinn merely grunted, deciding to be patient while the story of what had happened here unfolded.

When they entered the bedroom and Quinn saw the victim, he knew what Mishkin had meant when he said she'd had a lot to live for. Lilly Branston's address suggested she had plenty of money, and despite the gape-mouthed expression of horror on her face, she must have been beautiful. Quinn thought she was a bit older than the other victims, maybe even in her forties. But it was difficult to judge, with her staring eyes and the rictus of her mouth from which her panties, now crumpled on the pillow beside her head, had been removed by the assistant M.E. The attending examiner wasn't Nift this time, but a middle-aged woman who was tall and storklike yet had innumerable chins. Quinn knew her slightly and thought her name was Norma. She was treating the victim's horribly abused body with a cold precision and professionalism, through which now and then glimmered compassion and respect. So unlike her boss.

Quinn showed her his ID, which had his name on it, rather than the NYPD shield Renz had supplied.

"I'm Norma," the woman said. She had a high, nasal voice. "I know you from the Kraft case some years back."

"Ah, yes. Where's Nift?"

"You miss Dr. Nift?"

Quinn smiled. "Like a bad case of shingles."

"You know him, then," Norma said. "Dr. Nift is home in bed, and he won't meet Ms. Branston till well after sunrise."

"Seniority," Quinn said.

"Being the boss."

"Being a prick," Fedderman said.

Norma glanced at him, but nothing changed in her expression. She seemed a nice, if authoritative, woman and looked as if she should be principal of a school where the girls wore uniforms, instead of poking around a dead body.

Sal Vitali took a few steps into the bedroom. "Where's Pearl?"

"I decided to let her sleep," Quinn said. "Addie, too. That way we won't be bumping into each other like zombies tomorrow morning."

He propped his fists on his hips and looked closely at the victim. She was nude and had been bound with strips of torn sheet. Her nipples had been removed. A glaring X about twelve inches long was carved between her breasts. She'd suffered a terrible ear-to-ear slash, creating what looked like a horrible, greedy mouth straight out of a nightmare.

Then Quinn noticed something that made the nightmare more poignant and terrible.

He pointed to the white flower tucked in her tangled hair just above her left ear. "Was that there when they found her?"

"Yeah," Norma said. " 'Case you're wondering, it's a lily."

"I knew that," Fedderman said.

Norma glanced at him skeptically and continued to pick and probe.

"Our killer likes to pun," Fedderman said.

Norma said, "I don't concern myself with that kinda thing."

"Nift would," Quinn said. "He likes to play detective."

Norma shrugged. "*Play* is the operative word."

There was plenty of spilled blood, but it had the same

controlled look as that of the earlier victims. The killer had been deft and knew how and how much they were going to bleed, and how to avoid the blood as much as possible.

"Do you think the killer might have some kind of medical background, the way he seems able to predict and avoid arterial blood?" Quinn asked Norma.

"Not necessarily," she said. "Some reading, and of course practice, and it would be pretty simple to attain a butcher's skill."

"But he'd get *some* blood on him."

"It would seem inevitable."

"Looks like he washed up in the bathroom when he was done," Sal said. "Crime scene unit's gonna check the basin and shower drains. What they found with all their dusting for prints were mostly glove smudges, and a lot of the apartment looks like it's been wiped."

"They won't find any of the killer's blood or hair in the drain or anywhere else," Fedderman said. "He doesn't leave DNA, probably showers with a cap and maybe has his pubic hair shaved, the way some of these sickos do. And he's careful to be the cutter rather than the cuttee."

"The cuttee's name is confirmed as Lillian Maria Branston," Sal said. "Thirty-eight years old. A real estate agent—high-end stuff, judging by this place. Business cards say she was with the Willman Group."

Quinn had heard of the Willman Group. It was one of the largest and most successful real estate agencies in the city. And, as Vitali had said, it worked the high end of the market. And here they were on Park Avenue. Lilly Branston must have done okay.

"Keep one of her cards, Sal. We can check with the agency tomorrow." He smiled incongruously but warmly and turned his full attention to Norma. "Okay, dear, what've we got so far?"

Norma met his charm offensive with a meaningless smile, as if someone had reminded her of something remotely humorous that had happened years ago. "Body temperature puts the approximate time of death at about an hour ago. Maybe earlier."

"Good Christ," Fedderman said.

Quinn knew what he meant. It was as if they might be able to catch up with the killer if they hurried.

So close . . .

"You'll understand when I tell you how the squeal came in," Sal said.

Quinn might not have heard him. He was staring at the body with his arms crossed. The compression of time between the murder and the discovery of the body gave the impression they'd come close to nailing the killer, but of course it was only an impression. Time wasn't distance, and distance didn't mean much in Manhattan anyway. The sicko might be sitting in some all-night diner a few blocks away now, sipping coffee and basking in recent memories.

"Sexual penetration?" Quinn asked Norma.

"Thanks, but I'm gonna have to refuse," Norma said, deadpan. "As for the victim, there are no signs of sexual penetration. Nothing in the way of bruises. If there was any sort of sex, it was possibly consensual. As for the rest of it . . ." She waved a latex-gloved hand to take in the mutilated corpse.

"Nonconsensual," Quinn said.

"Murder usually is," Norma said.

Quinn didn't mind her short manner. She simply carried a cop's defensive humor in her black bag, along with her other medical supplies.

"We get her to the morgue and we can tell you a lot more," Norma said. "What she had for dinner, drug or alcohol content in her blood, precise cause of death . . . those kinda things. You know, clues."

" 'We' would be Nift?"

"Yeah, these are his cases. Instructions are that everything with these kinds of injuries goes through him."

"Carver victims."

"I would be assuming," Norma said, and began to gather her stainless steel instruments to place them in a sealed container and return them to her medical case. Every move was practiced and very businesslike.

The police photographer, a red-faced guy named Willis, poked his head in the door. He was wearing a wide grin. "Anything else in here I should shoot?" he asked, knowing he was teeing it up for someone.

Norma closed her bag and sighed, but shook her head no.

"I admire your restraint," Quinn said.

"I'm not built so sexy without it," Norma said. "Good night, good morning. Whatever the hell it is."

She left without looking back at any of them.

Quinn said, "Let's go talk to Stephen. See if he knows some jokes, since we're losing Norma."

Everyone other than Lilly Branston filed from the bedroom.

Nobody was smiling. Once again, comedy had not quite fended off horror.

On the way out of the apartment, Quinn told a paramedic eating a sandwich that it was okay now to remove the body.

The paramedic had removed a lot of bodies from a lot of crime and accident scenes, and had somehow found a way beyond tasteless humor to cope. He simply nodded and continued to chew.

53

Seated in a way that made him almost curled up on the hall bench, Stephen Elsinger looked distraught. Up close, he had bad skin and an overactive Adam's apple.

Quinn posed the questions.

"I already—" Stephen began with a weary impatience.

"I know," Quinn said. "But you know how it is. You must watch *Law and Order*."

Stephen smiled. "You kidding? I'm like an addict."

Quinn gave him the beatific smile that was a surprise on such a rough face. More like a priest's smile than a cop's. "I think you'd be more comfortable in your own apartment, Stephen. It's a short walk, is it?"

"A block down and around the corner," Stephen said. He uncoiled his skinny legs and stood up from the bench. His Adam's apple bobbed. These men were making him nervous. No, more than that—they were downright scary. "I got some beer, if you guys—"

"We appreciate the hospitality, Stephen, but we're on duty."

The Italian-looking cop, Vitali, who had already questioned Stephen, and the one who looked like a meek accountant were staring at Stephen in a way that made him uneasy.

The lanky potbellied cop with the bad suit smiled at him and shrugged, as if to say he would have liked a beer.

The big, tough-looking one who was their leader stepped away and made a sweeping motion with his arm. "Lead the way," he said

It took them about ten minutes to walk to Stephen's apartment building, a stark redbrick tower with a moldy green canopy over its entrance. Not the sort of place to have a doorman. The entrance was flanked by identical potted yews that had been trimmed into round balls of leaf. The lobby was so spare as to look like the reception area of some bureaucratic horror from Eastern Europe.

Stephen's nineteenth-floor unit wasn't in a class with the victim's condo, but in this part of town it had to be expensive. The apartment was also, Quinn noted, almost on a level with Lilly Branston's eighteenth-floor apartment. The furniture was utilitarian and mismatched. There was a poster of Albert Einstein next to one of the Three Stooges on the wall behind the sofa. The light had been left on in the kitchen, and an open takeout pizza box was visible on the table.

"We gotta go into the bedroom so I can show you how it was," Stephen said.

They all went into the bedroom behind Stephen. It was dim, and nobody switched on a light. Flimsy drapes were stirring in the breeze where a glass sliding door leading out to a balcony had been left open. There was a faint rancid odor in the air, as if Stephen had left his dirty socks lying about.

Quinn didn't wait for Stephen's invitation to step out onto the balcony.

There was a nice breeze out there, and a telescope, one of the big ones with a smaller finder scope, set on a tripod. It was made for serious study of the stars, only it wasn't elevated to look up at the night sky. It was a few degrees south of horizontal and aimed diagonally at a wall of windows a block away on Park Avenue.

"You an amateur astronomer?" Quinn asked Stephen, who had followed him out onto the balcony. Fedderman, Vitali, and Mishkin came out, too. Quinn hoped the small balcony would support all the weight.

"Yes, sir," Stephen said. "I like the stars. But with the lights in the city, this isn't the best place to view the heavens."

"So you've been viewing the windows in that building in the next block."

"Well . . . yes. People in New York do that all the time, right? I mean, it's not like I'm a peeping Tom or something."

"No, no," Quinn said. "Using a telescope to scan windows is a New York tradition. Take it from us, we see it all the time. Usually, though, the watcher settles on a select few windows. You settled on Lilly Branston's windows, and who could blame you?"

Stephen's Adam's apple worked furiously. "Yeah. Yes, sir. She's—she was beautiful."

"You watched her get undressed?"

"Yes, sir, I did."

"Who could blame you?" Quinn said again. "So describe exactly what you saw earlier tonight."

"She—Ms. Branston—came home around ten-thirty with some guy."

"You see what he looked like?"

"No, sir. I just caught like a glimpse of them, and then for a while I followed their shadows on the closed drapes. I know they were drinking, and I think they kissed. And she . . ."

"What did she do, son?"

"Got at least part way undressed in the living room. I mean, it looked that way."

"Like a shadow box show," Quinn said.

"That's right. Only not as clear. Then they went into the

bedroom, where the drapes were open, and I could see right
in."

"You can see the bed?"

"In a way, yes." He went to the telescope and aligned it
using the finder scope, adjusted focus. "Look. I don't have a
good angle, but I can see the bed in the dresser mirror."

Quinn looked. The window, over a block away, was
brought up as if he were right in front of it. The drapes were
open, and there was the reflection of about half the mattress
where the corpse had lain. The bloodstained sheets had been
taken for evidence, but Quinn could see the red stains on the
mattress.

"I never got a look at the guy because—Ms. Branston—
undressed standing in front of the window."

"She always do that?"

"Like most of the time."

"You think she knew you were watching?"

"Yes, sir. I think she suspected *somebody* might be watching." There went the Adam's apple. "One thing you learn
with a telescope is that women—a lot of them—like to show
off."

"So you watched her undress and get into bed."

"Yes, sir. Usually she slept wearing a kind of skimpy
nightgown. But tonight she didn't put on anything. She just
went over and stretched out on the bed, right on top of the
covers. She put her hands behind her head and was smiling.
I never saw her smile like that before."

"Like she was posing for somebody?"

"Yes, sir, like that. But not for me. More like for the guy
in her room."

"Then what happened?"

"I saw the guy come over to the window, just his arms
and hands, and he closed the drapes."

"You saw his arms. Did you get any idea of what he was
wearing? A shirt, a suit coat?"

"I got the impression he wasn't wearing anything, like Ms. Branston wasn't." Stephen moved back and leaned against the balcony's iron railing. Fedderman stood close to him. You never knew what people were going to do, and it was a long drop to the sidewalk. "It all went so fast," Stephen said. "It was impossible to make out exactly what was happening."

"Did you continue to watch?"

"No, sir. After the guy closed the drapes, there was nothing to see. Then after about an hour, I went back to take another look. And the drapes were open again. The window was open, too, like the guy was trying to air out the room." Sal looked over at Quinn without expression.

"The window hadn't been opened before?" Quinn asked.

"No, sir. I'm sure it wasn't. Is that important?"

"Who knows?" Quinn said, thinking the killer might not have wanted the body found right away, might have wanted fresh air in the room so the neighbors wouldn't smell the stench of putrefaction or feces so soon. If so, he'd gotten crossed up. He'd lost a measure of control.

Stephen swallowed several times and continued. "Ms. Branston was still in bed. But something didn't look right, even from this distance. Her face was like . . . distorted. And I thought she was wearing something red that didn't look right, either. So I really worked at focusing in, and"— Adam's apple time again—"I saw she wasn't wearing something red, that what I was looking at was blood. And her throat . . ." Stephen's voice became hoarse and cracked. He looked as if he might start to cry.

Quinn could understand why. With the powerful telescope, it must have been as if Stephen was right there in the room with the corpse.

"There, there, son," Quinn said, and gently patted his shoulder.

"That was when I called nine-one-one," Stephen said in a choked voice. Quinn could *hear* his Adam's apple working.

"Of course you did," Quinn said.

"When I saw the police cars start to arrive, I left here and walked over there, to where she lived. The police asked me who I was, if I was the one who'd called nine-one-one. When I told them I was, they sat me on a bench. That's where I stayed till Detective Vitali came and got my statement. Then you guys came and got me."

"A rough experience," Quinn said. "You did the right thing."

"You really think so, sir?"

"Of course. Say, Stephen, you ever take any photographs through that telescope of yours?"

"No, sir. Why would I do such a thing?"

"I don't know. I just wondered." Quinn smiled. "That's what I do a lot of in my job, Stephen. I wonder."

"I guess you do," Stephen said.

He agreed to come into the precinct house the next morning and sign a statement. Vitali and Mishkin would conduct the interview, and of course furnish transcripts to Quinn and company. It occurred to Quinn that this hybrid investigation was something like the government being in banking. Not always as efficient as it might be. But still in business.

54

It was raining lightly from a starless night sky when they stepped outside Stephen Elsinger's apartment building. The wet sidewalks shot back reflected light, and the street lamps were low stars in the mist. Sal and Mishkin had a city car. Quinn felt moisture cool on the back of his neck as he and Fedderman moved toward Quinn's Lincoln.

Then Quinn realized there was another reason for the chill he felt. Across the street stood the shadow woman in her usual hip-shot fashion, with her elbows out and her hands propped at her waist. She was in a doorway but up close to the sidewalk, and seemed surprised she'd been noticed. Her body gave a slight jerk, and she turned calmly and started to walk, then run.

All four detectives had seen her, and all realized that by the time they got into a car and got it started, she'd be long gone where a vehicle couldn't follow.

They all began running after her, starting slowly, as she had started, in for the long haul. If this was to be an endurance contest, the law would win it.

She was running downtown on Park, about a hundred yards ahead of them, and they were keeping pace. Everyone on the side of the law was already breathing hard, and this appeared to be a fairly young woman they were pursuing.

Quinn heard a leather sole slip on wet concrete, and someone—maybe Vitali—curse. The odds were slim that any of
them would be able to catch her. Quinn heard Mishkin use
his two-way to ask for help from any radio car in the vicinity.
He was difficult to understand between rasping breaths.

Male ego. Quinn wondered if that was what had caused
them to begin this pursuit with such high hopes. Cops and
ex-cops, no longer young. Flatfeet. For all they knew, the
woman ahead of them was an Olympic contender.

There was only sparse traffic at this late hour, and no one
driving past paid much attention to the footrace that was
going on along Park Avenue. Now and then the participants
encountered a pedestrian, usually carrying an umbrella, who
stood staring in surprise and curiosity as they plodded past,
rooster tails of rain at their heels.

Quinn knew that if the woman managed to flag down a
cab, and climb in with enough time and bullshit, she'd soon
be out of reach. Bunch of middle-aged creeps chasing her,
maybe drunk. Damsel in distress. The cabbie would buy into
whatever tale she told him and spirit her blocks away in no
time.

She crossed half of the street diagonally and was running
now alongside the grass median, staying on pavement where
the footing was better. Maybe hoping to be noticed easier by
a cab.

Quinn felt his legs weakening, and the familiar throbbing
pain in the one that had taken the bullet and was now supposedly healed. His ribs were beginning to ache. Mishkin
pulled even with him, as if they were competing with each
other, elbows pumping rhythmically as pistons. His droopy
wet mustache and the look of determination on his usually
mild features made Quinn think of a western gunslinger
headed for a showdown.

A showdown, Quinn thought. *That's what we need.* But he
knew the four of them were fading.

Posse of old bastards . . .

Then he heard a grunt, not so much of pain as of determination, and Fedderman was pulling away, his lanky, mismatched frame suddenly and amazingly graceful at high speed.

Quinn watched with astonishment, forgetting for a moment how difficult it was for him simply to keep running.

Fedderman was loping like a wolf, gaining on the woman, who glanced back in surprise and ran harder.

Fedderman ran harder, too. He was inspired.

Go, Feds!

Damn it! Here came a cab, its service light glowing. The shadow woman was waving an arm desperately as she ran, trading a little speed if she could just catch the cabby's attention.

Quinn watched the cab cross two lanes of traffic and head toward her.

Gonna lose her again!

Gonna lose her!

A siren yodeled, and a radio car turned the corner, roof bar lights flashing in the mist.

The shadow woman saw the police car and changed direction, trying to cross the grass median. She stumbled and fell to her hands and knees. Got up. Ran back out into the street, but away from the police car.

Toward the cab.

Damn it! She was going to make it.

Don't let her get in!

Don't—

She was suddenly on her hands and knees again, staring up at the fast-approaching cab. Its brake lights flared, and its wheels locked. The pavement was too wet for the tires to screech. They made a loud scraping sound, like fingernails clawing over cardboard, as the vehicle slid toward the immobile woman.

Its front bumper struck her hard enough to toss her body forward into an awkward cartwheel. She landed almost completely on the grass median, but not quite. Her head struck the curb, and she lay motionless with arms and legs splayed.

The driver was out of the cab and kneeling alongside her within seconds. He crossed himself, stood up, and moved hunched over onto the grass and vomited.

Fedderman was next on the scene, sliding to a stop and standing with his long arms dangling at his sides, gulping air and staring down at the woman's face.

Quinn ran faster as he got closer, even though pain sliced through his legs and burned like molten lead in his lungs. In his heart. All his attention was concentrated on the woman sprawled at the edge of the median.

Who are you?
Who are you?

PART
IV

Stars in the purple dusk above the rooftops
Pale in a saffron mist and seem to die,
And I myself on a swiftly tilting planet
Stand before a glass and tie my tie.

—CONRAD AIKEN, "Morning Song"

PART IV

55

Quinn joined the group huddled around the woman lying partly on the grassy median of Park Avenue and partly in the street. She wasn't moving, and there was a lot of blood puddled along with rainwater around her head.

Quinn stood in the cool mist and found himself looking down at the face of the woman who'd impersonated Chrissie Keller, the client who'd hired him in the first place and set all the pieces in motion. The woman who wasn't Chrissie Keller. Not according to Chrissie's mother, anyway.

Fedderman was kneeling next to her, feeling for a pulse.

He found one.

"Not dead," he said, sounding somewhat surprised. Her bloody head injury suggested something serious enough to be fatal. But then head injuries tended to bleed a lot.

"Could have fooled me," a uniformed cop from the patrol car said.

Quinn had to agree. The woman was pale, her eyes closed, with no apparent movement beneath the lids. Her features were peaceful and composed, and there seemed already to be about her the waxlike stillness of the dead.

"We got a call in for EMS?" Quinn asked.

"They're on the way," Mishkin said.

Fedderman peeled off his wrinkled suit coat and laid it

over the woman, as if, since he'd been the one to run her to ground, he was responsible for her. Quinn understood. It could be that way sometimes, and logic had nothing to do with it.

Sirens were closing in, and an ambulance preceded by two more radio cars turned the wide corner onto Park Avenue. They put on quite a light show.

While Fedderman was straightening up from spreading his coat, Quinn noticed something lying in the street, pinned partly beneath the woman's right thigh, as if it might have fallen from a pocket or had been tucked beneath her sweatshirt. He pointed, and Fedderman dipped low on shaky knees and pulled the object free. It was a small, zippered purse with a faded beaded design on it.

They backed away from the body and let the paramedics take over, two husky guys with incredibly gentle hands, charged with getting the injured woman to a hospital.

Fedderman handed the purse to Quinn, who unzipped it and examined its contents. There was a wadded tissue (as there seemed to be in every woman's purse he'd ever examined), comb, lipstick, pen, notepad, cell phone, and worn leather wallet.

Quinn searched through the wallet. Sixty-four dollars in bills. Credit cards in the name of Lisa Bolt. A Blue Cross card. Various other forms of identification, including an Ohio driver's license, all in the same name. And there was a dog-eared business card that surprised Quinn.

Stuffing everything back in the wallet, then the wallet back in the purse, Quinn handed the bundle to Fedderman, along with his car key.

"Our shadow woman and mystery client is one Lisa Bolt," he said, "a private detective from Columbus, Ohio. Take the purse and stay with her at the hospital, Feds. Use my car. I'll ride with Sal and Harold and catch up with you there later."

The paramedics were unfolding a gurney with practiced

efficiency and would soon have the woman in the ambulance.

One of them had a roll of thick blankets tucked under his arm. *Better than a body bag*, Fedderman thought. He recovered his damp suit coat. Holding it and the purse well away from him in one hand, he began trotting back toward the parked Lincoln.

Over his shoulder he yelled back at Quinn, "You better call Pearl."

It was as much a warning as a suggestion.

While he watched Lisa Bolt being loaded into the ambulance, Quinn called Pearl on his cell. She wouldn't like being woken at 2:10 in the morning. She'd like it even less if he *didn't* wake her.

He remembered her saying Yancy Taggart was on a lobbying junket or some such and she'd be at her apartment.

Pearl's home number was familiar enough to Quinn that he didn't bother with speed dial. He pecked it out rapidly without even having to glance at his phone's keypad.

Pearl ran true to form. She didn't at all like it when the chirping of the phone near her bed dragged her up from uneasy dreams. She pulled the damned, noisy thing to where she could grasp the receiver, fitted cool plastic to her ear, and emitted a sound something like a growl.

"Pearl?"

Quinn's voice. She squinted at the luminous numerals on her clock. Said, "Who the hell did you think?"

"Sounded like something fighting for food," Quinn said.

"Fighting for sleep," she said. Then in a clearer, deliberately more alert voice, knowing something important must have happened or was happening: "So why'd you call me as if I were somewhere in Europe where it'd be much later but still too early to call if it wasn't damned important?"

"I didn't follow that," Quinn said. "How about if you tell

me your Social Security number so I know you're wide enough awake to understand what I'm saying?"

Pearl expended considerable effort and sat up in bed. *The old Social Security number thing.* It went back to their early days together. She knew Quinn would keep picking at her until he was sure she was all the way awake before he unloaded on her.

She said, "Forget my Social. Get to the goddamned point."

Quinn did, filling her in on the Lilly Branston murder and the Lisa Bolt development.

"Why the hell didn't you call me?" Pearl said when he was finished.

"I just did call you."

"I mean earlier."

"It's two-fifteen a.m., Pearl. There is no earlier."

"You know what I mean."

"I wanted at least one detective tomorrow who was more than half awake. Then things developed fast, and I didn't have time. Get dressed. I'll find out what hospital Lisa Bolt's gonna be in and call you back on your cell so we can meet up there."

"If she's our shadow woman, make sure somebody keeps a close watch on her so she doesn't disappear again."

"If she disappears this time," Quinn said, "it'll be where nobody can follow. See you soon, Pearl. And, oh yeah, call Addie Price and alert her to what's going on."

"Yeah," Pearl said, "I'll be sure and do that."

She hung up the phone and then climbed out of bed and stumbled through darkness toward where she knew the door to the hall and the bathroom was located.

The geography of the night escaped her. She missed the door by several inches and stubbed her big toe so painfully she thought she might pass out. She stood still for a few minutes on one foot, propping herself dizzily on the door frame and holding the throbbing toe, uttering a string of ob-

scenities that would certainly have earned the shock and dis-
approval of her mother.

The pain brought her all the way awake, and she got
smart and flipped a light switch.

Owww!

There was her world in an abrupt illuminated clarity so
brilliant that it hurt.

Squinting and blinder than before she'd flipped the wall
switch, she limped on toward the bathroom, hoping not to
stub the toe a second time. That would be unbearable. If that
happened again . . .

What?

She made it all the way into the shower and stood beneath
the miracle of the water.

56

It was almost three o'clock when Pearl got to Roosevelt Hospital at Tenth Avenue and West Fifty-ninth Street. She joined Quinn and Fedderman in a nicely furnished waiting room handy to Critical Care. On the opposite side of the long room sat two large black men with their heads in their hands. One of them appeared to be silently sobbing.

Quinn was standing holding a paper cup of coffee. Fedderman had a cup, too, and was slouched almost horizontally in a gray upholstered chair with wooden arms. On a TV mounted to a metal arm above Fedderman, a guy in jeans and a black T-shirt was silently leaping around, holding himself and making faces as if he'd just been injured in the testicles. There were occasional close-ups of people in the audience laughing hysterically. The Comedy Channel. Oh, yeah. Pearl noticed that a damp heap of material on the floor appeared to be Fedderman's suit coat. It had blood on it.

"You two look like you've had a hell of a night," Pearl said.

Quinn said, "You call Addie?"

"Damn it! I forgot."

He glanced at his watch. "Too late now. Let her sleep."

Let her sleep all damned day, Pearl thought. She said, "So what's the latest on this Lisa Bolt, private eye?"

"Condition critical but stabilized. Internal injuries, fractured skull. She's in a coma."

"Anything in her possessions that provides a way to contact family?"

"Nothing," Fedderman said. "She was traveling light. If she has family, she probably didn't want them getting mixed up in whatever it was she was doing." He sounded down, so weary he might doze off any second. But more than that, Pearl thought. He sounded depressed.

"Doctors say how long the coma's gonna last?" Pearl asked. *Lisa Bolt's coma, not yours.*

Fedderman used the tips of his forefingers to massage the corners of his eyes. "Not only can't they say, they're not even sure she'll ever regain consciousness."

"But they know we need to talk to her if she does regain consciousness," Quinn said to Pearl. "That's why you're here."

"Let me guess."

"That's right. Feds and I are calling it a day—a night. Somebody'll relieve you later this morning. Then if you want, take the morning off and catch up on your sleep. If Lisa Bolt does regain consciousness, call me immediately."

"Any news?" a voice asked.

Addie Price walked into the waiting room. She was wearing tight jeans and a soft cotton blue sleeveless sweater with a neck so wide it had slipped down over a shoulder, making one of her bra straps visible. Her thick blond hair was mussed but looked styled rather than slept on.

No bed head for this cutesy, Pearl thought.

"How'd you know we were here?" Fedderman asked.

"Mishkin phoned and let me know. Probably Renz told him to. You get that coffee out of a machine?"

"Down the hall," Quinn said, and motioned with his head. He looked over at Pearl. "Now you've got company. You can fill in Addie; then the two of you can sit watch in case Lisa

Bolt comes around and talks. It'd be better if two people heard whatever it is she might say."

Pearl glared at him. *Fill in Addie and make her job of spying for Renz easier.*

Fedderman raised himself in weary sections from his chair, scooping up his wrinkled mess of a suit coat as he stood.

"We'll talk tomorrow," Quinn said.

He and Fedderman trudged from the waiting room. Fedderman was too weary even to throw a parting verbal jab at Pearl.

Addie said, "Those two look like train wreck survivors."

"No," Pearl said, "not the survivors."

"I'll go get some coffee," Addie said. "Then you can let me know what's going on. You want some?"

"Why not? We have to stay awake. At least one of us does."

While Addie was gone, a young nurse came in and picked up an empty glass coffeepot that Pearl hadn't noticed on a table over in a corner by the two black guys who were still silently fretting. She smiled brightly at Pearl as she flounced out with the empty pot, leaving a full one behind on the burner. It was probably better coffee than what Addie was getting out of the machine.

She and Addie could discuss that.

Pearl thought it was time that the two of them discussed a number of things.

Addie settled with her coffee into a leather chair and curled her long legs beneath her. Pearl was glad to notice that she had rather large feet.

Pearl was sitting nearby in a corner of a sofa, feeling tired but edgy. Now and then a hushed bell tone would sound and someone—usually a doctor—would be summoned to one part of the hospital or another. The occasional nurse or custodian would pass nearby in the hall. The two despondent black men had conferred with a doctor in scrubs and then left. Pearl and Addie were pretty much alone.

Pearl was wondering how to broach the subject of Addie's obvious flirting with Quinn when Addie spoke up.

"Congratulations again on your engagement," Addie said. "Yancy Taggart must be an interesting man."

"To be engaged to me, you mean?" Pearl asked.

Addie smiled. "Well, yes, that is what I mean. I don't imagine that you give of yourself very easily, Pearl, or to just anyone."

"Just anyone?"

"I didn't mean that how it might have sounded, or how you might have interpreted it." Addie sipped her coffee carefully, knowing by the almost untouchable cup that it was still almost too hot to drink. "I don't imagine that you end a relationship easily."

"No," Pearl admitted, "I don't."

"There isn't any reason for you to worry," Addie said.

"Worry?"

"About Quinn. You're worried that I might hurt him."

Pearl held her hot cup with both hands and looked at Addie over the rim. "My, my, you *are* a psychologist."

"It's obvious that you're still fond of Quinn. Not to the point that you won't marry someone else, but he's a good man and you know it and don't want to cause him pain. Or for me to cause him pain." Addie sipped, less cautiously. "The instant he learned you were engaged he became jealous, and on a certain level, you had second thoughts. That's only natural, for both of you. Now you're afraid I might be taking advantage of Quinn, amusing myself by getting him on the rebound."

"I'll admit to all of that," Pearl said. "So what?"

"So I want us to be honest with each other."

"That would start with you being honest with me," Pearl said.

"Okay. I'm extremely ambitious, Pearl. Maybe more ambitious than anyone you ever met. I'm drawn to Quinn, but that isn't going to stop me from using him to advance my career. I'm using him. I freely admit that to you and to no one else. I'm leading him on, but I don't intend to let him get too close."

"Why not?"

"I don't want him hurt badly when I drop him. He'll feel despondent and betrayed, but not for long. He'll realize I was just a conniving bitch. He'll tell himself that his thinking I was doing anything other than stringing him along should be a lesson learned. He'll be right. Within a few weeks after I'm gone, he won't even give me much thought."

"Meanwhile you're going to continue teasing him. There was a term for women like you when I was growing up."

"Prick teaser?"

"That's it," Pearl said.

"That's what I am," Addie said. "I use the elusive promise of sex to manipulate men."

"But you never come across."

"There would go the elusive promise," Addie said. "You're a big girl. You understand manipulating men, using them as stepping-stones to get ahead in life. You're not above that kind of thing yourself."

"True enough, though I can't say I'm always successful."

"Nobody's perfect."

"Thus our professions," Pearl said.

"Quinn's a big boy. He'll understand just as you do, after he has a little while to think about it. I know you're fond of him, and I'm telling you not to worry so much about him. He might get bumped when I drop him, but he won't be bruised."

"What about you?"

"Me? I don't bruise easily."

"I didn't mean that. Women like you, it's your inaccessibility that attracts. And once you deliver, that's gone. So you're afraid to deliver. You continue to tease because you're insecure."

Addie nodded thoughtfully. "Oh, on a certain level, that's true. But we know it and are used to that particular rough road. Having the ability to tease our way through life is our compensation for our insecurity."

"Hell of a realization."

"It's a realization that comes to most women, in one form or another. If we too freely lend ourselves, we might not maintain our value."

"We're not Swiss francs," Pearl said.

"Aren't we?"

"Let's not think about the answer to that," Pearl said.

"However Quinn views us—me—I can promise you he won't be badly hurt when our relationship ends."

"When it isn't consummated," Pearl said.

"I can promise you that, too."

"Insofar as anyone can promise such a thing."

"Insofar," Addie agreed. She took a long sip of coffee and smiled. "I'm glad we had this talk, Pearl. It clears things up between us."

"Yes," Pearl said.

"You're an honest woman and I'm not."

"Just so we've got that straight," Pearl said.

57

They were in the office at ten the next morning, Quinn, Pearl, Fedderman, and Erin Keller. Addie was still at the hospital, where she'd volunteered to wait for a plainclothes detective and a uniform who'd been assigned to guard Lisa Bolt. Lisa hadn't yet regained consciousness. Vitali and Mishkin were in the field, working the Lilly Branston case.

The air conditioner, already under assault by what was fast becoming a record heat wave, was making an underlying hammering sound as it hummed away. Indoors, condensation had appeared as a thin trail of rusty water trickling down the wall beneath the ancient unit. Nobody mentioned either the hammering sound or the stain on the wall. They didn't want to jinx the thing.

"That's her, all right," Erin said, looking at the photo on Lisa Bolt's Ohio driver's license. "Same woman as in the photograph you showed me earlier."

Quinn didn't doubt that it was, but he wanted Erin's official corroboration. He was building his case. Sooner or later, this mess was going be in court. He hoped.

"Are you sure you've never seen this woman before?" he asked Erin.

"She's a total stranger."

"And Chrissie never even mentioned her name?"

"Never."

"If you do remember anything—"

"I know," Erin interrupted. "I'll call you right away."

She left, probably to seek someplace cooler.

The door opened, and Addie came in. She was wearing the same clothes as last night. Except for what might be the slightest sign of bags beneath her eyes, she looked fresh and wide awake. Pearl knew that *she*, on the other hand, looked a premature sixty years old.

Everyone said hello or nodded good morning to Addie, and she smiled and returned their greetings. "Bolt is still out of it," she said, "but the doctors sound more optimistic."

She assured Quinn that Lisa was safely under guard, and then wandered over toward the coffee machine. She shot a sideways glance at Pearl with a slight smile. Co-conspirators, after baring their souls and ambitions last night. Members of the new sisterhood.

Pearl thought, *Screw that.*

When Addie had her coffee, she came back and sat on the edge of Fedderman's desk. Though her coffee mug had her initials on it, she still hadn't gotten a desk of her own. She didn't seem to mind. Not having a permanent workstation gave her the opportunity to flit around as she pleased.

"There's something I've been turning over in my mind," she said.

Quinn said, "Turn it toward us."

"When Lisa Bolt does come around and start to talk," Addie said, "I wouldn't expect too much. Whatever her reason for impersonating Chrissie Keller, she might not *know* it's an impersonation."

"Say what?" Fedderman said. He was seated behind his desk but had rolled his chair to the side so he had a three-quarter view of Addie.

Addie crossed her long legs. *Always with the legs,* thought Pearl, watching Fedderman's involuntary gaze shift to the roundness of Addie's derriere on his desk.

Got 'em comin' an' goin', girl.

"We all know about the amazing synchronism of twins," Addie said. "How sometimes they think or act almost as one person. If Lisa Bolt's impersonation of Chrissie is some kind of mental aberration, she might actually consider herself to *be* Chrissie—or the dead twin's counterpart."

"A third twin," Fedderman said.

"Mathematically impossible, but it captures the idea. We might have something like triplets on our hands."

"That sounds insane," Pearl said.

"Oh, it is," Addie said. "We also have a mother fixation here, demonstrated by the removal of the victims' nipples. The carved letter *X,* as if the victim is being negated out of existence and perhaps even memory. Not only that, if we have personality transfer, Lisa might do anything to maintain her delusion. If she thinks she really *is* the late Tiffany Keller's sibling, she might attempt to kill her mother, the one person who knows she's neither twin."

"Beyond insane," Pearl said. She didn't like it when investigations started straying into the occult. This world alone was hard enough to figure out.

"Maybe not," Quinn said. "Most of us here in this room have seen stranger things."

Pearl looked at Addie. "You must have done a lot of thinking in that waiting room."

"I'm sure we both did," Addie said.

"It's not a hypothesis we should work on yet," Quinn said. "It all depends on what Lisa Bolt has to say when she gains consciousness."

"If," Fedderman said.

The door swung open again, letting out more cool air to be devoured by the hot morning. Letting in Vitali and Mishkin. Both of them looked awake enough after their hard night. Mishkin nodded. His brown suit was pressed. His white shirt looked fresh and was neatly tucked into beltless pants held up by suspenders over his surprisingly flat stomach. Even his brushy mustache looked trimmer than usual.

Sal appeared rumpled but presentable. He winked at Fedderman. "Who'd have guessed you could outrun a gazelle?"

"State runner-up as a high school miler," Fedderman said.

"Long time ago, high school," Mishkin said.

"It comes back now and then," Fedderman said. "I even get the occasional pimple and want to do Mary Lou Minowski in the backseat."

"*You* knew Mary Lou too?" Sal said.

"Enough of this testosterone talk," Pearl said. "It's wearing."

Vitali walked over to where Quinn was seated and laid something that looked like a flattened lipstick on Quinn's desk.

"This is what?" Quinn asked.

"A flash drive, or memory stick," Vitali said. "The killer took Branston's notebook computer with him, but he overlooked this. It was down behind the cushion on the victim's desk chair."

"You plug it into a USB port on a computer," Pearl said, "and you can copy files to it. It's like a disk drive only smaller and without moving parts. Some of them have tons of memory."

Quinn brightened. "You mean Lilly Branston might have been backing up her computer with this thing?"

"Probably not automatically," Pearl said. "Flash drives are used more for storage than for systematic backup."

"An actual clue," Quinn said.

"The killer's first mistake," Fedderman said.

"Maybe," Addie said.

"Gimme," Pearl said.

Pearl worked at her desk with the flash drive until almost three o'clock, not even taking time for a proper lunch. She'd used a plastic fork to eat a takeout salad while exploring the world of Lilly Branston's deceptively tiny memory stick.

At first she'd been disappointed. Much of the little device's capacity was unused. What was there were mostly condo and co-op units listed with the Willman Group, sometimes entire residential buildings. The Willman Group's website was set up so a prospective buyer could take a virtual tour of the property, showing even the views out the windows. Pearl thought that if she was in the market for a million-dollar-plus apartment, she'd be in heaven—if she had a million dollars plus.

This wasn't heaven. She was a detective and would probably never see a million dollars that wasn't stolen.

Her spirits lifted when she opened a file titled "C and C." She soon learned the letters stood for Coffee and Conversation, and it was a matchmaking site for professionals and people with arcane interests, seeking companionship with people of the same ilk.

Not unusual in New York, where minutes moved faster than sixty seconds, and people didn't have time for the usual rituals of cultivating friends and lovers. The city had figured a faster way that suited its occupants.

C and C had a feature that distressed Pearl but must have had great appeal to its clients. Joiners posted their personal profile (photo optional) and ways to contact them—usually their e-mail addresses. There was no way for anyone else, including C and C itself, to track who had contacted whom. Clients made person-to-person contact without involving the company, which apparently made its money from advertising. Privacy was assured.

Pearl knew that the odds were good that Lilly had met her killer through C and C, but how to find him was a different matter.

She must have used screen grabs to transfer profiles to the flash drive. Lilly's e-mail history had disappeared with her computer. Her online service might have a record of it, but obtaining that was legally tricky. And there was always the possibility that she'd contacted another C and C client by phone. Maybe a public phone. Or maybe, as some of the C and C profiles suggested, anyone interested in the client could meet him or her at a certain place and time. And there was always the possibility that computers in Internet cafés were used to make initial contact. Those computers used the café's online service, ensuring anonymity in case extramarital lovers or pornographic sites were visited.

Pearl scrolled through the hundreds of "Male Seeking Female" C and C profiles. Who of these hopefuls might have interested Lilly Branston? Several were in sales, as she was. There were quite a few in real estate. There were CEOs, entrepreneurs, lobbyists, artists, scientists, inheritors of wealth, educators, Broadway producers, sports figures, government bureaucrats. No cops or private investigators.

Nothing here for Pearl. Too much here for Lilly. Quite probably Pearl had just seen the real or assumed name of the Carver. Perhaps even seen his photograph. But there was no way to single him out.

Or maybe there was. Maybe in the hands of a real expert belonging to the right generation, a computer might be able to narrow the search and hit pay dirt. The NYPD had such tech-nerd wizards.

Pearl decided to check with Quinn first. If he agreed, they could turn the matter over to Renz and his NYPD. Renz could make himself useful. Take credit for the idea. And at some point return the favor.

Pearl smiled. *Thinking like Addie now. Men as stepping-stones.*

Addie. Pearl thought it might behoove her, and maybe Quinn, to dig deeper into Addie's past.

The information after the attempt on Addie's life in Detroit was easy enough to find, and to verify. If her attacker hadn't broken off the assault, she surely would have been killed. Then, in truly heroic fashion, she'd come back from the brutality of the attack and earned her doctorate and become a criminologist.

There was plenty of press on her, and much of it generated by Addie. She'd become a relentless self-promoter and made herself into a local talking head on TV whenever crime was the subject.

Once Addie had almost lost her life and become truly focused, there'd been no stopping her.

It was Addie Price *before* the attempt on her life that interested Pearl.

There was no information on her before that date.

Nothing.

Pearl had a pretty good idea why.

58

Pearl showed Quinn the C and C documents on Lilly Branston's flash drive. After Pearl copied them onto her computer, Quinn took the flash drive with him and left to deliver it to Renz for expert analysis in narrowing the considerable list of suspects.

Alone again, Pearl called Addie on her cell and suggested they have dinner at a small Afghani restaurant on Amsterdam, not far from the office.

Eastern Starr was the name of the place. It was long and narrow, and there was a vaguely astrological feel to the décor. One long wall was all dark blue tapestries with quarter moons and backlit constellations. The scent of spices wafting from the kitchen was dominated by something unfamiliar and pungent that made eyes water at the same time it stimulated appetites.

"Meat and yogurt," Addie said, when their entries had arrived and she'd taken a taste. "I never dreamed they could be so good together."

"Just about everything here is good," Pearl told her. "Yancy introduced me to this place. He's a regular here."

"Ah, Yancy."

Pearl forked in a bite of her samboosak, watching how Addie obviously appreciated her food, which was made up of seasoned beef and noodles tossed in yogurt. She took a sip of Afghani wine, also surprisingly good, judging by the look on Addie's face.

"We here for another sisterly talk?" Addie asked, putting down her wine glass but not releasing its stem.

"Sort of," Pearl said. "I did some deeper research on you."

Addie seemed only remotely interested. "And?"

"Until you signed up for classes six years ago at the Metcalf Valley College of Criminology, there was no you."

Pearl had to give Addie credit. She saw the surprise in her eyes, then the quick calculation. There was no point in denials.

"I did find an Adelaide Price," Pearl said, "but she died thirty years ago of rheumatic fever. She was only five years old."

Addie pushed her food away and took a long sip of wine. "There's something you need to understand, and I don't know if that's possible unless you're me. After I was almost killed, I was afraid every minute I was awake, and I was afraid in my sleep—what sleep I managed to get."

"You mean Geraldine Knott was afraid," Pearl said.

"That's true," Addie said. "I am—was—Geraldine Knott. When I became something of a celebrity as well as a victim, the fear suddenly became worse. It wasn't idle fear. I even received threatening letters."

"I can understand your fear," Pearl said. "But the odds of being attacked by a serial killer twice are pretty slim."

"Oh, it can happen, though in my case it didn't. In order to be safe and anonymous again, I began using the name Addie Price. I did a search through death records and found someone who was born around the same time I was and died young. I appropriated her identity, even her early childhood. I became Addie Price."

"But why the fictitious second attack?"

"I realized that in becoming Addie Price, I'd also given

up the advantages of celebrity. So when it suited my purpose, I reclaimed them. I concocted a different, fictitious attack so I could draw on my experience as Geraldine Knott for professional purposes. Some of the details were the same. The man who tried to kill me was never caught. He wore a mask, so even if I came face-to-face with him again, I wouldn't know it."

"And this new identity helped you professionally?"

"Immensely. But I also created it for personal reasons. It sounds crazy, but being Addie Price empowered me so I could look at Geraldine's experience objectively, so I could deal with it. The new name, the new me, helped. You can't imagine how much it helped. I remain Addie Price."

Pearl continued to eat, but slower and with less enthusiasm. "So the story of Addie Price being attacked is just that—a story to help establish your bona fides as an expert with special, personal knowledge."

"Exactly," Addie said. "Based on the genuine Geraldine Knott attack for authenticity."

Pearl sipped her wine. She seemed to have had this all figured out before sitting down at the table with Addie.

"What are you going to do with your information?" Addie asked.

"Tell Quinn. Let him tell Fedderman. It doesn't have to go any further."

Addie let out a long breath and took another sip of wine. "I can live with that. And I mean it literally."

"Do you think it's possible that the man who tried to kill you was the Carver?" Pearl asked.

"It's possible but hard to say. He broke off the attack before he had a chance to . . . well, you know."

"That's why you're here in New York," Pearl said. "Why you politicked so hard for the job. That part of it's personal, too."

Addie toyed with her wineglass, using the crystal stem to rotate it in short but smooth intervals that did nothing to disturb the wine. "Yes, it's intensely personal, even though I'm not totally sure whoever attacked me was the Carver. I'm not his usual type, not part of his psycho scenario." She met Pearl's gaze and held it. "In fact, *you are*, Pearl, and that's something to consider."

"I've considered it," Pearl said.

There was a hitch in Addie's voice when she said, "There's enough of a chance it was the Carver who tried to kill me that I can't leave it alone."

Pearl smiled and shrugged. "Obsessive pursuit fits right in with our organization."

Addie cautiously tried another bite of her beef and yogurt dish. "I noticed."

"You mean Quinn," Pearl said.

"No," Addie said, "not just Quinn."

"So Addie's really Geraldine Knott," Quinn said to Pearl, the next morning in the office. He was gazing off to his right, the way he did when he was distracted and thinking. He'd been sitting that way almost from the moment Pearl had begun telling him what she'd learned about Addie Price.

The air conditioner was still making its hammering noise, but not nearly as loudly as yesterday. The day hadn't heated up yet. Pearl had made coffee. Its fresh-roasted scent permeated the office.

"We shouldn't be surprised," Quinn said. "She's a sort of show-business figure in Detroit. Celebrities more often than not change their names."

"You're a kind of celebrity in New York," Pearl said, "and you haven't changed yours."

"I've thought about it, though," Quinn said. "I'm trying to choose between Mike Sledge and Sherlock Spade."

"After the last couple of nights," Pearl said, "I might settle on Nancy Droop."

Quinn winked at her. "Not hardly, Pearl. Hey, what about Feds?"

"Oh, he's definitely Inspector Clu—"

"So," Fedderman said, standing just inside the door. "Caught you talking about *moi*."

"We were talking about Addie Price," Quinn said in a businesslike tone. "It's information that doesn't go past you."

"I'm a deep well of secrets," Fedderman said, sitting down behind his desk and fitting his fingers together tightly, as if preparing to show some kid the church and all the people.

"Aren't we all," Pearl said, not smiling.

Five minutes later, when Fedderman had heard about the Geraldine Knott–Addie Price identity switch, he shook his head. "Poor woman. She musta gone around scared shitless all the time. Maybe she still does, even with her new identity."

"That's why we keep her secret limited to us," Quinn said.

"And maybe the Carver," Pearl said.

Fedderman stared at his laced fingers and thought about it. "Addie's not his type." He looked up at Pearl in a way she didn't like.

"I know," she said, "I've looked in the mirror and seen photos of all the Carver's victims. I'm the sicko's type."

"You and a million other New York women," Quinn said.

"More than a million," Fedderman said.

"Those are comforting odds," Pearl said, but she didn't mean it.

59

Ohio, 1997

Miriam Grantland wished the wipers sweeping the windshield of her Ford Taurus would swipe away her tears along with the rain.

When she'd gotten the phone call, she left immediately. She was halfway to Cleveland and had sobbed through most of her journey.

Her thoughts nagged her like restless demons.

Why had Jerry been born? What had gone wrong? What had *she* done wrong?

Maybe nothing, considering the circumstances.

Maybe everything.

Damned trucks! An eighteen-wheeler swished past the Taurus doing over eighty miles per hour, trailing a deluge of rainwater that temporarily blinded Miriam so that she was driving sightless through the night and into the glare of oncoming headlights.

The truck became an object of her fury. She leaned forward to peer out the windshield, honked the horn, flashed her highlights. The Taurus's engine strained, and the steering wheel began to shimmy in Miriam's sweating palms. Inch by inch, she recaptured the highway lost to the truck, and on a gentle curve she passed it.

Her rage was unabated.

She glanced at the speedometer. Eighty-five. She held her speed, watching the headlights of the semi fall farther and farther back. There were only a few cars ahead of her on the dark, rain-swept highway.

On the straightaway now, she eased up slightly on the accelerator until the shuddering in the steering wheel and the car's front end went away. The sheet metal on the hood stopped vibrating. Eighty-two miles per hour. That was as fast as she dared to go without risking mechanical trouble. Any sort of delay was out of the question. Miriam set the cruise control. She needed to get to Cleveland, do what she had to do, and then get back home.

She thought about Jerry and all the problems he'd caused. It had to be him. Something was very wrong with him. His behavior wasn't normal. That was a fact she had to face.

He'd been born almost a month prematurely and weighed only slightly more than four pounds. Had that caused the problem? Maybe. Had it been her fault? Hardly.

Jerry's father? The bastard hadn't been around long enough to have much of an effect one way or the other. But then, who knew for sure about such things? And at a certain point, what did it matter? So maybe it had been Jerry's father. The past was impossible to change. Like it or not, we all lived in the present.

Miriam had nothing against gay people; that was obvious. It was an old friend in Cleveland who'd phoned her, a woman named Grace who'd for years lived with her lesbian partner she'd met in college. No big deal. Other people's sex lives were none of Miriam's business. It was nobody's concern what people did behind closed doors, in the privacy of their homes or in businesses that catered to such clientele. Miriam didn't doubt that eventually, even in Ohio, people of the same sex would be able to legally marry. That was fine with her. Times were changing, and Miriam could change with them.

But *Jerry*! Her own son.

She'd suspected something was wrong, known how he used to sneak out of the house at night and spy on the twins next door. Miriam never talked to Jerry about that. It was heterosexual and possibly not so unusual behavior for a boy his age. So he peeked, probably mostly out of curiosity. If the little teases didn't lower their shades that was their problem. Besides, Miriam had her own problems, and they were crushing and repetitious. Work, drink, sleepless nights, loneliness. Now and then a relationship that meant nothing other than sex and went nowhere beyond the bed. Work, drink, sleepless nights, loneliness. Over and over. Like a damned treadmill that would wear her down and someday leave her useless and hopeless. That was her life. It was difficult enough without Jerry coming up with ways to make it worse.

Of course he had come up with ways, but this was something she hadn't considered. And she was trying now to consider it only in a detached way. The time for recriminations and philosophizing was past.

Right now, she had to *act*.

The dark highway seemed to roll out before her forever. Talk radio matched her mood and kept her company. There was trouble everywhere. A man claimed the government was using silent black helicopters to spy on people. Code was spray painted on the backs of road signs to guide armies that moved by night. A secret global triad was running things, and was scheduled to reveal itself at the turn of the century—only three years away!

Miriam switched stations and encountered more talk radio.

By the time she reached the Cleveland suburbs, a formation of asteroids was speeding toward earth and would collide with the planet. They would arrive at the turn of the century. It was ordained. There seemed no way they could miss. Maybe that horrific event was what would cause the global triad to reveal itself.

Miriam got out the directions she'd scribbled on a blank envelope back in Holifield and followed them carefully through neighborhoods that were increasingly poor and more dangerous.

At last she reached the downtown street she sought, blocks of mostly brick commercial buildings, some of them boarded up with graffiti-marred plywood.

Ahead, blurred by the mist, was the red neon sign: EVERY LITTLE THING.

The rain and wet streets reflected the flickering red sign as well as streetlights that gave off an eerie orange glow. Through the sweep of the car's wipers, Miriam saw that several people were standing outside the club, beneath a fringed brown awning over its entrance. Some of them held glasses or bottles. Some of them were women.

Miriam slowed the car, veered it toward the curb, and parked. She would have to steel herself and go into this horrid place. She would have to come out with Jerry in tow and get him back to Holifield and make it clear to him that he was to stay away from . . . people like her friend Grace.

Maybe Grace was still inside the club, or whatever it was. She'd been there when she'd called Miriam.

Where Miriam had parked was about a hundred feet from the knot of people beneath the canopy. She left the engine running and the headlights and wipers on, watching the people she'd have to walk past to get inside. Even with the car's windows closed she could hear their loud voices, sometimes their laughter. They were milling around restlessly, as if they didn't want trouble but wouldn't mind it. One of the women, who looked overdressed for such a place, almost fell, and a man caught her and helped to steady her. He kissed her ear, and she grinned and grabbed his arm. Another woman, in a black cocktail dress like one Miriam owned, separated herself from the others and began shouting something unintelligible and lifting a beer bottle as if in a toast. She had long blond hair and a lineup of bracelets on each bare arm. Apparently she was drunk, because she was having difficulty keeping her balance in her black spike high heels.

She took a swig of beer, sashayed into the orange glow of the nearest streetlight, and noticed the parked Taurus.

Miriam switched off the headlights.

The blond woman hadn't moved. She took another long, slow pull on the beer bottle and then walked closer with a slight forward lean, as if to see who was sitting behind the steering wheel.

The glance, the meeting of gazes even through the rain-distorted windshield, was enough to force Miriam back into the car's seat, to gasp at what she saw.

Her dress,

Her bracelets.

Her son!

She opened the door and climbed out of the car without thinking, barely aware of the movements of her body. The gentle rain was cool on her face.

Jerry had turned around and was staggering back toward the club's entrance on his high heels, toward his friends, who were staring at him with puzzled and amused expressions.

"Jerry!" Miriam heard her voice call.

He tried to walk faster and stumbled, almost fell.

"Jerry! Goddamn you!" Miriam began to run. She knew what she was doing now, had her wits about her, and she was furious. That her own son should do this to her was unthinkable. It couldn't be happening. Couldn't be true. Yet there was the proof right in front of her, in a blond wig and high heels. Her heart was like an engine pumping rage through her blood.

She caught up with Jerry right outside the door, beneath the brown canopy. The people who were clustered there—

some of them women, others up close obviously *not* women—
moved back in stunned silence.

Miriam grabbed the back of her cocktail dress and ripped
it as she yanked Jerry back. He tottered on the high heels
and fell. Lying on the wet sidewalk, he stared up at Miriam
with made-up eyes, lipsticked mouth. His blond wig had
slipped sideways and appeared about to fall off. His mascara
was running.

Miriam spat at him, then kicked him hard in the side.

Jerry scrambled to his feet, wearing only one shoe.
Miriam shoved him hard toward the car. He opened his
mouth to complain, and she shoved him again.

"Mom—"

"Fucking pervert!" She struck at him with her fists.
Pushed! Hit! Pushed! Hit! Moving him toward the car.
Pushed! Hit! The other shoe had fallen off, and he held his
hands over his head and the blond wig, his body bent so low
to avoid the blows that he was almost duckwalking.

Miriam opened the passenger-side door and shoved him
inside the car. He shut the door himself. Anything to stop the
rain of blows her clenched fists and tired arms continued to
launch with the force of her disgust and desperation.

After stomping around to the driver's side of the car,
Miriam screamed at the people near the club entrance.
"Fucking perverts!" It was all she could think of to shout.
The objects of her insult merely stared at her, as if there were
something wrong with *her*. A few of them laughed.

The car's engine had died, and it took three tries to get it
started. Finally Miriam crammed the shift lever into drive
and spun the tires on the wet pavement.

As the Taurus sped past the club entrance, Miriam saw almost all laughing faces now. One of the women shouted at
her and raised her skirt high with both hands. She, or he, was
wearing nothing underneath but black net pantyhose. Miriam
had pantyhose like it at home in her dresser drawer. She

glanced over at Jerry's drawn-up legs. They were clad in black net pantyhose.

"Why?" Jerry's mother asked him, driving automatically and retracing her route out of town. "For God's sake, *why?*"

Jerry didn't answer.

"Your father," she said. "Where was your goddamned father? This is *his* fault!"

Neither Jerry nor his mother exchanged another word all the way back to Holifield.

They managed to get inside the house without anyone seeing them. Miriam hoped. There were some nosy people in this neighborhood. People who peeked through windows.

Miriam made Jerry remove his—most of them *her*—clothes, and then climb onto his bed on his hands and knees. He was so embarrassed, so demolished by what had happened, that he couldn't offer even token resistance. He was a little boy again.

She got a thick leather belt that had been her husband's from the closet and whipped Jerry's buttocks and the backs of his thighs until she was exhausted. Neither of them said anything while this was transpiring. Jerry did not so much as whimper.

Afterward Jerry's mother sat in front of the TV in the living room and began to drink gin. Before her on the television screen was an old black-and-white movie, Humphrey Bogart kissing Ingrid Bergman. Jerry's mother seemed more interested in her bottle.

Jerry waited until she was sleeping soundly on the sofa before he packed a suitcase and crept from the house.

He didn't leave a note.

He never returned to Holifield.

60

Norton Nyler was the computer nerd from the NYPD. He'd brought his laptop to the office on West Seventy-ninth to demonstrate the program he'd developed to narrow the list of C and C clients who might have met with Lilly Branston and then killed her.

He was a short, chubby guy in his twenties, with a scraggly little mustache and an errant lock of dark hair that made him look like an obese actor portraying young Adolf Hitler.

"I'll download all this to your computers when I'm done demonstrating it," he said. His voice was surprisingly screechy. Quinn and his detectives gathered round and exchanged uneasy glances. Pearl was the only one of them who possessed better than basic computer skills. Of course, she wasn't in the same league as young Hitler.

"You do have your computers networked, don't you?" Nyler asked.

Quinn shrugged. "I, uh—"

"We don't think so," Pearl said.

Nyler looked at her strangely, then must have seen something in her eyes and looked away. "No matter. I can check after I'm done here and we can deal with it." He grinned hugely, and Hitler disappeared. "Whatever issues you might have, we can deal with them."

Quinn wondered if anyone had problems anymore instead of issues.

With what looked like a surgeon's pale fingers, Nyler worked his laptop's cursor and keyboard, and up popped thumbnail shots of about twenty male C and C clients. "I used certain protocols to zero in on the clients most likely to get in touch with the victim; then I further honed the list by pinpointing those clients the victim herself might have initially contacted in hopes of a prospective romance."

Pearl thought, *You little old matchmaker.*

"To hone the list even more, we factored in geography," Nyler said. "Then came the hard part. It was tedious and time consuming, but we obtained most of the remaining clients' addresses. Sometimes we had to rely on Homeland Security; sometimes the names and addresses were simply in the phone book."

"You should have been a detective," Fedderman said.

Nyler glanced over at him. "I am."

My God, Pearl thought, *the new breed.*

Nyler brushed back his *fuehrer* lock of dark hair from his forehead and got back to business. "I overlaid a city map marked with the addresses and sites where the murders occurred." He right-clicked his computer's mouse, and a detailed map of Manhattan came on screen. The image grew larger as he zoomed in to Midtown and South Manhattan.

"There are seven suspect C and C clients living in near juxtaposition to the murder sites," he said. The cursor danced and blinked over one flagged address after another, and information, names, and addresses of seven men came on the screen.

"Are you saying one of these men is probably the Carver?" Quinn asked.

"No. I'm saying that of the C and C clients on the final

list, the circumstances of personality, compatibility with the victim, appearance, age, and geography make these men the most logical for you to contact first."

"Does it make sense that they'd kill close to home?" Pearl asked.

"Close, no. But it also doesn't make sense that they'd kill farther from home than necessary. Everyone, even serial killers, tends to fall into patterns. Even a cautious killer will leave their house or apartment and turn either right or left most often, take a subway or cab or bus or not. Eat and shop at some of the same places. If they're driving, they'll avoid certain one-way or narrow streets, heavy traffic, or predictable long-term construction delays. In short, we all unconsciously choose the easiest route to wherever we're going. We seldom *unnecessarily* go out of our way, even while going somewhere to commit murder." He looked at each of his listeners in turn. "Remember, we're only discussing probabilities here."

"Possibilities," Pearl said.

"Okay," Nyler said. Again the un-Hitler smile that made him look like a mischievous child. Had the real Hitler smiled like that? "Odds," he said.

"We don't even know for sure it was a C and C client who killed Branston," Quinn said.

"Well, it's an imperfect world," Nyler said. "And difficult to predict. I'm just trying to chart you the easiest possible way to get where you want to be."

"Like the killer choosing a victim," Fedderman said.

"Or the victim moving toward her killer. Starting at any of those seven addresses, and the victim's address, my computerized victim and killer should think and act somewhat in conjunction, whether they know it or not."

"And you came to this conclusion by starting at the crime scenes and working backward," Pearl said.

"Er, not exactly. But yes, that's pretty much how it works."

"That's how we work," Quinn said.

"There you go," Nyler said.

"Whaddya think?" Pearl asked when Nyler had gone.

"I think it's mostly bullshit," Quinn said, "but we oughta go to those seven addresses and talk to those seven guys."

"Funny if they turn out to be seven brothers looking for brides," Fedderman said. "Or three feet tall, like in *Snow White*. Hey, maybe I'll get Dopey."

"I get him all the time," Pearl said.

Quinn gave her his warning look.

"If they have something else in common," Pearl said, "it'll give me more confidence in Nyler and his computer program." She gave Quinn a look to let him know she was dubious about this turn in the case. "It seems to me this is a good job for Vitali and Mishkin."

"No," Quinn said, "I'd rather have them looking for the real Chrissie Keller. Besides, you're the closest thing we've got to Snow White."

61

Pearl drew a guy named Fred Levin who lived on Fifth Avenue near the park. It was an impressive address. Everything in the lobby was drastically oversized, as if to make smaller and intimidate anyone who happened in uninvited. She showed the six-foot-plus doorman one of the badges given out by Renz, and he called up and explained to Levin that she was a detective.

Levin told the doorman to send Pearl up, and after signing in to the building she rode the big elevator to the big seventeenth floor.

The hall was carpeted in rich brown that felt a foot thick under Pearl's feet. The apartment doors were cream colored and gilded, with gleaming curled brass handles rather than knobs. One of the doors down the hall was open, and a medium-height, slender, dark-haired guy was standing just outside it smiling at Pearl. He was wearing tight designer jeans and a white golf shirt with a turned-up collar. From this distance, he appeared quite handsome.

Fred Levin wasn't a disappointment close up. He had chiseled features with full lips for a man, and a head of wavy black hair. His dark eyes took in Pearl with obvious interest. She saw that he was wearing leather deck shoes without socks. He was thirty-five, according to Pearl's information, but he might have passed for twenty-five. Pearl thought *smoldering* would describe him pretty well. Maybe there was something to this C and C operation.

She introduced herself, and they shook hands.

"You're a detective?" he asked, as she approached. "Like on *Law and Order*?"

"Uh-huh. Just like."

Levin stepped aside so she could enter, then closed the door and motioned for her to sit on a light tan leather sofa. There were matching chairs and a low coffee table the size of a small airport. Works of modern art hung on the walls. They were mostly prints, but a few were definitely oils, and something about them suggested they'd been carefully chosen.

Pearl sat. "Nice apartment."

"I hired a decorator," Levin said. "A few years ago, when things were going well."

"Things aren't going well now?" Pearl asked.

Levin shrugged. "You know, Wall Street. I worked for Lehman Brothers, and then a smaller firm after Lehman went under. Five months ago the smaller firm went under."

"So you're unemployed?"

He smiled. "'Fraid so. But the smaller firm ran hedge funds and I walked away with scads of money, so unemployment doesn't stop me from offering you something to drink."

"These hedge funds were legal?"

"Barely. Coffee? Something stronger?"

"Water would be good," Pearl said.

She watched him walk into the kitchen. So slender and athletic. On a tall bookcase near a window was what looked like a skiing trophy.

"You ski competitively?" she asked, when he returned with a tumbler of water with crushed ice in it.

"Used to," Levin said. "Downhill slalom. Till I tore up one of my knees a few years ago."

"That's too bad." Pearl sipped her ice water. She remained on the sofa. Levin remained standing. "Do you recognize this woman?" she asked, and stretched out an arm to hand him a photograph of Lilly Branston.

She watched his handsome face as he studied the photo. If he did recognize Branston, there was no sign of it.

He handed the photo back to Pearl. "She looks vaguely familiar, but I don't think I know her."

"Her name's Lilly Branston."

He looked a little less blank.

"She's the Carver's latest murder victim."

He looked genuinely surprised and then smacked his forehead with the heel of his hand. "Jesus! Yes. Of course. I think I might have seen that photo—or one like it. There's a bulletin board in the subway stop. It's got her name and photo on it. Said something about her being missing, I thought."

"No," Pearl said, "must be another woman on the subway wall. Lilly Branston isn't missing. We know right where she is—in the morgue."

Levin made an ineffective pass at looking appropriately grieved, and then he appeared puzzled.

"What?" he asked. "I should care more than I do?"

"I don't know how much you care."

"Not much, tell you the truth. Of course I feel sorry for the victim, but I don't get overemotional about that kind of thing. I mean, about a woman I never met. Is there some connection with me? Did she live around here?"

"Not far away." Pearl placed her water glass on a cork coaster, part of a stack placed for convenience on the coffee table. The table was oak and gave the impression that it might be antique and expensive. "Have you ever used the services of an Internet matchmaking company called Coffee and Conversation?"

She watched the changes in his eyes. He was thinking furiously. Wondering how he might possibly be involved. Or wondering how to lie so he'd seem uninvolved.

"*That* Lilly Branston!" he said.

"The dead one," Pearl said.

"She was next on a list of women I was going to get in touch with." Levin began to pace, three steps this way, three back, swiveling neatly on the plush carpet. The leather soles of his deck shoes looked as if they'd never been outside. "I didn't mean to lie to you. It came to me gradually who she is. Was. Lately I've looked at a lot of photos of a lot of women."

"So you've met a number of women through Coffee and Conversation."

"No, only two. I'm very selective. I've been divorced for three years. I've learned to be careful about my relationships. Maybe too careful." He made a sweeping motion with an arm to take in the vast, well-furnished living room. "As you can see, I'm what you'd call more than reasonably wealthy."

"You're concerned that women might be after your money instead of you?"

"Yes. But only insofar as they might turn out to be a waste of my time. Fact is, I wouldn't want a woman who didn't at least take my wealth into consideration. I like very smart, very aggressive women. When I saw that Lilly Branston was a real estate agent with the Willman Group, I knew she had to be both those things." Levin tried a smile. "Have you ever noticed how aggressive female real estate agents are?"

"Like female cops," Pearl said.

He gave her a speculative up-and-down look. "I do read the papers. It's interesting that a cop who's the serial killer's type—and quite beautiful, I will add—is searching for the monster. Kind of like the baitfish seeking the shark."

"We won't go to that part of the ocean," Pearl said. "We were talking about your search for a soul mate."

"Yes. Anyway, what I liked about Coffee and Conversation was that, if things didn't work out after your first meeting, there were no loose ends. I mean, nobody had anybody's address or phone number. Maybe not even their real name. They had only rudimentary information, and maybe the photo that was on the C and C website, and that was it. Nobody was going to . . ."

"Stalk you?"

"Not so much that. More cling to me. I've found women to be clingy."

"You're not short on ego."

"No, I am not. But I do attract women on the hunt. That's why the C and C concept appealed to me. You contact C and C, and if the other party is willing, they set up a time and date for coffee and a get-acquainted meeting. You are literally strangers when you meet. If either of you so chooses, you can keep it that way."

"Did your meetings with the first two women on your list go any further than caffeine and conversation?"

"No. I think I was way too aggressive for them."

"You didn't mention their names."

He gave Pearl two names that she jotted in her notepad. She would check later and make sure they were C and C clients.

Pearl placed her notepad and pencil in her lap. "When you say you were 'too aggressive,' do you mean sexually? In your sexual practices?"

Levin stopped pacing and appeared genuinely shocked. "No, no, nothing like that. What I mean is that I don't apologize for wanting to make even more money, for wanting even more prestige and power. More of everything. It's part of Darwinism, part of being human. Too many people don't accept that. You'd be surprised how many women out there want to turn the world green, or spray paint people wearing fur coats, or eat nothing but arugula lettuce and beans—and all to the exclusion of everything else." He looked sincerely at Pearl. "Detective, I don't give a flying flip if the world is two degrees hotter in twenty years or if the ocean rises six inches. I want to be the guy who gets rich building dikes."

Pearl looked at him. *Hoo, boy!*

"So you were what . . . too honest for those women?"

He laughed. "You might call it that. I don't want to get involved with any woman under false pretenses. Best to get our beliefs and ambitions out there in the beginning. Do I want to be fantastically wealthy and take over the world? Be the king of everything? Sure, if the opportunity presents itself."

"Are you legally sane?" Pearl asked.

At first she thought he was going to get mad, but he simply laughed again. "We both know I can't answer that one, so why did you ask it?"

"You, uh, remind me of someone." She picked up her notebook again and glanced at what she'd jotted down. "Did you meet either or these women night before last?"

"Sure did." He gave Pearl the woman's name, which she underlined. "We spent three hours learning about each other in the Weekly Grind coffee shop, and then we had a late supper and strolled around the city for a while. Till well past midnight, actually."

"Sounds romantic. You must have hit it off at least somewhat."

"I thought so. Three lattes' worth, anyway. She even gave me her phone number, but when I called yesterday she said she'd thought about it and didn't want to carry the relationship any further. It was because I'd kicked at a stray cat while we were walking. The thing might have had rabies, for all we knew. She confessed she was a member of PETA. I told her I liked animals and would join PETA myself, but it didn't impress her."

"Maybe for some reason she thought you were being insincere."

"But I *do* like animals. Enough, anyway."

"Maybe it was the caffeine talking. Do you still have her phone number?"

"I think so, sure." He walked to where a phone sat on a table near the foyer and flipped the top page of a stack of yellow Post-its. He read a phone number to Pearl. "You can call and check. She'll verify what I assume is my alibi."

"I will," Pearl said, writing down the number

"That's when Lilly Branston was killed, wasn't it? When I was with my C and C friend?"

"That's the time frame," Pearl said. "By the way, did you lie about not recognizing Lilly Branston when I showed you her photo?"

"No, no! The photo really didn't ring a bell. Then I did mistake her for some woman whose photo is in the subway stops. But when I heard you say her name, it all came into focus."

She asked him about his whereabouts at the times of the other Carver murders. He couldn't remember where he was during most of them, but he was out of town at a shareholders' meeting at the time of Joyce House's murder. Witnesses and charge account statements would back him up.

Pearl figured that was probably true or he wouldn't have been so bold about it, but she dutifully wrote down the information to be verified later.

She slipped her notebook back in her small leather purse and stood up. Slung the purse with its strap sideways across the front of her blazer. She thanked Levin for his time and went to the door.

"Maybe you would have gotten along with Lilly Branston," she said.

Levin gave her a bright smile. "A woman real estate wolf? You betcha."

Pearl wondered why she couldn't help having a shred of sympathy for this thoroughly reprehensible human being.

But she knew why, and it had to do with the diamond engagement ring on her finger.

She remembered that Yancy—she and Yancy—lived not far from here.

Levin escorted her to the elevator when she left. A real gentleman. She thought about telling him what a shallow and obvious cad he was but realized that would be unprofessional.

And useless.

He'd been her second interview of C and C clients. Neither interview had been productive.

Late as it was, Pearl decided to call it a day's work and walk the half dozen blocks to Yancy's apartment. She could call the woman who was Levin's alibi from there. Or maybe tomorrow morning she should go interview her in person. Be thorough.

As she descended to lobby level in the elevator, she found herself humming a song from long ago in her life. At first she couldn't place it, and then she did:

"Love Is Strange."

Pearl had dropped by the office to work up her report on her interviews when Fedderman came in exhausted and gleaming with sweat.

"You look like you've been sprayed with WD-40," Pearl said.

"It's damned hot out there."

"Have any luck?"

"Naw! I drew a lover boy named Gerald Lone. Only I followed every avenue and there is no Gerald Lone. Well, I take that back. There's one in Queens who's ninety-three years old. Not our man. It's a dead-end search for a guy using a made-up name and address so he can make out."

"You shoulda been able to get to him some way."

"I tried every way. He used an Internet café or library computer to register his alias on C and C. Then they did the rest for him, secure as the CIA. He's covered his tech tracks like a terrorist hacker. He might as well not exist."

"To the law, maybe."

"More likely to his wife, when he's out being whoever he's pretending to be to get in somebody's knickers."

"Knickers?"

"Yeah. They're catching on again, I hear."

"Only with you, Feds. And whatever it is you're dating." Pearl finished her word processing and shut down her computer. She could print tomorrow. "Speaking of long shots, what do you think of this computerized dragnet?"

"I think it doesn't work, because the computer nerds at C and C are smarter than the ones at the NYPD."

Pearl nodded. "Love will find a way."

Quinn took his yellow legal pad to study after eating an early and light dinner at the Lotus Diner. He ordered a second cup of coffee. He wanted to smoke a cigar but didn't. The other diners might turn on him.

He was reading where he'd left off on the pad:

Shadow woman appears again at crime scene.

As he was about to put pencil to pad, Thel arrived to top off his coffee. She squinted down at the pad as she poured.

"What's that? You writing a book?"

"Sort of," Quinn said.

"Either you are or you ain't," Thel said.

"Who said that? Plato?"

"Plato's our Greek salad, right at the top of the menu."

The coffee ran over, and Quinn had to move the pad fast to keep it dry.

"Sorry," Thel said. "I was philosophizing."

Quinn hadn't had any dessert. "Are there any doughnuts left from this morning?"

"Sort of," Thel said, and retreated with the glass coffeepot.

Quinn returned his attention to his legal pad, figuring either he'd get a doughnut or he wouldn't.

He wrote:

Pearl engaged to Yancy B.

Then he crossed that out. It had nothing to do with the investigation.

He took a sip of coffee and resumed writing with his stubby yellow pencil:

Lilly Branston's body found. Carver's M.O.
Witness—Stephen Elsinger. Telescope.
Shadow Woman caught. Lisa Bolt. Coma. One
  Chrissie accounted for.
Geraldine Knott, Addie Price, same person.
C & C site found on Branston's flash drive.
Comp. nerd's software program, seven names.

Thel reappeared and placed a plate containing a damaged cake doughnut in front of Quinn.

"Last one," she said.

"It looks as if mice have been at it."

"They know what's good," Thel said. "You want a warmup on your coffee?"

"No thanks." He was staring at the legal pad, trying to pull some sort of pattern or meaning from it.

"Book got you stumped?" Thel asked. To her, the pad was upside down. "Looks like a mess. Like you don't know how it's gonna end."

"I don't," Quinn said.

"What kinda book's it gonna be?"
"Mystery."
"Right up your alley."
"Should be," Quinn said.
"I wouldn't try to dunk that doughnut."

62

The uniformed doorman at Yancy's building was half a block down the street, chatting with a woman trying to control a huge fluffy dog on a long leash. The leash was looped around one of the doorman's legs. *Some security*, Pearl thought, as she pushed through the glass double-door entrance to the lobby.

Yancy was due back later tonight. He'd be surprised to find her in his bed, but he wouldn't mind. He liked those kinds of surprises. He'd no doubt wake her up. That was the kind of surprise she didn't mind.

As she rode the absolutely silent elevator, she mused that she was moving up in the world literally as well as figuratively. Yancy had money and, like Fred Levin, would probably always have it. The similarities between the two charm dispensers were still kind of unsettling. But she loved Yancy. She was sure that would be impossible with Levin. The differences between the two men might have to do with the heart. Something about Levin hinted that he harbored malice, that he found a subtle sadistic enjoyment in being detached and purely pragmatic. Yancy might have the substance of shadow, but there wasn't the slightest hint of maliciousness in his carefree soul.

After stepping out of the elevator, she walked soundlessly

down the carpeted hall. There was no one else in sight. She
still hadn't met her and Yancy's neighbors on either side.
Hadn't seen them in the halls or even heard them through the
walls. Maybe rich people were like that, leading lives insulated by their wealth.

She keyed the apartment door and pushed it open. It
made a soft brushing sound over the thick throw rug in the
foyer in a way she liked. Careful not to muss her hairdo, she
lifted her purse strap over her head and laid the purse on a
small, marble-topped table. Then she removed her blazer
and held it in her right hand, planning on draping it over the
sofa arm before going to the kitchen and getting something
cold to drink.

Two steps off the foyer tile and onto the living room carpet, Pearl knew something was wrong.

But she didn't know what. Didn't know how to react.

She did know with a thrill of fear that she wasn't alone.

Something struck her hard just above the small of the
back, causing the breath to *whoosh* out of her, momentarily
paralyzing her. She dropped to one knee, bending over as if
trying to find something on the floor. She tried to breathe but
couldn't. Her brain was struggling to work, to comprehend
what was happening.

. . . *Gun's in my purse.*

She was thinking self-preservation and self-preservation
only. All she knew for sure was that she was in deep trouble.
The rest of her mind was a muddle.

A hand from behind cupped her chin and yanked her hard
so she was lying on her back on the floor. She involuntarily
drew up her knees, still trying to breathe.

He was standing over her, slender but strong-bodied,
wearing a loose-fitting dark sweatshirt and matching sweatpants. Jogging shoes that were black but for their white soles
and toe caps. He had on a black knit balaclava so that nothing of his face was visible other than his eyes. Pearl thought
the eyes might be familiar, but she couldn't be sure.

She also, for a moment, thought about the careless doorman. That carelessness must be how the man had entered the building and found his way to Yancy's apartment.

The intruder straddled her, yanked her arms sideways, and kept them that way as he scooted forward so he could place his knees on her upper arms and bring his full weight to bear on them, pinning them, and her, to the floor.

Pearl immediately recognized the method and knew who he was—the Carver. She knew how much danger she was in and how precious life was.

At first she thought he had no fingernails, and then she saw that he had on skin-tight latex gloves that were flesh colored. From the pouchlike pocket of his sweatshirt he drew a knife with a long, slender blade.

Moving her arms only feebly from the elbows down, Pearl helplessly clawed the air. The strength had left her arms quickly in her awkward position under the man's weight. She was starting to regain her ability to breathe and considered screaming, but she was sure that if she made any noise he'd use the knife. He was leaning slightly forward, staring down at her and slowly waving the knife blade back and forth before her eyes, as if trying to hypnotize her. She somehow got the impression that beneath the balaclava he was smiling.

He wants my full attention. He wants me to grasp what's going to happen.

Not the eyes this time, but something about the man seemed familiar. It was in the way he moved.

Who is this bastard?

She kicked out with her feet, trying to loosen the crushing weight on her arms. He simply bore down harder with his knees. Her upper arms ached so badly they began to go numb.

Think, Damn it! You're running out of time. Out of life. Think!

If I can't use my arms, I'll use my legs!

She brought both knees up sharply and suddenly, and did

manage to make contact with his back with one knee. But it wasn't enough to do anything but anger him. Or perhaps amuse him. He held the point of the knife close to her right eye and shook his head no, letting her know she'd better not kick again.

From beneath the black knit that covered his mouth, he said in a deep muffled voice, "I'm going to explain to you what I'm doing while I'm doing it."

He used his free hand to yank up her blouse, and then with the knife he deftly sliced through the material between the cups of her bra. He flicked the cups away right and left with the point of the knife, and her breasts were bare.

Pearl knew the ritual, and knew that once he began it the pain and terror would render her completely helpless.

She was determined to keep struggling as long as possible. She controlled her breathing, drawing air deeply so she could muster her strength for one more attempt to buck the man off her and somehow try to put up a fight. Maybe she could kick him in a vital spot, slow him down, and reach her gun in her purse.

Slowly she drew her knees up as far as she could, then kicked straight out with her legs and dug her heels and elbows into the carpet.

Her sudden, spasmodic effort had some effect. She heard the man's grunt of surprise and felt his weight shift inches forward so his crotch was almost in her face. His weight had lifted slightly, and she thought she might be able to free one arm.

She clenched her eyes shut with the effort of trying to work her arm free, kicking out again with her legs. The killer's weight rose from her almost completely, as if he might be positioning his body and seeking balance, maybe getting ready to hit or kick her.

She opened her eyes and looked up into the perspiring, determined face of Yancy Taggart.

* * *

Yancy's eyes were wide with surprise and anger, but not fear. He was gripping the Carver's sweatshirt with both hands, pulling him off Pearl.

"Got the bastard!" Pearl heard him say.

Then she saw the flash of the knife as the killer writhed and twisted his body to gain leverage. The blade winked through the air, and Yancy made a sound like a harsh intake of breath. Pearl felt something warm on her face, and saw what the CSU techs called a slash pattern of blood on the wall.

The killer was standing completely upright. He kicked Pearl hard in the side of the head, and she went blank for a few seconds with pain. She saw in slow motion the killer conceal the knife again in his sweatshirt pocket and then pirouette like a ballet dancer toward the door.

Then he was out the door and into the hall.

Pearl crawled over to where Yancy lay on his back. His throat was sliced almost ear to ear. He was staring at the ceiling, making soft gurgling sounds and desperately feeling with his fingers the edges of the gash in his throat, as if trying to piece himself back together.

Pearl was sure he saw her and that he tried to say something, but he went silent, and the life in his eyes dimmed.

She heard herself whimpering. Her limbs wouldn't move as directed. She managed to stand up and take a few steps before stumbling. The room lurched, and she fell hard on the carpet, bumping an elbow. Fighting dizziness and nausea, she crawled the rest of the way toward her purse on the table. Like an infant who could walk some but still found crawling the easiest and most direct way to a destination.

She wanted her cell phone now, not her gun.

63

Quinn sat on the floor with her, holding her so close and tight that it hurt her ribs.

Pearl was infuriated because she couldn't control her sobbing. Each breath she drew caught in her throat and turned into a deep, wretched moan. Tears tracked down her cheeks so freely she could feel them spatter on her forearm. Grief was so real, like a horrid creature that had taken up residence inside her.

She couldn't help it; she dug her forehead into Quinn's shoulder and sobbed. Fedderman was somewhere nearby. The CSU techs were bustling around, and a couple of paramedics were waiting to remove the body. Remove Yancy. For now, everyone was giving Pearl and Quinn a wide berth.

"It'll be all right," Quinn crooned to her, his huge right hand patting her back ever so gently. "All right . . . all right . . . all right . . ."

"It won't be!" Pearl managed to blurt. "Goddamn it, it'll never be all right!"

"Better, then," Quinn said, not breaking the rhythm of his patting. "It'll be better in a while. Better, Pearl . . ."

I'd settle for tolerable! Oh, God, just tolerable!

She sobbed for a while longer, as Quinn patted and crooned.

Finally, when she'd managed to calm down enough not to completely lose control if she attempted to speak, she told him what had happened. So much more than she'd said over the phone.

"That's all for now," Quinn said softly when she was finished. "You don't have to say anything more, Pearl."

But the words, suddenly freed from her constricted throat, kept spilling out of her. "Yancy came home early," she said in someone else's voice. Grief was pulling her strings. "Came home early and didn't know what he was walking into. Didn't know . . ."

Is this the new me? Forever?

"He came home early and saved your life," Quinn said. "He was a good man, Yancy. Worthy of you."

"Oh, Quinn, damn it! Will you stop with the Hemingway bullshit? Yancy's dead. I want him alive!"

"We all do, dear, but that's impossible."

God! Oh, Jesus!

She heard and felt Quinn sigh. The heft and heat of his body shifted. "There's nothing I can say that will help enough, Pearl. We both know that."

Pearl nodded and pushed away from him. He leaned toward her, and she felt him kiss her forehead, the furnace heat of his breath.

"But you helped," she said. "I'm grateful."

She was speaking in her own, familiar voice now.

Quinn noticed the change, too. Her voice was so calm it was jarring. But it didn't surprise him.

He understood Pearl. She was in hell. She wouldn't burn for an eternity, but the embers would never really die.

Quinn looked at her seated next to him, so small, so crushed, and yet somehow more vivid than ever. It was as if she were lighted in some ghastly way from within.

He felt a chill and thought about pulling her close to him again, but he didn't. He knew what she was thinking. Knew the world she was in. In some ways they were like twins. He knew her reactions by blood and by brain. Knew her passions and obsessions.

If the Carver didn't have something from hell after him before, he did now.

The killer sat on the end of a bench in Washington Square Park, his elbows on his knees, his head bowed. His hands seemed to be steady enough except for the tips of his fingers, which were trembling.

It had been so close. All his planning, his reading of fate, and then a door opened and everything had spun out of control. It was frightening that this sort of thing could happen to him.

Of course, he knew that it happened to other people who made no mistakes.

They cross with the light and are struck and killed by a car. They get on a plane, and it reaches the end of the runway and rams into the ground. They take a bite of food they anticipate enjoying, and a heart attack kills them before they taste it.

That was the sort of thing that had *almost* happened to him. That, in fact *had* happened to the man whose throat he'd cut.

You open a door and step inside and you die.

Not that he could complain about his reaction to the intruder. He'd identified the new and unexpected threat immediately. Body obeyed mind. Blade obeyed body. So fast had he been moving that not a drop of blood had gotten on him.

He rocked back and forth for a moment on the bench.

Pearl. He'd so wanted Pearl.

She'd been concerned about her lover. So concerned with him that she hadn't given chase.

He knew that for a while, anyway, he'd have to leave Pearl alone. She and his other pursuers would be on their guard. Continuing to stalk Pearl wouldn't be smart. Besides, his failure to claim her as one of his victims would dull the pleasure of having her.

He found solace in the knowledge that the assault on Pearl hadn't been a complete failure.

If his pursuers' time and anxiety would now be wasted protecting Pearl instead of hunting him, that was fine. The attack on her had at least served a purpose.

The bench bounced slightly, jouncing him out of his thoughts. Its iron legs weren't resting on level ground, and someone had sat down on the opposite end and created the seesaw jolt.

He looked over and saw a small woman with dark hair and eyes. Her hands were working to open a white paper sack that was tightly wadded at the top. She was wearing jeans and a sleeveless pink T-shirt. Her arms were smooth and tan and strong looking. Her breasts were ample.

She got the sack open, dipped in a hand, and, with an arm motion as if she were sowing seeds, tossed an arc of popcorn out in front of the bench. Pigeons appeared immediately and began flapping and strutting about, pecking at the unexpected feast. The woman tossed out more popcorn, causing more pigeons to materialize. Feeding them seemed to please her immensely, judging by her smile.

Then she glanced over, and the smile was for him.

Something in his heart moved. The woman was not unlike Pearl.

Not unlike her at all.

He smiled back and introduced himself with the name he was now using. "I'm Gerald Lone."

She seemed a bit surprised by his impulsive introduction. After all, this was New York. He could see her appraising him. He might have been jogging in the park and was resting on the bench. He looked respectable enough. A handsome man (or so he saw himself) in a big and lonely city. This was the way lives casually intersected. This was the way things began.

Would she take a chance and acknowledge that he existed? Would she be polite and reply?

How could she be cool to him while proffering her heart to pigeons?

"I'm Elana Dare," she said.

"As in take a chance?"

"It's spelled that way."

Her voice was like Pearl's.

64

Quinn told Pearl she should take some time off and pull herself together. He wanted her to wait until Yancy was buried before even thinking about returning to work. Of course she ignored his advice. She was at her desk the next morning.

Pearl was locked on.

Even the afternoon after Yancy's funeral in New Jersey—paid for partly by Pearl but mostly by the Wind Power Coalition, as Yancy had no living relatives—Pearl came in to the office.

Quinn walked in and found her there, alone. They'd all attended the service and funeral. Afterward Vitali and Mishkin had left to tend to NYPD business for Renz. Probably they were filling Renz in on every detail of the attempt on Pearl's life, up to and including Yancy's funeral. Fedderman was re-interviewing Pearl's neighbors to see if anyone had recalled some minor detail that might have major significance.

Fresh news, much of it inaccurate, would be in tomorrow's *City Beat* as well as in the major papers. Cindy Sellers had been at the funeral, wearing a tight black dress accessorized with a small black digital camera. There had been no gathering after the funeral. Some of the mourners had gone on their own to an upscale Manhattan bar near Grand Central Station to drink and reminisce about Yancy. They were mostly men, expensively dressed, neatly groomed and with styled haircuts. If they weren't staying in Manhattan they had trains to catch to upscale communities back in New Jersey or in Connecticut. Quinn didn't know who they were. Neither did Pearl. Brother lobbyists, maybe.

The office was hot and damp, but Pearl didn't seem to notice. Her world was internal. Quinn walked over and switched on the air conditioner. The metallic hammering began, and he slapped the side of the unit. The hammering noise remained, but it was softer, as if in respect for Pearl's grief.

Quinn's shirt stuck to his perspiring back as he settled into the warm leather upholstery of his desk chair.

Sitting slouched behind his desk, he looked over at Pearl. There was a sheen of perspiration on her forehead and above her upper lip. She'd stopped at her apartment, or brought clothes, and had changed from her funereal black dress into tan slacks and a white tunic gathered at the waist with a maroon sash. Her eyes were slightly puffy, but other than that there was no sign that she'd been crying disconsolately only hours ago in New Jersey. The funeral, Yancy, were part of the past now, on the continent. Manhattan was another place altogether, an island. A hunting ground more sophisticated than veldt or jungle, and every bit as deadly.

On a corner of Pearl's desk was a lush floral arrangement Quinn remembered from the funeral home, though it hadn't been transported to the gravesite. The mortuary must have given the cut flowers to Pearl, and she brought them here, where they should last about a week if she kept them watered in their pressed glass vase. Quinn wondered what Pearl thought when she looked at them. Was she fondly remembering Yancy, or using the sight of the flowers to stoke the fire in her heart so she could find his killer?

Quinn said, "You all right, Pearl?"

"Um."

Apparently she didn't want to talk.

The phone rang, and Quinn punched the glowing line button and picked up before Pearl had a chance to answer. He saw by caller ID that the call's origin was Roosevelt Hospital.

"Quinn and Associates Investi—"

"It's Fedderman, Quinn. How's Pearl doing?"

Quinn glanced over at Pearl and caught her lowering her eyelids. She'd been staring over at him, curious.

"Okay," he said.

"What I called for," Fedderman said, "is Lisa Bolt is conscious."

"Is she—"

"She's slightly addled, but the doc says that's natural and there's no apparent brain damage. You know head injuries, how they bleed. It was bad, but not as bad as it looked. The rest of her's about healed up, too. She's in pretty good shape, Quinn, considering."

"What about her tongue?" Quinn saw Pearl glance over again.

"It can wag at us this afternoon, if we don't push her too hard."

Quinn looked at his watch. "It's afternoon now."

"So it is."

"See you shortly."

Quinn replaced the receiver and stood up behind his desk.

"Want to go for a drive?" he asked.

Pearl looked at him with her puffy eyes. "Where to?"

"The hospital. Lisa Bolt is awake."

A change came over Pearl's features. Within seconds, grief had given way to a hardness and determination. "Let's go."

"You sure you're up for this?"

"You sure you can stop me?"

"Actually," Quinn said, "I'm not."

As they were leaving, she turned back and lifted the vase

of mortuary flowers. She deftly removed the tag and black ribbon without damaging a flower.

"For Lisa Bolt," she said. "They might help make her more talkative."

Quinn grinned at her with a kind of sadness. "Pearl, Pearl . . ."

"I can't think of a better use for them," Pearl said.

"Nor can I."

Quinn put up the BACK SOON sign and locked the door behind them.

They got in the Lincoln, Quinn at the wheel. On the drive to the hospital Pearl was quiet, but he could feel the energy coming off her damp flesh like waves of high-tension electricity. It reminded him of the way you could put your fingers up close to a TV screen and see the individual hairs on the back of your hand rise.

Lightning stitched the gray summer sky, bright enough to hurt the eye even in daylight. Quinn wondered if it was a coincidence.

He lay in agony, the edge of the knife blade resting lightly on his chest. He'd thought he was in control, but it hadn't turned out that way. The need had always been there, and now it was alive.

Unknown forces, driven by shame and guilt, were in control. He could see his fate moving like clouds across the ceiling.

This must not happen.

He should have known, should have been more careful, should have planned better.

Didn't he think he'd someday reach this point?

"Should have" is in the past.

The past that he'd thought was dead. That he feared so that it ruled his dreams. The past.

It must not happen again. It must not!

He had said the words aloud the first time to gather courage. Now he said them again, this time only in his mind.

I am a fool.

He applied the knife.

I must wash the sheets carefully.

65

Lisa Bolt's hospital room smelled like Lysol and spearmint, as if it had just been disinfected by a cleaning lady chewing gum. Lisa was sitting almost completely erect in her cranked-up bed, her back propped against a pillow. She looked thin but surprisingly well. There was a flesh-colored strip of adhesive tape on the side of her neck. A beige turban was wound around her head, obviously to conceal a bandage. She was wearing light makeup but had her eyebrows penciled in as dark slash marks.

The nurse, who was middle-aged and looked like a gaunt, predatory bird, informed them that only two visitors would be allowed in the room. Quinn settled on himself and Pearl.

"Please keep in mind that she's still weak," the nurse cautioned Quinn.

"Of course we will."

The nurse glanced at him from the corner of her eye and seemed dubious.

"These are for you, Lisa," Pearl said with a smile. She placed the vase of flowers on an otherwise bare windowsill and deftly and lovingly adjusted the arrangement.

"Do you want some water?" Quinn asked Lisa, motioning with his head at the plastic glass and pitcher on the tray table rolled close to the bed.

Lisa kept her head on the pillow as she moved it slowly back and forth once to decline. Her head didn't move at all as she looked at Pearl and then at Quinn.

"I owe you an apology," she said. Her voice was raspy from disuse, or perhaps from the feeding tube that had been recently removed.

"We're glad you're alive," Quinn told her.

"You owe us the truth," Pearl said, pushing too hard too fast.

Quinn gave her a look, signaling her to ease up and listen for a while without butting in. She understood it perfectly, and he knew it. Both of them thought it was scary sometimes, the way they could almost read each other's thoughts.

Pearl moved a step back from the bed as Quinn continued. "It is time for the truth, Lisa." His tone was not at all threatening.

"I know," Lisa said. She took a deep breath and swallowed, wincing as if it hurt.

"You're sure about the water?" Quinn asked.

She nodded and then closed her eyes. "I'm trying to organize my thoughts before I tell you about this."

"Of course . . . of course . . . we understand."

"It's as if I've been away on a trip."

"Of course, of course . . ."

Lisa waited almost a full minute before beginning: "It started when Chrissie Keller came to my office in Columbus and hired me to see if I could somehow get her murdered twin's case reopened. She told me about her slot-machine windfall and waved a lot of money at me. Enough to convince me to take her on as a client even though I thought there wasn't a chance in hell I could reexamine the NYPD's old investigation and find something that would get them to reactivate the case." Lisa turned her head to the side, and her eyes teared up. "Since I didn't think I could help her, I shouldn't have taken her money. I know that."

"I think it's understandable," Quinn said. "You were in

business to make money, and someone wanted to hire you. That's how it works in our occupation." *We're all in this together. Allies.* "Go right on with your story, dear."

Lisa gazed up at him and managed a slight smile. Pearl could hardly stand watching this.

"I knew that to help Chrissie I'd have to be creative," Lisa said. "I did some research and decided that since I wouldn't have much pull with the NYPD, maybe I could sort of sublease the case to somebody who would have pull. Somebody like you. To do that, I'd have to be convincing, the way Chrissie was convincing with me. I struck on the idea of pretending at first that I *was* Chrissie, the surviving twin. Chrissie liked the idea."

"And why not? It's quite clever."

Lisa signaled silently that she would like some water now, and Quinn helped her to take a few dribbling swallows.

That earned another smile from Lisa, as if Quinn were Father Teresa. "My job was to gain your trust," she said in a somewhat revitalized voice, "and then shadow the investigation and eventually tell Chrissie who and where the killer was before the police got to him. That last part was important."

Quinn understood why. Chrissie wanted to get to her sister's murderer first. "She wanted to be ensured of justice. Her kind of justice."

"Yes," Lisa said. "Chrissie is consumed by a yearning to avenge her twin's death. It's almost as if she herself had been molested, mutilated, and murdered."

"I take it you mean she feels that way . . . beyond the norm."

"Far beyond. If there is such a thing as a norm in this kind of situation. She's obsessed. You know how it can be with twins. It's spooky, almost like two bodies sharing a common mind. And it doesn't seem to stop after death. At least, that's the way Chrissie sees it. And there's something else."

"Else?" Quinn said, wishing Addie or maybe Helen the

NYPD profiler was present to decipher some of the deeper motivations floating around here.

"During the twins' childhood, Tiffany was molested by her father. And whenever that happened, Chrissie was badly beaten where it didn't show. Chrissie, of course, was confused and intimidated and did nothing about it. Nothing to help Tiffany. She feels extremely guilty about that."

"When you say extremely . . ."

"Chrissie is driven by guilt and feels she can find redemption by locating, torturing, and then executing Tiffany's killer."

"So she's using us to try to commit murder."

"She wouldn't call it murder," Lisa said.

"I'm not sure I would either," Quinn said. "But the way for us is clear: We've got to find and stop her."

Pearl moved closer to the bed and spoke looking down at Lisa. "Do you think she might want her kind of justice so badly she'd kill in order to get to the Carver?"

"I do," Lisa said without hesitation.

"You and Chrissie have been in touch?" Quinn asked.

"I have no idea where she is," Lisa said.

Sort of an answer, Quinn thought.

The door opened, and the nurse who'd allowed them access to Lisa Bolt entered the room. There was a smaller, younger nurse standing off to the side and behind her. The younger woman, who looked about twelve, was holding a rectangular metal tray containing a lot of rigmarole that included a large hypodermic needle.

"I'm sorry, but we think the patient needs to rest," the older nurse said.

"Of course," Quinn said. He started to pat Lisa's hand and then saw all the bruising from intravenous needles. He patted her shoulder instead. "You rest now, and we can talk later. I hope you feel better having told us this. I know we've been heartened by seeing you awake and looking so much better."

The older nurse, who knew bullshit when she heard it, pointedly moved out of the way so there was room for Quinn and Pearl to leave.

"Take the best care of her," Quinn said, as he and Pearl edged past both nurses.

"We will indeed, sir," the older nurse said. "It's what we're doing right now."

Quinn smiled beatifically at the nurse as he held the door open for Pearl.

"Watch out for that one," Pearl heard the older nurse say to the younger, as she and Quinn found themselves in the hall.

They walked a little way toward the nurses' station and stood near a drinking fountain.

"You know we still can't believe anything Lisa Bolt says," Pearl told him.

"Of course not. On the other hand, maybe she's had an epiphany. That can happen when you're struck by a moving vehicle."

"Or you can wake up in a hospital and be as big a liar as before you were struck."

"That too," Quinn said. He paused and felt at his shirt pocket, as if absently seeking a cigar. "Do you think whoever attacked you could have been a woman, Pearl?"

Pearl gave it some thought. "It's possible. It all happened so damned fast. He—or she—was slender, maybe short to average height for a man, but damned strong. I'd guess an athletic, wiry man. But a woman . . . possibly."

"Tiffany's postmortem has her at five-feet-nine. Chrissie would be the same height."

"Might fit. I never saw whoever killed Yancy stand up straight, so I could only guess within several inches either way."

"And madness, obsession, gives people strength," Quinn said.

You should know, Pearl thought.

They were quiet for a moment as a trio of nurses bustled past.

"Lisa Bolt's going to be out of here soon," Pearl said, "and she needs to be watched."

"Your job and Fedderman's," Quinn said. He laid a hand very lightly on her shoulder, as if concerned that she might drift away like a balloon, and looked down into her eyes. "How are you doing, Pearl? Really?"

"I don't want you worrying about me."

She was determined not to let Quinn find his way back into her affections by way of her grief for Yancy. She didn't think he'd do that deliberately, but it sure as hell could happen. She couldn't trust him, and she couldn't trust herself, so she had to play it tough.

"But I do worry, Pearl. I can't help it."

"And I can't help it if you do," she said. "So worry away. Just don't involve me."

66

Quinn sat in Renz's office and watched sunlight angle in through the blinds and cast slices of brilliance swarming with dust motes. The office was warm, crowded as it was and with the invasion of the sun. Renz, seated behind his desk and wearing navy blue suspenders and a white shirt with the sleeves neatly rolled up, appeared cool. There was in the air the faintest scent of cigar smoke, as there was the whiff of political corruption.

Quinn had suggested the meeting, but Renz was pretending he'd summoned him. Quinn knew it was some kind of ruse to maintain dominance. Renz was full of such minor stratagems to help him become or remain top dog. Quinn used to enjoy deflating Renz, but he'd become bored with that and usually let the dog have his day.

"This investigation is turning into a disaster," Renz said. "The media wolves are all over it and all over me. The mayor's office calls half a dozen times a day." He leaned forward over his desk and glared at Quinn, who was seated in one of the chairs facing the desk. "What the bejesus is going on?"

"Progress," Quinn said.

"Do illuminate me."

Quinn told him about Lisa Bolt's recovery and what she'd said yesterday at the hospital.

"And we still don't know where the real Chrissie Keller is?" Renz asked.

"Not yet," Quinn said.

"Then the only actual progress I see is you found the woman who conned you into thinking she was Chrissie. And you needed a careless cab driver to do that."

"Not quite."

He told Renz about Tiffany Keller's childhood molestation by her father, and about Chrissie's guilt over doing nothing to stop it. Watching Renz's flabby features, Quinn was glad he'd decided to present this information to the Machiavellian police commissioner face-to-face. It opened up all sorts of possibilities.

Renz sat running a fingernail over his close-shaven, overflowing jowls. Anyone listening closely could hear the sound of the nail scraping minute gray stubble.

At last he said, "You proposing using the father as bait?"

Renz hadn't quite proposed the idea himself, which was what Quinn had wanted. But this should be close enough.

"Addie gave me the idea," Quinn said. Since Renz had assigned Addie to the case, he had to at least pretend to give serious consideration to a strategy based on her theory.

"What's the wife, Erin, say about this?" Renz asked.

"Nothing yet. She doesn't know we're considering it."

"Does she know her prick husband molested their daughters?"

"Probably. That's usually the case."

"She'd go along with using him as bait, then. Might even be enthusiastic."

"Might be ecstatic."

"Where's hubby now?"

"We haven't tried to locate him yet. I wanted your opinion first."

"Tell me more."

"We could leak it to the press that he's in town, leak where he's staying. If Chrissie really did commit any of these murders, making it look like the Carver's back in action, she might go after old dad. She's already got blood on her hands, and she *is* out to avenge her sister's death. Why not also avenge her sister's molestation? Assuage at least some of that guilt she's suffering for keeping quiet about what was going on?"

"Might work," Renz said. "But if we try it and fail, I'll be chewed up like dog food by the media. You understand that politically this will be a risk?"

"Sure. But it might be a bigger risk not to act and make something happen."

"There'll be no way to keep it out of the media."

"No," Quinn said. "But that's okay. At least some of it has to be public knowledge for it to work."

"Do you even know where Dad is?"

"He should be easy to find."

"Hah! If you do find him, how will you make him go along with being bait?"

"I don't know yet. We might ask the twins' mother."

"Maybe you could hold a child molestation charge over Dad's head, so he cooperates or does prison time."

"The statute of limitation's expired," Quinn said. "He couldn't be prosecuted even if there was enough evidence."

"*He* might not know that."

Quinn stood up. "So I've got the okay to do this?" He wanted no mistake about Renz's involvement. He and Renz would own this decision, and suffer their respective consequences if it failed.

"Do it," Renz said, also standing. "It's better than what we've been doing, which seems mostly to be going around finding fresh victims."

Quinn nodded and moved toward the door.

"How are Vitali and Mishkin working out?" Renz asked behind him.

Quinn stopped and looked back. "They're good cops."

"And Addie Price? How's she working out?"

"She's the reason I'm here," Quinn said.

Renz grinned. "I can pick 'em. Right?"

Quinn said, "That's the reason you're here."

He went out the door, wondering if the twins' father was still alive and could be found.

"He lives in Detroit and uses the name Edward Archer," Erin said. She elevated her chin slightly. "We have very little contact."

Quinn and Fedderman were in the office, along with Helen Iman, the NYPD profiler and psychologist Renz had insisted sit in for Addie, who was with Renz today, helping him prepare for his regular briefing of the press. She was becoming something of a media consultant to him. Helen was a lanky six feet tall with choppy red hair and looked like a natural basketball center. She was also the best at this kind of thing, and the only profiler Quinn trusted.

Erin was seated in a chair angled toward Quinn's desk. Her long auburn hair was neatly combed, and she was wearing a light beige pantsuit, tan high heels, and a dainty silver and pearl necklace inside the V-neck of her white blouse. She was a compact package next to Helen. Quinn could detect the subtle scent of her perfume. It made him think of the flowers Pearl had taken to Lisa Bolt.

"But you do know how to contact him?" he said.

"Not directly," Erin said. "I'd have to make a few phone calls." She smiled in that secretive way of hers, as if she was a move ahead of him. "But why should I? He has no interest in either me or Chrissie now. I haven't seen him since Christmas three years ago, when he dropped by unexpectedly. I think he'd been drinking."

"What does your husband do in Detroit?" Quinn asked.

She crossed her legs so her calves were close together. "*Former* husband. He's in the insurance business, has his own agency. Doing quite well. I was told that he has political ambitions."

"Political?" Quinn sensed a vulnerability.

"He wants to run for city council or some such thing. Maybe alderman. Whatever they have in Detroit." She absently fished about in her matching tan purse and then stopped and looked around. "Mind if I smoke?"

"Yes," Pearl said, from where she sat behind her desk.

Erin shrugged and snapped the purse closed. "Why are you asking me about Ed?"

Quinn told her what they had in mind, touching on the regular molestation of Tiffany, witnessed by Chrissie. Not asking if Erin had known about it.

But the question remained in the air, unasked.

Erin reached again for her purse, opened it, and snapped it shut. She sat thinking, neither confirming nor denying that she'd been aware of the molestations and beatings that had dominated her children's young lives. The truth was a beast better kept caged.

She addressed Quinn calmly. "You want Ed to come to New York and let you make it known that he's here."

"Yes. Under his real name: Keller."

Erin crossed her legs even tighter. "To avoid unfavorable publicity, he might agree to do that. He's an ambitious bastard. But I can't believe Chrissie—"

"I know," Quinn said. "But you must consider that you're the poor girl's mother. And she's not been thinking straight. Our psychologist"—he nodded toward Helen, all strung-out six feet of her leaning casually on a wall—"believes that if she knows he's in town, Chrissie might break cover and go after her father."

"You mean try to kill him."

"Perhaps. Though that might be putting it too dramatically. She might at least want to see him and have it out with him."

"At which point the police will step out from behind the curtains and Chrissie will be arrested."

"Melodrama again. But yes. I'm being honest with you. Your daughter is a murder suspect. That's not to say she's guilty."

"But you think she is."

"Not necessarily. What I think is that we can't find her, and nothing else seems to be working. You *do* want her found?"

"Of course I do. Found and not hurt."

"That would be our objective. I promise you that none of us wants to see the slightest harm come to Chrissie."

"And you want me to talk Ed into this."

"If that's what it takes, yes."

Erin rearranged her legs and stood up. "I need to think about this."

"Of course." Quinn stood also. "But can you let us know as soon as possible?"

"I'll do that," Erin said.

She glanced around at everyone, gave a tentative nod, and left the office.

"Best follow her," Quinn said to Fedderman.

Fedderman snatched up his suit coat and shrugged into it. Buttoning his shirt cuff on the run, he hurried from the office.

Nobody said anything for a while.

Then Pearl said, "Do you think she'll go for it?"

"I don't have a clue," Quinn said. He looked over at Helen.

"You handled her very well," Helen said, pushing away from the wall. "Odds are she'll do what you asked. One way or the other, she does want her daughter found."

"We don't need her to do this," Pearl said. "Now that we know Edward Keller is Edward Archer, he should be easy enough to find. We can make him cooperate."

"Erin can be far more persuasive," Helen said. "We need her to pull him back into the past and pressure him into co-operating. He knows she can blow his cover any time, make public the fact that he beat and molested his own daughters. With a few words she can ruin him in his new life as Edward Archer."

"The past can be a son of a bitch," Pearl said, maybe thinking of Yancy.

Helen nodded. "Even though Erin professes to hate Keller, he's her former husband. She's got a difficult phone call to make. It won't be easy for her to put him in a vise and squeeze."

"Oh, it might be," said Pearl.

"Do you think she will squeeze?" Quinn asked.

"I think she's a woman who can," Helen said.

Half an hour later, Fedderman called.

"When Erin left the office she got into a cab," he told Quinn. "She went to Fifth Avenue and did some window-shopping, and then hailed another cab. She just went into her hotel."

"Window shopping," Quinn said. "That's interesting."

"Maybe it helps her think."

"Hang around a while longer," Quinn told Fedderman. "Make sure she doesn't come back out, but if she does, tail her."

"Done," Fedderman said, and broke the connection.

Quinn slowly hung up the phone. "She's going to make us wait for her answer," he said. "In her own way, our Erin's something of a control freak."

"You think?" Helen said. She was smiling.

"Those twins," Quinn said, shaking his head. "They must have gone through hell when they were kids."

"One of them's still in hell," Helen said.

"How long do you figure it'll be before Erin makes up her mind?"

Helen shrugged. "You might think in terms of hours or days. It depends on what Erin wants and how much she wants it."

Twenty minutes later Erin called Quinn and gave him Edward Archer's cell phone number.

"See how he reacts to your proposition," she said. "Then I'll talk to him."

Quinn told her he thought that was reasonable.

68

Twenty minutes past noon in Manhattan. It was the second day in a row the killer had returned to the same park bench at the same time. He'd brought a small white paper sleeve of popcorn both times, purchased, he guessed, from the same street vendor Elana Dare had frequented.

It was another warm day, and the scent of blooms on nearby bushes carried on the gentle breeze. People bustled past, and traffic roared like distant lions and was visible beyond the low stone wall that marked the park's boundary. The sidewalks were crowded with worker drones striding to and from lunch. The walkway in front of the bench wasn't as busy as the sidewalk, but plenty of people were in the park.

The bench rocked as a ragged homeless man plopped himself down on the opposite end. He smelled of urine and booze and needed a shave almost to the point where you'd have to say he had a beard. His untucked shirt was bunched where the neck of a bottle in his pants pocket protruded. His eyes were fogged but alert.

"Don't sit there," the killer said.

The man looked at him in surprise from beneath a ledge of bushy gray eyebrows; he was used to being ignored.

"Not your bench," he said, his voice gruff from infrequent use.

The killer remained firm. "I've got it leased for the day."

"I'm subleasing it."

The killer reached into his pocket, and the man looked alarmed. Seeing this, the killer smiled. This kind of person lived outside the system and in almost constant fear. Dealing with him should be easy for someone who knew how to use that fear.

"Let's say I've got an NYPD badge in my pocket and I'm going to show it to you," the killer said. "At that point, things will start to happen. Is that really what you want?"

The man stared at him for a long time; then he stood up unsteadily and walked away, He walked slowly and without glancing back, preserving what was left of his shredded dignity and saving the killer the two dollars he was going to pay him to leave.

Seizing opportunity was an art. So was recognizing it.

The killer absently reached into his narrow paper sack and pulled out a few puffs of popcorn and poked them into his mouth. The burned salt aroma rising from the bag triggered his hunger, and he was glad he'd brought the popcorn even though it was a prop.

Propcorn, he thought, smiling. Maybe he should patent it. *Propportunity?*

A hundred feet down the path, two skateboarders rushed and rattled along, flanking three walkers who had to bunch tightly together to avoid being bumped. One of the skateboarders veered away and stepped off his board in a manner that caused it to nose up at a sharp angle. He snatched it out of the air and began an easy, youthful jog.

Behind him, walking, she appeared.

She hadn't seen him yet and was watching the other skateboarder, who'd shot far ahead. The killer noticed with satisfaction that she was holding a bag of popcorn identical to his.

Her clothes were more casual today—jeans, sandals, a red T-shirt with FDNY printed on it. She was small, narrow-waisted, and busty. Her long dark hair had a slight wave in it. Like Pearl's.

She saw him and paused, pretending, he was sure, that she was surprised. He knew then that she'd thought he might be here. That she'd come hoping he was here. There was a tingling satisfaction and anticipation in his mind and body, as if he were a fisherman whose hook had just set. The fun part was ahead.

She continued to the bench and sat down, not on the opposite end but about two feet away from him. She hadn't completely lost her expression of surprise. "Small park," she said.

He smiled. "Wouldn't want to mow it."

Her laugh was music. "That joke has a familiar ring to it."

"Happens every spring," he said.

She opened the paper sack she was carrying and began tossing popcorn out onto the bare earth and littered pavement in front of the bench. As before, pigeons magically appeared.

When a squirrel came close, she stopped throwing popcorn. She bent low, picked up a small pebble, and threw it in the direction of the squirrel, deliberately missing it but scaring it away.

"Not a fan of squirrels?" he asked.

"No. They scare away the pigeons."

"Some people think they're cute."

"I'm not one of them. Squirrels are rats with decorative tails."

"I agree."

"Really?"

"Yes. I agree with everything you say. That's so you might have lunch with me, Elana."

With the squirrel observing from about fifty feet away, she began tossing popcorn again. "You remembered my name."

"It's the most beautiful name I ever heard."

"That's Maria."

"No, no. It's Elana. I once met a girl named Elana." He put on a horror-stricken expression. "You forgot *my* name!"

"Gerald Lone," she said.

"Wow! After two days. That must mean you'll have lunch with me."

"After the pigeons are finished eating."

"Fair enough, especially for the pigeons." He reached into his paper sack and, like Elana, began feeding the insatiable birds. "Are you on your lunch hour?" he asked.

She shook her head no. "Like a lot of other people in this city, I'm between jobs."

"Firefighter?" He pointed at the T-shirt lettering distorted by her oversized breasts.

"No," she said. "Just a fan."

"So am I."

"What about you?" she asked. "Are you gainfully employed?"

"I'm in software. That means I have to travel a lot. What was—or I guess I mean what *is*—your field?"

"Accounting. I was junior accountant for a chain of shoe stores. When they cut expenses, I was one of them."

"Heels. They should have kept you around just to look at."

She gave him a phony demure look and giggled.

"Women aren't supposed to be good at math," he said.

Now her look was anything but demure. "I'm good at lots of things women aren't supposed to be good at." Playing him while he was playing her. Not knowing he was way, way out of her league. He was going to enjoy this.

He smiled at her. "Isn't that bag about empty?"

She grinned and dumped the remaining popcorn onto the ground. He did the same with his popcorn.

He knew this was going to work. This was going to work just fine.

As they strolled from the park, they crumpled the popcorn bags and dropped them into a trash receptacle. They walked closer together. Both of them knocked salt from their fingers by brushing their hands together, as if in strange, hushed applause to celebrate the end of loneliness.

Behind them the pigeons went into a feeding frenzy, and the squirrel returned.

69

"Let me get this straight," Ed Archer/Keller said, when Quinn had contacted him via Archer's cell phone. "You want me to come to New York and register at a hotel under the name Edward Keller? And then you want to let it be known that I'm there?"

"It's a simple request," Quinn said. "Since Keller is your real name."

Silence for a few seconds. Then: "That's not exactly a state secret."

"It is in your state. And in your city. Where you're in business and have political ambitions."

"This is beginning to sound a lot like blackmail, Detective . . . Quinn, is it?"

"It is. And I wasn't thinking so much in terms of blackmail as in asking a father to help his daughter find safety in a dangerous situation."

"Daughter?"

"Chrissie Keller. We've been unable to locate her."

"You've been speaking to Erin, my ex-wife. That's where you got my number."

"I'd assumed she told you I was going to call."

"No, I haven't heard from her. She's in Ohio."

"Erin's in New York," Quinn said. "Doing what a good

mother should do. And a good father. Trying to protect her daughter."

"Chrissie's really missing?"

"Yes. She came to New York to find help in bringing the killer of your other daughter to justice."

"Jesus!" Keller said. "You do know a lot about me."

"Enough for my purposes," Quinn said.

Let the bastard know he's between a rock and a rock.

"This is a rotten thing you're doing," Keller said. "You're mucking around in a world I left behind. I even legally changed my name, built another life. Now you're threatening to rip it all apart if I don't cooperate in some kind of impersonation of my old self."

"Your true self," Quinn said. "I'm giving you a chance to be a real father. To stick your neck out for your daughter."

"What's the neck-sticking-out part?"

"She's a suspect in several murders," Quinn said.

"Come off it! Chrissie?"

"The same."

"I don't believe it."

"Of course not. She's your daughter. And you might be right. She might be innocent. But either way, you can help her. We think if you come to New York and she finds out about you being here, she'll come to you."

It took Keller a few seconds to process that. "And when that happens you can apprehend her. You're using me as bait."

"I can't argue with that assessment."

"Listen, Quinn, this is almost like you asking me to do this for a stranger. After Tiffany was killed . . . well, everything came apart. For me, for my wife, for Chrissie. We all wanted, *needed*, new and separate lives. For all of us, the past is poison. Apparently more so for Chrissie than for anyone else. You don't understand what you're asking of me."

Quinn considered bringing up the child molestation, but

thought better of it. The police would need Keller's cooperation, so let Erin call and put the knife in him and twist it.

"I know what I'm asking," Quinn said. "And I know that
once you've weighed your options you'll comply."

"I need to think about this," Keller said.

"That sounds reasonable, but the sooner you say yes, the
better for everyone—especially Chrissie. I need to know tomorrow. I'll give you my number to call."

"I have it on my cell phone from your call," Keller said.

"Fine. I expect to hear from you by three o'clock."

But Keller had broken the connection.

Quinn wasn't dissatisfied with the call. He knew Keller
would come around eventually. But he didn't want eventually to be too eventual. He pecked out Erin's cell phone number.

She answered immediately.

When Quinn described his conversation with Keller, she
laughed in an ugly way that was so acidic Quinn thought the
phone might melt in his hand.

"I'll call him," she said. "I'll put that bastard right back in
the poisonous past and then yank him into the poisonous
present. And I'll remind him he helped create them both.
He'll do as we ask, if he doesn't want his spiffy new life and
his standing in the community shoved right up his ass."

"Just be sure to let me know—"

Quinn realized Erin had abruptly broken the connection,
just as Keller had done earlier.

Maybe it was a family thing.

Quinn had just finished hanging up after his conversation
with Erin when Pearl called from the hospital.

"Lisa Bolt checked herself out of here an hour before I
arrived," she said.

Quinn opened his desk drawer and reached for a cellophane-wrapped cigar. "Say again, Pearl." Anger sizzled in his voice.

"You heard me the first time, Quinn."

"What time exactly did she leave?"

"Hospital records have her leaving at eleven thirty-one."

Half an hour after you were supposed to be at the hospital. Are you slipping, Pearl? Is it grief over Yancy, or something more?

Only because of Yancy, Quinn didn't ask Pearl why she'd been late. "Why did the hospital let her leave?"

"They couldn't stop her. They say she's well enough anyway."

"What about the uniforms who were supposed to be guarding her?"

"She waited until they were between shifts and yakking away down the hall by the coffee machine. They figured it'd be okay for a minute or two because they were between her room and the elevators. She must've taken the stairs down a floor before getting on an elevator. The uniforms couldn't have made her stay, even if they'd been there to try."

"Didn't it occur to them that somebody might have come *up* the stairs to get to her?"

"I'm sure they've been asked that question."

"Did she leave with anyone?"

"No. I'm told she got into a cab."

"Does the hospital have an address or contact number where she can be reached?"

"Address is an apartment in the West Nineties. Phone number's to a pet shop on Amsterdam."

"Would it be safe to say she's missing again?" Quinn asked, keeping his anger on simmer.

"Unless she's turned into a puppy. I'll check out the pet shop and the apartment address and let you know."

"There won't be an apartment at that address. Or if there is, it won't have anything to do with Lisa Bolt."

"Undoubtedly."

"Are we in the wrong business?" Quinn asked, looking at the wrapped cigar and changing his mind about lighting it.

"It's the only business we know."

"Sometimes I don't think we know it very well."

"It's hard to keep strings attached to people who don't want it that way," Pearl said. "Stop being critical of yourself and kicking yourself in the ass."

"I was being critical of you, Pearl. Kicking you in the ass."

"Oh. Well, that won't work."

70

Quinn stopped at the Lotus Diner the next morning and had a breakfast of eggs, toast, and coffee. He read the *Times* over a second cup of coffee and then read a *City Beat* he'd gotten out of a machine down the street.

He wasn't surprised when he saw the headline: SHADOW WOMAN OUT OF HOSPITAL. The piece went on to say how Lisa Bolt, strongly suspected of being the so-called "shadow woman" in the Carver murder investigation, had checked herself out of the hospital and again dropped from sight. A certain little NYPD bird had informed the reporter (Cindy Sellers, according to the byline) that the police had no way to guard Lisa Bolt around the clock, nor could they legally hold her if she decided to check out. Sellers went on to say that it was still a free country, for the most part, and even someone of interest to the police could come and go as they pleased.

All of this deliberately downplayed the momentary negligence of the NYPD uniforms assigned to keep watch on Lisa Bolt. That was to lessen the embarrassment of the department and of Renz in particular. Renz was, Quinn had no doubt, the talkative little NYPD bird.

How did it happen, Quinn asked himself, as he laid the folded paper aside in a puddle made by his water glass, that both he and Renz were indebted to Cindy Sellers? She could obtain information from either source and then cross-check it with the other. The opportunistic muckraker must have been born making a deal.

Quinn glanced around and decided the diner was too crowded for him to make a call on his cell phone and not be overheard. He slid from the booth and handed enough money for breakfast and a tip to Thel the waitress.

"In a rush, Captain Quinn?" she asked, slipping the bills into her apron pocket.

"Always," Quinn said.

"Somebody being murdered?"

"Always."

"Want a coffee to go?"

"Al—"

"Never mind," Thel said.

He walked back to the counter with her and waited while she filled a white foam cup full of coffee and fitted it with a tight plastic lid. He accepted it and thanked her. "Thel," he reminded her, "I'm no longer a police captain."

"In my mind," she said, "always."

Outside the diner, he strode through the warm morning and the sweet spoiled smells of trash waiting to be collected, to where the Lincoln was illegally parked with his NYPD placard on the visor. Inside the car, he placed his steaming cup in a holder and watched the windows immediately begin to fog up. It was time to play dumb. Or at least uninformed. He pecked out Cindy Sellers's direct number.

"It's your other little bird," he mumbled impatiently, waiting for her to pick up. She must know from caller ID who was on the other end of the connection.

When she did pick up, she said, "What've you got, Quinn?"

"Lisa Bolt checked herself out of the hospital yesterday. She's in the wind again."

Cindy let a few moments pass before replying. "You read *City Beat* this morning?"

"Haven't had time," Quinn lied.

"Pick up a copy and read it. Learn all about Lisa Bolt checking out of the hospital and dropping from sight again. The shadow woman's back in the shadows. If she really *is* the shadow woman. You gotta do better, Quinn. You got scooped on this one."

"You're serious?"

"Sure am."

"Damn!" Quinn said.

When he got to the office, Pearl was already at her desk. Her coffee mug was steaming away alongside her computer, and he realized he'd left his to-go cup in the car.

"Renz dropped a word in Cindy Sellers's ear already," he said, sitting down behind his desk and swiveling the chair this way and that as if to fasten it firmer to the floor. "Doing damage control."

"No surprise," Pearl said, eyes still on her computer monitor as she maneuvered and clicked her mouse.

"Anything?" he asked.

"World of knowledge, but none of it any help."

Quinn got up, walked over to the brewer, and poured some coffee into his initialed mug. He was returning to his desk when Fedderman walked in. He looked overheated and rumpled already, and it was still three hours till noon.

"The windows on your car are all steamed up," he said to Quinn. "Looks like just the place to lose the crease in your trousers."

Quinn nodded. "Been having trouble with that," he said, not wanting to explain, thinking nobody but Fedderman still said *trousers*.

He settled back down in his desk chair with his coffee. Sipped. *Yuk!*

"Erin's got form," Pearl said.

Quinn and Fedderman looked at her.

"Not the kinda form you guys are dreaming about," Pearl said. "She got into trouble in a little town in Florida twelve years ago when she was on vacation with her girls. Assault charge. A small-town cop pulled her over for speeding, and they got into a spat. Erin broke his nose."

"She doesn't seem the type," Fedderman said.

Pearl smiled at him. "She said it was self-defense, that she was trying to push him away and hit him accidentally."

"While she was swinging at him," Quinn said.

"Twelve years ago," Fedderman said. "And it could have happened to anybody. Doesn't mean much now."

"You're cutting her a lot of slack," Pearl said.

"Jesus, Pearl! She lost a daughter to a monster. You don't understand how that feels."

"I think I might," Pearl said.

Fedderman sighed. "I'm sorry, Pearl. I mean, about Yancy."

Pearl's eyes teared up, and Quinn thought she might leave her desk to go into the half bath, or at least use a tissue. She simply continued working her computer, maybe reading more about the old assault charge. Tough Pearl. Quinn felt a swelling admiration for her.

His desk phone rang. As he leaned forward to reach for the receiver he glanced at caller ID and recognized Edward Archer's cell phone number.

"Mr. Keller," he said, when he picked up.

"Archer," Keller corrected. "Until I get to New York. That's part of the deal."

"There's a deal, Mr. Keller?"

"I'll rearrange my schedule and fly in to LaGuardia to-morrow morning."

"That would be fine."

"How long will I be staying?"

"That's impossible to say. Bring plenty of clothes."

"You don't make it easy."

"It isn't going to be easy. It's what you should do."

"*Have* to do," Keller said. "Where do you want me to stay?"

"The Belington Midtown. It's on Twenty-fourth Street."

"That isn't Midtown."

"Few things are what they seem," Quinn said. "Remember to check in as Edward Keller. I'll be in touch."

"I don't want Chrissie harmed," Keller said. "That's why I'm doing this."

"Of course."

Quinn hung up on Keller before Keller's cell phone could be shut off. It felt good.

"We've got him," he said, thinking, *Thank you, Erin Keller.*

Pearl was grinning. Fedderman looked glad but thoughtful.

Quinn had a connection at the Belington. He remembered when it had been a flophouse. Then it had become gentrified. Now it was on the way again toward becoming a flophouse, but hadn't gone so far that it wasn't still respectable. Years ago Quinn had saved the manager's son's life in a shoot-out in a Chinese restaurant. The manager at the Belington would provide a room for Keller, and whatever else Quinn might want.

Vitali and Mishkin had to be brought in on this, and soon. Before that happened, Quinn knew he had to make a phone call to Cindy Sellers.

She'd been using Quinn and his team to sell papers. Now it was time to use her.

71

As Quinn was parking the Lincoln across the street from the office the next morning, he saw Addie walking on the other side of the street. She was wearing blue slacks, a white blouse, and a tailored gray blazer.

He turned off the engine and sat for a moment admiring her walk, the play of leg and derriere muscle beneath the taut blue material. Half walk, half dance. Did women know what they had—really had—that was rooted in time and desire that went back to before the first scratches in the sand on some distant shore? The depth and timelessness of their simple but powerful magnetism reached through the ages with the power of ancient goddesses. It was a wonder more people weren't killed as the result of passion gone wild.

It was a wonder there weren't more Carvers.

On impulse, Quinn tapped the horn.

Addie turned and saw him and smiled, making the early afternoon brighter.

When she saw he wasn't getting out of the car, she looked both ways and crossed the street toward him. Another symphony of motion. He pressed a button, and the window glided down.

"Going in to the office?" he asked, knowing it was an

inane question. She hadn't taken a leisurely stroll and happened to find herself right outside the building.

"I was," she said. Her smile widened. "Am I still?"

"Depends on whether you've had lunch." He raised his wrist and glanced at his watch. "It's already five minutes to eleven."

"Is this *Honk if you like the Early Bird Special*? Or is it work?"

"Some of each."

She nodded and walked around to get in on the passenger side.

"It's still cool in here," she said. "You must have just arrived."

"You were the first woman I honked at."

"You must be hungry."

He drove three blocks to Simone's, a French restaurant that specialized in desserts. Scents from the kitchen teased the appetite. The tables were round and impracticably small, and there were polished wood partitions that lent privacy and created a maze for the servers. Silver and crystal glinted on white tablecloths.

"This is nice," Addie said, glancing around. "Did you and Pearl come here?"

"Never," Quinn said.

"Ah!"

She seemed to catch a meaning he hadn't yet discerned.

A waiter arrived, poured water, and offered to take their drink orders. Addie stayed with water. Quinn ordered a coffee. Neither of them was really hungry, so they agreed to go straight to the desserts.

When the waiter returned with Quinn's coffee, Addie ordered raspberry sorbet. Quinn chose the crème brûlée.

"I thought we might talk," Quinn said, when the waiter was gone.

"That'd be nice."

"About work," he said.

"Only work?"

"No. But you never did weigh in on what you thought about setting up Ed Keller as a method of luring Chrissie. Or even whether Chrissie's guilty of murdering in the manner of her twin's killer in order to kick-start the Carver investigation."

Addie didn't hesitate. "I think Chrissie could well have killed Maureen Sanders precisely for that purpose. Sanders was a homeless woman. Chrissie might have thought she didn't have as much value as other potential victims."

"A less serious murder?"

"In some people's twisted view."

"But in Chrissie's view? I'm not so sure."

"Remember, Chrissie isn't thinking straight. And if you were going to choose a victim for the purpose of attracting attention so you might find the person you *really* wanted to kill, what kind of victim would *you* choose? A woman with something to live for? Or someone like poor, homeless Maureen Sanders? Someone suffering on the streets, and who might not have lived much longer anyway."

"Playing God."

"We all do it sometimes," Addie said. "In small ways and large."

"But most of us know deep down we're only pretending."

"As Chrissie might, in unguarded moments." Addie took a sip of water, little finger extended. "This is all supposing, of course, that Chrissie is a killer."

"That she killed Maureen Sanders, at least," Quinn said.

"As for there being enough hate generated by Chrissie's history with her father, I agree with the NYPD profiler Helen on that one, too. That kind of hate can take total control of a person. I think Chrissie will go for him." Addie took another sip of water. She left a crescent of lipstick stain on the glass's rim that held Quinn's attention.

Their desserts arrived, and he and Addie were quiet for a moment.

"Do you have everything set up at the hotel?" Addie asked, after a spoonful of sorbet.

"We do. And it should work, as long as Keller cooperates."

"He will," Addie said. "Partly because of his ex-wife's instructions. She knows too much. He's afraid of her."

"Relationships never really end, do they." It wasn't a question.

"Never."

Addie took another bite of sorbet. Quinn was fascinated by the pink of the raspberry melting against the red of her lips. She caught him watching, looked right into his mind, and smiled.

He was suddenly uncomfortable, perched on his miniature chair at a tiny table. He felt oversized and out of place, and trapped in a silence that badly needed to be filled.

"It's something, what we do to our children," he said. "The way it eventually comes around in pain and anger. It makes for a hell of a world."

"Is this the part of our conversation not about work?"

He grinned. "I guess it is. On the other hand, maybe it's what our work is all about. Especially this case."

She used her napkin to dab at her lips and then surprised him. "You're still in love with Pearl, Quinn."

He sat for a while without breathing.

"How do you know?" he asked.

"It's obvious."

"Does Pearl know?"

"Oh, God, yes!" Addie sat back and waited for the question he had to ask.

Quinn didn't disappoint her. "Does Pearl still love me?"

"Yes, she does. But she doesn't know it. She's in denial, just like you. Only her denial is deepened and complicated by the fact that she's grieving." Addie leaned forward and rested her fingertips lightly on the back of his hand. Her eyes held a depth of sadness that made him curious. "Whatever personal relationship we have has to take that into account, Quinn. Take Pearl into account."

"Are we headed toward a personal relationship?"

"We both know we are. That's how we came to be here."

Quinn thought about that. He'd been the one to suggest lunch together, and not only for business reasons. It had seemed the most natural thing in the world.

"We need to be honest with ourselves," Addie said.

"And careful." *Am I ready for this? Do I really want it?*

"That, too."

"There's a mutual attraction," Quinn said, "but you and I can't have much of a relationship." His words seemed inadequate. They didn't nearly express what he felt about Addie. The strengthening undercurrent of conflict and confusion that made him hesitate on the brink.

"I know," she said sadly. "But we'll wait."

"For what?"

"To see what time permits."

After a few more bites of sorbet, she stood up.

"I'll walk back while you finish eating," she said. "It'll look better if we don't arrive at the office together."

"We have nothing to hide." *How many times has every cop heard that?*

Addie answered him with a smile.

"I'll go," Quinn said. "Stay here and finish your sorbet."

"You finish it." She bent down and kissed his cheek.

Her lips were still cool from the sorbet, but beneath the ice was fire.

"People really in love aren't hungry," she said, and walked from the restaurant without looking back.

Quinn sat and sipped his coffee for a while. He knew he was being worked. Oh, Christ, was he being worked!

Lunch with Addie had seemed like such a good idea, but it had made him uneasy. More tentative. He knew about how human experience was doomed to repetition. One fall after another.

When he closed his eyes he could almost see his toes hanging over the abyss.

He wasn't hungry.

72

Lisa Bolt crossed the street toward her hotel, where she'd left her luggage after checking out. Surely they must have held it while she was in the hospital. She'd registered under another name, so they wouldn't connect her with the Lisa Bolt in the news. But had the fact that she'd not returned for so long attracted suspicion? Would the hotel contact Homeland Security and have the suitcase treated as a possible bomb?

Lisa doubted it. The last thing a down-and-out hotel like hers would want is a posse of authorities searching the place with everything from metal detectors to dogs.

If anything, hotel personnel might have opened the suitcase to see what was inside—maybe to find out if there was something valuable. If that had happened, they had been disappointed. They'd have found nothing but Lisa's limited and well-worn travel wardrobe.

She was about to enter the lobby when a hand gripped her arm just above the elbow, squeezing hard enough to hurt.

"Quiet and you won't be harmed," a man's voice said.

She turned to look at who had her. A medium-height man, middle aged but trim, wearing dark dress pants, a blue shirt with the sleeves rolled up. His eyes were barely visible behind darkly tinted glasses. They were steady and serious and made her a believer.

"I have a knife," he said. "Start a fuss and I'll use it."

The way she was bent at the waist from the pain was attracting attention. A woman came close and asked in a concerned voice if she was all right.

"She's fine now," the man said. "I won't let her fall again."

He led her away, toward a narrow walkway that ran alongside the hotel. Shaded as it was by brick and stone walls that seemed to converge above them, it was dim as evening in the confined space. There were a few plastic trash bags piled there, and a Dumpster squatted in the light near the opposite end of the passageway. She knew there was a fire door somewhere along the hotel's wall, but she didn't think they were going inside. That didn't seem to be what the man had in mind.

Though badly frightened, she tried to gather her courage.

"Listen," she said, when he'd loosened his grip on her arm. "Don't think you—"

His fist hit her ribs like a hammer, and she sagged against the wall.

"Don't have any doubts about who's in charge here," he said. He leaned in close to her, supporting his weight with one hand against the bricks, his face inches from hers. As if they were lovers.

That was what anyone glancing in the walkway would see, a lovers' tryst, away from crowded streets and prying eyes. Two people who wanted to be left alone by the rest of the world.

They stood that way for what seemed a long time while she managed to catch her breath. His breath smelled like a combination of onions and mint-flavored mouthwash.

"What the shit do you want?" she finally managed to gasp.

"That's easy," he said.

* * *

Quinn parked the Lincoln illegally in the same loading zone where he'd been parked when he'd seen Addie and called her over. His mind was still working on their conversation in the restaurant. Parsing words, reading meanings and messages that probably hadn't existed. Trying to figure out how he felt.

He entered the office and caught a glimpse of Addie over by the coffee brewer, but he didn't look directly at her. Fedderman was at his desk, going over something in a file folder. Pearl was seated at her computer, staring past it at Quinn. There was a gleam of curiosity in her eyes. Pearl sensing that something had shifted in some subtle way, but she didn't yet know what, how, or why.

"Anything?" Quinn asked. His standard question.

"Nobody else has been murdered and had her nipples cut off," Fedderman said. "That's the good news."

"And the bad news?"

"Everything else."

Both women were silent.

"I had Sellers wait till tomorrow morning's edition before planting the info about Keller's presence in the city, and at the Belington," Quinn said. "She promised to do it subtly enough that it won't seem an obvious trap."

"Can she bring that off?" Addie asked.

"She's an artist at that kind of thing," Quinn said. "She—"

He was interrupted by the door flying open and banging against the wall.

Lisa Bolt staggered in. Her left eye was swollen, and she was limping with one foot cocked out at an odd angle.

Fedderman jumped up and kept her from falling. He led her to his desk chair and sat her down.

Quinn had picked up the phone and was about to peck out 911. Lisa shook her head violently from side to side and held up a hand in a signal for him to stop.

He placed the receiver back in its cradle.

"I'm not hurt that bad," she said. "Nothing's broken. Not like the accident."

But the way she was wincing and holding herself, it obviously pained her to talk.

"You've been beaten," Quinn said.

She nodded and then whispered something no one understood.

Quinn moved closer and bent low so he could hear. She turned her head so her lips were close to his ear.

"Archer."

73

"You mean Keller," Quinn said.

Lisa shook her head no again. Her breathing was ragged. "He's here in New York, been here a while, under the name Archer. You called him on his cell phone thinking he was in Detroit. He's been *here*, and he must have found me somehow, maybe followed me from the hospital."

Addie arrived with a glass of water and handed it to Quinn, who held it in front of Lisa. Her throat worked noisily as she took half a dozen swallows, spilling most of the glass's contents onto her blouse. Quinn saw what might have been specks of blood on her blouse along with the water.

"Take your time," he said, still holding the water close. "Tell us about it when you're ready."

She pushed the glass away. "He approached me on the street near my hotel. I didn't recognize him at first, but Chrissie'd told me about him, shown me some of the old family photos."

"You're sure it was Keller?" Pearl asked.

"Yeah. No doubt about it. He's been in New York trying to find Chrissie, and he figured I'd know where she is. He didn't believe me when I told him I didn't know, so he tried scaring me into telling him. Then he tried to beat it out of me, kept hitting me and asking over and over."

"You told him?" Quinn asked.

"I couldn't. I didn't know Chrissie's whereabouts. Still don't know. Keller's afraid that if she's taken alive, not only will his dual identities come out, but so will his darker secrets. He'll be professionally, politically, and personally ruined."

She made a fish mouth and strained to move her head forward. Quinn tilted the glass so she could slurp down more water, feeling some of it slosh coolly over his thumb.

"I'm sure Keller intends to kill Chrissie," Lisa said. "He has to. She's the only eyewitness to what he did back in Ohio. He wants to short-circuit any investigation or testimony that will substantiate Tiffany's childhood molestation."

"Makes sense," Fedderman said, giving Quinn a look.

Quinn didn't have to be told. "While you were shadowing our investigation so you could get prior information to Chrissie, Keller was shadowing you so he could locate Chrissie."

"Right," Lisa said. "I knew somebody was tailing me, but I didn't know who. It wasn't a pro, so I ruled out anybody here, and Vitali or Mishkin. I wouldn't have known I was being shadowed at all if it was someone like that. I also had no idea what my shadow wanted."

"But now you do."

"Yeah. I'm sure I always shook him; it was easy. And I never led him to Chrissie. He must have gotten frustrated and decided to confront me. But I couldn't give him what he wanted."

"Of course not." Quinn patted her arm.

Lisa drew in a deep, harsh breath and braced herself with her hands on the chair arms. She stood up, swayed, and then remained steady. She smoothed her clothes, brushing futilely at the stains on her blouse.

"I had to come here and tell you," she said. "I thought you should know about Archer putting one over on you."

"Keller," Quinn said.

"Whatever. Long as we're talking about the same creep. Long as you know his real purpose is to see that Chrissie's killed before she can talk about him. About the past. He'll tell you he has her best interests at heart, that he wants to keep her safe. But he's lying."

"Everyone seems to be," Quinn said. "Are you sure you don't know where Chrissie is?"

Lisa's blood-rimmed eyes met and held Quinn's gaze. "I do not know."

"And we believe you."

She shuffled toward the door.

"Where are you going?" Addie asked in alarm.

"My hotel. Gotta rest."

"You shouldn't be alone," Quinn said.

"I'll be all right. Archer—Keller—finally believed me when I said I didn't know where Chrissie was. In my job, I've been beat up before. I'd know if I was hurt bad. If I just get some rest I'll be okay. Company's the last thing I need."

"We can't force you," Fedderman said.

Lisa managed a painful grin. "I always hear that, then damned if somebody doesn't try."

"If you say you're not badly hurt, we'll take your word for it," Quinn said. "But at least let one of us drive you to your hotel."

"No, I'll take a cab."

"We can call one."

"They're easy to hail down at the corner."

Quinn knew that was true. Lisa could walk to the corner, and within minutes she'd be gone. "That address you gave the hospital," he said, "it isn't accurate."

"I was afraid of whoever was shadowing me. It turned out I was right to be scared."

"You surely were. What's your hotel?"

"The Middleton Towers on Eighth Avenue."

She made her way to the door, moving normally now except for a slight limp. She turned and smiled. "Thanks, all of you. And I'm sorry for any trouble I've caused you."

A few seconds after she went out the office door, Quinn heard the street door open and close.

"Follow her, Pearl," he said. "And do a fine job of it."

"Always do," Pearl said, and went to the door and then stood for a few seconds, playing out some time and distance for Lisa Bolt.

When Pearl was gone, Quinn phoned the Middleton Towers and asked to be connected to Lisa Bolt's room.

The desk clerk told him there was no Lisa Bolt registered.

Quinn hung up the phone and gave a grin that was more of a grimace. "Is there no one in this screwed-up world who isn't a liar?" he asked the room in general.

"No one," Addie said.

74

True to her word, Lisa limped to the corner and waved a cab over to the curb. By that time, Pearl was sitting behind the steering wheel in the unmarked with the engine running.

Traffic was heavy, and from time to time Pearl lost sight of the cab. Once she thought she'd lost it completely. But she'd memorized its number, and after easing the car around vehicles stalled at a traffic signal, she was able to find the cab again. It was traffic-locked as she was.

The familiar silhouette of Lisa's head and shoulders was still in the cab's rear window. Lisa didn't once turn around to check and see if she'd been followed. Pearl guessed the beleaguered woman figured nothing worse could happen to her and was all out of apprehension. That could happen sometimes. It was actually a kind of surrender.

The cab pulled to the curb on Columbus Avenue, and a few seconds later Lisa got out. She stood up gradually, as if her back hurt, and now she did glance up and down the street. Pearl had parked half a block away, but hadn't yet climbed out of the car. Lisa's gaze slid right past her.

Lisa began limping along Columbus. She posed no problem for Pearl, who locked the unmarked behind her and casually began to follow. There were enough people on the sidewalks that, even if Lisa glanced behind her again, it was doubtful she'd pick out Pearl, who was nimble and a bit of a chameleon.

At a side street at the end of a line of small shops, Lisa stopped. She opened the brown leather purse she was carrying and appeared to study a slip of paper, as if double-checking an address.

Then she turned the corner and began walking faster and with more purpose.

Pearl watched her ease her way up some concrete steps and enter a four-story stone and pink granite apartment building that looked as if it contained eight units.

Maybe sixteen small units, Pearl suddenly thought. She'd better work her way closer if she was going to find out which apartment Lisa entered.

Trying to time it just right, she jogged down the street to the building and didn't hesitate going up the steps. If the place had a security door and Lisa had to be buzzed up, Pearl might find herself face-to-face with her in the foyer. On the other hand, if Pearl waited, she might not be able to follow Lisa up the stairs, staying out of sight while she saw which apartment she entered.

Pearl drew a deep breath, pulled open the heavy wooden door, and stepped inside.

No security door. And no Lisa. Not in the foyer or on the stairs.

The building had an elevator. Pearl saw a tentative brass arrow climbing a set of faded numerals. It was at the two.

Immediately Pearl started up the wide wooden stairs, taking them two at a time. She hesitated on the second-floor landing, peeking around the corner to see if the elevator had stopped.

It hadn't. The brass arrow on that floor was still climbing. If the arrow was accurate, the elevator was almost to the third floor.

Pearl took the steps three at a time, using the slickly worn banister to yank herself along.

She reached the third floor just in time to peer around the corner and see Lisa step from the elevator and walk away from her, down a dim hall with a linoleum floor patterned to look like gray tiles.

Pearl watched her knock on a door and get no reply.

She knocked again, waited a full minute, and then dipped into her purse and came up with what looked like a lock pick. As she bent over to use the pick, she reflexively turned the knob and pushed to make sure the door was locked.

It was unlocked.

Lisa replaced her lock pick in her purse and entered the apartment.

Pearl grinned. *Gotcha!*

She walked quietly down the hall and noted the apartment number, 3-S, then returned to the stairwell.

What to do now? Her instructions were to follow Lisa, not to confront her. But what was Lisa doing there? It obviously wasn't her apartment, or she would have had a key.

And she'd knocked and gotten no response. She was almost certainly the only one in the apartment.

So what was she doing in there? Waiting for a friend who lived there? Burglarizing the place?

The friend was more likely. But maybe Lisa wasn't waiting.

Pearl decided the apartment was probably only a brief stop for Lisa. She might be on the move again soon. Maybe with different clothes. Maybe with a new identity.

The logical thing was to go back outside and wait for Lisa to emerge. See where she went next.

Before leaving the building, Pearl made sure there was no rear exit. Then she went outside and walked back to the corner, where she could stand and not be noticed, and where she could see the concrete steps to the building Lisa had entered.

Lisa was in a box. If she came down the steps to the sidewalk and turned toward Pearl, all Pearl had to do was duck into a doorway or otherwise make herself invisible until Lisa passed, then resume tailing her. If she came down the steps and turned the other way, there was plenty of time for Pearl to catch up with her before she disappeared down the street. Limping Lisa didn't cover ground fast.

Pearl put on her knockoff Gucci sunglasses, crossed her arms, leaned against a NO PARKING ON CORNER sign, and waited.

75

Quinn and Fedderman pushed through a heavy plate-glass revolving door and entered the lobby of the Belington. The bustling hum and rush of the city suddenly became quiet.

The lobby was not only hushed but surprisingly cool and vast. An array of ornate brass bars was affixed to the long registration desk in a way that suggested tellers' windows in an obsessively secure bank. The marble floor was patterned with fine cracks. The ceiling was vaulted, with a graceful design of arched wooden beams. Artificial green vines tumbled from large terra-cotta pots next to groupings of deeply upholstered furniture. On a table in front of a fan-shaped mirror were chipped and yellowed plaster busts of Artemis and Apollo, gazing away from each other like the arrogant bookends they were.

"Looks like an ancient Greek ruin that's been spruced up," Fedderman said.

Ignoring a bellhop and curious desk clerk, they made their way to the elevators.

Vitali and Mishkin had met Keller at LaGuardia and driven him to the hotel. They'd ensconced him there according to Quinn's instructions and explained the rules. Mishkin had later dropped by the office and left a room key card for Quinn. He'd assured him that Keller was being cooperative, and everything was set up at the hotel. Quinn, being Quinn, wanted to make sure of that. He also had plenty of questions for Keller. Such as: How long had he been in New York? Had he actually flown in to LaGuardia, or taken a cab there so he could pretend? And had Lisa Bolt been telling the truth about him beating her? Lisa was a smooth liar.

"He's in two-twenty-one," Quinn said, leaning on the glowing up button as if it were a doorbell and he might speed things along inside.

Speed wasn't a feature of the Belington. Quinn and Fedderman got tired of waiting for an elevator and took the carpeted stairs to the second floor.

The halls in the old building were wide and long, lined with pale blue doors with raised panels. Quinn and Fedderman went to 221 and knocked.

When there was no response, Quinn knocked louder, keeping an eye on the door's glass peephole for any change of light.

Nothing.

Quinn pulled his wallet from his hip pocket and extracted his key card.

It worked on the first swipe, and they pushed the door open.

Quinn went in first, eyes darting left and right, taking in the neatly made bed with the closed suitcase on it, the hanging bag in the otherwise bare closet. Unlike the hall doors, the closet door was a cheap hollow-core panel that slid on tracks. The Belington's rooms didn't match the lobby's grandeur. They were small and plain and modestly furnished.

Both men stood motionless and listened. There was no sound of a shower or bath running. Fedderman went to the bathroom door, knocked twice, and then eased the door open. He looked back over his shoulder and shook his head. The bathroom was unoccupied.

Like the rest of the room.

"Keller agreed to stay in his room until we contacted

him," Quinn said, annoyed by yet another missing partici-
pant in his plans.

"He probably stayed about twenty seconds," Fedderman
said. He opened and closed the dresser drawers, all of them
empty. "Didn't even bother to unpack."

"So many people disappearing at one time or another, we
oughta turn the case over to Missing Persons," Quinn said.

He walked to the connecting door leading to the adjacent
room and opened it to make sure it was unlocked. That room
was to be occupied by whoever would be listening to
Keller's bugged room, and would provide a staging area for
the police if and when Chrissie did show up to take out her
rage on dear Dad. Quinn let his glance roam over the room,
identical to Keller's, and then closed the door, leaving it unlocked. He wandered over to the bed and checked the luggage tag. It said the suitcase belonged to Edward Archer.
Quinn was getting used to this, people with at least two identities.

"Maybe he went out for something to eat," Fedderman
said.

"The agreement was for him to use room service."

"Ever notice how our agreements never seem to work
out?"

"Hard not to," Quinn said.

"The people we meet in our business, crooks and killers
and such, they're dishonest."

"Can't count on them."

"I guess we shouldn't be surprised that Edward Keller is a
lying bastard."

"I'm not surprised," Quinn said. "But I am pissed off."

Quinn returned to the suitcase on the bed and reached
over to open it.

"Careful," Fedderman said. "It might be a bomb."

It wasn't a bomb, but it was empty.

76

Pearl was getting tired of waiting.

The first fifteen minutes, nobody entered or exited the stone and pink granite building. Then a woman with what looked like a greyhound on a leash came down the concrete steps. Ten minutes later, a man in a blue Windbreaker and white golf cap exited and jogged down the steps, flipping away a cigarette and opening a dark umbrella as he descended. Pearl noticed for the first time that there was a fine mist. Her blouse was lightly spotted, and the back of its collar felt damp and tacky on her neck. She hunkered down and decided not to move to shelter unless it began raining harder.

Five minutes later an elderly lady pulling a two-wheeled folding grocery cart approached the apartment building. There were three brown paper sacks stuffed into the cart. She wrestled the contraption up the slippery wet steps and disappeared inside.

Pearl shot a look at her watch. Lisa Bolt had been in the apartment building for half an hour. It obviously wasn't her apartment, but despite the business with the lock pick, maybe she was staying there. Or visiting someone who *was* staying there.

Like Chrissie Keller.

Pearl decided to go check. It seemed the thing to do, without an umbrella.

She encountered no one as she took the elevator to the third floor and made her way toward apartment 3-S.

When she was ten feet away, she noticed the door was open about an inch, as if someone had pulled it closed but not hard enough for the latch to engage.

Somebody leaving in a hurry?

It hadn't been Lisa, Pearl was sure. There was no way she could have slipped past without being seen.

Except for the time I spent in the elevator.

Pearl hadn't worn her blazer or shoulder holster, so she removed her Glock nine-millimeter from her purse and held the gun tight against her thigh. Then she pushed the door open, raising the gun at the same time, and went in fast, holding the Glock in front of her with both hands, hearing the door bounce off the wall behind her.

She crouched and swept the barrel of the gun this way and that.

But her dramatic entrance had played to no audience and brought no response. The apartment, what she could see of it, *seemed* unoccupied.

Only *seemed,* because there was someone else in here. She was sure of it. Be it gut feeling, stirred air, the additional fraction of a degree of body heat, subliminal sound . . . whatever, she knew she wasn't alone.

Her throat was dry, and it was an effort to swallow as she decided to explore.

There was nowhere to hide in the living room. The furnishings were shabby, and there was dust on the matching tables at each end of the long green sofa. On a windowsill was a lineup of small potted plants, all of them wilted. An empty Diet Pepsi can lay on its side on one of the tables, and a copy of Oprah's magazine lay open on the floor as if it had been tossed there. Somebody was a lousy housekeeper.

Still holding the gun at the ready, Pearl held her breath and negotiated the hall. It took her only a moment to glance in the tiny bathroom and assure herself that it was clear.

On to what must be the apartment's only bedroom.

It also appeared unoccupied.

There was an odd burnt scent in the air, as if someone had been smoking here recently. Or cooking.

The bed was made but somewhat sloppily, and was too low for someone to hide under.

The closet. If she really wasn't alone, he, she, it, would probably be in the closet. Hiding behind the clothes draped on hangers. Waiting.

Pearl steeled herself and yanked open the closet door.

No clothes at all. There were only a few wire hangers inside, an old coupon for pizza on the floor, nothing on the wooden shelf above. The faint scent of mothballs wafted from the closet.

Pearl shut the closet door, turned around, and saw the foot.

It was barely visible on the floor on the other side of the bed, as if someone had fallen out of bed and was lying there.

The foot was bare and had toes with chipped red enamel on the nails. There was a callus or blister on the side of the big toe.

Pearl eased over until she was against the wall and peered at the narrow space between wall and bed.

Lisa Bolt was crammed into that space, her left foot beyond the bed, her right leg jammed sideways with the knee crooked. She was wearing her jeans, but that was all.

Pearl squeezed in to where she could reach Lisa. She called her name several times to see if she was conscious.

"Okay, okay," Lisa mumbled, though there was no movement and she didn't open her eyes.

Pearl reached Lisa's perspiring arms and began pulling on them. They kept slipping out of her grasp.

"Try, will you?" Pearl said, after one of her fingernails had been bent back. The finger continued to throb.

Begrudgingly, and after much flailing around, Lisa cooperated enough so that she was turned and on her knees. Pearl gripped her around the waist and got her standing upright, and Lisa collapsed onto the bed.

Pearl eased her around until Lisa was lying lengthwise with her head on the pillow. That was when she saw the pattern of cigarette burns on Lisa's breasts and recognized the scorched smell she'd noticed in the bedroom. It hadn't been from something cooking. Not exactly.

Someone had tortured Lisa by holding a lit cigarette to her bare flesh.

The realization in the hot bedroom with the smell of burned flesh made Pearl's stomach turn, and for a moment she thought she might vomit. When she swallowed, she tasted bitterness at the back of her throat.

"Who did this to you?" she asked.

"I'm sorry," Lisa said, and started to sob.

Pearl almost slapped her, and then thought better of it. "There's no time for this sorry bullshit now," she said. "Tell me what went on here. Tell me now, Lisa."

Lisa struggled to control herself and went from sobbing to gasping to ragged breathing. She was calming down.

"Get a grip," Pearl said.

"Yeah . . . I'm okay now."

She might have thought she was about to be slapped, and that had done the trick.

"What are you doing here?" Pearl asked.

"I thought Chrissie might be here. This was a place where we met once, but she's moved. Must have been scared."

"Scared of us? The police?"

"Yeah. You, of course. Scared of her father, too. She must have seen in the news that he was in town."

"Was it Keller who did that to you? With the cigarette?"

"Yeah. He left a while ago."

The man in the blue Windbreaker, with the umbrella. Flicking his cigarette away as he went down the steps.

"Damn it!" Pearl said.

"You screw up?"

"Royally."

"Welcome to the club," Lisa said. "I knew Chrissie would be here or in another apartment where she's been staying. She wasn't here." Her gaze roamed around the room, and her eyes widened slightly, as if fear had set in again. "Keller was suddenly behind me. The bastard had been hiding. I couldn't put up any kind of resistance." She sounded ashamed.

"You were surprised," Pearl said. "And you probably should still have been in your hospital bed to begin with. Don't be so hard on yourself."

"He tied me up, took off my blouse, and started in on me with the cigarettes. He jammed a pillow over my face whenever I tried to scream. Punched me around, too. I think he broke something in me. I heard it crack. He demanded to know where Chrissie was. Said he'd kill me if I didn't tell him, and that he'd find me and kill me if I lied to him."

Lisa started to shiver, maybe going into shock. Pearl laid the other half of the old bedspread over her to warm her up. The shivering got worse.

"It's okay," Pearl said. "He's gone."

"Of course he's gone. I gave him what he wanted, the address of the apartment where he could find Chrissie." Lisa pointed feebly toward the door. "He left to find Chrissie. I told you he wanted her. I told you."

"You told us," Pearl said, feeling for her cell phone in her purse. She punched out 911 to get an ambulance in a hurry for Lisa.

"Now tell me the address you gave Keller," she said, when EMS had an ambulance on the way.

Lisa lay with her eyes closed, as if reading from the insides of the lids, and told her.

Pearl called Quinn, filled him in on the situation, and re-layed the West Side address. Then she called Vitali and clued him in, along with Mishkin. They were Midtown in their un-marked car. She asked Vitali to have a radio car sent to where she was with Lisa as soon as possible, and another to the address where Chrissie was supposed to be staying.

"They're on the way," Vitali said. "The uniforms will make sure Lisa gets back in the hospital. Maybe she'll stay there a while this time."

"She will," Pearl said. "She's got broken bones this time. Cigarette burns in bad places." Over the phone she heard the unmarked's siren kick in, parting the traffic in front of Vitali and Mishkin.

"What are you figuring on doing, Pearl?"

"Soon as the uniforms get here, I'm leaving for where you and Mishkin are going—Chrissie's apartment. We need to get there before Keller."

"You wouldn't realize it over the phone, but right now Harold has our car doing ninety on Broadway. We only slow down when we have to get up on the sidewalk."

"He'll kill her," Lisa said in a pain-weary voice behind Pearl. "That bastard, her father's gonna kill her."

Pearl said, "A couple of cops doing ninety think other-wise."

77

Pearl had to park the unmarked a block away from the apartment address Lisa had given her. The street was cordoned off by twisted strands of yellow crime-scene tape, along with a striped blue and white sawhorse. Two big uniformed officers were standing nearby with their fists on their hips.

The cops stood very still, made so much larger by what they represented, and watched Pearl approach. Cops were like that at times like this; sometimes she forgot they were on her side—for the most part, anyway—and that she was one of them. She couldn't shake the feeling that she was defying their shall-not-pass posture and attitude.

They represent the law, but not always justice.

Quinn's kind of bullshit.

She flashed her ID, and one of the uniforms, a young dark-haired guy who looked like movie star material, raised the tape so Pearl could bend at the waist and edge beneath it. She knew him from her years in the department but couldn't remember his name. Dexter or Derrick . . . something like that. He smiled and winked at her. These guys never gave up.

The block was clear of traffic, and the knots of onlookers that had gathered were all behind her on the other side of the tape and sawhorse. As Pearl walked along the deserted sidewalk toward the apartment building that supposedly contained Chrissie Keller, and possibly Chrissie's father, faces gazed at her from the other side of windows. Some of the faces looked bored, some concerned, others amused.

Every hundred feet or so a uniformed cop stood or paced, making sure the citizens stayed inside, away from any potential line of fire. Most of those caught inside the cordon who'd requested in the beginning to get out were gone, leaving those who for some reason couldn't leave, along with the usual gawkers who were thrilled that their day had been juiced up by a hunt for a killer. Something was going to happen here. Somebody might die.

Up ahead were flashing lights and an assemblage of emergency vehicles parked at various angles, as if they were toys scattered along the curb by a young child. Pearl saw another, smaller collection of vehicles beyond the first, so that the two gatherings of cops and cars flanked the building where they had finally found Chrissie Keller. Figures moved among the nearest array of vehicles. One of them was Quinn.

When he saw Pearl approaching, he moved away from the cluster of people he'd been talking with and assumed a waiting attitude.

"Looks like everybody beat me here," she said, slightly out of breath.

"And everybody was too late," Quinn said. "Edward Keller's up on the fifth floor with Chrissie."

"Shit!" Pearl said, and actually kicked at the sidewalk.

Quinn understood her disappointment.

Pearl glanced around at the army of cops. "Keller's holding her hostage?"

"That's how it was supposed to be," Quinn said. "But it didn't work out that way. Chrissie was waiting and ready for trouble. She's up there holding a shotgun on Keller."

Pearl saw a white windowless van parked closest to the building. She knew a hostage expert was inside, possibly talking to Chrissie.

"She demanding something?" Pearl asked. "Or is she working up to killing him?"

Killing her father. Pearl tried to imagine how that must feel. It was something her mind didn't want to touch.

"She's not saying," Quinn said. "She's agreed to talk, though, if we send someone upstairs to her."

"Who's the someone?"

"She didn't specify who or how many. Hostage control says two or three of us can go, along with the person most likely to be able to talk Chrissie out of pulling the trigger."

It didn't take Pearl long to figure out who that might be. "Her mother?"

"Yeah. At least Erin thinks so."

As if the pronunciation of her name were magic, an unmarked car pulled up to where a uniform raised a resolutely waving arm to halt it, and Erin got out on the passenger side. Sal Vitali climbed out from behind the steering wheel, Mishkin from the back of the car. Sal took a cautious look up at the face of the brick apartment building, calculating angles and gripping Erin's arm with a firm gentleness as he escorted her toward Pearl and Quinn.

He and Mishkin must have made a detour after they'd talked with Pearl, to pick up Erin and rush her to the scene.

Erin looked pale and frightened. "Sal's explained the situation to me."

So they're on a first-name basis, Pearl thought.

Quinn quickly and precisely told them the plan. Pearl realized he must have given it a lot of thought while waiting for Erin to arrive.

As he was talking, a uniformed cop was fitting a Kevlar vest on Erin, making sure it was adjusted for a tight fit. The Velcro straps made harsh ripping sounds in the warm afternoon.

"Pearl, Feds, and I will take Erin upstairs on the elevator," Quinn said. "We'll take our time. Sal and Harold will climb the fire escape in back and let themselves into the apartment while we're diverting Chrissie's attention. We'll be in the living room, and both of you try to move to that end of the apartment, where you might be able to get a bead on Chrissie. Nobody fires a shot unless it's absolutely necessary."

Erin adjusted the bulky vest so it fit more comfortably. A breeze ruffled her red hair, and she didn't look so scared now. Her square jaw was still set like a rock, but her eyes were different. She looked determined. Quinn was staring at her. She gave him the slightest of nods, as if assuring him that she was up to this. Quinn figured she probably was up to it.

"Everybody be careful," Quinn said. "We screw this up and the SWAT team'll take their turn."

And somebody will die.

"Bullet city," Vitali said.

"Seldom are you so poetic, Sal," Mishkin said.

"It's the moment, Harold."

Vitali and Mishkin moved away, toward the passageway that led to the rear of the building and the fire escape. Staying close to the front of the building so anyone firing from a window would have an impossible angle, Quinn led the way as he, then Erin, Pearl, and Fedderman made their way toward the entrance. Pearl saw that Erin was gripping Quinn's belt at the small of his back, as if he were leading the blind.

They entered, crossed the small tiled lobby, and rode the tiny, stifling elevator to the fifth floor. It seemed warmer and more confining as they rose.

Pearl absently touched the bulk of her handgun beneath her blazer, as if checking to see if her heart was still beating.

Thinking of Yancy.

78

When they exited the elevator, Quinn led them only a few feet down the hall to 5-D. The apartment had windows facing the street. Windows that he thought offered the SWAT snipers maybe too much opportunity. If everything went right, there would soon be a lot of people in the apartment.

If everything went right, no shots would be fired.

But if anything went wrong . . .

He stood off to the side of the door and knocked.

"Coming in, Chrissie!"

There was no sound from inside, but he was sure she'd heard him. At least heard the knock.

He reached over, rotated the knob, and pushed on the door.

It was unlocked and swung open wide.

He breathed in deeply, knowing it might be his last breath, then stepped into the doorway.

Edward Keller was standing awkwardly with his arms at his sides, leaning slightly to his right with his knee braced against the arm of a pale green easy chair for balance. He was a medium-sized man, wearing gray pants and a white shirt, red tie. The tie was loosened. The shirt was plastered to his body with perspiration so the pink of his flesh showed through. What was left of Keller's thinning dark hair was mussed, as if he'd been raking his fingers through it. His eyes were red-rimmed from the sting of the rivulets of sweat that were tracking down his face. It was an ordinary face, made stiff as a mask by terror.

He didn't look at all mean or dangerous now.

That was because his daughter, Chrissie, stood calmly ten feet away from him, holding a twelve-gauge shotgun trained on his midsection.

Keller stared with slack-jawed fear at Quinn and the others who filed in behind him. Something was going to happen here, and soon. He didn't know what, but it scared the hell out of him.

Scared Quinn, too.

A shotgun. Just what we need. She must have brought it with her from Ohio.

Quinn sensed the others spreading out behind him. They knew the shotgun, which looked like a semiautomatic, would, if fired wildly over and over, turn the apartment into a bloody death trap.

He turned his attention to Chrissie. She seemed calm, almost in a trance. Speeding along tracks leading to a train wreck and unable and unwilling to stop. The shotgun rested light and easy in her hands. She'd grown up in a small town in bird-hunting country. Quinn hoped she was familiar with guns and wouldn't go crazy with the thing.

Keller broke the silence by stammering, "Please get her to stop pointing that shotgun at me."

"It wouldn't hurt you to drop the barrel a few inches, dear," Quinn said to Chrissie.

There was no change in her posture or expression. The gun remained steady. Quinn noticed she was standing in one of the few areas of the room where there was no chance of a sniper's shot from outside hitting her. She'd thought this out. Her eyes darted to Quinn, back to her father.

"It would be better for all concerned," Quinn said calmly, "if you lowered the gun and we talked."

He was suddenly aware that Pearl had unobtrusively removed her handgun from its holster and was holding it down
and slightly behind her right thigh, where Chrissie wouldn't
see it.

Jesus! Yancy!

Shouldn't have let Pearl come up here . . .

Quinn pushed Pearl from his thoughts and smiled at
Chrissie, moving a few feet to his right so she could see him
in her peripheral vision while looking at her father. Keller
was trembling now. There was a spreading urine stain on the
front of his gray pants.

"What is it you want?" Quinn asked Chrissie.

Her answer was spat from behind clenched teeth. "Justice."

"Then we're on the same page," Quinn said. "So let's talk
about this and see if we can arrive at justice."

"I don't want to talk."

Quinn saw Keller stiffen as she spoke, asking himself the
same question Quinn was asking: *Then why did she let these
people come up here?*

And suddenly he knew why.

The shotgun roared, and Keller's body leaped backward
and spun, spewing blood as it fell.

Chrissie brought around the long barrel of the shotgun,
drawing a bead on Quinn, then Erin, Quinn, then Erin. Erin
began to scream.

"He's dead, Chrissie!" Quinn said, almost screaming
himself so he could be heard with Erin making all that noise.

Erin had figured it out, too. Chrissie had known she
would come into the apartment, and Chrissie knew *why* Erin
would come. Even though hers had been a sin of omission,
Erin wanted Chrissie's silence as much as Ed Keller had.
She wanted to make sure of that silence.

Or maybe Erin would have settled for simple forgiveness.

But forgiveness was out of the question now.

Quinn tried again to make himself heard. "You can stop it now, Chrissie! Stop!"

"Kill her!" Erin shrieked. "Shoot her, goddamn it! Shoot her!"

The shotgun barrel stopped moving where it was aimed at a point precisely between Quinn, who was the hunter and authority figure who'd come for Chrissie perhaps in the way her father had, and Erin, her mother. It didn't waver. But Quinn knew that it would soon move a foot or so one way or the other. Chrissie was making her choice.

"Don't do it, dear. . . ."

"Shoot her, goddamn it! Shoot her!" Erin shrieked again.

Quinn heard Fedderman's nine-millimeter bark beside him. The bullet struck Chrissie in the side and jerked her half around so she staggered back a few steps. The shotgun barrel flew upward, and a round exploded into the ceiling, bringing down a shower of plaster or drywall powder.

Now she was lowering the gun, her finger still on the trigger. It would take a second for the long barrel to swing around.

Quinn's old police special revolver was out of its holster and blasting away. He'd known he had no choice and had acted automatically.

A halo of red mist appeared around Chrissie's head. Her eyes rolled back, and she collapsed.

The silence was complete for several seconds. Then Quinn's ears began to ring.

He looked at Fedderman, then at Pearl. They both seemed all right. Erin was slumped on the floor, the side of her head pressed to the wall. Quinn went to her, bent low, and looked into her wide, uncomprehending eyes.

"Are you hit?" His own voice, coming from far away. He screamed it again but could still barely hear himself. "Are you hit?"

She shook her head no and then said something. He read her lips: *My baby was going to kill me.*

Quinn straightened up and glanced at where the winner of the Tri-State Triple Monkey Squared Super Jackpot lay dead with the lower half of her face missing. He went to Pearl. She was still holding her Glock at her side, pointed at the floor. He gently removed the heavy gun from her hand and checked the breech, then the clip.

The gun hadn't been fired.

He gave the Glock back to her and then gripped her shoulders and smiled down at her.

"Damned thing jammed," she said.

He wondered if it had.

She looked away.

He kissed her forehead, and she smiled back at him.

Not much of a smile, but something.

79

Quinn was in Renz's office the next morning, seated before Renz's wide desk. Renz was ensconced in his plushy upholstered chair, looking plump, satisfied, and permanent. Heat lay over both men in slices of sunlight from the slanted blinds.

"It worked out well," Renz said. One eye shone brighter than the other in the light from the blinds.

"It worked out," Quinn said.

Renz appeared puzzled by Quinn's lack of enthusiasm. "Addie has it right. Chrissie murdered the homeless woman, Maureen Sanders, to make us think the Carver was active again and prompt a vigorous investigation that might lead Chrissie to him. That was why Chrissie shadowed your activities. Then she committed the other two murders as a way to keep the investigation moving. Or maybe—and Helen thinks this is *very* possible—after doing Maureen Sanders, Chrissie developed a lust for blood and couldn't stop."

"Helen's been wrong a few times," Quinn said.

Renz leaned back in his chair, tucking in his chin so his fleshy jowls spilled over his stiff white collar. "*If* Chrissie didn't commit the other copycat murders, and the real Carver was active again, Chrissie's death and assumed guilt will probably induce him to return to his state of what he considers to be retirement."

"Those sound like Helen's words."

"They are. And with the Carver's last two murders—three, if you count Yancy Taggart—attributed to Chrissie, he'll be safe. And the city is safe, comparatively."

"And your political aspirations are safe."

"Comparatively."

"You are a bastard, Harley."

"Sure. But I said *if* Chrissie didn't commit the other murders. I think she probably did, and the Carver only had to outsmart us once, a long time ago."

"Sounds like you admire him."

"Well, he beat us," Renz said. "That's the only thing I admire about him."

"So you're satisfied with this outcome," Quinn said.

"Everybody's satisfied with it. Ask them."

"I have."

"And?"

"They're satisfied."

Renz grinned and shrugged. Then his expression abruptly changed, as if he'd suffered some slight pain. Or realized one might not go away. "*You're* still not satisfied, right?"

"It fits together," Quinn said. "But just."

"Like the killer was shot through the head, just." Renz tilted forward in his chair and propped his elbows on the desk. "Don't poke around at this, Quinn. It's a sleeping dog you'd best let lie."

Quinn smiled. "Because the dog might reveal some inconvenient truths?"

"Because the sonofabitch might have rabies."

Elana Dare twirled before the full-length mirror mounted on the back of her bedroom door, glancing over her shoulder so she could see the action of the silk skirt she'd bought only hours ago. The smooth, lined material draped from her hips as gracefully as it had in the shop's mirrors. It moved just right, was just revealing enough. Any tawdriness that might be suggested by the brief hemline was mitigated by the overlapping panels and dark gray color. The skirt was sensual yet subdued.

Sexy with class, Elana decided.

Perhaps the most momentous thing she'd done in her life was to mention during a conversation with Gerald Lone the date of her birthday. He'd phoned later and asked if he could take her to dinner on that night to celebrate. He'd also promised there would be no strings attached, that he simply liked and admired her and wanted to contribute to her happiness.

No mention of how they'd grown closer on discovering how much they had in common, or of the electricity they could almost see when bare flesh touched bare flesh. And of course there was no mention of how his charm had finally overwhelmed her.

So they had a dinner date. No strings.

And after dinner, though Gerald might not know it yet, they would come here to her apartment—which she'd better start cleaning, since there wouldn't be much time tomorrow.

Elana smiled at her image in the mirror. It was still an attractive image, but no longer a young one. For God's sake, she'd be twenty-seven years old tomorrow! How had it happened?

Time was such a clever thief; she understood that now, and she knew that a person had to anticipate that stealth. Time would have you before you knew it. Well, that wasn't going to happen to Elana. She wasn't going to grow old too fast and smart too slow, while year after lonely year passed faster and faster.

She had her mind made up that tomorrow night things would be different. Those strings Gerald had mentioned would attach themselves, and bind them one to the other.

Elana could be clever, just like time. After a good meal, good wine, it would be easy to make it seem like Gerald's idea to come home with her.

But it was Elana's idea. She'd be the one in control.

She was determined that tomorrow night she would make of Gerald Lone a birthday present for herself.

80

Quinn left Renz's office in a glum mood. It was true that everyone else who'd been involved in the investigation was satisfied with the outcome. Satisfied enough, anyway. Renz was certainly content with his cemented and powerful political position.

Fedderman was a realist and resigned to a gray world.

Helen the profiler would get a pat on the back and maybe a raise in pay.

Addie Price would have something to chatter about during her TV spots in Detroit, and no doubt her speaking fee would increase.

Vitali and Mishkin were in line for commendations and might be kicked up a notch in rank and pay.

Bribes to let the sleeping dog lie.

Even Pearl seemed comfortable with the result of the investigation. There seemed to be no doubt in her mind that Chrissie had killed Yancy. Pearl had come to the hostage site ready to find any excuse to avenge Yancy's death by killing Chrissie. She'd been burning to kill Chrissie. Only Pearl could have stopped Pearl from squeezing the trigger. And Pearl had.

But that didn't change the way she felt about Chrissie Keller.

Well, maybe they all had it right, Quinn thought. Justice had been served here in a number of ways. Chrissie's death might mark the end of the new incarnation of the Carver, and Chrissie had found her revenge. She'd killed her father, and her mother had to live with her guilt for not speaking up years ago, and with the image of her daughter's head exploding from the impact of a bullet that took brain matter with it as it exited the skull.

Maybe worst of all for her, Erin would always remember that shotgun barrel moving back and forth between her and Quinn, and she'd always wonder who would have been her daughter's choice to die next in the West Side apartment.

With the later murders attributed to Chrissie, the Carver's time of bloody rampage was finally over.

The victims' families would find peace and the much-mentioned closure. Mary Bakehouse would cease to be afraid and have two good and loyal friends in the large golden retrievers she'd bought as her protectors, dogs that would probably never under any circumstances bite anyone.

Maybe Renz was right, and Quinn shouldn't poke and probe.

Quinn believed that.

Sure, he did.

81

Addie phoned Quinn and told him she was returning to Detroit on a late flight out of Kennedy. He asked to see her one more time. About the case, he assured her. It was already afternoon; could she drop by his apartment to discuss the investigation in private?

"The investigation's over," she said.

"I'm not so sure."

He could hear her breathing into the phone as he sat watching the only thing moving in the quiet office, dust motes swirling in a sun beam that had penetrated the front window.

"Have I made you curious?" he asked.

She laughed. "I'll admit that."

"Because you have doubts, too?"

"Because you're always sure of everything. That's what attracted me to you in the first place."

"So we can talk about it? Maybe we can discuss it over dinner someplace."

"I'm having dinner on the plane."

"What? Peanuts and miniature cookies?"

"I'm flying first class, Quinn. It'll be steak."

"My apartment, then. Afterward we'll stop by your place for your luggage, and I'll drive you to the airport."

"Okay, your apartment," she said. "For a drink and a chat. And we can leave from there for the airport. I only have a couple of carry-ons. I travel light and unburdened by baggage."

"Then you're lucky," Quinn said.

She laughed again. "So philosophical for a cop. That's something else that drew me to you."

"So what's scaring you away?"

"So dark," she said.

When they'd broken the connection, he wondered if she'd been kidding.

She was wearing a light beige blouse with a white scarf knotted loosely at her throat, dark brown slacks with brown high heels that made her legs look longer. A large black leather carry-on was slung by a narrow strap over her shoulder. She smiled at Quinn in a way that wounded him, and he would always remember.

She pecked him on the cheek and slid past him into the apartment, dragging an arm. At the end of the arm was the handle of a red rolling suitcase that would be maximum size for a carry-on.

"I'm going to miss you," she said.

"And I you."

He stepped well out of the way of the suitcase, then relieved her of the handle and sat it upright near the door.

Quinn led her to the living room, and she crossed to the upholstered green chair that long ago had been his wife's favorite. She sat down and crossed her legs, placed her arms on each arm of the chair, and looked expectantly up at him.

"You should be the prettiest passenger on the flight."

"That's nice of you to say, Quinn."

"Can I get you a drink?"

"Anything but gin."

He went into the kitchen, and a few minutes later returned with a scotch and water over ice in an on-the-rocks glass. In his other hand was an opened bottle of Heineken.

After he handed her the glass, they sipped their drinks, then Quinn went over to the sofa. He didn't sit down on the cushions, though. Instead he sat perched on the wide sofa arm, facing Addie.

"When we're finished with our drinks," he said, "I'd like for us to go into the bedroom."

Addie seemed to stir without actually moving, and for only a second seemed alarmed. "I didn't think that was our deal."

"Do you realize," Quinn said, "that despite our attraction to each other, we've never even kissed? I mean, really kissed?"

She took another sip of her drink and then nodded. "I realize that." She sat back, but it was as if she was trying to get as far away from him as possible. "I made a mistake coming here."

"Why's that?"

"I thought better of you."

"I would like for us to have sex," Quinn said.

She gave him a calm, level look with eyes he'd never seen before. "That isn't going to happen." She moved to stand up.

"Sit down, Addie."

His voice was calm, his tone moderated, but it carried authority. She sat back precisely in her previous position.

Quinn said, "This hypothesis that we're left with after the investigation, do you agree with it?"

"That's a rather awkward change of subject, but I'll take it."

"Do you agree with it?" he repeated.

"Of course I do."

Quinn placed his Heineken bottle on the lamp table, not caring if it left a ring, and crossed his arms. "Want to hear my hypothesis?"

"That's really why I'm here, isn't it?"

He ignored her question and continued, but there was a note of sadness in his voice. "Here are some facts," he said. "You were with the Michigan state police when you sought out your assignment to this case. Ed Keller traveled to New York from Detroit. You worked skillfully in guiding the investigation, gaining credibility each time you were right about something. You have an impressive résumé, but there's a hole in it during the first period when the Carver was active years ago here in New York. When Erin Keller visited the office the first time, you wore a pair of reading glasses. You haven't worn them before or since. You succeeded in avoiding Erin after that. And I noticed that whenever we saw the shadow woman at or near a crime scene, you weren't with us."

Addie sipped again at her drink and met his gaze directly. "Anything else?"

Quinn smiled but his eyes didn't join in. "Yes, Addie. You were never in the slightest really interested in me."

She became smaller in the chair, wounded by his words.

Then she put down her glass and began to unbutton her blouse.

"Addie—"

"Be quiet, Quinn."

She continued to work the buttons, and then used both hands to open the blouse wide.

He could only stare at the false breasts that were some kind of foam creation.

"That's why the Carver broke off his attack on you," Quinn said.

"No one knows for sure. Perhaps something surprised him, frightened him away. As you know, he's the reason why, as Addie Price, I became a police profiler. I wanted revenge, and I thought I could finally attain it by getting assigned to this case. I could do what Chrissie Keller wanted to do, use you and your detectives to locate the killer. Chrissie must have murdered that homeless woman and mutilated her in a way that would draw out the Carver, or at least cause the police to reopen the investigation."

"It worked too well," Quinn said.

"The Carver murdered Joyce House and Lilly Branston," Addie said, "and that allowed us to get closer to him."

"We still didn't get him," Quinn pointed out.

"We did," Addie said. "You summoned Keller as Edward Archer to New York on his cell phone, but Lisa Bolt, who at a certain point had begun working for me, will attest that Keller didn't fly to New York. He was already here. You were using him to bait Chrissie, while he was using *you* to bait her. If he could kill Chrissie, his secret would be safe no matter what anyone else said. If you check Keller's résumé, you'll find a hole in it, too, for the same time period when there was a hole in mine. While I was trying to fit the fragments of myself back together after he attacked me and was scared away before he could slit my throat. You'll also find he was in New York at the time of the Carver murders."

Quinn stood all the way up from the sofa arm and paced a few steps back and forth. He stayed standing. "You're telling me Edward Keller was the Carver? Your attacker wore a mask when he almost killed you years ago in Detroit, so how can you possibly be sure?"

"I recognized his voice. And Lisa Bolt saw him undressing for bed through the cracked door of the cheap hotel where he was staying here in New York."

"And . . . ?"

"Call your medical examiner. Ask him about the corpse."

Quinn called the morgue and eventually was put through to Nift.

"Anything unusual about Edward Keller's body?" he asked.

Nift didn't say anything for a while. Then: "It's got bullets in it, Quinn. That's unusual."

"Something else," Quinn said.

Again the long silence. "Call Renz," Nift said, and hung up.

Carver called Renz, who also played dumb.

"It's going to be in the news tomorrow anyway," Quinn lied. "You might as well tell me."

"What news?"

"Nift knows it. He's sitting on the goddamned body. How do you think the word got out?"

"That asshole!" Renz said.

"You've realized what he was for years, so why'd you try to keep a secret with him in the know?"

"I shouldn't have. Let Cindy Sellers have her way."

"She usually gets it," Quinn said.

"I wanted to keep it out of the media, didn't want more questions, more attention drawn to the fact that we carried this thing in the cold-case file for years."

"What are we talking about?" Quinn asked.

"Keller's torso. His nipples have been removed. And there's a large letter X carved into his chest."

"Jesus!"

"The wounds are recent, and were almost certainly self-inflicted."

Quinn stood quietly, putting it all together.

"Jesus!" he said again.

Renz was saying something else, but Quinn hung up. He knew the real reason Renz wanted Keller's self-inflicted injuries kept secret. It was critical to his political ambitions that Chrissie remain the latest and last Carver. He wanted the case to stay on the record exactly as it was, wrapped tight and neatly filed away, a fading part of the city's ignoble past.

Quinn looked at Addie, who had the answers. Who'd from the start had most of them.

"There you have it," she said. "Insofar as anyone ever has all of anything."

"Keller might have been the Carver all the way through. Chrissie might have been innocent."

"Might," Addie said. "We'll never know for sure."

"Other things we can know for sure," Quinn said.

"But are you sure you want to know them?"

"I'm sure I have to," Quinn said.

82

Addie finished her drink and then stared at the ice cubes, as if there might be some revelation there now that the liquid was gone.

"Nothing between us was real," Addie said.

Quinn nodded. "I somehow knew that from the beginning."

"But you didn't know you knew."

"I still can't be sure. Not yet."

"Yes, you can," Addie said. "Nothing's been real for me since Edward Keller. I'm afraid nothing ever can be. I followed him to Detroit, then from Detroit to New York, unsure he was the one who attacked me, who later killed Tiffany. I knew he wasn't someone named Edward Archer, though I wasn't sure he was the Carver. But I became sure."

"Why did he try to kill you, of all people, in Detroit?"

"My watching him must have attracted his attention, and something about me disturbed or attracted him."

"But why, after attacking you, did he come here to New York to stalk and kill more victims?"

"I don't know for sure," Addie said. "Maybe it was because he was almost caught and he realized the risk he was taking, so he wanted a bigger city to disappear in. Or a larger pool of prospective victims. Maybe he followed Tiffany in

New York. Maybe there was something special about me. I'd been a surprise to him, and he ran from it. He was sure I hadn't seen his face, and he wouldn't know I recognized his voice. I couldn't prove anything. After he killed Tiffany, he'd be safe. No one would believe Chrissie in a he-said, she-said confrontation about childhood molestations, even if she did work up the courage to speak out. He didn't see her as a threat, and I'd hardly make a credible witness. But when he became successful and got political ambitions, he had to eliminate all his vulnerabilities, including Chrissie, which is why he agreed to your request to act as bait. He wanted to draw Chrissie to him so he could kill her."

"You joined the case after Lisa Bolt disappeared," Quinn said.

"At that point I hadn't seen her. I assumed she was the real Chrissie, and I was afraid she might recognize me. Just like I was afraid Erin Keller might recognize me."

Quinn stared at her. "So that was the reason for the reading glasses when Erin first came into the office. Why their lenses were unground."

"You noticed that. It's just like you to notice things."

"Addie Price wasn't the first time you changed your name, was it?"

"No," she said, lowering her head and smiling sadly.

When she looked up at him there were tears in her eyes. Her mascara was running.

"Are you satisfied now?" she asked.

"That's a hell of a question."

She laughed. From somewhere she produced a wadded tissue and dabbed at her eyes.

After an awkward silence, Quinn said, "What Keller did to himself . . . why?"

Addie shrugged.

"Guilt," she said.

"Shame," Quinn said.

"They're twins," she said.

83

Cindy Sellers's throat was dry. So fascinated was she by Quinn and Addie Price's conversation that she'd almost forgotten to breathe.

As she listened to the recording from the digital micro-recorder she'd secretly planted in Quinn's apartment, she knew she had a major story, the kind that could make a career. Of course it had been obtained unethically, not to mention illegally, but her standing as a journalist should prevent her from having to reveal her source.

Like Pearl, Sellers had researched Addie Price and found a false record of her birth.

Unlike Pearl, she'd continued her research and discovered the real reason; the reason for both name changes. And the reason why the Carver inexplicably stopped his attack on Geraldine Knott in Detroit. Why her assailant *couldn't* bring himself to kill Geraldine.

Geraldine wasn't Geraldine.

Not even close.

The question now, in Sellers's mind and balanced in her conscience, was whether she should reveal the recorded conversation she'd just heard.

She searched her soul for almost ten seconds before deciding to phone in the story.

* * *

Addie Price had missed her flight, so the next day Quinn drove her to Kennedy. They had a good-bye drink in an airport bar before walking to the security checkpoint.

They shook hands, and then Addie impulsively kissed Quinn's cheek and turned away to join the security line. She didn't look back at Quinn. He didn't look back at her.

Back in his apartment, Quinn sat at his desk, fired up a cigar, and got out his yellow legal pad.

He found a stubby yellow pencil.

Beneath *Computer nerd's software program, seven names,* he wrote:

> *Pearl attacked, Yancy killed.*
> *Lisa Bolt checks herself out of hospital.*
> *Edward Keller agrees to come to NYC.*
> *Lisa Bolt says Keller is in NYC to kill Chrissie so he*
>   *can keep past hidden.*
> *Keller not in hotel as agreed.*
> *Pearl finds Lisa Bolt badly beaten by Keller.*
> *Lisa gives police address she gave to Keller.*
> *All hell. Keller, Chrissie die.*

Quinn leaned back and surveyed the entire page. Something was still wrong. It wasn't anything in his notes.

There was something missing.

He realized what just as the phone rang, startling him out of his reverie. As he lifted the receiver, he saw on caller ID that Renz was on the line.

"I thought you oughta know," Renz said, "the Detroit cops found a hidden room in Keller's basement in Detroit. There was a freezer there, with plastic bags containing guess what?"

"Grisly souvenirs," Quinn said.

"What looked like shredded flesh," Renz said. "Each bag was labeled. We're waiting for DNA, but blood type and other forensics make it just about certain the labels are correct and what we've got are the severed nipples of all the Carver victims up to and including Tiffany Keller."

"He killed his own daughter."

"People do that kinda thing, Quinn. Especially under the circumstances. She was a liability."

"Yeah. Look at the good it did him."

"He was a sicko," Renz said. "End of story."

"I guess you're right, Harley."

"Time for you to stop guessing, Quinn. Get drunk and get laid, if you're not too old to get it up, and put this one away."

"I'll do that, Harley. Maybe not all of it."

Quinn hung up.

He turned his attention back to the legal pad, thinking back on his conversation with Renz.

. . . up to and including Tiffany Keller.

The souvenirs in Keller's freezer in Detroit were all older than five years, stopping with the macabre reminders of Tiffany.

Where were the missing body parts from the later victims?

If Keller had resumed his activities as the Carver, why wouldn't he have resumed his old M.O.? His hotel room, his belongings, had all been thoroughly searched. No body parts.

If Chrissie had committed the later murders and taken the nipples as souvenirs, which seemed unlikely, where were they? Had she simply removed them so she could emulate the Carver's M.O. and then disposed of them?

That was the most likely thing, Quinn decided. And if they hadn't been destroyed, actually finding them, proving what he thought to be true, would be too much of a long shot, especially if it meant reopening a case virtually everyone wanted to stay closed. And of course the courts would be in the position of having to prove that Keller and Chrissie *hadn't* murdered anyone after Tiffany's death. Not easy to do, since both were dead.

So the case would remain closed. Everyone involved who was still alive would have to live with that.

Quinn used the phone in his den to call Pearl's apartment.

She didn't answer, but he sat for a while and let her phone ring.

Then he abruptly hung up. He decided the loneliest sound in the world was an unanswered phone after the fifth ring.

Miles above the earth, Addie Price soared with her eyes closed. She dreamed about a sultry night and a knife blade held tightly by pinched fingers close to the point so the cuts would be shallow and seem tentative. There was a gray homeless woman in the dream, her eyes wide and glittering with horror, her sagging breasts revealed . . . the snick of blade nicking bone, carving flesh. Human flesh, so fragile . . . so temporary.

Human flesh . . . first a trickle of blood, then the deluge. The others—

The plane hit an air pocket, and Addie awakened, glanced about, realized where she was, and smiled.

Human flesh, so fragile . . . it had to be packed carefully in ice in order to be shipped.

That evening, in a Holifield, Ohio, gin mill, Jerry Grantland's mother Miriam, who was also the mother of Geraldine Knott, Loren Ensam, Gerald Lone, and Addie Price, read the New York papers, then buried her head in her arms and wept.

At the same time in New York, Elana Dare sat alone at an Upper East Side restaurant table, trying to ignore the stares of the other diners, who by this time had to know she'd been stood up. Her second cocktail, a prop to mitigate her embarrassment, sat before her on a damp paper napkin on the table. Between sips of what was now melted ice, she was desperately using her cell phone to call Gerald Lone.

His phone rang and rang.

EPILOGUE

Detroit, one year after New York

Jerry Grantland, wearing a buzz cut, dark business suit, and yellow power tie, entered the CookRight culinary supplies store and made his way to a display of carving knives arranged in a glass showcase.

He was standing studying the knives, his forefinger touching his chin, when a sales clerk approached. He was a chubby man about forty, stuffed into a cheap gray suit and wearing a cheaper white smile. He moved around behind the counter so he could open it should Jerry decide he wanted to examine the merchandise further.

Then his expression changed, and his magnified blue eyes widened behind rimless glasses.

"You sure remind me of somebody," he said. A tentative kind of recognition entered his eyes. "That television personality that used to be on the news commenting on local murders. The one who got into some kinda trouble. Why, she could be your sister."

"If I had a sister," Jerry said, and bought a knife.